HALF ASLEEP
ASLEEP
in
FROG
PAJAMAS

HALF ASLEEP
in
FROG
PAJAMAS

Tom Robbins

BANTAM BOOKS
New York   Toronto
London   Sydney   Auckland

Half Asleep in Frog Pajamas

A Bantam Book / October 1994

All rights reserved.
Copyright © 1994 by Tom Robbins

Book design by Donna Sinisgalli

Library of Congress Cataloging-in-Publication Data

Robbins, Tom.
  Half asleep in frog pajamas / by Tom Robbins.
    p. cm.
  ISBN 0-553-07625-6
  I. Title.
PS3568.O233H35   1994
813'.54—dc20   94-11549
                                                               CIP

Published simultaneously in the United States and Canada

Bantam Books are published by Bantam Books, a division of Bantam
Doubleday Dell Publishing Group, Inc. Its trademark, consisting of the
words "Bantam Books" and the portrayal of a rooster, is Registered in U.S.
Patent and Trademark Office and in other countries. Marca Registrada.
Bantam Books, 1540 Broadway, New York, New York 10036.

PRINTED IN THE UNITED STATES OF AMERICA
BVG   0 9 8 7 6 5 4 3 2 1

For Maestro Rudolpho.
For Our Man in Nirvana.
And for the "visiting faculty."

It has been demonstrated that some amphibians are able to use celestial bodies for orientation.

—The Encyclopaedia Britannica

No doubt the world is entirely an imaginary world,
but it is only once removed from the true world.

—Isaac Bashevis Singer

HALF
ASLEEP
in
FROG
PAJAMAS

Thursday
Evening
April 5

Just Back from Timbuktu

Four P.M.

The day the stock market falls out of bed and breaks its back is the worst day of your life. Or so you think. It isn't the worst day of your life, but you think it is. And when you give voice to that thought, it is with conviction and a minimum of rhetorical embellishment.

"This is the worst day of my life," you say, as you drop a salted peanut into your double martini—on better days, you drink white wine—and watch it sink. It spirals downward more slowly, more gracefully, than your own plunging fortunes, the pretty little gin bubbles that gather around the peanut a marked contrast to the lumps and burrs and stinging things that are attaching themselves to your heart.

It has been approximately four hours since the market slid off the roof, and the shocked and, at times, hysteric roar that had filled the Bull & Bear earlier in the afternoon is starting to give way to a slightly dimmer din of elaborate survival strategies and cynical jokes. You share neither in the desperate ploys nor the false mirth. You hold your prematurely graying head in your hands and repeat, "This is the worst day of my life."

"Come on, kid," says Phil Craddock. "The market'll be back."

"Maybe the *market* will be back. But *I* won't. I've left my clients so far underwater, they're going to need gills to breathe." You gulp a fireball of martini. "Posner knows it, too. He passed me in the hall right after the bell and asked me if I didn't think nursing was a noble occupation."

"Maybe he meant for *him*."

You laugh in spite of yourself. "Posner emptying bedpans?

Before that happens, the Pope will star in an X-rated movie shot on a mink ranch. No, Phil, the old man sent me a signal that said, 'Sell your Porsche, baby, and line up for food stamps.' If there isn't a major bounce-back on Monday, I am puppy chow."

"Monday's four days off."

"Thanks for reminding me. A whole extra day to go crazy in. Well, Good Friday's famous for its executions."

"Settle down, little lady," says Phil. "Now's the time to slip into your bulletproof bra."

At the reference to intimate apparel, you redden. It was fine and dandy for you to joke about X-rated movies, you've never *seen* an X-rated movie, X-rated movies are unreal to you, but when a man, even a man like Phil Craddock, looks you in the eye and speaks of things personal, things private and tinged with naughtiness, your inevitable fluster paints such dollops of pimento on your olive cheeks that they would be fit to garnish a martini—in this case, the third one of the afternoon, all doubles—and when you attempt to stem the blood, it makes you blush all the harder. Your propensity to be easily, blatantly embarrassed is one of the several things that annoys you about your lot in the world, one more example of how the fates love to spit in your consommé. The company at your table is another.

Phil Craddock trades soybeans and pork bellies and, except for the loosely knotted tie around his neck, looks as if he might farm them, as well. Come to think of it, the tie is rather a farmer's tie, a chronically unstylish, country-prayer-meeting kind of tie, broad and outdoorsy and turned up at the tip. (There is only one person in the Bull & Bear more slovenly attired than Phil, and that is the man at whom Ann Louise, your other tablemate, is staring.) Actually, Phil is considerate and congenial, but that annoys you all the more because he reminds you of your annoying supposed boyfriend, Belford Dunn. Phil and Belford are really very much alike, except Belford is a decade younger, and, of course, one could hardly imagine Phil sharing his apartment with a born-again monkey.

As for Ann Louise, you don't know her well. She joined Posner

Lampard McEvoy and Jacobsen about six months ago, moving from New York, where, apparently, she was a house-afire broker, and where, gossip would have it, she indulged an inordinate fondness for sodomy, practicing it with practically every bigwig on Wall Street, including a few who are household names. Ann Louise is middle-aged and squat, but not unattractive, and you suspect you could learn a thing or two from her—in the area of business—but Ann Louise has a *reputation*, and, moreover, she's barely acknowledged your presence, having spent the past half hour staring at the back of a long-haired stranger (strange to you, that is), who appears to be holding court at the bar. You lack the angle and the eye-power to see him clearly.

In any case, it is no wonder you're irritated. Of all the brokers, managers, and investment bankers in the Bull & Bear with whom you might hold mental hands at this critical, even historic moment; before whom you might pour out your singspiel of personal defeat, why did you have to end up at a table with these two . . . *outcasts?* It is unfair, although not untypical, an insult pasted to your injury, and further evidence, you think, that this is the worst day of your life.

The worst day? Gwendolyn, you are forgetting, perhaps, that day—was it eight years ago?—when in the same mail you received notice that you had been rejected for graduate study at Stanford, Harvard, Yale, and the University of Pennsylvania's Wharton School of Business; in the same morning's mail, turned down by all of your top choices, and you a female member of an ethnic minority at a time when institutions, in a befuddled, heavy-handed attempt to compensate for past injustices and in an almost panic-stricken scurry to be perceived as sociologically correct, were falling all over themselves to add persons of your description to their folds.

The worst day? Surely it would require more than the market's free-fall, with you in its arms, to eclipse that day when your mother scribbled one last sonnet in her lavender notebook and stuck her head in the oven.

The worst day? You are only twenty-nine years old. There will be other days, other catastrophes. Perhaps in the very near future. In fact, something may be building at this exact minute, something connected to, if not wholly precipitated by, the born-again monkey.

Four-Fifty P.M.

Located in the failing heart of Seattle's financial district, the Bull & Bear restaurant and lounge is an old-school, masculinized establishment, with pressed zinc ceilings, dark wood paneling, and passages of velvety maroon wallpaper dotted with rows of spiky gold fleurs-de-lis, which some patrons, after a few cocktails, habitually perceive as mutating dollar signs, money symbols grown lush, radiant, and, they hope, prophetic. On any Friday afternoon, its bar is crowded with noisy "bookies," as they call themselves, winding down at the end of a stressful week in a stressful occupation, but on this "Friday," which is actually a Thursday, the population of drinkers has nearly doubled—and it gives no indication of thinning out. Indeed, many of the brokers will remain in the Bull & Bear until it evicts them at two in the morning. It isn't simply a matter of pouring alcohol on their wounds or of a reluctance to go home and look the family in the eye. There are practical reasons. Everyone is on pins and needles (or fleurs-de-lis) waiting to learn how the foreign markets will react. Then and only then will it become clear whether or not this plunge is the Big One, the Death Crash, the financial apocalypse that will put the "broke" back in "broker" once and for all and leave the United States of America's standing in the international economic community somewhere between that of Portugal and Mongolia.

To that end, all eyes are on Tokyo, where, due to the sixteen-hour time difference, the international date line, and daylight saving time, the Nikkei is just now beginning to light the gas under its morning teapot. Every brokerage house in downtown Seattle has left a scout or two in the office to watch the wire, and throughout the evening the spotters will phone in to the Bull & Bear or, in some cases, deliver in person, the latest report on the state of the Nikkei. It is Good Friday already in Europe; markets there closed long before it became apparent how much of America's doo-doo had hit the propeller, and they will not reopen until Sunday night, Seattle time.

When a bartender shouts, "Gwen Mati! Telephone for Gwen Mati!" a momentary hush falls over the room. Could this be the first dispatch from the front? As you scoot your chair from the table and rise, people from Merrill Lynch, Prudential Securities, and other prominent firms gaze at you with eager, almost envious orbs, not stopping to consider that were you a major player, you would have had your personal satellite phone alongside your martini glass. Your colleagues at Posner Lampard McEvoy and Jacobsen suffer no illusions about your importance, yet because they are aware of your ambitions, they do pause to wonder if you might have bribed the office sentinel to call you instead of Posner with the early numbers from Tokyo.

"Here!" you yell, and wave your arms. The phone is attached to the wall at the far end of the bar, and you set out for it, gingerly threading your way through the mob. As soon as you are out of earshot, which is a matter of inches, Ann Louise turns to Phil and says, "That girl is finished in this business."

"Why you say that? You hear something?"

"Let's just say I have a feeling in the seat of my pants." Ann Louise grins lasciviously.

On you push, sustaining an occasional elbow to the breast or blast of cigarette smoke in your face. Inebriation is rampant. Liquids are being spilled. Glasses shattered. Confessions exchanged. Cocaine—when is the last time you've seen cocaine in this milieu?—snorted. Brokers are openly necking with their sales assistants, managers are caressing their secretaries' thighs. It is akin to the sudden outbreak of war, when all social rules are temporarily suspended. As you squeeze past the table where Sol, your firm's chief analyst, is sitting, he gives you a faint, rueful smile and says, "*Après nous le déluge.*

The fun has stopped, *mon amie.*" You pat his shoulder and press on, but as you near the telephone, you hear his voice behind you. "The fun has stopped."

You reach for the receiver. There will be no co-worker on the line, no exclusive flash from the Nikkei wire. It will be, rather, Q-Jo Huffington, your supposed best friend, calling to tell you she is waiting for you at the Virginia Inn. You are well aware that Q-Jo is waiting. You had arranged to meet at four-thirty at that arty tavern among whose bohemian clientele Q-Jo is very much at home. You don't much like the place, since it reminds you of your supposed parents, the kind of place they would have frequented, but it is far, far preferable to having Q-Jo, all three hundred embarrassing pounds of her, show up at the Bull & Bear. You are annoyed that she is impatient. Could she really expect you to keep your date on a day such as this? Not if she has listened to the news, she couldn't. Alas, Q-Jo listens only to the music of the spheres.

"Hello," you snap, sounding as gruff as your little schoolgirl candy valentine voice can manage. The voice on the other end belongs to Belford Dunn, your assumed beau. "Gee, honey," he says, "sorry to trouble you with this on a terrible day"—Belford has heard the news—"but André's got out. He's run away!"

Belford is virtually sobbing. Yet, you feel more annoyance than sympathy. Leave it to Belford! Your career is sailing down the greased chute to Hell, the entire American economy is sailing down the chute, while Belford goes to pieces over a runaway pet. On the other hand, André is no ordinary pet. André is a monkey with a past.

And he has not so much run away as escaped.

"Belford, please," you hear yourself plead. Somehow, the alcohol has distanced you from your voice just enough so that you can listen to it as if it had been prerecorded. Still, you can't be entirely objective about it. Nothing about yourself annoys you quite so much as your voice. *This is the way,* you think, *a package of Hostess cupcakes would sound if a package of Hostess cupcakes could speak.* Q-Jo, on the other hand, says your voice is your lone saving grace. She claims you are the only career woman she has ever met for whom Dental Drill was not a second language. You explain that businesswomen have to talk harshly in order to compete with men. And if your voice is as airy and warm and vulnerable as Q-Jo says, it is only because you have been unable to alter it. Once, you took up smoking in an attempt to produce deeper tones, but cigarettes made you nauseous. What Q-Jo hears as sexy, you perceive as squeaky. That, regrettably, was your childhood nickname: "Squeak." Your mother never called you anything but "Gwendolyn," but to your dad and everybody else, it was "Squeak"-this and "Squeak"-that. Made you feel like a goddamned mouse.

"Please, Belford. . . ." You make it clear that while the market has been closed since one p.m., that while its sudden nine-hundred-point decline probably has given you a permanent haircut, that while you may be in a swell saloon swilling gin, you, nonetheless, are technically still working. You owe it to your clients as well as to yourself—your personal account has been bled of some relatively serious juice—to remain on duty, as it were, until the heathen Japs, for whom the anniversary of Our Lord's crucifixion is just another day in the shop, demonstrate whether or not they intend to follow us to the bottom of the lake. However, not wishing to appear insensitive to Belford's plight, you, in spite of your responsibilities and woes, offer him a deal. To wit: if André hasn't turned up by supper time—and you are confident that he will not forgo his raisin bread and banana Popsicles—you will join in the search. Furthermore, you will bring Q-Jo along so that she might apply her considerable psychic powers to the determination of the monkey's whereabouts.

Relieved, Belford thanks you profusely. So profusely it annoys you. "Meanwhile," you say in your most efficient manner, "you can scour the neighborhood. And better notify the police."

"Yeah, I guess I better," he concedes unhappily. "I don't think André would . . . *revert* or anything. But I guess I'm morally obliged to tell the authorities."

You are about to ring off—expressions such as "morally obliged" rather irk and embarrass you—when he says, "At first, hon, when you talked about waiting for news from Japan, I thought you meant Dr. Yamaguchi."

"Who?"

"You know. Dr. Yamaguchi. He's due in town tonight."

"Oh, that cancer guy. What would he have to do with any of this?"

"Well," Belford says, "he's from Japan. And he's bringing good news. That could help the market."

You sigh your best long-suffering sigh and hang up. Since you are in the vicinity, you go to the ladies' room and urinate as hard as you can, forcing a stream against the porcelain that would knock a small animal off its feet or put out the eye of a cyclops. Then, you commence to fight your way back through the crowd. As you move parallel to the bar, you find yourself directly behind the man at whom Ann Louise has been staring; a tall, slender man with bleached, stringy hair hanging halfway down the back of a worn leather jacket. He's in tight but frayed jeans, and you notice a gold earring in his left lobe, as well as some sort of tattoo on the back of his hand. If it is incongruous that a fellow of uncouth appearance would be standing at the bar of the Bull & Bear, it is all the more unusual that throughout the afternoon other, more acceptably attired, people, people in the business (Posner, even!), have been stopping to chat with him. There are a couple of brokers around him now, schmoozing it up, and you think, *This couldn't have happened in the eighties, this could only happen on the worst day of my life.*

When, on the spur of the moment, the stranger spins around to leer at you, a high-pitched little yelp Minnies out of your throat, and you flinch as if you were a ripe tomato that's just heard the creak of the garden gate. Small wonder you are startled. The smile that slices across the bony plain of his stubbled jaws is as fierce as a paper cut, and his eyes are as reddened as bedsores, as probing as coat hangers. You feel their gaze in your uterus. Before you can move away, he lays a single bony finger against your wrist and nods toward Sol, the analyst. "The fun is just beginning," he whispers confidentially, and his bad grin widens like a rip in a wetsuit.

Back at your table, you slide with exaggerated helplessness into your chair and slump there. "Good grief!" you exclaim. "Who *is* that scumbag?"

"Why, that's Larry Diamond," says Phil.

And Ann Louise adds, as if it explains everything, "He's just back from Timbuktu."

FIVE-FIFTEEN P.M.

Because you feel a trifle queasy after draining your third martini, you decide to order food. For years, you have subsisted largely on green salads made from exotic plants with astringent flavors and unpronounceable names (try saying "arugula" or "radicchio" after a hard day riding the range) and drizzled with vinegars that cost more than good champagne; but today the rules have been suspended, and your taut tummy is crying out for animal protein. Being a traditional meat-and-potatoes kind of cookery, the Bull & Bear's kitchen is quite prepared to fill your request for chopped round steak with carmelized onions and steamed asparagus.

While the waitress is arranging your utensils, your bread basket, and butter dish, Phil volunteers some information on this distasteful Larry Diamond character. Seems Diamond used to be an ace, quite possibly the hottest broker in the Pacific Northwest, but he threw his darts a bit recklessly and lost his job and his assets in the last crash, the crash of '87.

"We knew about him in New York," Ann Louise interjects. "For a hooterville like this, he generated jumbo juice. But basically, he was a churner, and smiling-and-dialing will always bury you in the end." At that, she shoots you a pointed glance. You cannot help but blanch.

"Yep," says Phil, running his clunky farmer's fingers through his white hair. "Ol' Larry was prone to go dialing for dollars. Wonder what he's doing nowadays."

"He's just back from Timbuktu."

"Yes, Ann Louise, you mentioned that. But why?" you ask. "What would a guy from the business be doing in a place like that?"

It is Phil who answers. "Maybe he knows something we don't."

"About Timbuktu?"

"Hey, we got a global economy."

"But Timbuktu? I mean, that's supposed to be the end of the earth."

"Well, everywhere else has already been tapped. Thailand. Argentina. Turkey, now, and Vietnam. Maybe Timbuktu's a play."

"What's their economic base?" asks Ann Louise. "I don't think there's very much there."

And you say, "Mr. Diamond doesn't strike me as a man on the prowl for a foreign market play. He looks more like a biker, like a . . . like some kind of wild . . . musician or something." Try as you might, you cannot say the word *musician* without thinking of your father—but that is a separate issue.

Ann Louise smiles indulgently. She is on the verge of responding, when a wave of noisy excitement rolls over the establishment. The crowd starts to mill, individuals pivoting first one way and then the next, as if a famous movie star were about to enter the room naked, but nobody is sure through which door. The looks on some faces, however, suggest they expect an armed terrorist instead of a celebrity. Obviously, a rumor is loose in the room, running amok, goosing people, biting their ankles. The hubbub mounts, then, in an ever softening smorzando, peels away like sonar panty hose when an elderly man, a senior vice-president at Merrill Lynch, climbs precariously atop a table and croaks the announcement, in a hoarse old voice, that the Nikkei has opened sharply lower, yet not as low as many had feared, and that it shows signs of stabilizing.

There are scattered cheers, there is cautious applause. Then everyone begins to speculate at once. Your meal arrives, and you are ready to masticate your initial hesitant forkful of meat, only to have your jaw muscles lock when you overhear someone at an adjacent table remark, "I'll tell you why *I* think the Nikkei's holding. I think it's because of Dr. Yamaguchi."

Six-Ten P.M.

By the time you have finished eating, there have been two more flashes from Tokyo. The earlier of these has the Japanese index pissing off a pier. News of this downward trajectory is greeted with resignation if not fatalism at the Bull & Bear. A subsequent report that the Nikkei has turned upward again is met, depending upon an individual's temperament, either with optimism or disbelief.

Not knowing how to react, you order a glass of port, just to keep some sugar in your tank, and repositioning your chair, join Ann Louise in her scrutiny of Larry Diamond. "Is that what happens to brokers who get the ax?" you ask. "Am I going to end up a bum like that in a few more years?"

It is a rhetorical question, but Phil responds. "Larry was some kind of genius," he says quietly. Ann Louise nods, looks at you, and smiles.

Well, excu-uuu-se me! you say to yourself. But you regard the "genius" with a bit more care. What did he intend when he said the fun was just beginning? For that matter, what did Sol mean when he said the fun had stopped? As far as you are concerned, the real fun stopped back in the eighties. Before your time. In those days, some-body in your position could earn major money. Jumbo money. You read about it, dreamed about it, all through college. How typical of your luck that when you finally arrived in a position to poach your golden eggs, the goose had a hysterectomy. Seems as though the day you got your license, America's economy started to unravel. Well, if it can *unravel* it can *reravel*. Right? No, you vaguely recall you heard somewhere that *unravel* and *ravel* mean the same damn thing. In that case, you don't have a Chinaman's chance. Or, to be more precise, a Filipina's chance. Ah, but, Gwen, that won't do,

13

either. If you refuse to acknowledge your race, how can you blame your misfortunes on it?

Rather drunkenly, you contemplate the bad sign under which, you are sure, you were brought forth. Although self-pity usually annoys you, you are mainlining a veterinary-sized syringe of it when it registers on you that Larry Diamond has left his station at the bar and is shuffling toward your table. *How disgusting*, you think. *He even walks like a derelict.*

"How's it going, Larry?" asks Phil.

"Mr. Diamond, I presume," gushes Ann Louise. Suddenly, she is as bright as the tip of her little cigar.

Mr. Diamond ignores them both. He just stands there for a while, shuffling in place, looking as loose as the collar around the neck of eternity. Then, he says to you, "I'll wager you and I have something in common."

"Oh, I doubt that," you say. "I haven't been canned—yet."

His grin is alarming in that it is simultaneously violent and generous, antagonistic and admiring. His red eyes, which resemble Spanish peanuts, dance demoniacally as they look you up and down.

"I didn't come over here to talk shop," he says. Then, still grinning, he nods toward the spot where your dinner plate recently sat. "I ate asparagus, too," he confides. "Do you realize that for the next five hours, our urine is going to smell exactly alike?"

Six-Thirty P.M.

At least the weather is nice. Seattle's winter rains—which usually follow hard upon the fungus-infected, blackberry-stained, spectacularly mildewed heels of its autumn rains—had petered out the previous week, and with each passing day, the sky seems to be getting lighter and higher, as if the sky has come unmoored and is drifting away from Earth: the Chicken Little syndrome in reverse. It is said that in the crash of '29, the sky was dark with the falling bodies of erstwhile millionaires who had thrown themselves out of windows, but this evening when you look up, not so much as the button off a Brooks Brothers suit lands on your pretty face.

And, yes, Gwendolyn, you *are* pretty, a fact that periodically irks you because it can lead to encounters such as the one that has caused you to flee the Bull & Bear. Of course, you've never attracted an admirer quite so vile as Larry Diamond before. After Diamond's perverse remark, which Ann Louise and Phil found surprisingly amusing, you grabbed your purse, arose with as much dignity as you could muster, blushing all the while, and attempted to stalk off to the powder room. He blocked your path. Perhaps he wished to apologize but you didn't give him a chance. "Out of my way, Bozo," you said.

Now, you intended to speak coldly, and with good reason. On the other hand, how much frigidity can be conveyed by a voice that seems to have been designed to incubate baby bluebirds? Yet, Diamond reacted as if you had both slapped his cheek and handed him the key to the treasure. His leer folded faster than a lawn-sprinkling service in Bangladesh, and his wickedly glinting eyes became abruptly sober, suspicious, imploring. "Do you mean," he asked softly, "Bozo as in tribe or Bozo as in clown?"

You couldn't answer. For some reason, he scared you more now than when he was acting lecherous. You stood there dumbfounded until he seized you roughly by your shoulders and stuck his stubbly face into yours. You had thought, from his appearance, that he would reek, but when you gasped, involuntarily sucking in his aroma, you discovered that he smelled metallic and sugary, rather like a tin of fruit cocktail. Did that reassure you? Not in any way. He was shaking you gently. "Bozo tribe or Bozo clown?"

"Clown," you blurted, fully expecting him to pay back the insult by causing you bodily harm. However, with a disappointed little smile, he released you instantly and stepped aside so that you might proceed. And proceed you did, on wobbly knees, to the front door and through it to the street. Where now you stand, letting the mild April breeze blow your hair and skirt about, while you watch the sky float off beyond the stars.

15

Six-Forty P.M.

Wisely, you elect not to drive your car. You still owe thirty grand on that Porsche, and with your current streak of luck, you definitely could count on bashing it against something inflexible—and collecting a DWI citation into the bargain. The Virginia Inn is within walking distance, but after a thorough survey of your surroundings, you decide that pedestrianism also is out of the question.

Downtown Seattle has come to resemble the slums of Calcutta, so dense is its population of beggars, vagabonds, hustlers, buskers, maniacs, thugs, winos, addicts, and the physically and mentally impaired. Now that the rains have ceased, they have staggered, crawled, hobbled, or strutted from doorways, overpasses, condemned buildings, sewers, and vacant lots into the finest streets of the city. There they hawk their merchandise, play their accordions, and petition, vocally or via cardboard sign, for alms, alms, alms.

Some of these wretched creatures are threatening, others merely pitiful. For example, the family sitting in a semicircle in front of a cheese shop: Papa Panhandler, Mama Panhandler, Junior Panhandler, and Baby Panhandler, festooned in rags, twinkling with snot, squatting there weathered and sore, yet hopeful; waiting for the Good Samaritan (church-sponsored or governmental) who, they firmly believe, will show up sooner or later to sponge their brows and buy them a color TV. In your favor, Gwendolyn, you entertain a flicker of compassion. Largely, however, it is bewilderment you feel. "What's the matter with these people?" you ask yourself. "How did they let themselves get in this fix? Where are their tidy cottages, where are their cute farms? Where, oh where, has all the money gone?"

The money. The lovely money. Q-Jo contends that it is your grasping for material wealth that has caused twenty-three gray hairs (she counted them) to sprout on your black Filipina crown—but you know it isn't so: it is the Welsh blood from your mother's side of the family that is to blame. Anyway, there is no grasping on your part, no vulgar greed. Rather, it is a biological drive. That's right. Pushing

16

thirty, you hear the clock ticking. Only it is not babies you want to make, it's cash. You long to swell up with a pregnancy of moola and expel silver dollars like a slot machine.

Alas, the money is going away. It is leaving America as fast as its stubby green legs will carry it. America, who loved it so dearly. It has already left the lazy and the stupid—and now it is leaving you. You are heartsick about it, and you'll be damned if you will give Baby Panhandler that five spot you have semi-drunkenly, semi-guiltily pulled from your purse. Hey, folks! You've got financial problems, too. Have you ever! At least these people don't have Porsche payments and a condo mortgage to worry about.

Before you reach the taxi stand on the corner, however, you give the five-dollar bill away. You give it to a decrepit old geezer whose beard is like a shock of hazardous asbestos blowing in the wind. The gentleman has a placard around his neck. Grotesquely lettered, the sign reads, MANY THINGS ARE DESTROYING ME. With that, you can identify.

SIX-FIFTY P.M.

The cabbie who picks you up sports a Jamaican do, having wasted untold productive hours teasing and rolling his hair until it looks like an infestation of elongated woolly worms. Worse, he smells like your dad. Which is to say, he stinks of freshly burnt marijuana. Jesus! Why you? What is there about you that attracts such people? Well, you suppose that if one is indiscreet enough to rendezvous with Q-Jo Huffington, it is only fitting that one's transport to that rendezvous be weirdness on wheels.

Briefly, you consider ordering the driver to carry you directly to Belford Dunn's, but you realize in time that it is the gin working in your glands that is responsible for this annoying urge. There was a year in which you drank a fair amount of scotch, in hopes that you would develop a nice, low whiskey voice. Alas, you learned that

17

hard liquor arouses you sexually, so you switched, naturally, back to white wine. Better squeaky than horny. "Driver!"

"Yes, sistah?"

"Oh, never mind." In any case, Belford would be otherwise occupied with the location and repatriation of a backsliding primate.

The cabbie, who, despite his Caribbean accent, speaks better English than the average American fraternity boy, begins to talk to you about Rastafarianism. Just to be polite, you ask him how come Haile Selassie, a modern-day but quite dead Ethiopian emperor, for goodness sake, came to be regarded by the Rastas as their high priest and principal saint? He explains that once upon a time—he thinks it was in the fifties—Jamaica was experiencing a devastating drought. People couldn't remember when they had last seen a raindrop. Then, Selassie flew to Jamaica on a state visit. The instant his plane touched down, there was an unexpected cloudburst. And it rained every second Haile Selassie was in the country. It poured for three straight days. And when his plane took off again, it stopped. "There you have it, sistah."

All you can do is shake your head. *Good grief!* you think. *Guy has a bad vacation, and they found a religion on it!* You shake your head some more. The twenty-three gray hairs shake with it.

Indeed, Gwendolyn, it is a very strange world. And it's getting stranger by the minute.

**Thursday
Night
April 5**

Barking at the Moon

Nine P.M.

It is night now, no longer evening but fully night, as in "black as," if not precisely "dead of." Evening usually has the afternoon hanging on its coattails, has actual flecks of daylight clinging like lint to its lapels, but night is solitary, aloof, uncompromised, extreme. The safe margins of the day, still faintly visible during eventide, have been erased by night's dense gum, obscured by its wash of squid squirtings, pajama sauce, and the blue honey manufactured by moths. Is the night a mask, or is day merely night's prim disguise? Most of us are born in the night, and by night most will die. Night, when tangos play on the nurse's radio and rat poison sings its own hot song behind the cellar door. Night, when the long snake feeds, when the black sedan cruises the pleasure districts, when neon flickers "Free at Last" in a dozen lost languages, and shapes left over from childhood move furtively behind the moon-dizzy boughs of the fir.

It is the night of the alleged worst day of your life. Have things gotten any better? Not appreciably. While the American eagle flops like a headless chicken in the stock exchanges of the Orient, panicking the traders with a globby shower of blood, you hold your girlish breath, cross your fingers—and watch Q-Jo Huffington devour pork chops as if pork chops were about to follow money down the road out of Dodge.

You are seated in a padded plastic booth at the Dog House, a downscale restaurant whose motto is "We Never Close," a declaration whose truthfulness is reflected in the weary pantomimes of the waitresses, some who appear to have been on duty around-the-clock since the restaurant opened for business in 1934. For the most part,

21

the Dog House caters to an aging blue-collar clientele, although in the cracked hours after midnight, it is heavily infiltrated by the more extreme elements of the youth culture: by punks and bassers, grungettes and metalheads, thrashers and ninja boys, and by slumming high-school thrill-seekers from Mercer Island, Hunts Point, and other ritzy suburbs. Battle-hardened waitresses keep the kids in line, but you are relieved that the hour is still early and the diners less disturbing than déclassé. Which is not to imply that you are anything but annoyed to be here.

When Q-Jo named the Dog House as her dinner destination, you assumed it was a joke, a silly pun relating to the fact that so many people in the Virginia Inn were barking. Yes, *barking!* There they were, Seattle's poets, painters, musicians, and filmmakers; people whom one would guess might be cultured and sophisticated; but were they discussing Gödel, Escher, or Bach; were they casting a particularly illuminating light upon the stock-market crash, relating it to McLuhanian technology theory or "The Fall of the House of Usher"? Maybe they were at that. One hardly could account for every nuance of every conversation in the tavern, especially with the recorded music of African-American bluesmen being played at a volume that would have prompted those old Negroes to drop their homemade guitars and run into the forest with their hands over their ears. In fairness, there might have been at any given table intellectual speculation of invigorating quality. All you know is that you failed to hear the words "Dow Jones," "*deutsche mark,*" or "Michel Foucault" pass through any lips—but you did hear an inordinate amount of barking.

And when some bespectacled gallery poof, all certifiably hip beneath his crimson beret, would let loose a little bark, many around him would join in. Then, and this was the oddest part, everybody would beam in a bemused fashion, as if they were delighted yet did not understand in the least the source of their delight. Good grief! Was this some new fad? When you queried Q-Jo about it, she shrugged and said, "Oh, Dr. Yamaguchi," and brought up the Dog House.

Naturally, you kept expecting hidden connections to assert themselves. In time, and quite synchronistically, they would. But for the present, it was a matter of pork chops.

"Gwendolyn, you went ahead and ate without me, you thoughtless bourgeois bitch. Now, you gotta step aside and watch the big dog eat."

It is something to see, all right. Q-Jo glides into the platter of pork chops like a killer whale nosing into a school of salmon; smoothly but deadly, taking a bite out of first one chop and then another in turn, chop by chop; leaving them maimed, unable to flee; then circling back to finish them off, one at a time, fat and all; finally sucking every last droplet of gravy from the bones so that what remains is clean and white and polished, like markers in a Chinese board game.

And when you leave the table to use the telephone, she orders a second platter.

The bathroom scale does not exist that can instrumentally accommodate the poundage of Q-Jo Huffington. She pegs the needle at its furthest reach and would have to transfer to a commercial scale to determine precisely how far beyond the three-hundred-pound barrier—set by mechanical limitations and public decency—her weight has actually wandered. As for her cholesterol level, it is not in four figures but very nearly. Moreover, she smokes at a ruinous rate cigarettes that she rolls herself from black, coarse, sinister-looking shreds of Indonesian tobacco; smokes them at a pace that leaves you woozy and wondering if differences other than volume exist between her lungs and the tar pits of the Mesozoic.

One would presume that a woman as sensitive and aware as Q-Jo, a woman whose precognitive abilities are so convincing that they have made a believer of a skeptic as skeptical as you; one would suppose that such a woman—a professional tarot reader, for goodness sake—would take a special interest in nutrition and good

23

health. And she does, as long as it is the health of others. She denies, however, that either altruism or hypocrisy is involved. True, she is a giving person, and eating is one way of getting something back, a way for her to be nourished in return; but there is more to it than that. "I smoke and eat so that I don't fly away," she explains, meaning mentally fly away, although you picture her bulk hovering over the city like the Goodyear blimp. "When you're on the astral plain as much as I am, you need food and tobacco to bring you back into your body. For me, they're a grounding device." They are also protection. Apparently, Q-Jo is an emotional sponge, a walking psychic antenna who, even as she rips pork chops asunder, has to struggle to block the unconscious transmissions of fellow Dog House diners from her screen. Obesity affords her a measure of insulation, an extra layer with which to reduce her vulnerability. Tucked away in a sanctuary of fat, her psyche does not feel quite so exposed.

Privately, you have always found Q-Jo's size appealing. From the day you met, you have experienced—and rigorously suppressed—a strong impulse to jump onto the perfumed acreage of her lap, to rest against the buddhas of her breasts and let her rock you in her baobab arms. But while others also are fascinated by her, by her purple turbans, her multicolored caftans, her welding-spark eyes, cavernous dimples, Santa Claus laughter, patchouli effluvium, ebony cigarette-holder, and rings whose stones are the circumference of goiters, you nevertheless are embarrassed to be seen with her in public. God forbid that your employers or clients should ever discover that this baggy flake considers herself your companion. It continually humiliates you that the fates have seen fit to match you with such a friend. Once you have moved into your new condominium—if by some miracle the stock market's duck-dive has not annihilated those plans—you intend to see less of her, although less of Q-Jo is still aplenty.

NINE-TEN P.M.

"So what did you find out?" Q-Jo wants to know when you return to the booth and your recently refilled coffee cup.

"About André or the market?"

She looks at you incredulously. "André, of course. The stock market don't mean shit to me."

"It means more than you know. If this collapse is as lethal as it could be, it'll impact the lives of everybody in this country."

"Haw!" she guffaws, and licks a temporary cold sore of mashed potato from her upper lip. "It'll screw up the lives of those people who *allow* it to screw up their lives. The rest of us will get along just dandy."

"Yeah? How dandy will people get along when their investments fail, when their pension funds are belly-up, when federal programs run dry, and factories and banks slam doors in their faces and they're out of a job? You have a mortgage yourself, do you not?"

"They'll get along just like they've always gotten along. Before there was any such thing as banks and mortgages and factories and jobs. Before they bought into this bogus melodrama."

"What bogus melodrama?"

"The one you've based your life on. Now drink your coffee. I want you sober as a judge when we go out that door."

"Good grief, Q-Jo! You are just so . . . naive. You live in your own little world . . ."

"It ain't so little."

". . . and think everybody else can do the same. Well, anyway, even though you're not interested, a guy at the office told me that it's rubber-ball city in Tokyo right now. Index hits the floor, hits the lid, hits the floor, hits the lid. Every time the Nikkei starts down the drain, the pharmaceuticals rally and fish it out. Where it's going to close is anybody's guess." You are visibly excited.

"Gwen, baby, please ask the waitress to bring us three walnut shells and a dried pea. I know a fun game we can play."

"Look, my whole future's at stake here."

"Yes, yes." Q-Jo sighs a sigh as big and luxuriant as a bargeload of catnip. "You've been saying that all night. Confusing 'future' with 'career,' confusing 'career' with that roulette wheel you spin every day. A crash could be the best thing that's ever happened to you."

"You've been saying *that* all night. And I don't want to hear it anymore. If you aren't going to do the cards for me, let's forget it."

"I'm eating," Q-Jo says. It is a statement impossible to refute.

NINE-FIFTEEN **P.M.**

Q-Jo gnaws. You sulk. What gall she has, criticizing your profession. She a fortune-teller, one cut above a grifting gypsy in a dusty store-front. Then there is that other "job" of hers, the one nobody in the whole world does but Q-Jo Huffington, a job so wacko it doesn't have a name. What would a person call it, anyhow? Travel agent after-the-fact? Surrogate boredom victim? Marginal employment any way one slices it. Yet she insists that *you* are trafficking in illusions. What nonsense. Confused, whimsical, baroque, her aspirations are immaterial in the truest, and most regrettable, sense of the word; whereas you dream on solid ground, pure, clean: the sweetly insatiable yearnings of a young bride. In a little ruffled apron yodeling with strawberries that you embroidered yourself, you kneel at the oven door of the world, keeping a nervous but hopeful eye on the money soufflé. Q-Jo's version of this scene has you a vampire wrapped in the curtains.

"Well," she says, interrupting your pout, "did you get hold of Belford?"

"Yes. I reached him on his car phone. He's still driving around Queen Anne, looking for André. Rather upset that we aren't helping. I'd promised him we would."

"Almost done," she says. From her full red lips, she wipes the last stains of the flesh of the pig. "Let me just grab a dish of their tapioca pudding. A body can't hardly find old-fashioned tapioca pudding anymore."

26

"Belford's in a state. I've never seen him worked up like this. He's usually so calm." You pause. Reflect. "Naturally, I hope he finds André, but you know, it might be a positive thing for him if he's rid of that monkey."

"Oh, I disagree. The brutal truth is, that monkey's the one and only interesting thing about Belford boy. Without André, he's the duke of dishwater, the earl of dull." She pauses. Reflects. "As far as I know, that is. I have no idea what he's like in the sack. It's a fact that some men conceal the greater part of their personality between their legs." She flashes a grin you could slide a dictionary into. "Care to comment?"

Good grief, Gwen! Your face turns so red you can see it reflected in Q-Jo's silverware. The vice squad could hire you as a smut detector. You are sputtering toward an irritated response when, thankfully, a beehived waitress bustles over to take Q-Jo's dessert order. You excuse yourself and set off toward the lavatory, passing en route the ice machine, the milk dispenser, and a case in which humble proletarian bowls of pudding and Jell-O quiver with passive resentment in the shadows of opulent slices of pie. If this amounts to a confectionery model of impending class warfare, it is no secret where your sympathies lie. You all but nod hello to a particularly patrician wedge of coconut meringue.

The toilet is a shock to your sensibilities, not because it is in the least unsanitary but because it has been freshly painted with untold quarts of yellow enamel the color of a canary with liver disease. Blinking at the unrelieved brightness, wrinkling your nose at the perfume machine—fifty cents for a squirt of Evening in Paris—remembering with a sudden fondness the understated elegance of the Bull & Bear's facility, you, fully sober at last, let yourself into one of the twin screaming-yellow stalls, hike up your dress, pull down your panties, vigorously scour the seat with a wad of tissue, then sit. Although the cocktail lounge is at the other end of the restaurant, you can hear Dick Dickerson at the organ as plainly as if he is being piped through the plumbing. Dick is offering a rendition of "Lazy River," and a few of the customers are singing along. Your father used to listen to "Lazy River" (a jazz version, of course), accompany-ing the recording on his bongos—those cursed drums that ruined your chances for a normal childhood.

You are sitting here, half in reverie, half in annoyance, when your body abruptly twitches in a mild startle reaction. Cutting through the residual aromas of stale tobacco smoke, cheap perfume, oil-based paint, and piney woods deodorizer; cutting through the loo-air with a golden track, comes the smell of your own micturi-tion, a smell heightened a hundredfold by your recent ingestion of asparagus. And the instant your brain identifies the odor, it thinks of Larry Diamond. Just as the perverse bastard knew it would! You are disgusted with yourself and furious with him. And, as you discover when you wipe your labia, recognizably and quite inexplicably aroused.

NINE TWENTY-FIVE P.M.

You storm past the pie cabinet, where the Jell-O has started to look alarmingly upwardly mobile, and catch up with Q-Jo at the cigar counter. She is chewing on a toothpick and paying the tab.

"Belford Dunn is the nicest, most decent man I know, his sex life is nobody's business, and besides, *you* don't even have a boy-friend!" You say this through clenched teeth while practically balling your tiny hands into fists.

"Whoa. Whoa, there. Take it easy, lady. No need to get defen-sive. Belford's a sweetheart. The whole damn town knows Belford's a sweetheart. If the nimble-minded should ever put him on trial for terminal dullness, I'll testify under oath that he's twice as nice as he is tedious. Fair enough?"

Your inclination to vigorously condemn this faint praise is tempered by the embarrassment you feel at the way the cashier is regarding the pair of you. You make an edgy move toward the door, and Q-Jo says, "Good. Now let's go try and reunite our boy with his red-assed ape." She lays a thick, sweaty palm on your shoulder. "I suggest we begin by checking the jewelry stores."

NINE FORTY-FIVE P.M.

Near the crest of Queen Anne Hill, Q-Jo pulls over and eases her Geo Storm (the fact so many fat people drive small cars might be worthy of a behavioral scientist's attention) right up to the rear bumper of Belford's huge Lincoln, like an ambitious cocker spaniel sniffing out the estrogen level of a Doberman bitch. When she turns off her headlamps, you can see the silhouette—the squarish head, the wide shoulders—of the man you have vowed to ease out of your life by July 4 (Independence Day!), yet whose honor, if not élan, you have just passionately, though incongruously, defended. The ambiguity is not lost on you. It irks you, in fact. And there may be more to come. Any moment now, this man will spread his mouth over your mouth, and, duration depending upon how distracted he is by André's disappearance, mash it about. To what extent will you find that agreeable? Considering that obsolete boyfriend or no obsolete boyfriend, market crash or no market crash, worst day of your life or no worst day, your glands are blithely brimming.

Q-Jo opens her door and, like a discount Houdini trying to escape from a golf bag, begins pulling herself free of the car. Belford opens his door, slides out, and rushes to Q-Jo's assistance. You sit there. You look him over. You wonder.

Belford Dunn used to be a logger. What in earlier, more colorful times was called a lumberjack. He resided near his birthplace on the Olympic Peninsula and felled cedar and fir for his livelihood. At some point, he read the handwriting on the sawmill wall. It said, "Timber is a dying business."

Right next to it was a wall upon which was written, "A tree farm is not a forest." Belford put two and two together, concluding that at the rate Americans were selling logs to the Japanese, it was merely a matter of time before we ran out of woods and that the

29

"plantations" that were being established in their stead were without appeal, being devoid of wildness and beauty, diversity and danger, curiosity and reverence, that primal reverence that has forever been inspired by the Unknown Place; the place unknown, that is, to all but such messengers of our psyche as the moon and the mushroom and the owl and the stag.

When Belford packed up and left Port Angeles, it surprised his parents, who always thought of their son exactly as he was described in his public school evaluation: "Lovable but average." (Perhaps, Gwen, that is the way you think of him now.) Lovable though he may have been, however, he was, at thirty-three, unmarried, and he had only a few compunctions about leaving less foresightful buddies behind to whine and howl about the eventual loss of logging jobs. He did try to talk some sense into them, but their vision extended no farther than the nearest tavern, the length of a pickup truck, the panel of a VCR. So, adios, amigos. . . .

Once settled at the Seattle YMCA, Belford enrolled in real estate classes. He earned a Realtor's license, landed a job, and within eighteen months was selling more properties, both residential and commercial, than all but a handful of Puget Sound agents. He proved to be a natural salesman, primarily because he liked people and they liked him. They trusted him. Belford's brain chewed its cud as placidly as a moo-cow behind the broad, open facade of what is commonly known as an "honest face." Indeed, he *was* honest. From his thin, sandy hair to his shoeshine. He was active in the Lutheran church out of genuine piety, not as a ploy to make contacts—although contacts he did make in abundance. And money he made in abundance, as well. Ten years later, he still generates what you, Gwen, call jumbo juice. But most of it he gives to the church or to charities. And even more disturbing, in your estimation, he is planning to quit his job in September so that he might go back to school to become a social worker. Good grief! The upside, you suppose, is that if nobody can successfully apply the Heimlich maneuver to an economy that is choking on a dinosaur bone, America will need more social workers than real estate salesmen. But who is going to pay them? And how much?

It was from Belford Dunn that you bought your apartment. At the time, it was *his* apartment, but having proclaimed it too fancy, he moved several blocks away to smaller, simpler digs. His idea of "fancy" hardly coincides with yours. The building, a 1930s low-rise, is solid, and each of its units has leaded-glass windows, exposed beams, tiled fireplaces, and Swedish hardwood floors; in short, old-fashioned charm galore, but no one could claim it is a chic address. How could it be? Q-Jo Huffington lives there. Some months ago, you put your unit up for sale and signed a contract to buy a marine-view condo in a desirable upscale high-rise downtown. Good-bye, marginal neighbors, hello, *concierge!* The deal is scheduled to close next week. But next week, you—and the fellow stockbroker who is negotiating to buy your current place—may be sipping your morning coffees in the unemployment line. The timing of the crash could not have been worse. When you think about it, you scarcely can prevent yourself from screaming foul language and stamping your little feet.

At any rate, Belford seemed like a good catch at first. Even today, you are not prepared to admit that personal wealth and emotional stability are inadequate substitutes for *savoir-vivre.* Nor that unrelenting decency can wear on a person's nerves. What you will admit is that if you knew you had to spend the rest of your life with a social worker, you would blow your brains out. You might do that anyhow. Your mom did.

Out on the curb, Q-Jo is giving Belford a high five. "Hey, you big flamboyant, fun-loving, spicy guy!" He knows she's joshing him, he's not stupid, but he smiles good-naturedly. It's a smile a girl could bring home to mother, if she had a mother; a smile a girl could pet like a pony, sip like a lemonade, hum like a popular tune; a smile a girl would feel safe with in a dark alley. Not that Belford would ever take you down a dark alley. Except for assorted camping trips and fishing expeditions, which you found tiresome, dirty, and boring,

Belford has never taken you *anywhere*. Belford is not given to the romantic vacation, the luxury resort, the spontaneous weekend in Palm Springs. Three years ago, shortly after you met, he went to Europe. He thought he ought to see it. You were annoyed, frankly, that he didn't invite you—you slept with him earlier than you might have in the hope that he'd ask you along—but, alas, it was a package tour. Pre-sold and all that. You didn't sulk for long. *It will polish him,* you consoled yourself. *He'll be more sophisticated after he's seen London and Rome.* What you hadn't counted on was that he'd spend the entire month in Saint-Tropez fighting to gain custody of a monkey too hot for France to handle.

TEN P.M.

On Queen Anne Hill, there are a lot of places where a monkey might hide. It's a residential area, an area of yards. To be sure, the hill is ringed with apartment buildings—yours is one—but it's primarily a neighborhood, an extensive neighborhood, of single-family dwellings. And single-family dwellings have yards. Front yards, back yards, side yards. In these yards there are shrubs, bushes, hedges, trees. Bordered by toolsheds, garages, patios, gardens. There are schoolyards, too. And a couple of parks. There are even several wild wooded patches, spacially limited, yet adequate habitat for small animals. If opossum and skunk and raccoon can hide there, survive there, year after year, decade after decade, almost in the middle of a teeming metropolitan chockablock, think how an enterprising monkey might fare.

As distraught as he is—the kiss with which he greeted you turned out to be no more than a matrimonial peck—you would suspect that Belford would be driving around willy-nilly, mistaking for André every pussycat that darted behind a rosebush, yet surprisingly, there is a modicum of organization to his efforts. A modicum. His method has been to motor very slowly up and down one section of Queen Anne streets for twenty minutes, then to speed back to his apartment to see if the prodigal simian might not have returned; then, disappointed, to select a different section and repeat the process. You could greatly improve the efficiency of this operation, and normally you wouldn't have rested until you had done just that. Tonight, however, you haven't the starch for it. Fate has sicced the witches on you, and only a miracle in Tokyo can keep your innards out of their menudo.

So, Belford continues to do what he's been doing for hours, only now while he scans one side of the street, you halfheartedly scan the other. And behind you, taking up most of the Lincoln's roomy backseat, sucking on shaggy, smelly cigarettes, tugging at the folds in her caftan, Q-Jo cranks up the psychic radar.

"Getting anything, Q-Jo?" Belford asks.

"*Nada.* But that's hardly surprising. I don't read monkeys."

Over your shoulder, you shoot her a glance. "Since when?"

"Jackasses, yes. And jackals. Maybe a baboon now and again. But just the two-legged kind."

"André's only got two legs," Belford objects.

"Well, yeah, I suppose that's true. He'd have to have hands and fingers to do the things he's done."

Now would be the perfect moment to segue into a discussion of André's past activities and the possibility that he may be *trying*, at least, to resume them; the ideal time to bring up Q-Jo's proposal that the search party cruise the downtown gem shops, the museums, and first-class hotels—but neither Q-Jo nor you dare pursue it. There's something intimidating about a strong man on the brink of tears. Moreover, Belford has yet to contact the police. *He's refusing to face reality*, you think. Turning back to the window, you recommence your monkey watch with half-open eyes, reviewing in your mind the mistakes that left you so personally vulnerable to a market meltdown. Facing a little reality of your own.

Easter falls on the first Sunday after the first full moon following the vernal equinox. Therefore, as it is a cloudless night, there must be a moon in the sky. And whether waxing or waning, it must be virtually full. Sure enough. There it is. Poking over the tip of the

Queen Anne communications tower, big and bulbous and shiny and pitted, like the nose of a vaudeville comedian.

You, alas, are unmoved by it. A tissue of worry lies like a layer of cirrostratus between you and the moon. Your eyes are oblivious to the heavens, but when the Lincoln, on its way back to Belford's place, glides past several couples socializing in the moonlight outside the popular 5 Spot Cafe, your ears are reasonably certain that they hear people barking.

TEN TWENTY-FIVE P.M.

"Yamaguchi-san," says Q-Jo, in a fake Japanese accent. She chuckles.

"Right," Belford agrees. "Dr. Yamaguchi." He, too, manages to cough up the husk of a laugh.

"Hey! What is this with Yamaguchi and people barking?" you demand. Something is afoot, something silly and stupid, no doubt, but you are irked that you seem to be the last soul in Seattle who isn't in on the joke.

"I didn't personally catch it on the tube," Q-Jo explains, "but—"

"Look there!" Belford interrupts. "Is that him?"

"What?"

"Where?"

Belford brakes the Lincoln and angles it to the right so sharply that its front tire black-faces the curb. You entertain a whiff of burnt rubber and the feeling that the curb is down on one knee about to sing "Mammy." Then you see it: an anthropoid shape scrambling on all fours across the lawn of a duplex. Only a millisecond separates the synapse that falsely registers the silhouette of André from the one that accurately informs you that the shape is much too large for a monkey.

"It's a man," says Q-Jo.

"Yeah," Belford reluctantly agrees. The bellows of a huge sigh fills the car with the vapid carbon dioxide of his disappointment.

As the three of you look on, the man crawls into the shadow of a rhododendron shrub and all but vanishes there.

"Think it's a burglar?"

Q-Jo scoffs at you. "Gwen, the guy's in his *underwear*."

"The poor fellow's drunk," says Belford. "Or disturbed."

"Probably a stockbroker, then," you say. You check your gold Rolex. "In another thirty-five minutes, there could be a guy like him behind every bush in town." You issue a bitter little laugh and lay your hand on Belford's. It's the first time you've touched him tonight. "Let's keep moving, dear."

Belford, however, is already reaching for the door handle. "He may need help," he says. "He might be in pain."

There's no use trying to restrain the socially responsible once they are locked in on their suffering target. You pull back and let him go. Q-Jo makes a move to follow him, then thinks better of it and lights up another noxious cigarette instead.

"You're wise to stay in here," you say. "What if he's on drugs?"

"Belford's lucky if he is. People on drugs are always less trouble than people on booze."

As your supposed boyfriend slowly approaches the night crawler—for an ex-logger, it's amazing how daintily, almost primly, he moves—you strain to remember if your father was more trouble when he was drinking dago red or smoking Humboldt weed. "Trouble" may be the wrong word. Seldom was Ferdinand Mati trouble, he just wasn't much of a dad.

Out of the shrub-shadow, an arm suddenly materializes. Long and alabaster in the moonlight, it is reminiscent of those disembodied appendages that in old horror movies strangled, one by one, the occupants of Gothic mansions and played tortured Rachmaninoff solos on grand pianos in the middle of the night. The arm is vigorously, frantically waving Belford away. Belford does stop but failing to get the picture, asks the flailing arm, "Friend, are you okay?"

At that instant, the front door of the lower duplex flies open, and onto the tiny porch bursts a man in a postman's uniform. The man is wielding a croquet mallet and appears agitated and potentially dangerous, except for the fact that his progress is impeded by an equally agitated woman, wearing a red bra but no underpants, who has a firm grasp on his collar. The woman is weeping and wailing, and the man is attempting to shake her off while his vision adjusts to the dimmer light outdoors.

"There's two of 'em!" the man yells. He lunges forward so forcefully that the woman falls, releasing his jacket. "Were you fucking *two* of 'em?" As he bolts down the steps, brandishing the croquet mallet, you call out, "Belford!" Your voice sounds so high and tweety to you that you are embarrassed to add anything further.

At the same time as the disembodied arm is retracted into the shadows, Belford raises his own arm in a conciliatory gesture. Belford wishes to pacify, Belford wishes to reason. However, neither reason nor logic nor gloom of night shall stay this courier from his appointed rounds. The postman takes a running swing that grazes the sleeve of Belford's placating gesture. Now, it is Q-Jo's turn to holler. "Get behind the wheel!" she orders.

For some reason, you cannot move. You sit there as if mesmerized by numbers on a computer screen while the mallet whizzes around Belford's head. "Goddamnit, Gwen! Get behind the wheel and start the car!" Q-Jo pokes you hard between your shoulder blades with her cigarette holder. Thus prodded, you slide across the seat, turn the ignition—and whimper. Will the worst day of your life never end?

Whump! The sound of the mallet smacking Belford's face mimics the sound of a fastball landing in a catcher's mitt. Belford has not tasted so much cellulose since a limb fell on him his first week at work in the woods. Spotted owls circle his skull, chased by miniature *putti* with their diapers on fire. Belford is staggering, the mallet is rising for another *whump*, when the night crawler darts from his hiding place and lopes off down the street. Switching attention, the presumed cuckold follows him in hot pursuit. Prodded by Q-Jo, you inch the Lincoln forward. Q-Jo opens the door for Belford, whereupon you experience simultaneous horror at the blood he is dripping and jealousy at the way he waves good-bye to the pantless blond on the porch.

Ten Fifty-Five P.M.

Although Belford's apartment is clean and tidy, it reeks so of monkey that it turns your stomach. Q-Jo's sinister cigarettes will soon mask the animal odor, but the tobacco has been punching your nausea bag, as well. You slip out onto Belford's narrow balcony for a suck of fresh air. The night is coolish, but mild enough to be restrained by your Armani trench coat. Trees, newly leafed, block your view of downtown and its lights, but you can see (good for you!) that the sky is aprickle with stars and that the moon looks like a radiation blister that a primitive physician has treated with sulfur. That your brain cells might be catenated to those distant fossilized fireballs would strike you as preposterous, but only slightly more preposterous than your emotional links to the fellow who is lying on the sofa with an ice pack on his face.

Neither you nor Q-Jo can claim any first-aid experience—the stricken soul who relies on either of you for CPR can kiss his tush and his ticker good-bye—but between the two of you, you accurately determined that Belford's nose was merely bloodied, not broken, and that the cut in his lip should not require stitches. Q-Jo made him pinch his nostrils together until the blood flow clotted, you sponged his features with a wet hand towel. You weren't as gentle as you could have been—damn Posner if he thinks you'll take up nursing!—but Belford didn't complain. When he spoke at all, it was to express pity for those involved in the duplex triangle. Which, of course, annoyed you since you believe that the sordid of the world get what they deserve.

Now, he's speaking again. Muffled by the ice pack, no intelligible word makes it as far as the balcony. Intuitively, perhaps, you shoot another curious look at the stars, as if the constellations might hold an answer for you. (And, could you project your gaze all the way to the suburbs of Sirius, indeed they might—although not to any question that you have so far thought to ask.) Then you go back inside.

"What were you saying, Belford?"

"He said," Q-Jo replies for him, "that he wants to look for André some more. He wonders if you'll mind driving him."

"I guess I could," you consent with a minimum of enthusiasm. "What time is it?" You follow the rhetorical question with a glance at your watch. "Good grief!" you exclaim. "It's . . .

ELEVEN-THIRTEEN P.M.''

You knock over a chair and bounce off an ottoman in your explosive sprint to the phone. Good grief, good grief, good grief! How could you have allowed the crucial moment to pass unnoticed? Damn Belford and his meddling, damn proletarian immorality, damn the monkey, and damn the stars!

At Posner Lampard McEvoy and Jacobsen, the phone burbles, burbles, and burbles some more. The first few burbles mimic electronically the sound of neurological urgency, the next few the sound of the heart's frustrations. *They sure as hell got out of there fast,* you think. *The Nikkei not closed fifteen minutes and they've already blown the disco? What does it mean?* Banzai or hara-kiri? A hollow recorded voice comes over the line, informing you that the offices are closed until Monday and wishing you a happy Easter. Slamming down the receiver, you wonder if God doesn't have an answering machine to screen out the prayers of the venal and the boring? And in which category has he placed you?

Ignoring the encouragement that Belford mumbles through his ice pack, you let your fingers run not walk through the yellow pages. "R" is for "restaurants." There are so *many*. The only yellow-pages list longer than the restaurant list is the one for attorneys. So one eats out, one breaks a tooth or finds glass in the chowder or gets food poisoning; one sues. What does that say about America? Here it is, Gwen. The number of the Bull & Bear. Punch it in.

Once again, you are privy to a crosstown attack of chronic burbling. You try to imagine conditions under which the Bull & Bear might have emptied out, but you are not quite that creative. At long last, the receiver is lifted off its cradle, and you hear the aviary gabble-gobble of a crowded lounge, followed by the bartender's curt hello.

You ask to speak with Phil Craddock, good ol' Phil, and while he's being paged, strain to hear if you can pick up any clue concerning the Nikkei's performance from the tone of the barroom babble. It is definitely not subdued. But is that a skinny blade of panic snickersneeing through the roar?

"Not here," grunts the bartender.

As clearly as if he were on closed-circuit camera, you can tell he is hanging up the phone. "Wait!" you scream.

"Yeah?"

"Try Sol Finkelstein, would you? Thanks."

Phil is a commodities trader, a different breed, he's probably home in bed snoring like an overturned tractor. You should have asked for Sol in the first place. Good ol' Sol. As you await him, you hear, or think you hear, from somewhere so deep in the phone that it might well have emanated from a source other than the Bull & Bear, might have danced off like a stray spark from another conversation on another circuit, perhaps in another city, you hear, or think you hear, the word "Bozo." It gives the back of your neck a most puzzling tingle. You are still trying to make sense of it when the bartender comes back on the line. "Sol's not here," he says.

"Well, then, would you please page—"

"Lady, for Christ's sake, I'm not your social secretary! I'm busy!" He bangs down the receiver, leaving you with an earful of dead but vibratory air.

You bury your head in your hands. You can almost feel random hairs, strands that a moment ago were glossy black, turning gray in their follicles. Number twenty-four. Twenty-five, twenty-six. Your presumed friends hasten to console you.

"We haven't consulted the cards yet," says Q-Jo, stubbing out a cigarette in a thick vortex of gagging smoke. "Could put this whole affair in a different perspective."

"Gwen, honey," says Belford, removing the ice bag and sitting upright on the blood-flecked sofa, "let's think about this for a minute. There's got to be someplace else you can get the information you need."

"Oh, it doesn't matter," you say, your voice as burnt-out as a picnic marshmallow that's fallen off its stick. "It doesn't matter how Tokyo closed. I'm doomed anyway. Goddamn doomed!"

"Baby, baby, that's not so," Belford says. He puts a blood-stained arm around you.

Q-Jo just looks at you. She is hardly astonished that the Wall Street quake is rattling skeletons in your personal closet. She—and the tarot—have suspected for quite a while that you've been picking toadstools without a field guide.

MIDNIGHT

Obviously, a birthday candle's worth of optimism continues to flicker in your heart, else why would you be stopping by the Bull & Bear on the way to fetch your car? Belford had dropped you off at the parking garage, and while he'd been occupied with emptying his wallet for a delegation of the derelict, the dipsomaniac, and the dispossessed that had found in him a sympathetic ear, you slipped around the corner, still intent on reception of a report from Asia.

Q-Jo had gone home to bed. She had scheduled an early morning tarot reading, for which she must be rested, plus a noon appointment to eat cucumber sandwiches and watch out-of-focus videos of an elderly widow's tour of the gardens of England. For pay. This was Q-Jo's second "job." As you hugged each other good-bye, the two of you had made a tentative date for a midmorning consultation with the cards and a firm date to go out together Friday evening; to a nice escapist movie if you have your way, to the Werewolf Club to catch Betty Spaghetti & the Meatballs if Q-Jo is allowed to choose. "After weak tea and underexposed vistas of anal-retentive planting habits, I'm gonna require loud sounds and plenty of them," she said. You hate music clubs for any number of reasons, including the distinct threat of encountering your father in one of them, but you consented to consider the Werewolf, since it has a state-of-the-art ventilation system and since substantial persons—*real* persons, persons with incomes above five figures—have been known to show up there (although should they observe you in the company of Ms. Huffington, it could do you more harm than good).

Once Q-Jo, trailing a plume of acrid smoke, had been seen safely into her building, you had suggested to Belford a change in the André strategy. "Two cars can cover twice as much territory as one," you reasoned. Regardless of how he might covet your companionship, he could not argue. And regardless of your fatigue, a result both of the day's blows and the martinis with which you sought to soften them, you were intent upon demonstrating your often unappreciated goodwill. Thus, Belford eased the Lincoln down the Queen Anne incline, carrying you to retrieve your beloved Porsche so that you might enlist it in the sweep of the monkey-haunted hilltop.

Belford hates his automobile as much as you adore yours. For the present, a luxury car is a necessary accoutrement to his Realtor's image, but he is looking forward to the day when he can exchange it for an unassuming little egalitarian model such as Q-Jo's. He had mentioned this again as you neared the bottom of the hill and the cardboard lean-tos of the homeless came into view. As usual, it annoyed you. The trouble with Belford, in your opinion, is that he achieved financial success without ever dreaming of it, a situation contrary to the American way of life. The American dream is wasted upon those who never dreamed in the first place. Now that the schism between rich and poor has grown so wide, the old-style, anything-is-possible-in-America dreams are falling through the

41

crack. Today, the road to the pot of gold is paved with lottery tickets and frivolous lawsuits. A thoroughly cheesy way to go. How grand, how noble your dreaming has been in comparison. If only you had had a whit of fortune, had not been forced by circumstance to cut corners, bend rules . . .

"What happened today, sweetums?" Belford's question had jarred you loose from your musings. "I mean, how could the stock market fall apart like that?"

At last. He had finally got around to it. He was pooping the question. (As opposed to "popping the question," which he had done on a couple of occasions as well, meeting with an evasive response: you wanted to keep your options open.) "I should've seen it coming," you confessed. "I did see it coming, only I didn't do anything about it. Why? If I had pulled my clients out of the market and it shot up, which it did last year, they would've hated me, deserted me, I would've been the lone dumb wimp who missed the rally. On the other hand, if I'd stayed in and the market sank, everybody would've been in the same boat, it wouldn't have been me in the dunce corner all by myself. So I kept my people in. Worse, I stayed in myself. Yesterday, we tested HIV-positive. Today, we landed in Intensive Care."

"Yeah, but why, exactly?"

"Well, it's no big secret the economy's been skating on thin ice all year. Stocks overpriced at the same time that earnings have been weak. Money flowing out of this country, not much flowing back in. In their hearts, most Americans believed the government would sooner or later do something to reverse the stream. That's giving the government credit for more brains and more integrity than it's obviously got. The equities market's been chugging along on faith alone. There was a real vile character in the Bull and Bear this afternoon, a former hotshot broker, disgraced now, really . . . vile; but anyway, I overheard this creep say, 'Faith is believing in something you know isn't true.' And he's probably correct. Yesterday—God, it seems so long ago—that faith was badly strained when two cities in Pennsylvania and one in Maryland defaulted on their municipal bonds. The Street was skittish and set to stampede, and this morning one of the top analysts fired the shot. He predicted New York would also go into default and that Trace Manhattan Bank would turn toes up. That's all it took. The institutional and pension fund investors lit out for the hills, with the little guys running right behind them, hanging on to their suspenders."

"Down what? Eight hundred points?"

"Eight hundred and seventy-three, to be precise."

"That's awful. But I thought that after the crash of eighty-seven, they fixed it so that couldn't happen anymore. They put in safeguards, automatic circuit-breakers, or something like that. Wasn't it something like that?"

"From what I've heard about eighty-seven—I was a mere schoolgirl at the time—that carnage was the result of internal factors. A market discrepancy between the New York exchange and the pit in Chicago. A result of hedging short-side in futures. The futures market didn't have an uptick rule. It could short into weakness. In a down market, Wall Street traders had to wait for an uptick to go short. So to stay in the game, they would hedge their portfolios in Chicago. What with the volume increase brought about by programmed trading, it simply caught up with them."

Had Belford understood what you'd just said? And if he had not, how could he expect you to marry him? How could he expect that, in any case? In the shine of passing street lamps, you had tried to project what Belford would look like in ten years. Belford the social worker. Jaws gone to jelly, wire-rimmed spectacles, bald on top, tufts longish and gray on the sides. Benjamin Franklin without a kite.

"And you're right, the SEC did fix it so that internal causes couldn't pull the rug out again. But protection against *external* events is virtually impossible. What are they going to do, tape that damn analyst's mouth shut? Trading limits can't stand up to massive redemptions from mutual funds. They can slow it down, maybe; but once it's got momentum, they can't stop it. On top of that, there was some kind of atmospheric interference today, sunspots or something, that caused safeguard equipment to fail. Just a lot of bad luck, basically. Probably because *I* was so heavily invested."

When Belford had admonished you for taking the crash personally, you laughed as if you'd been joking—but you had been partially serious. There are people, you have noticed, who have money genes. Posner, for example. Even Belford. It isn't that they always inherit fortunes, although they are inclined to do that, too; but that they are genetically disposed toward wealth, connected to it on a molecular level. There's an extra, golden chromosome attached to the helix of their DNA, and it attracts money the way that a chipped or blemished chromosome will attract disease. You were not born with it, alas, and attempts to have it implanted have inevitably resulted in rejection. The grafts won't hold. Therefore, in order to keep your system green, you are forced to have regular, frequent, painful injections. Might it have been different had your daddy been Ferdinand Marcos rather than Ferdinand Mati, had your mom cared less for poetry? Maybe. As it is, however, you relate to cash the way a diabetic relates to insulin: absorb it artificially at a particular rate or run the risk of shock. Even then, you experience periodic allergic reactions, as if your white corpuscles have been mobilized to fight dollars off.

In any event, talking about the crash in a broad, somewhat objective fashion had made you feel better. Inspired, you'd been ready to treat Belford to a rehash of the Gwendolyn Mati theory of economic riptide—what happens when the push and pull of concentrated wealth collides with the stagger and swoon of excessive poverty and why it is imperative that you in the middle class swim like hell toward the channel of prosperity—but the Lincoln had arrived downtown, and its driver had become distracted by the very real, nontheoretical spectacle of poverty in the streets.

You had kissed your fingertips—a totally safe practice since your nails are chewed down to the quick—and touched them to Belford's busted lip. What color was the striping on that mallet, did anybody notice? Would it ever be employed again in a sunny Sunday afternoon of croquet on the duplex lawn, the postman and his wife paired off against in-laws or friends, calm now, reconciled, concentrating on wicket angles; while half a block away, hunkered down behind the wheel of a parked car, her lover glowers through dark glasses; and high up in the spire of a cedar, his eyes burning like joss sticks, his carat-sensitive fingers parting his fur in a silent harvest of fleas, a monkey also is spying?

You had wanted to share this vision of André's whereabouts (a premonition—or have you been made silly by your association with Q-Jo?), but Belford had been busy, cooing to the underprivileged as if they were his own baby kin, so you'd slipped away and rounded the corner of Union Street to rummage for one more frayed piece, perhaps, in the solid gray jigsaw puzzle of your destiny.

Now, as you near the Bull & Bear, a bank's digital reader board informs you that the temperature is forty-nine degrees, the hour exactly midnight. The watershed hour. The volatile stroke. Superstition's chime. Midnight, when the monotonous tick-tock of diurnal progress is for one throbbing moment replaced by the cool but smoky honk of a saxophone, alternately seductive and threatening. Midnight. The black growth on the clock face that has to be biopsied every twenty-four hours to see whether it is malignant or benign.

TWELVE OH-ONE A.M.

The affable Sol Finkelstein and the even more affable Phil Craddock are standing on Sixth Avenue, in front of the Bull & Bear. If they have been out here for a while, it would explain why they didn't come to the phone. It is hard to imagine what would keep them in the night air so long, but happily, as far as you can tell, neither of them is barking at the moon.

Great! you think. Now you won't have to go inside, breathe more tobacco fumes, face Posner, or encounter that Larry What's-his-name, that geek who has managed to ingrain himself in your

45

bladder so that every time you take a pee (pardon your French), his portrait wafts up from between your knees.

"Hi, guys."

Phil nods to you, but Sol looks away. That's odd, but then it is apparent that they are both quite drunk.

"Listen, I've been tied up at my PC," you lie, "correlating historical performance rhythms with debt levels to see if I can get a higher resolution on a recovery scenario, and I guess I worked right through the Nikkei close, silly me. Can you tell—"

"How long you been in this business?" Phil interrupts.

"Me? In the business?"

"Uh-huh."

"Four years."

Phil grins at Sol. Sol rolls his eyes.

"When you've been in the market four years, you think you know everything there is to know. When you've been around twenty years, you realize you don't know shit. Am I right, Sol?"

"Never knew shit. Never will."

Where is this coming from? Must be whiskey, the great ventriloquist. You force a smile. "Okay, I'll bear that in mind. But I'm still understandably anxious for the numbers from—"

"I'll tell you something, little lady. Sol and me are the only ones in the firm who can stand you."

"Right," says Sol. He looks you in the eyes for the first time. "And we hate your guts."

Twelve Oh-Three A.M.

As you hurry away, lips trembling, eyelids slapping down every teardrop that pokes its head out of a duct, you hear a voice call after you, the voice of Ann Louise.

"Churn and burn, baby," she calls. "Churn and burn."

HALF ASLEEP *in* FROG PAJAMAS

Twelve Oh-Seven A.M.

Folded like a sack of kittens over the wheel of your Porsche, you sob until you can sob no more. Then you sob some more. You haven't cried like this since your mother died. Not even the kiss-off from Harvard and Wharton pumped this much tearwater. When at last you feel composed enough to drive, you squeal out of the parking garage, your nose in a Kleenex, your blurry eyes on the road. You head straight home, monkey mission aborted, as far as you are concerned.

You do telephone Belford as soon as you let yourself in. He'll worry when you don't show up at the rendezvous point, and you don't want him calling you, catching you unaware and detecting pain in your voice. As expected, you get his machine. Someday, even the "call of nature" will be answered by a machine. For the time being, however, one must attend to it personally, but you wait until you have brushed your teeth and creamed your face before you brave that final pee of the day and the name that it surely will sing in the bowl. Just back from Timbuktu.

You dig out your old flannel pajamas for the comfort that is in them, put them on, and pad to the bed, stopping en route to em-power the TV set and switch its channel to CNN. Good grief, Gwen! There is something in you that just won't let go.

Sure enough, before five minutes have passed, there is a report on the market crisis. You feel embarrassed and amateurish, you feel *marginal*, to be relying on public media for market information, but at least you're no longer in the dark. Hong Kong suspended trading, you learn, Singapore and Taipei remained active and were beaten to a pulp. The news from Tokyo is as oddly inconclusive as it had been earlier. Down, yes, but still not lower than Godzilla's kneecaps. What to make of the Nikkei's relative buoyancy? The announcer quotes an analyst as guessing that it could be because of the reve-nues expected to be generated by Dr. Motofusa Yamaguchi's cancer cure, revenues that the good doctor has promised to spread evenly throughout the Japanese health sector (drug companies, hospitals, medical suppliers), and from which other stocks (transportation, hotels, banks, etc.) are bound to benefit.

Well, there you have it. Rather indefinite, but it could be worse. "Whether or not Tokyo's relative resilience will help ease our own financial crisis remains to be seen," the announcer says. "We won't begin to know before Monday morning—and that's a long Easter weekend away.

"Meanwhile, in Seattle, Washington, Dr. Yamaguchi met the American press on Thursday evening, and the suddenly famous Hokkaido clinic director had something, ah, *unusual* to say. Stay tuned."

You switch off the television and slide into bed. Ah! No sweetness like the sweetness of smooth, clean sheets. No protection quite so arrow-proof as a fluffy quilt. Hardly has your head dented the pillow, however, than you slide out and turn the set back on.

ONE OH-SIX A.M.

When news seeped out nearly nine months ago that a physician at an obscure clinic on Japan's northernmost island was curing colon cancer on a routine basis, the word "quack" was pronounced so often, the international medical community sounded like a duck farm. Eventually, as more and more cures were documented and as Motofusa Yamaguchi's theories, if not his methods, were made public, experts conceded that there was some scientific validity to the program at Fugetsudo Clinic but insisted that Yamaguchi's work was only experimental and that the marketing of experimentation as approved treatment was unethical, constituting as it did a profit-motivated exploitation of the desperate and the ill. The fact that *Fugetsudo* translates as "the wind and the moon" reduced nobody's suspicions, although why a simple reference to the natural world should foster mistrust in a profession founded upon observation of nature was a mite unclear.

Nevertheless, the healings continued. The tabloids were full of them. Should Princess Di give birth to a three-headed baby, the story would play second fiddle to the latest Yamaguchi "miracle"— unless one of the heads belonged to Elvis Presley, of course. The reticence of *The New England Journal of Medicine* on the subject was exceeded only by the reticence of Yamaguchi himself.

It turned out that Dr. Yamaguchi was not "marketing" his cure, nor was he refusing treatment to those without means. In a rare interview granted to *Texas Monthly*—he had received his medical training in Houston—he professed a willingness to share his discovery with the scientific world as soon as it was technically feasible to do so: it was not quite as easy, he said, as chalking a secret formula on a blackboard or handing over the blueprints for some machine. Paradoxically, he hinted that his treatment was so straightforward that a layperson could comprehend it. If his former patients understood it, however, they were as inscrutable as their physician. Not one of them had anything revealing to divulge to the prying press, although this may well be attributed to the opium with which Yamaguchi admittedly anesthetized them. A gentleman from Kyoto did make reference to a "ninja enema," a phrase that delighted tabloid editors as much as if they had invented it, but serious parties dismissed the reference as further evidence of the inadvisability of opium as a clinical sedative. Or else something that got terribly lost in translation.

In time, Fugetsudo Clinic was overrun, the town of Kushiro was overrun, the island of Hokkaido was overrun. The genuinely afflicted were exceeded in number by the self-diagnosed and the hypochondriacal, and those were exceeded by reporters and entrepreneurs. Logistical problems became so immense that they forced the clinic to shut down altogether. Yamaguchi said he would confer with his nation's leaders about what to do next.

Meanwhile, people were dying. Colon cancer is the third most common deadly form of malignancy, and only cancer of the lungs takes more lives. Victims and their families put pressure on the U.S. government to import Dr. Yamaguchi's technology but the National

Institutes of Health turned a plugged ear, and the Food and Drug Administration would only cluck about Yamaguchi's "regrettable use of smokable opium." As for the highly politicized, highly competitive American Cancer Society, it seemed openly pleased that Fuget-sudo Clinic was out of business. Out in Seattle, however, researchers at the Fred Hutchinson Cancer Research Center took a more positive, open-minded approach. They were impressed both with Yamaguchi's results and his expressed knowledge of MCC, a newly discovered gene that, in its normal state, produces the protein that regulates colo-rectal cell growth, but when defective, acts as an impetus to polyp and tumor formation. Hutchinson gambled and sent a team of investigators to Japan. When it returned the previous month, it proclaimed, with only token hesitation, what even the Japanese Health Ministry, although increasingly enthusiastic, was reluctant to admit: Motofusa Yamaguchi could cure cancer of the colon.

How? Well, the Hutchinson researchers were not completely certain. There were still many questions. However, Dr. Yamaguchi had consented to appear at a conference to be hosted by Hutchinson in early April—yes, the man who would leave his clinic only for late-night walks in the woods was coming to Seattle!—and perhaps he would explain everything then. Meanwhile, let us rejoice.

And now here he is. Meeting the press upon his arrival at Seattle-Tacoma International Airport. A hero's welcome. Strobe-flash fireworks. City fathers jostling to get into every picture. Lots of American flags, as if America is so desperate for something to feel good about, it will try to transform a foreigner's medical break-through into an excuse for a patriotic rally.

Not much to look at, you think, as a man, short, fiftyish (about your dad's age and height, though lacking your dad's ponytail), in a nondescript business suit, blinks and smiles shyly at the big bouquet of microphones that is being shoved stem by nodding stem in his face. When he speaks, his voice is as strong as his build is slight; his reasonably fluent English is lightly barbecued with a Texas drawl. His front teeth, now revealed, are the size and color of sugar cubes, and he has the odd habit of periodically tapping them with a Bic lighter that he seems to carry for no other purpose.

ONE OH-SEVEN A.M.
(Prerecorded and rebroadcast)

"Thank you, thank you. I am happy as catfish in muddy water to visit in U.S. again. Thank you." Dr. Yamaguchi taps his teeth with the Bic.

"You are having many questions. As time pass, I will try best, my best, to answer them each one." Pause. Tap, tap. "But we must bear in our minds that best of answers is not always reliable. Answers can be open to interpretation. Answers are tricky things." Yamaguchi says "things" the way a Texan would. "Thangs." It is rather disconcerting.

Yamaguchi widens by a centimeter or two his almost painfully shy smile. "Please indulge me to tell a small story. In the eighth century there lived Joshu, a great patriarch of Zen. One day, a monk ask Master Joshu, 'Does a dog have Buddha-nature, Master?' " Pause. Tap.

" 'Does a *dog* have Buddha-nature?' To that, Master Joshu was said to answer, '*Wu.*'

"Now, please, *wu* is in Chinese language a negative response. Negative. 'No,' yes? But the word have many fine shades of meaning. Many nuance. So, depending upon inflection, subtle nuance in pronunciation, *wu* could mean 'absolutely not' or 'probably not' or 'possibly not' or 'usually not.' Could mean emphatic 'no' or could mean 'Am rather incline to doubt it.'

"So, for twelve hundred years, scholars have argue. Exactly what did Master Joshu intend by *wu*? What inflection, what shade of meaning? Twelve hundred years, they argue and argue. But I am here to tell you." Long pause. No tap. Dr. Yamaguchi is, in fact, gripping the Bic with both hands.

"When ask if dog have Buddha-nature, master did not answer,

51

'Wu.' That is big misunderstanding. When ask if dog have Buddha-nature, master answer, *'wuf!'* "

For a second, Dr. Yamaguchi beams merrily at the reporters and dignitaries. Then he throws his head back until the slits of his eyes are pointing toward the ceiling. *"Wuf!"* he barks. *"Wuf! Wuf! Wuf! Wuf! Wuf!"*

Friday
Morning
April 6

In the Temple of Busted Luck

Five-Thirty A.M.

"Sears, Philip Morris, Merck, General Electric, American Express, Coca-Cola, International Paper, AT and T . . ."

You are sitting on the side of your bed, eyes closed, breath shallow, little titties still rising and falling to the tempo of sleep, but you are reciting the Dow Jones Industrials just as you have first thing every morning since you were a sophomore in college.

". . . Alcoa, Du Pont, McDonald's, Exxon, General Motors, Texaco, Woolworth, Boeing, Goodyear Tire . . ."

On the West Coast, stockbrokers must begin work early in the day in order to be in sync with Wall Street time. At the university, you trained yourself to awaken at five-thirty a.m., even though your first class was not until nine. Wake. Swing bare feet out and plant on floor. Chant.

". . . Union Carbide, United Technologies, Chevron, Three M, Eastman Kodak, Westinghouse, Walt Disney, Procter and Gamble . . ."

You were strict from the start. The morning after you lost your virginity—you were a junior then—it was, "Sears, Philip Morris, Merck, General Electric," etc., while the boy, a rugby star (you would have preferred a golfer, frankly), lay there dumbfounded, wondering if he had deflowered a saint or a kook: he was young enough to think there was a difference. At "Exxon," you felt a warm trickle down your inner thigh, and for a moment you were dumbfounded, too.

There was a time when recitation of the list expressed a sacred passion. Behind the pennaceous curl of your long lashes, you entertained visions of golden smokestacks, taller than the Himalayas, saluting the heavens with holy smoke; of tires that turned like prayer wheels, of cash registers that chimed like temple bells, of vats of molten metals illuminating the void. The incense of distant pulp mills enlivened your pious nostrils, your being was enveloped by that Buddhistic calm that only a substantial line of credit has the power to sustain. Today, you remain in awe of the Dow and its throbbing green aura, but, like Grandma Mati running laps around her rosary beads, you have come to invoke its pantheon by rote.

"Caterpillar, J. P. Morgan, Bethlehem (in whose steel manger an exalted profit was born), I . . . B . . . Mmmmmm." You always save IBM—poor old Big Blue—for last, because of its long-held position of honor in the hagiographic hierarchy and because the energizing manner with which its mantric syllable reverberates in your diaphragm serves to alert the frontiers of your consciousness and shake you fully awake. "I . . . B . . . Mmmmmm." As the final droning *m* rumbles out of your torso and into the ether, your eyes slowly open, and you face the world. But not for long.

The sun is rising like it isn't street legal. The sun is coming up sneaky. Finding not a single cloud behind which it might take cover, it seems hesitant, furtive, afraid to pop its clutch. The feeling is contagious. As soon as it dawns on you that this is not only a holiday but also the morning after the worst day of your life, you dive back into bed and cover up your head. If, however, you fear you will only lie there and fret, you are pleasantly mistaken. By the time the sun drags its tailpipes over the speed bump of the horizon, you are sound asleep again.

EIGHT-FOURTEEN A.M.

The Buddha is walking his dog. The dog's name is Sparky, and her leash is a long silver thread.

The Buddha is walking his dog on a golf course. "Hey! Hey you!" the golfers yell. "Somebody please get that fat fool off the green." On the seventeenth hole, the Buddha picks a mushroom. On the eighteenth hole, he eats it.

Now, the Buddha is flying his dog like a kite. The silver string snaps, and Sparky floats away over the pitched slate roofs. Her bark is a yappy kind of thunder. She rummages in a cumulus as if it were a garbage can.

In the restaurant district, cooks bang on their pots and pans and toss scraps of meat into the air. "Buddha's Dog Soup" would fetch a fancy price, if they could just coax her down. Famous chefs scurry up ladders and fire escapes, striking woks with wooden spoons. The banging grows louder, louder. Then you are awake. The banging wakes with you.

"Okay, okay. I'm coming." Your new condo will be in a security building, complete with twenty-four-hour doormen; Belford won't be able to barge in like this. You are positive it is Belford at the door. Claiming a need to marinate her psyche in the deepest, thickest marinade for the longest possible time, Q-Jo is never, ever up before nine. Highly improbable that it would be anyone from the disco: should Posner want to can you, should Phil or Sol wish to apologize, they would attend to it Monday at work.

You are correct, of course. It is Belford. And he looks a wreck.

EIGHT-FIFTEEN A.M.

Rough of cheek, bleary of eye, Belford obviously has been awake all night. His Men's Wearhouse suit is rumpled and bloody, his nose and lips are swollen, for the first time in his adult life his hair is uncombed, and his left hand and left cuff are coated with a sticky yellow substance, the result of his having sat on the steps of his building wagging a banana Popsicle—André's favorite breakfast—in the dawn's early light. You are disgusted, but then you suspect that you, too, are functioning below the summit of your grooming potential. You withhold criticism of Belford while you flee to the bathroom for a consultation with the mirror.

The eyes that blink back at you are puffy and red from weeping, but aside from that, your reflection reveals nothing untoward beyond the usual surprise at your Philippine demeanor. In all these years, you still have not gotten used to it. Thanks to your mother, who was mostly Welsh, you managed to avoid growing one of those flat-bridged noses that cause all Philippine women to look like tomboys, even those with truckloads of black lace bras and two thousand pairs of high-heeled shoes. Your crisp little nose is your mother's gift, but everything else—your skin, your hair, your eyes, and mouth—came over on the gene boat from Manila Bay. While growing up, you made several attempts to home in on your heritage, to no avail. First, you were born in Oakland and reared in Seattle, in a milieu more bohemian than ethnic. Second, there was the pervasive lack of self-definition that characterizes the Philippine Islands, in general; a result of three centuries of Spanish occupation and half a century of nestling under America's iron-feathered wing, not to mention the Japanese invasion, prolonged Chinese emigration, and two decades of drastic dictatorship. Moreover, your ancestral homeland was the only nation in that part of Asia to be colonized by the West before it had developed a centralized government or an advanced culture. While still a teenager, you decided to deal with the identity problem by ignoring your packaging and focusing on its contents, which you are convinced is Yankee through and through. It is understandable that others do not always see you as the all-American girl, but what is really annoying is the smirky way that mirrors regard you, as if to say, "Who are you trying to fool?" You wish you knew.

Face washed, teeth brushed, hair flounced, bladder emptied (not a whiff of asparagus enzyme to taunt you during the meeting of waters), you check your reflection again and decide that the flannel pajamas must go. Off they come. Then right back on. Better frumpy than naked, you reason, as you return to your beau.

Belford is lying on the bed, eyes closed and an expression on his face that could end three Italian operas and still have enough anguish left over to butter an existentialist's toast. You lie down beside him. You wish only to comfort him, you tell yourself—as if Belford could not be comfortable with his fly fully buttoned. He grows in your hand the way money ought to grow in your account. Well, time to take some profits. Belford's eyes pop open. He scarcely can believe you are being this bold. You can't believe it, either. You are blushing, in fact, while you shimmy out of your pajama bottoms and lower yourself onto him. Ooops. A tad off-center. His burgundy knob bangs hard against your perineum. A quarter inch to the south and you'd be following the path, so to speak, of Ann Louise. You raise up, adjust, and try again. This time you close around him like silo doors closing around a heat-seeking missile. You bite your lip to keep from squealing. Admit it, Gwendolyn, you needed this. You really needed this one.

Spine arched, head thrown back, your own hands cupping your breasts, squirming and jouncing all the while, you ride into the morning. It's a short ride, actually, and none too smooth, but it takes you where you want to go. As a lover, that is pretty much how you regard Belford Dunn. Cheap transportation.

Eight-Forty A.M.

Q-Jo claims that you have never had a genuine orgasm. How would she know? Even with an ear against your bedroom wall, she wouldn't know. Moans and groans are not your style. On the other hand, she could be right. How would *you* know? What you do know is that at some point in the coital embrace, you reach a stage where you think you have been plunged waist-deep into bubbling hot chicken fat. And afterward you feel embarrassed and a little soiled. If that isn't orgasm, what is it?

Mercifully for you both, Belford falls asleep immediately following ejaculation. Careful, lest you rouse him, you slip out of bed and back into the bathroom, where you shower long and hard, as you always do after sex. Then, creamed and powdered, you stare into your closets for a while, surveying the Chanel suits, the Ralph

Lauren blouses, and Donna Karan blazers, many of which are not paid for yet. The longer you stare at your wardrobe, the more strongly it occurs to you that you ought to be nice—very, very nice —to Belford Dunn.

With all the quickness in your Porsche, you zip to the Queen Anne Thriftway and return with the makings of a traditional breakfast; one of those deadly bacon and fried-egg repasts that lumberjacks (and Filipino drummers) seem to enjoy. Q-Jo claims that the thing men enjoy most in all the world is what vulgar people call a "blow job." Q-Jo says, "Show me a wife who doesn't suck cock, and I'll show you a husband I can steal." The very thought of it causes you to spit, albeit daintily, into the sink.

NINE-THIRTY A.M.

It turns out that Belford has given up bacon for Lent, but he relishes the eggs, even though you fried them so long and so hard that their edges are as black and lacy as one of Imelda's bras, and their yokes have the texture of gum eraser. In the process of devouring five slices of jam-lavished toast—he hasn't eaten since lunch on Thursday—he compliments your cooking to the point where you start to get annoyed. You would be annoyed even if he weren't spraying crumbs. Ah, but you spoon your yoghurt and hold your tongue, and after he has done the dishes—you couldn't dissuade him—you put your arms around him and say, "Now, dear, I realize you want to rush out and drive around some more, and we can do that later on, but first don't you think it's in André's best interest, as well as everybody else's, that we go downtown and file a report with the police?"

Belford grimaces. You are rather pleased. You prefer a look of agony to his customary placid grin. "I realize it's the right thing," he admits. "But what if the police find him and won't give him back? I mean, even if he hasn't done anything, once they learn about him, they might not give him back to me."

"No, that's silly. You convinced the French to trust you with him. And you couldn't speak their language."

"I *bribed* the French."

"Belford! You never told me that. Well, then, there's no problem. You think the cops in Seattle would turn down your dough?"

Your boyfriend, whose stock appears to be ascending in reverse ratio to IBM's steep slide, is pensive for a moment or two. "Okay," he says at last. "Let's go."

"Maybe you ought to stop at home on the way and change clothes." It is a prudent suggestion. In addition to its bloodstains, the rumpled wad of a suit now sports about its fly an encircling white crust of dried semen and vaginal juices, like an alkali lake on the moon.

"No time," says Belford, with a glance at the kitchen clock. "We should get downtown and right back. Else we'll get tied up in traffic."

"It's a holiday."

"Yeah, but there's a parade at noon."

"Are you kidding me? A Good Friday parade?"

"Not exactly, no. It's some kind of celebration for Dr. Yamaguchi."

Ten-Twenty A.M.

You take the Porsche because you don't believe Belford is in any shape to drive. You are in less than pristine condition yourself. Oh, you look fine enough, in your Italian jeans, Anne Klein blouse, and cashmere blazer, but there's an albatross around your neck as big as Mount Rainier, the volcano whose titanic snow cone is filling the southern quadrant of the sky with such massive majesty that even lifelong Seattle residents are compelled to gawk. Of course, due to the rain clouds that customarily cling to the city like clods to a hopper, nobody gets to see the mountain very often. On the rare clear day, such as this April morning, when not so much as a cellophane pasty censors the mammary display (the frost-nipped breast of the queen of the Sasquatch?), Seattleites are caught wondrously off guard, a fact attested to by a concomitant escalation in traffic accidents. You keep one eye on the road, one on the peak, but take delight neither in technology nor in nature. In your present situation, both seem hostile, threatening forces. To your mind, an American could no longer count on either technological advances or natural resources to generate glad gobs of gelt.

Once at the Public Safety Building, you are directed to the fifth floor. There, the elevator discharges Belford and you into a small, shabby, windowless lobby. There are doors, forbiddingly closed, with signs on them that read POLICE ONLY. Everything is gray: the walls, the linoleum, the three wooden benches. You have the feeling that while it may be spring outdoors, it is always winter in the house of the law. You actually shiver. Maybe you are remembering the several occasions when your father came home with his skull split open. It couldn't have been his fault every time. When you and your little brother would ask why the cops beat him, he always answered, "Brown eyes, black hair."

Around the corner, there is a reception window. The two of you don't get much of a reception. Belford is disheveled and obsequious; you, as is your custom in the presence of public servants, haughty. Persons who are haughty to porters and clerks are thought to be expressing an overt sense of superiority, although it is more likely that they are trying to widen the distance between themselves and their servers, to make the gulf so broad that fate would have logistical problems freighting them back across it. Inside every career woman who stiffs a waitress is the lingering fear that she herself might have to wait tables someday. The haughtiness is a pathetic attempt at protective voodoo.

The receptionist—she probably has a different title—is a fortyish matron who looks as if she might have spent a lot of time in a freezer locker. Her face is ashen, flat, and lopsided, like a stone-axed cut of caveman meat, a reptile steak for a prehistoric barbecue. Her eyes are spots of gristle, and her thin mouth is an ax wound in the fillet. When she learns that you are here on behalf of a monkey, it is her turn to be haughty. "Don't you know the police are busy with important matters?" she asks, as if you are so dumb you have learned nothing from all the cop shows on TV. "You should've gone to animal control."

Belford turns on his Realtor's charm, but she keeps repeating "Animal control. Animal control." She wants to send you to what used to be called the "pound" to present your problem to an animal control officer: a "dogcatcher" in less self-important times. Eventually, poor Belford bites his busted lip and commences to fill her in on André's background. He doesn't get very far before, smirking all the while and rolling her dead yellow eyes at the other clerks in the office, she rings for a detective. You have the distinct impression that she is acting out of suspicion rather than compassion. In fact, you hear her stage whisper "Harborview" to the girl at the next desk, Harborview being the hospital where the cops dump indigent citizens who have blown their bonnets.

For more than half an hour, you wait on one of the hard gray benches, with not so much as an out-of-date magazine to help you pass the time. You are annoyed by the delay but hardly surprised. Undoubtedly, the woman with the face of singed saurian sirloin was speaking the truth when she said there was only one detective on duty in that division. The city can no longer adequately fund its service agencies. Everywhere, everywhere, the infrastructure is deteriorating. Fiscal funeral directors circle America's largest municipalities like buzzards, archaeologists are pointing shovels at towns that aren't even buried yet. In any case, with no distractions other than Belford, you are forced to sit there and dwell on Monday morning's market, weighing whatever slim chances you think you might have to cover your badly exposed ass. A wave of nausea gasses your gobble.

When the detective finally shuffles out, Belford has the presence of mind to hand him his business card, and you quickly follow suit. The cards have a positive effect—a Realtor? a stockbroker? why, these silly shits might tip cocktails with the mayor—and the red-faced, white-haired detective, who looks like an Irish priest who has banged his nose a few too many times against the grille of the confession booth, listens politely, even interestedly, to Belford's tale.

Eleven-Ten A.M.

"You ask me what kind of monkey is this lost monkey? Well, officer, if you know your monkeys, you'll have a good idea of André's description when I tell you he's a tailless macaque of the type commonly called a Barbary ape. An Old World monkey. About yea tall and yea wide. Fur's a dark brown. Sweet-tempered unless provoked. Crazy over banana Popsicles, raisin bread, those little packaged apple pies—from the convenience store, you know? A regular macaque type monkey, I guess. Little or no tail. But, excuse me, officer, if that's all there was to it, we wouldn't be using up your valuable time, we'd be over at animal control."

Belford pauses to compose himself, and in the interlude, the detective looks up from his notepad and stares at you. It's a hard stare. The detective is wondering, you surmise, whether a young, spotless, well-coiffured professional woman such as you could possibly be responsible for the mess *en soleil* around Belford's fly. How embarrassing! On the other hand, he could be glaring at you because he has his savings invested in stocks. Or is it the brown eyes and black hair? You shudder and shift your weight from left cheek to right on the derriere-numbing bench.

"You see, I brought André back from France. Over three years ago. He'd been in some trouble over there. A whole tub of trouble."

"Exactly what kind of trouble would this ape have been in, sir?" For some reason, he stares at *you* again. Good grief! What disgusting thoughts might this public servant be entertaining? And how can you stifle your blush?

"André was not a new monkey. By which I mean, he was a

previously owned monkey. And his previous master was a Belgian animal trainer turned bad. Turned jewel thief, to be frank. *Famous* jewel thief. Or would that be *infamous*?"

"Go on." The detective apparently did not moonlight for the grammar police.

"You may have heard of the guy. Kongo van den Bos. No? Really? Well, in any case, it was entirely Kongo's fault. I mean, what would a monkey want with a movie star's emerald necklace or some old Aztec jade? Or the Hope diamond, for that matter? I mean, you know, a monkey may be kinda smart, but they're only animals when all is said and done, and they don't have any idea that these brightly colored stones and golden metals are so valuable to us human beings. André was just doing what Kongo van den Bos—I'm surprised you never heard of him in your line of work—taught him to do. It was like a circus trick, you know, as far as little André was concerned. There's absolutely no way a monkey could comprehend it was criminal activity. From a law enforcement perspective, wouldn't you say that's so?"

"Go on, sir."

"Okay, you see, I was in France on a tour a few months after Mr. Van den Bos got himself busted. He was caught red-handed in Saint-Tropez—that's a town on the Riviera, not the sort of spot where I normally hang out, ha-ha—and it was at that time that the authorities finally realized he had trained this monkey to do his dirty deeds for him. It explained his success. I mean, you know, who's better than a monkey for getting in and out of billionaires' bedrooms? Well, there was a trial, and Kongo was convicted and sent to prison. But then there was the question of what to do with André. André is the monkey's name. I guess there was a big to-do over it, because the authorities wanted to put André to death. They swore up and down that he now had ingrained criminal habits and couldn't ever be trusted. But the animal rights groups over there intervened, and eventually they turned this poor, exploited creature over to the Saint-Tropez municipal zoo. This was about a week

65

before my tour hit the Riviera. Well, unfortunately, André was only in the zoo a couple of nights before he, uh, escaped and, uh. . . ." Belford lapses into a sorrowful silence.

"Please go on." At this point, you have the feeling that the detective is less hurried than curious. "Go on," he orders, so on Belford goes.

Making annoying excuses all the while, he tells the detective how the monkey broke out of the zoo and went on a rampage. In one night, André tore through half a dozen villas and nearly as many hotels, stealing watches, rings, and brooches, only the finest stuff, selecting and rejecting with the eye of a connoisseur, although sometime before dawn he snatched the false teeth from a glass of water on the police chief's dresser. The police chief took it as a deliberate personal insult, and when André was captured the next afternoon in the midst of a siesta in the crow's nest of an anchored yacht, the chief vowed that the monkey would die. It was difficult to argue for André's life. Heretofore, he had presumably been carrying out the commands of his master, a poor dumb beast under a villain's control. Now, however, he had robbed of his own volition, had robbed discerningly, expertly, and, most of all, voluminously. (When Kongo was directing him, he seldom made more than a couple of heists a month.) Clearly no ordinary animal, André was, in the police chief's words, "diabolically clever and a threat to priceless private property." Wags claimed the chief clinched his repatriated dentures as he said it. Nevertheless, animal rights activists came once more to the monkey's defense. Led by a former film star, protest demonstrations erupted all over France. Belford watched one such protest from the balcony of his hotel room in Paris. Belford saw, in the streets and on television, photographs of the condemned monkey. In his heart, Belford felt something shine, like a hot but distant planet. Involuntarily, Belford reached out toward the monkey in the picture, as if to take its tiny hand in his.

André's execution hour arrived. The police chief and three of his men held the animal in place for the veterinarian's "hot shot."

The needle was centimeters away from shaved haunch when there was an explosion of breaking glass, and Brigitte Bardot herself leapt through the vet's window, followed by a dozen fellow activists. While the two sides scuffled, a judge in a hearing room a few blocks away granted a stay to Bardot's lawyer. The attorney raced to the vet's, pulled the chief off his client, and presented the document. When his tour group arrived in Saint-Tropez, Belford learned that the "little rascal," as he had begun to refer to the macaque, had been temporarily spared. Belford shouted, "Hallelujah!" Right there on the French Riviera. He could not help himself.

"I've always loved animals, officer. Somebody mistreat a dog, it'd really get my dander up. This French monkey was so cute, and its life had been so unfair. Well, right away I got me an interpreter and went down to city hall, to the police station, and to the court, and offered to take André off their hands. To bring him to America. Land of the free and home of the brave." (*Good grief!* you think. *When will the corn stop, and the ball begin?*) "At first, they wouldn't even listen to me, but I was persistent. You learn that in salesmanship. Persistent and polite. My tour went on to Spain, but I stayed behind, and nearly every day I stopped by the office of some official or other in Saint-Tropez and made my pitch. I don't know which the chief got the most tired of, the controversy in the media or me on his doorstep, but one day, after about a month of hard lobbying, he called me in and said in perfect English, 'If you can get this damnable brute out of France by tomorrow night, it is yours.' Those were his very words. And with great joy, I complied."

The detective scowls. "The Frenchman didn't file a report with U.S. authorities? Nor you neither?"

"No, officer, he did not and I did not. Maybe I was in the wrong, but I wanted to give this poor monkey a new lease on life. Why bring his past with him to Seattle? You see, I was convinced I could reform him. And I did. As Miss Mati is my witness, I did."

The glance the detective gives you is like a coin tossed to a leper. To Belford he asks, "Now, how do you know that, sir?"

" 'Cause after six, seven months or so—these things take time —I could leave baubles and beads and imitation jewels lying around all over the place, and André wouldn't even touch 'em. Why, if I dangled a rhinestone bracelet in front of his face, he'd screech and run out of the room." (*Maybe*, you think, *he was screeching at your bad taste. You believe that monkey can't tell rhinestones from diamonds?*) "How did I accomplish this? Well, part of it was conditioning, simple rules of animal training, although it isn't always real simple, it requires a heap of patience. And part was my faith. I'm talking about prayer now. Lord, how I prayed and prayed over that monkey! And I taught André to pray, too. Okay, you can look at me funny, but for the last year and a half, André has been kneeling down beside me every night at bedtime and bowing his head, and folks may say, 'Monkey see, monkey do,' but I believe sincerely there's more to it than that. André is devout. He is. You should see the way the little rascal reacts to pictures of Jesus Christ. I know, I know, it's only a dumb animal, but who's to say André does not have a soul, a little monkey soul? Sure, he's been retrained, but I'm prepared to go further than that. André's been *reborn*."

The detective clears his throat. Scarcely looking up, he asks Belford about the circumstances of the monkey's disappearance— "Yesterday morning while I was at work. He unlocked the apartment door and just took off. No warning, no nothing"—and then assures him that the police would not, could not, hold André, once apprehended, unless he has committed an offense. In fact, in the absence of a crime, the only action the detective can take at all is to issue an information report. A non-emergency (read "low-priority") bulletin would be broadcast to patrol cars advising them to be on the lookout for an unrestrained monkey. At this point, appearing a trifle stunned, like a priest who's heard the confessions of a dormitory of hormone-laden schoolgirls, the detective excuses himself and scurries away to the safety of his office.

"Gee," says Belford. "That wasn't real satisfying, was it?"

"Well, didn't I tell you to mention the bribes? Might have given him some inspiration."

HALF ASLEEP in FROG PAJAMAS

Eleven-Thirty A.M.

Outside, it has gotten surprisingly warm. And, not so surprisingly, hazy. The air tastes of sauerkraut, the metropolitan ozone layer wiggles like a mold of rat jelly. Although there's barely a cloud in the sky, Mount Rainier has virtually vanished. It is a spook summit now, a ghost tit behind the haze, and the sun is ghostly, too, its blazing oceans of nuclear radiation no match for the spew of tens of thousands of little Japanese cars. "Don't breathe this air," you say. "You don't know where it's been." Behind a hydrocarbon hood, the city is outlined like the features of a robber under panty hose. "I can remember," says Belford, "when Seattle didn't have any smog. It was not that long ago." "We shouldn't complain," you say. "It's the smell of money."

Happily for you, Belford pays for parking. You suppose you are going to have to start pinching your pennies now, a thoroughly depressing idea. For some odd reason, you think of that creep in the Bull & Bear and what he said about the fun just commencing. "Harborview," you hiss. And Belford, believing you are referring to the police receptionist, hastens to add, "We probably did strike her as a bit demented, poor woman."

By driving along the waterfront on Elliott Avenue, you manage to avoid any congestion generated by the Yamaguchi parade. It turns out not to be a parade, anyhow, but a rally at the downtown Westlake Mall. The mayor gives Dr. Yamaguchi the key to the city. Cancer patients from a five-state area and British Columbia mill about, crying out to be blessed. The good doctor promises the crowd and the press that he will reveal findings of some importance at the conference on Monday—and then, with shy smiles and Bic-taps, relates a little story about how his parents consented to his studies in Houston only because they thought "Rice University" sounded sympathetic to a homesick Asian's dietary needs.

On the climb up Queen Anne Hill, you stupidly ask Belford if he has considered the possibility that André might have been stolen. He shakes his head assuredly, but his confidence turns quickly to panic when you elaborate. "I'm talking plot here. A professional job. I mean, there're criminals all over Europe who know about André and his special talents. Maybe one of them traced him here. Okay, so they wouldn't know how to control him, what commands to give, and so forth. But what if Kongo van den Bos informed them? Suppose he sold the information to one of his jailmates, or they beat it out of him? Suppose Kongo's been paroled? It's been three years. Early release happens all the time in America, so why not France? Suppose Kongo's here? Suppose . . . ."

"Lord," Belford moans. "Lord, lord, lord, lord! Why didn't I think of that?" He insists that you turn the Porsche around and fetch him right back to police headquarters so he can alert the detective. It taxes your powers of persuasion to convince him that he can accomplish it just as easily over the telephone. "Call as soon as you get home. Then take a nap, for goodness sake. Drink a glass of cooking sherry. You're a load of nerves." You are not as nurturing as you ought to be, perhaps, but you have devoted the entire morning to Belford at the expense of your own agenda. You simply must catch Q-Jo before she leaves. Her tarot deck awaits you, with its lurid colors and obscure archetypes, an extravagantly fashioned if spitball-plugged keyhole in the door to your temple of busted luck.

Eleven-Fifty A.M.

You don't make it. Her appointment with the garden club tourist is at noon, and it appears as if she is going to be on time for a change. To you, whose creed is to never ever be late for *anything*, she once quoted Oliver Goldsmith: "Punctuality is not an admirable trait in a woman of grace." You surveyed her beanbag rolls of bouncing flesh and saw a travesty of grace, but the best you could come up with in response was, "The early bird gets the worm." Naturally, she had some fun with that at your expense.

In any event, today of all days, Q-Jo Huffington has left for work on time, her "work," in this case being not in her primary capacity as tarotmancer but in her secondary role as professional one-woman captive audience for travel bores.

Nearly a decade ago, on a Metro bus, Q-Jo slid her tectonic plates of tootsie-wootsie tonnage onto a seat next to a (fortunately) tiny, black-clad crone who, it turned out, had recently returned from a visit to her ancestral home in Greece. When Q-Jo responded with some semblance of enthusiasm to the already dog-eared snapshots the old woman pulled out of her purse, the woman said, "You come to my house, look at my pictures, I pay you ten dollars." And Q-Jo, because she felt sorry for the lady and because she could use ten dollars, complied. Later, it occurred to her that the world was full of people with similar needs. Some were old and alone, some were weird and friendless, some had friends but were in danger of losing them if they subjected them to another illustrated account of their last vacation, some were simply incorrigible show-offs. What they had in common was that each of them had been somewhere and wanted to tell somebody about it. In great detail. So, Q-Jo hired herself out. She would sit in their parlors or dens or cramped apartments—occasionally in an executive suite—and pore through their scrapbooks and photographs, applaud their slide shows and video presentations, ooh and ahh at their souvenirs and mementos, listen attentively to journal entries and passages from guidebooks and hyperbolic brochures, and generally exhibit appreciation and curiosity. (She learned early on that the more questions she asked the better tips she earned, although it was prudent to ask only those questions she was reasonably certain a client could answer.) From family reunion picnics in Iowa to the Folies-Bergère in Paris, from the magic mice of Disneyland to the killer rats of Kabul, Q-Jo had had occasion to comment on them all. Sometimes more than once. Her clients tended not to travel often—some took only one trip in their entire lives—and it was fairly common for her to be invited to review the same journey twice or thrice or more.

If you have told her once, you have told her forty times, her little scam may be creative and clever, but there's no money in it, no *serious* money. She says she doesn't mind. "It's supplemental income.

The tarot business seems to fluctuate a lot, according to the alignment of the planets." According to the state of the economy, in your opinion. "Anyhow, my clients rely on me emotionally," she maintains, a sentiment not appreciably different, it seems to you, from the bleeding-heart attitudes of Belford Dunn, which she often joins you in ridiculing.

No matter. Q-Jo has gone off on a job, just when you need her most. However, as you discover when you walk down the hall to your own more spacious unit, she has left you a note.

Eleven Fifty-Three A.M.

Wedged in your threshold is a small rectangle of black rice paper that when unfolded reveals the following message handwritten in silver ink:

> Gwen Baby,
>
> Regret we missed connections. I'll be back by three. Meanwhile, the cards are spread on my reading table. I've shuffled them, meditating on you and the questions I'd bet the ranch you're dying to ask. So pick a card. You know how. Study it and we'll get together later.
>
> Ta-ta,
> Q the Huff

She wishes you to select a single card. That's the way you do it these days. Now that you have grown close, she has difficulty giving you a full-scale reading. Her feelings, her fears and hopes for you, show up as static in the psychic transmission. She says the tarot can have a plethora of meanings, and when she looks at the cards that come up for a friend, she, due to a protective instinct, tends to lose her objectivity and overaccentuate the positive. As a result, the friend is misled, and Q-Jo's gift is compromised. "Tarot with a stranger is kinda like a one-night stand," she explains. "It's usually both more dangerous and more honest than sex with the partner you love."

Recalling the first time she ever read you, you have to concur. That was nearly three years ago. You were new in the building, having recently purchased your apartment from Belford Dunn. You were also fairly new at Posner's disco, and it was a mix of career anxiety and career ambition that led you to ring Q-Jo's bell, although she contends it was actually other concerns altogether.

Just as the University of Washington was the only school of any consequence that would accept you in its graduate program, Posner Lampard McEvoy and Jacobsen was the only brokerage house that would hire you. God knows you applied at the jumbos first. Granted, you had not been any academic whiz, but you earned your MBA fair and square (except for that teensie bit of cribbing and brown-nosing to which every pressured student occasionally resorts), and you were confident of eventual success. After all, it was the only thing you had ever wanted. Okay, if you were forced to launch your career at a regional firm, so much the better. You could become a big fish in a small pond and soon be invited to swim downstream. To the sea where the big bucks splashed. Of course, it irked you to no end that Posner was unimpressed by your MBA. "We're here to sell," he said, "and I'm giving you a chance because of your experience in selling." You had paid your way through college by working afternoons, weekends, and summers at Nordstrom. The store had started you out in the lingerie department, but you became so blushingly flustered whenever a male questioned you about intimate apparel that they had to transfer you to outdoor wear. Oh, yes, you moved a mountain of ski jackets over the years, but that's another story. If Posner couldn't differentiate between Gore-Tex and government bonds, that was his problem.

Your problem was that your performance that first year at the disco hadn't quite lived up to your expectations. True, you were better off financially than you'd ever been in your life, but the major juice seemed annoyingly just out of reach of your dipper, and Mr.

Dunn, as you called him then, had had to pull some strings at the bank to get your loan approved.

At exactly what juncture you became aware that your neighbor down the hall was Seattle's most highly regarded tarotmancer escapes you now. Vivid, however, is your recollection of the evening that you, with hesitation, cynicism, and more than a dollop of shame, pressed the chewed tip of your index finger against her buzzer. Disoriented by her size and attire, you blurted out that you would like to schedule an appointment—"Just for the fun of it, you know"—and she said, "How does immediately strike you? My six-thirty gig just canceled." Stammering excuses, you attempted to back away, but she looped the lumpish loaf of her arm—the baguette of the behemoths—around you and drew you across the sill. "Come on, you look like a girl who's into instant gratification. Why procrastinate when we can precognitate?"

Before you could protest further, you were being seated at an oval cherry table in a living room—"parlor" is a more descriptive term—that might have been decorated by a Midwestern grandma on a shopping spree at Sears in 1939. Furniture in the room was covered with that nubby upholstery that is mildly but incessantly irritating to both the skin and the spirit, sofa pillows were stiff and scratchy, curtains were of dingy lace; and adorning the walls, where you expected to see, if not heathen mandalas at least inspirational slogans superimposed over pictures of rainbows and sunrises, there were landscape paintings of the type sold in perpetually-going-out-of-business furniture stores in the gritty parts of town. When she noticed the way you were scowling at the decor, she waved her arms and said, "Psychic forces find this atmosphere hospitable." *Good grief!* you thought. *Is she implying that the Higher Self sleeps under chenille?*

How ill at ease you were as you shuffled the cards! Q-Jo could tell that you were totally unfamiliar with the tarot, but she provided very little that evening in the way of history or background. In the years that followed, she lectured you extensively on the subject, although as you would be quick to admit, most of it went in one ear and out the other. You returned the deck to her. "Listen," you said. "I'm a stockbroker, and the reason I came to you is, well uh, I'm wondering . . . my timing has been off lately vis-à-vis the market, and uh, frankly, I've picked some sinkers and thrown some wide darts, and. . . ." You fumble in your purse. "I don't have a stock guide with me, but I can run down the hall and get it. I was hoping that we could look it over just a little bit and you might—"

Q-Jo put a plantain phalanx to your lips, issued a brief, derisive chortle, and said, "Now *you* listen, honey, and listen good. Do you really believe that if I could pick stocks that are gonna double—or winning lottery numbers or racehorses—that I'd be living in this one-bedroom apartment smoking rot-lung tobacco and wearing last year's turban? Come on! I'd be styling and smiling in a nice little villa in the Himalayan foothills; fountains, peacocks, Ram Dass in the guest suite, both a French chef and a weight-loss doctor on duty around the clock, so forth and so on. You get the picture. And another thing: I cannot accurately predict your future. We need to get that straight, too. I can't, no psychic can, and any that claim they can are swindlers."

She rapped the deck with the same musaceous digit she had employed to shush you. "A crystal ball, this is not, and you damn well ought to be glad about it. It isn't tea leaves or goat entrails, neither. What it is is a highly refined, highly efficient system of symbolic knowledge. The symbols that were carefully chosen over the centuries speak directly to the deeper levels of the mind. The western mind. In the East, the *I Ching* cuts the very same mustard, but with a more, shall we say, intricate turn of the knife. Never mind that. The images here in the tarot will serve to open up and free certain aspects of your subconscious. Once the symbols have un-locked your subconscious, I can use my own psychic vision to read what the hell's going on in the recesses of your pumpkin. I read your subconscious thoughts—they're damn near as legible to me as *The Seattle Times*—but I don't read the future. *Comprende?*"

As intimidated as you were disappointed, you nodded in the

affirmative and upon Q-Jo's direction, cut the cards. One by one, off the top of the deck, she began to turn the cards over and lay them out systematically in an arrangement that soon approximated the shape of a Celtic cross. "Now, for one reason or another, your subconscious knows things your conscious mind doesn't. Oftentimes it's ahead of your conscious mind in regards to the direction you're leaning regarding a particular situation or decision. So in that respect, the information I glean for you tonight may, at a later date, seem to you to be a prediction coming true. Follow me? Mmm . . . what have we here? Likewise, if the tarot and I detect trends in your behavior, such as patterns and that kind of thing, we *can* be at least semi-predictive. You know, if you see that somebody is driving down I-Five seventy miles an hour blindfolded, you can safely 'predict' that relatives of that person will be coming into money, providing that the person's adequately insured. Okay, Gwen? But if a psychic claims she or he can actually *know* future events, well, that's denying that there's free will, and I happen to believe in free will. The future's not preordained. Anything that I reveal to you tonight can be changed. You, of your own free will, can change it. Reverse it, redirect it, whatever. You can remove the blindfold and slow the hell down. Remember that. Now, let's have a look. Mind if I smoke?"

Although tobacco fumes tend to turn your stomach, you signaled that it was permissible. She fired up her stinkweed, filled her sails, and fell into a light trance. In that state, her voice became soothing, almost hypnotic; her manner of speech more articulate and formal. Nevertheless, it didn't take long for her to ram her supertanker into your amusement pier.

"In the number three position, which is the card representing current concerns and influences, you see we have the Four of Pentacles. What's happening in that picture, Gwen? Don't try to analyze it. Just look at it as if it was an illustration in your favorite children's book. That's the way I want you to *always* look at the cards. Okay? What's the figure doing? Grasping, right? He's holding down two pieces of gold with his feet, he has his arms tightly wrapped around another piece, and a fourth one is balanced on his head: gold on the brain, in other words. What the Four of Pentacles in this position suggests is insecurity about money, fear of financial loss. There are basic security issues here. You seem to be worried about accumulating sufficient funds or of losing what you have already. And if you should lose your money, what would you be worth as a human being, who would you be? Your identity is wrapped up in material wealth. The problem here, Gwen, is that the more desperate you are to achieve financial success and the tighter you hold on to what you've got, the greater your chances of losing it. Money's like love in that respect. You might want to focus on other aspects of life for a change. It could benefit you to loosen your grip."

Shock of recognition? Not enough to matter. Neither informed nor impressed by what you'd heard, you thought, *What a scam! She could have extrapolated everything she said from the comments I made when I first walked in.* You were decidedly annoyed, and it wasn't destined to get any sweeter. It seems that a four-inch tag of pasteboard called the Five of Rods was familiar with your modus operandi to the degree that it could accuse you of causing problems for yourself without realizing it, of tripping yourself up, of struggling too hard, and spreading yourself too thin. There was yet a third card representing stress around matters financial, while in the position that was alleged to disclose how others viewed you, there thundered an almost comically aggressive dude on a charger, the Knight of Swords, whom Ms. Huffington described as consumed and pushy, a type who wouldn't allow anyone or anything to block his or her path to the payoff.

If there was a crouton of fact in that nettle salad—and you had had to admit there was *a* crouton—it could be dismissed as temporary and trivial, from your point of view, certainly not deserving of the hulking hankyhead's conclusion that you either had chosen the wrong goals or the wrong way to pursue them. You had been on the verge of compensating her—"Do you accept Visa? Now *that's* a card that knows how to treat a woman"—and fleeing to the comforts of home when she proceeded to the Queen of Cups and regained your attention in a prime-time way.

A slender, fair-skinned blond in royal robes sits on a carved wooden throne at the edge of the sea. Clams have gathered about her feet, caroling, perhaps; the tide sucks her toes. Oblivious to salt and shine, to ships on the horizon and pearl-making in the surf, the queen gazes intently at an ornate golden chalice that she balances in her hands. She gives the impression that the sky could burst without interrupting her fix on the grail, her fidelity to its hard beauty.

"This woman, the Queen of Cups, is delicate and dreamy," said Q-Jo. "She's a romantic, an aesthete, though sometimes in a morbid way. She can be gentle and nurturing but obsessed with philosophical questions she can't understand." Q-Jo looked up from the layout. "Gwen, this woman obviously isn't you. She must be your mother. Yes, she's your mother. Your mother was a loving person but emotionally imbalanced. Probably tried to be there for you but didn't know how to, because she couldn't even be there for herself. I say 'tried' because I sense she's gone to the other side, with which she was always very intrigued. Your mother took her own life. You still are unable to say why."

How could this fat fraud know that? How dare she know? It was the future she was hired to scan, not the past! You were outraged. But the tears you were choking back were not of fury.

Q-Jo found your father in the layout—the immature and unreliable Page of Cups. She pointed to the Five of Cups and the Seven of Swords, the former indicating the loss and loneliness she said you've experienced in family matters, the latter suggesting anger and separation. She alluded to ducked landlords, bare mattresses, and spilled Chianti, to revolutionary rants and thrift-shop school clothes, even to mimeographed poetry magazines and those all-night bongo parties that had caused you to fall asleep in freshman algebra. She spoke of a "forgiveness card," but you couldn't tell which one. By that time, you'd lost control, your sobs growing wet and muscular. The arms with which the psychic enveloped you were like inflated beach toys: rubber horses pumped up with molasses.

You pulled away, but you were both purged and comforted, and you knew you would visit her again.

Eleven Fifty-Five A.M.

You let yourself into Q-Jo's flat. It has the same tiled fireplace and exposed beams as yours, but whereas your red maple floors are bare and polished, hers are nearly hidden by threadbare Oriental rugs; whereas your leaded windows sparkle unadorned, hers are draped with dry-rotted lace; whereas your apartment is airy, modern, minimalistic, hers is dense and itchy. As ever in her quarters, you experience oddly mixed sensations of solace and suffocation.

The tarot deck is on the cherry table, twiddling its tens of thumbs, tapping its tens of feet. Instead of the cruciform layout, it is spread facedown across the tabletop in a gambler's fan. Not bothering to pose a question—what could possibly be on your mind other than the market crash and the extent of its repercussions in your life?—you immediately point to a card. As you're about to pick it up, however, you withdraw your hand. Somehow, that card doesn't feel right.

Giggling nervously, you glance around the room as if you're being watched. You feel suddenly foolish. The nation, if not the world, is in economic turmoil, your career's on the bubble and with it your dreams, your security; and you're wasting your time consulting a deck of picturesque cards provided by a roly-poly occultist, *in absentia.* Oh, but what the heck. Q-Jo complains that you never take the tarot's advice anyhow, so where's the harm? It's a game, a frail amusement, and who couldn't use a diversion?

Slowly, you pass your hand over the deck. Until . . . it experiences a slight tug. You've never felt *that* before. Like a water witch's Y-stick that has sniffed out an underground spring, your pointing finger, bobbing and twitching, is pulled downward until it touches a particular card. You pick up the card and without examining it, clasp

79

Tom Robbins

it to your heart, as Q-Jo has encouraged you to do, and return to the less cloying oxygens of your own place.

Eleven Fifty-Nine A.M.

As you enter your apartment, the phone is ringing. You elect not to answer it. You fear one of your clients could have gotten your unlisted number and is calling to berate you, although more likely it's Belford. André has come home. André has not come home. André is a hostage. André is kaput. André, in a blond wig and glasses, has been spotted in Vegas; or onstage with the gospel choir at a Billy Graham crusade. Give you a break. Right now you aren't interested in André.

The voice that crackles out of the answering machine speaker, its intonations afuzz with auditory hairballs, is not Belford's, however, it's Q-Jo's. "Gwen, baby, it's Huff," she says. "I stopped by Fratelli's for a sundae and a shake, so I'm running a little late, but I wanted to let you know we're probably gonna miss the early movie 'cause I've scored another job and won't be home till six or so. Guy's hiring me to look at some interesting slides for a change. At least, they *could* be interesting. He's just back from Timbuktu."

80

Friday
Afternoon
April 6

Tell 'Em Salvador Dali Sent You

Four P.M.

The afternoon lasts approximately as long as fourth grade. However long it takes a *wuf* of light from Sirius the Dog Star to reach its reflection in a puddle of tar on the Dog House roof, that's how long it takes the afternoon to go by. The afternoon is a million-car train rattling at half-speed through a crossing in a prairie town. The boxcars are empty, and you try to fill them up with market research. At least that's what you tell Belford each time he phones. "No, I can't help you hunt for André right now. I'm doing market research."

What you actually are doing is reading Friday's edition of *The Wall Street Journal*, poring over every paragraph in a largely futile quest for salvation. The experience is both disheartening and marginalizing. There was a time when you could have gone to the disco on a weekend or holiday and availed yourself of the tools and materials of the trade, but five or six months ago, Posner asked for your key back, saying that the partners no longer felt it was in the firm's best interest to have its brokers working overtime when they should be relaxing, replenishing their energies. At that moment, you thought it a well-intentioned if misguided policy. Now you can't help but wonder if he confiscated anybody's key but yours.

The post-crash *Journal* is a gray blizzard of statistics, studies, casualty figures, history, forecasts, and interviews. They must have interviewed a hundred analysts, managers, regulators, marketers, investors, and consultants of all stripes (including that two-faced Sol Finkelstein), and although they were busy bear-dancing on hot coals, they were cogent enough to offer plenty of rational explanations for what went wrong. Most cited the "magnitude of government and corporate debt" and the "slow growth in the nation's money supply." There were the usual references to overvalued stocks, flat profits, and escalating foreign competition. A few complained anew about the perils of computerized trading, while a couple of financial-newsletter writers wanted to lay the blame on institutional criminality. "Jesse James got himself appointed to the bank's board of directors. Saved wear and tear on his horse." Sol Finkelstein was quoted as saying, "On a fundamental valuation basis, America's been in economic never-never land since Reagan's first term in the White House." Funny, you never heard Sol bring that up in a meeting.

The afternoon is as sunny as it is interminable. You open a window to let the sunbeams in. They behave like tourists, which, in Seattle, they practically are. Dressed in panties (white with two tiny pink bows) and an Exxon Corporation sweatshirt, you prop yourself up against a cloudbank of pillows that rises above the ridge-line of your headboard. There on the bed, the newspaper spread about you like a wino bride's dowry, a pitcher of Filipino-style iced tea within reach, you ought to be serene, but of course, you are not. You are anxious. You could just as well be balanced on a spider-infested log in a sewage lagoon, that's how anxious you are. And it is virtually impossible to separate the work-related anxiety from the anxiety about Q-Jo.

On second thought, it isn't impossible at all. Although you are sincerely worried about Q-Jo, it's not a looming, career-crumbling-sized worry. To be honest, it is not so much worry as outrage. And bewilderment. Is this a monstrous coincidence, another of those tasteless practical jokes that the Fates love to spring on you and then roll on the linoleum with laughter? Or is there some cause-and-effect in operation here? Was Larry Diamond—that was the creep's name, wasn't it?—aware that Q-Jo and you are supposed to be friends? And if he was aware of that supposed friendship, wouldn't it stand to reason that his employment of Q-Jo was in some perverse way connected to, or directed at, you? But why? You suppose it could be the other way around: he approached you at the Bull &

Bear in the hope that you could grease the rails to Q-Jo. There are men, descendants of the New England whalers, perhaps, who are aroused by women of scale. If only you had answered the phone in time, you might have warned her. The Huff moves surprisingly fast, especially after taking on sugar.

Fretting, you change position on the bed, causing your sweatshirt to ride up and expose abdominal flesh. The sunbeams, cameras around their necks, immediately form a line to get into your navel.

Four-Thirty P.M.

The afternoon drones on. The specialists in *The Wall Street Journal* drone with it. Management blames labor: "The American worker is underproductive and overpaid." Labor blames management: "When a guy's wearing a golden parachute, he doesn't care if the plane's on fire." Whereas the prudent might cite "the international wild card of oil prices," the cynical refer to such things as "the thick blindfold of patriotic optimism that the military-industrial complex and its political flunkies have wound around our eyes." One overwrought pundit charges, "America's economy is a sinking ship deserting the rats." *Harumph,* you harumph. *Who's he calling a rat?* Until yesterday, none of these experts foresaw anything more traumatic than a keen correction. "We were expecting a spanking and got a beheading," one admits. Annoyed, you toss aside the interviews and return to the charts. Technical analysis was never your forte, and you are struggling to comprehend a particular configuration of linear data when the telephone rings, causing you to jump so sharply you spill iced tea in your belly button. The less said about sunbeams the better.

You are reasonably certain it is Belford on the line, but unless he's reporting that the born-again monkey has fetched home a diamond as big as the Motel 6, you have scant interest in answering another of his calls. On the other hand, it could be Q-Jo, a desperate Q-Jo in the clutches of a fiend. Refusing to consider the possibility that Q-Jo might *relish* the clutches of a fiend (blotted from your memory is the time you walked in on her with not one, not two, but three Russian cadets from the training ship *Pallada* climbing about in her rigging), you spring from bed and hover above the phone. If it is Q-Jo, time could be of the essence, but you chance it and wait.

Following the fifth ring, you hear your own voice and cringe. You spent hours recording and re-recording the message, and you still hate the way you sound. "Hello. You've reached the temporary residence of Gwendolyn Mati. I'm not home right now, but if you'll leave your name, number, and time that you called, I'll get back to you the instant my busy schedule allows. Speak slowly and distinctly as soon as you hear the beep." *Click. Beep.* "Hey, Squeak! Dat you? Where you, Squeak?"

Good grief! *Him.* Are you ever glad you resisted the temptation to pick up the phone!

"Hey, man, I don't dig talking when there nobody there. You want record me, you got see my agent. Ha-ha. But, Squeak, hey, I playing tonight, man. Yeah. New club in Belltown. Woman Ray's. It so cool you think you someplace else. Hey, dey got dis Andy Warhol robot tending da bar. A real robot, man, but dis robot got Andy Warhol body parts in it. Look just like him but it a robot. I not sittin' in with da band, I solo, man. Drums and poetry. Read some your mama's old poems. 'Love is like a snowmobile racing across the tundra / It flips over, pinning you underneath / At night the ice weasels come.' Bop-boppa-wop! You know. So drop in see you papa, Squeak baby. Tonight, tomorrow night, Woman Ray's, okay? Dey got 'nother robot working da door. Dis one call Marcel Duchamp. He strict, but he let you in. Tell 'em Salvador Dali sent you. Okay. *Ciao.*"

FIVE-TEN P.M.

The next time the phone rings, it really is Belford. As you listen to him apologizing profusely for interrupting your work, you have to laugh. You laugh with irony because you have been unable to focus on the charts since your father called, you laugh with something approaching genuine amusement because you cannot imagine you and Belford Dunn applying for admittance to the Woman Ray Club. Belford has never even heard of Salvador Dali. Which is perfectly all right. Salvador Dali and fifty cents will get you a cup of clock melt. In any case, André remains at large, it seems, and Belford has come to the conclusion that your suspicions are well founded: to wit, the monkey has been abducted by its former owner or associates of its former owner. André would not have flown the coop of his own volition, his character is simply too strong, too loyal, too loving for that. Belford has been trying to reach the French consul general in San Francisco to ascertain whether or not Kongo van den Bos is still incarcerated, but the consulate is closed for the Easter holidays. So, your alleged beau has booked himself on a late-night flight to San Francisco, where he will attempt to track down the consul general and persuade him to provide information and assistance. It is an international matter now, after all.

"I'd love to invite you along for the weekend, sweetums—there's supposed to be a really inspirational sunrise service in Golden Gate Park—but I'm going to beseech you to stay here and keep searching for the little rascal in my absence. You know, just in case."

You flash a smile that could polish every winesap in Happy Valley. This is the best news you've heard since the last time the Fed lowered interest rates. How lovely to have Belford out of town, out of your hair, for the remainder of the weekend! Now you'll be free to devote all of your attention to your shaky career and the external and internal factors that are shaking it. In Belford's absence, moreover, you ought to be able to get a clearer perspective on his role in your future. As fiercely as you might wish to deny it, you are compelled to admit that an abba dabba honeymoon with Mr. Dunn is a feasible solution to your current problem.

Oh, but what if you should marry Belford and he discovers that your problem is a tad more . . . shall we say, "complicated" than that of the average broker caught in the crash? Upon the stage of worry that dominates the theater of your mind, you imagine a

87

scene in which a distraught hubby comes home—from his flourishing realty office, you would hope, not from some grubby cubicle in the Department of Social Services—to confront you. "Gwendolyn," he says in his sternest manner, "it's common knowledge that brokers push stocks and other instruments based on what the brokerage firm wants to peddle on a given day or week. It's also common knowledge that unsuspecting customers are sold specific securities—mutual funds are a good example—that result in the highest commission for the broker. It's a fact of life, sad but true, that most brokers have their own interests at the forefront of every buy and sell recommendation that they proffer. That just goes with the territory, I guess. But, Gwen, Mr. Posner has informed me that you were unethically churning your accounts. He was concerned about that possibility from the start. Posner hired you not because of your MBA or your unusual voice or your good looks, but because once at Nordstrom you sold his daughter three pairs of ski pants when she only needed one. He both liked it and feared it that you were so money-motivated. And his worst fears came true. You solicited orders night and day, pressing to switch accounts from one mutual fund into another, but rarely explaining trades properly. You set up portfolios with an atrocious disregard. You had the wrong clients in the wrong stocks at the wrong amounts and with the wrong expectations. When the market finally fell, you left a killing field in your wake."

It's erythrophobia time. And as usual, your fear of blushing causes you to blush. But there's no pigment of guilt in the puccoon that reddens your cheeks. Instead of shame, you feel resentment. You would have operated differently had conditions been different. As it was, you were tricked by circumstance, cheated by history. Were you supposed to just surrender to the zeitgeist? Be a pebble? Go where you were kicked?

In your fantasy, your groom forgives you. Belford Dunn is nothing if not forgiving. Of course, you have to *earn* your redemption. "I want you to get down on your knees," Belford orders. Not for a blow job but something equally degrading and distasteful. "I want you to pray to Lord Jesus, Gwendolyn. André and me will pray with you." So you kneel between the fleabitten macaque and the square-headed hulk in his Men's Wearhouse suit, and you endure the triple ordeal of confession, contrition, and avowal. Then, new leaf smartly turned, you are released. Off the blasted hook, wahoo!

By the time this simulated confrontation has played itself out, you are feeling pretty swell. Certainly the best you've felt in forty-eight hours. Actually humming a little ("Lazy River"), you pull jeans on over your panties, close the window against the cooling air, fold and set aside *The Wall Street Journal,* exchange your iced tea for a goblet of chardonnay, check the clock—half an hour until Q-Jo's due home—and turn on the television in pursuit of further hope. If the President has taken extraordinary measures, if he and his administration have acted boldly for a change, marriage to Belford could be an option whose bristles you no longer are obliged to caress.

Alas, it is neither the President nor one of his economic advisers whose face fills the incandescent glass rectangle. Rather, it is Dr. Yamaguchi.

"Doctor!" a reporter calls. "Doctor! You've come here from a small clinic on the northernmost tip of Japan, and our mayor's given you the key to the city, the governor's planning to wine and dine you, there's been a huge public rally in your honor, people cheering you, clamoring for you, press from around the world constantly shooting your picture. How does all this attention feel, Doctor? How does it feel?"

With that tiny, furtive smile peeking out of the corners of his mouth, Dr. Yamaguchi lowers the Bic, sighs, and shrugs his shoulders. "Another day," he says, "in the life of a fool."

FIVE THIRTY-ONE P.M.

You suck in a breath that could tatter every squash blossom in Happy Valley. The card! The card, the card, the card! You had put down the card while you were listening to Q-Jo's message, and so frazzled were you by the implications of that message—"He's just back from Timbuktu"—that you forgot about it. All afternoon, as you itched and fumed about the fate of the market, the audacity of Larry Diamond and the safety of the Huff, the card has lain on top of the bookcase, facedown, unexamined, ignored. Goodness knows when you might have thought of it again if it hadn't been for Dr. Yamaguchi.

"Fool," he said. *Fool.* Three of the last four times you have selected a card from the tarot deck, it has turned out to be the Fool. Three times in four. "Baby, the tarot's got your number," said Q-Jo. "This is *your* card."

"Gee, thanks a lot. That's encouraging as shit." You must have been upset: you said the "s" word.

"Hey, I've always suspected you were a closet Fool. If I hadn't, I'd have given up on you long ago."

If that is a compliment, then a rapscallion is a hip-hop onion. However, you ought to be grateful, you suppose, that Q-Jo maintains a more positive view than you do of that figure some experts regard as the beginning of the tarot and others regard as its end.

A giddy youth is skipping through the wilderness, seemingly oblivious to the dangers around him. His cap is on backward, as if he doesn't know—or doesn't care—whether he is coming or going. Dum-dum-de-dum. Skip along, skip along. In his left hand he holds, as though presenting it to society, a white rose, the apple's opposite, emblem of purity and innocence. Over his right shoulder, tramp style, a stick with a bag hanging from it. What is in your bag, Fool? Dum-dum-de-dum. We will trade you a kilo of gold for the contents of your bag, sight unseen. Dum-dum-de-dum. He is an admirer of clouds. And with his eyes turned upward, he has skipped right to the brink of a deep and rocky chasm. The promontory is crumbling beneath his boots. Yet forward he goes, clear eyes squinting in the sun, a smile on his lips, his bag of useless trinkets swinging wildly.

According to Q-Jo, the whole tarot deck, or at least the twenty-two trump cards of the Major Arcana, may be read as the Fool's journey. "On one important level," she explained, "the major cards are chapters in the story of a quest. I'm talking the universal human quest for understanding and divine reunion. And it doesn't matter whether the quest starts with the Fool or ends with him, because it's a loop anyhow, a cycle endlessly repeated. When the naive young Fool finally tumbles over the precipice, he falls into the world of experience. Now his journey has really begun. Along the way, he'll meet all the teachers and tempters—the tempters are teachers, too—and challenging situations that a person is likely to meet in the task of his or her growing. The Fool is potentially everybody, but not everybody has the wisdom or the guts to play the Fool. A lot a folks don't know what's in that bag they're carrying. And they're all too willing to trade it for cash. Inside the bag, they have every tool they need to facilitate their life's journey, but they won't even open it up and glance inside. Subconsciously, the goal of all of us out-of-control primates is essentially the same, but let me assure you of this: the only ones who'll ever reach that goal are the ones who have the courage to make fools of themselves along the way."

Now, that is all fine and dandy, you suppose, but the word "fool" plays whoopie-cushion music in *your* ear. It's a label you would hasten to scrape off your pigeonhole with the first sharp object at hand. When you learned that in medieval tarot decks the Fool sometimes was identified as the Beggar, you knew for certain you wanted no part of him. Anyone who heralds poverty is no friend of yours. The Brinks truck, not the circus wagon, is your transportation of choice. It's not enough to be "in the money," you want to be in money, inside of it, like one of those dead presidents looking out. "Anybody who doesn't build themselves a fortress of money is a fool," you once said.

"Exactly so," quipped Q the Huff.

FIVE THIRTY-FIVE P.M.

With forced nonchalance, you saunter up to the bookcase. Every book on the shelves is about investment strategy, save for an encyclopedia of wine, a Porsche picture book, and a skinny volume of your mother's poetry: *Cupid Reflected in the Drool of a Zombie While the White Butterfly Attends the Lilacs After the Heat Has Gone.* Published posthumously. The card is on top of the case, next to the Bauhaus vase, and with continued nonchalance, you lift it up. *If I get the Fool again, you think, I may go stick it back in the deck and take another card.* Psychic or not, Q-Jo would never know.

Wait a minute! Hold on! "What the fu——?" You come within two consonants of pronouncing the "f" word. Who could blame you? This card . . . why, you've never seen this card before. At one time or another, you've at least glanced at every card in the tarot, and you are absolutely positive this one has not been among them. What the . . . fun?

To a degree, it resembles the Star card, except that the nude female who is kneeling beside a pool has, on this card, green scales over the lower half of her body, and her hands and feet are webbed like a frog's. Moreover, she's wearing a headdress that resembles the tail of a fish. At the bottom of the card, where it would normally read THE MAGICIAN, THE TOWER, THE EMPRESS, or in this case, perhaps, THE STAR, it reads, in the usual block letters, THE NOMMO. *The Nommo?* What the . . . ?

Looming in the sky above the kneeling nude, there are the same seven silver stars and the one giant central gold star that you remember from the Star card. Only now the silver stars are very faint, as if clouded over, and the big bold gold star has some kind of markings on it. After a minute, you recognize the markings as the dim outline of the head of a dog. *Huh?*

Like the maiden on the Star card, this one holds a pitcher in each hand—or, should one say, flipper. With the pitcher in her left . . . appendage, she pours water onto the ground, with the pitcher in the right, she is pouring water back into the pond. As you walk toward the window, where the light is better, you notice that the pitcher on the left is gold, the other, silver. And then you notice something else. In the background, behind the pool and beneath the dramatic sidereal display, there is a little tree with a bird perched in its uppermost bough, exactly as there is on the Star card. But here a word is inscribed on the bird's body. And the word (oh, how many goose bumps does it take to cobblestone the epidermis of a full-grown Filipina?), the word is *Bozo.*

Perplexity lines your face like the type in an arrest warrant. You collapse into the nearest chair like a reverse phoenix sinking back into the ashes. Q-Jo Huffington had better get home soon.

. . .

Friday
Night
April 6

. . .

The Dream Ain't Over
Till the White Dwarf Sings

Seven-Fifty P.M.

Why aren't we as smart when we wake up as we are in our dreams?

The sunset had been spectacular. In recent years, pollution has both expanded and intensified the solar palette, and tonight, without the customary clabber of cloud to diffuse its hues, to make it resemble, as it so frequently does in Seattle, a poultice of quicksilver and peach juice, it spread the full length of the western horizon like the *nuée ardente* bloodspill of a Day-Glo Christ. It was the definitive Good Friday sunset, and you had watched it from your chair until the last sanguineous drop of it was absorbed by the greasy gray waters of Puget Sound. The sky had been as crimson as any of your blushes, plus a great deal more luminous, and at one point you actually had thought about Jesus and how Belford and Grandma Mati both referred to him as "the Light of the World." You were on the verge of being consoled, maybe even uplifted—but then the darkness rolled in from every direction, and you said to yourself: *That figures.* Shortly thereafter, you nodded off.

You dreamed that you were holding up that weird maverick tarot card—the one that in actual fact was lying on your lap—only in your dream the card seemed ancient and worn, as if it were made of parchment or papyrus or something, and there was a kind of aura around it. But it had not puzzled you in your dream, you intuited its meaning, you understood it perfectly. A man was standing behind you, looking over your shoulder. He was never identified, but his voice was familiar. Even now, awake, you are within one synapse of recognition. This is what he was saying:

"Sarah Bernhardt was such a powerfully popular, awe-inspiring actress that when she toured in North America her performances invariably sold out, even though she spoke hardly a word of English. Whatever play she did, Shakespeare, Molière, Marlowe, or whatever, she did in French, a language few nineteenth-century Americans could comprehend. Theatergoers were provided with librettos so that they might follow the action in English. Well, on at least a couple of occasions, ushers passed out the wrong libretto, a text for an entirely different drama than the one that was being staged. Yet, from all reports, not once did a single soul in those capacity crowds ever comment or complain. Furthermore, no critic ever mentioned the discrepancy in his or her review." At this point, you distinctly remember, the man nudged you. Then he went on.

"We modern human beings are looking at life, trying to make some sense of it; observing a 'reality' that often seems to be unfolding in a foreign tongue—only we've all been issued the wrong librettos. For a text, we're given the Bible. Or the Talmud or the Koran. We're given *Time* magazine and *Reader's Digest*, daily papers, and the six o'clock news; we're given schoolbooks, sitcoms, and revisionist histories; we're given psychological counseling, cults, workshops, advertisements, sales pitches, and authoritative pronouncements by pundits, sold-out scientists, political activists, and heads of state. Unfortunately, none of these translations bears more than a faint resemblance to what is transpiring in the true theater of existence, and most of them are dangerously misleading. We're attempting to comprehend the spiraling intricacies of a magnificently complex tragicomedy with librettos that describe barroom melodramas or kindergarten skits. And when's the last time you heard anybody bitch about it to the management?"

Those were his exact words, you recollect them with a peculiar clarity. And sure, it was just some pseudo-philosophical, nugatory babble, but where had it come from? Even if such a man existed, you had dreamed his speech; thus, the words had had to have come from *you*. Was there some part of you that entertained ideas such as those? How annoying, if true. And what of the inner you that seems to know so much about Sarah Bernhardt? You vaguely recall your mother once dropping her name. Before your mother dropped all those barbiturates and sank into the Big Snooze-a-roo.

SEVEN FIFTY-THREE P.M.

Abruptly, you switch on the floor lamp by your chair. When your eyes have grown accustomed to the glare, you reexamine the aberrant tarot card—and in the 150-watt beam of full disclosure make a significant discovery. To wit: the card has been altered.

Yes, it is as plain as the Welsh nose on your Filipina face. Watercolor marking pens and a black stylus were used to transform an ordinary Star card into the fishy anomaly that so astonished you. A pale blue wash dimmed the silver stars, a bright green felt-tip turned the maiden's feet into flippers, the words, THE NOMMO, were superimposed over the whited-out original title, THE STAR. In a sense, your discovery is a big relief. It means that you had neither overlooked this card in the past nor that something, uh, *supernatural,* had occurred. Good. However, you are left to wonder why Q-Jo would do such a silly thing, why she would deface the tarot, for which she harbors a profound respect. And you must wonder, further, about the intrusion of that word *Bozo.* Frankly, *Bozo* has become a bit of a bother to you.

When at last you check your Rolex, you are bothered all the more. Q-Jo is almost two hours overdue. And she has not had the courtesy to phone. Oh, but what if she is unable to phone? What if she is bound to a fumigated mattress, the victim of unimaginable probes and squirts perpetrated by that . . . that pee-sniffer? Once again, your emotions vacillate. Anger. Concern. Anger. Concern.

NINE P.M.

Anger. Concern. The upsetting oscillation continues, and now, with each swing of the pendulum, the to and the fro are escalating in scale. ANGER! CONCERN! Well, to be scrupulously exact, it is more like, ANGER! concern. Because you do have more faith in the Huff's ability to take care of herself than you do in her reliability; at least where men are involved. However, when the phone rings a few minutes after nine, you do not hesitate. You are at that phone like a trout at a gunk-filled fly.

"Oh, sweetums, you're home. I just called to leave a good-bye message. I thought you and Q-Jo were going out. I thought that was why you weren't helping me tonight. Look for André."

"I'm here. Q-Jo is out. Way the hell out. And the reason I'm not helping you look for André is. . . ." Your voice trails off. Just as well. Your tone is sour enough without getting specific about what you wish Belford would do with his monkeyitis.

After a pause, Belford says, "I don't read you."

"Listen, Belford, I'm worried about Q-Jo. She had an appointment this afternoon with a really weird guy, and she hasn't come home yet or called or anything."

"So that's it. Well, honey, I'm sorry you're worried, I don't like you to worry. But Q-Jo is a willful woman, a *lot* of willful woman if I may say so, and nobody's likely to make her do anything she doesn't want to do. And what makes you think this client of hers is weird?"

"I *know* him to be weird."

"Oh? You're personally acquainted with the gentleman?" Under the fingernails of his voice, there can be detected the green cheese of suspicion.

"The *gentleman?* Yes! No! I mean, I met him yesterday at the Bull and Bear. He tried to. . . . He referred to. . . . Never mind. Trust me, he's an unstable individual. Q-Jo's three hours late and hasn't called. And strange stuff is happening."

"What kind of strange stuff?"

He had you there. Should you attempt to articulate it, the "strange stuff" would sound pretty innocuous. How could you explain why a doctored tarot card and the stupid word *Bozo* were distracting you from business and turning your Easter into Halloween? "Belford," you say at last, "do you think we're trying to follow the show with the wrong libretto?"

There is silence on the line. Then he asks, "What exactly is a libretto?"

Good grief! Get that man out of town before you marry him. "What time's your flight? When do you come back?"

"Plane's at eleven. I get back late Sunday night. And honeykins, since you're available now, I wonder if you'd be up for driving me to the airport? In my car, if you don't mind. I'd kinda like to leave you with the Lincoln so's that when you're driving around looking for André, he'd be able to, you know, recognize the car. Are you aware"—he chuckles in a sad, proud way—"that sometimes the little rascal sits on my lap while I drive? I think he wants to steer."

"When do you want to pick me up?" you ask coldly. Anything, even this, is better than waiting around for the slut of the occult.

"Nine-thirty."

"I'll be ready at nine forty-five."

TEN-FORTY P.M.

On the way home from the airport, you ease the Lincoln up to eighty miles an hour. You aren't in *that* much of a hurry, despite your acute curiosity about Q-Jo's circumstance; it is only that you are certain Belford has never pushed the town car over fifty-five, and for some reason that irks you. "How do you like it, baby?" you ask the speeding vehicle, then blush all the way down to the gas pedal at the sexual innuendo in your remark.

On a whim, or maybe not, you take the Seneca Street exit and find yourself downtown. From there, it's as natural as buying low and selling high to drive past Posner Lampard McEvoy and Jacobsen. You just want to see if the lights are on. Oh, my goodness, they are! Moreover, as the fates would have it, there is a parking space right across the street. You pull into it and kill the engine. You are so nervous your nipples are vibrating. But, hey, you have every right in the world to go upstairs and check out what is happening—and if no one is watching, to make an effort to cover some of your tracks.

Uh-oh. The entrance to the elevator lobby is blocked by what is called a "street person." And he is armed with one of those high-tech weapons that were so popular after the last Gulf War. No, no, calm down, it's not a mini-missile after all, it's a telescope on a tripod.

"One dollar, lady, you can see the man in the moon. Two dollars, you can look at Sirius."

"Why's it more for Sirius?"

"It's farther away."

You can't argue with that. Well, a gander at the stars is better than a serenade on a squeeze box (a street person last week wanted fifty cents to play "Strangers in the Night" on a Jew's harp), and if you humor him he might step aside and let you pass. His face is kindly, if a trifle hollow-eyed and dissipated: he is probably an astronomy professor who has lost his job in the crunch. You fork over two bucks, bend at the waist, and put one brown orb to the lens.

"Where? I don't see. . . . Wait, I think I've found it." You press your eye against the eyepiece until, like the row of stiff bristles on the leg of a psocid, your lash rakes and combs the optical glass. "There's a bright dot there. Is that it? Not much to look at."

The astronomy bum snorts, and then he hacks, spitting onto the sidewalk a glob of such substance that you hear it splat. "Lady, there's eight-point-six light-years between it and us."

"That doesn't sound so far. Is this a good telescope?"

"Shit, lady, that's trillions of miles. I said trillions. Even so, it's pretty damn close. It's relatively close and relatively big. Brightest star in the sky."

"Oh, come on." Who does this tramp think he's kidding? "I've seen a lot brighter ones. Without a telescope, too."

There comes a cackle, a snort, a cough, and a splat. You shudder, imagining something the consistency of pancake batter and the color of the life-forms in a bachelor's refrigerator, but you keep your eye on the dancing point of yellow fire at the end of the tube. "What you may have seen, missy," the vulgar fellow dares to correct you, "was Venus or Mars or Jupiter. They're *planets*, for Christ Almighty's sake. Sirius there is a *star.*"

Okay, he may be right about that. You aren't going to enter into a discussion with a marginal astronomer. By his aroma, you can tell he has moved nearer. "Fact is," he says, "Sirius is a binary star. There's two of 'em. Sirius A, the Dog Star so-called, is the big sparkly one. But he's got a teenie-weenie buddy. Sirius B. The little one's a white dwarf. That's a technical term, but I can understand how a person like you might think it's poetic."

"Can I see it? The little star?" You really aren't that interested, but you want to get your two dollars' worth.

"Maybe, if you squint real hard. It's to the lower right of the big one."

As you strain to pick out Sirius B, there is a pop and a flash, as if Sirius A has exploded—and the heavens and all that doth loom and lurk and leap and lie beneath them disappear.

When you regain consciousness, minutes later, you are flat on the sidewalk, your jeans and panties down around your ankles, the contents of your purse strewn about you like a dead pharaohette's favorite things.

ELEVEN P.M.

Everybody in town has a front-row seat at the first public showing of your twat: each and every hair countable, labial road map unfolded for consultation, clitoris a gleaming morsel awaiting cocktail fork or chopsticks. Yet, you are not blushing. You are beyond blush. You have fled that which blushes. It is the Worst Day of Your Life, Part II, and you have crossed the river and climbed a tree.

Gradually, however, for better or worse, you are winched back into your body. The pavement is frigid against your bare derriere, and the glare of a street lamp beats against your vision like a board. You sit up slowly. There is no spear of pain, nothing flops around as if broken. Tugging up underpants and pants, you rise to your feet. Buckling your belt, you look around you. To your surprise and relief, you are alone on the street. The shabby Sagan has vanished, and with him the assorted beggars and buskers who previously had populated the block, although in the distance you perceive a clump of shadowy figures from whose midst there floats the unmistakable refrain of "Strangers in the Night" being played on a Jew's harp. You scoop up your possessions and fling them into your purse.

I've been raped and robbed, you think, *and I must notify the police.* But not here. Not on the pay phone in the lobby, and most assuredly not upstairs in Posner's disco. Looking over your shoulder all the while, you hurry across Sixth Avenue to the car. Once inside the Lincoln, doors locked, engine running, you begin to shake and sob. You also begin, as the shock wears off, to doubt that you've been raped. Your crotch is neither sore nor damp. The sting, the scent, of violation are nowhere upon you. Wary as a worm-yanking robin, lest any of the homeless sneak up on the car, you take inventory in your bag. The cash is still there, all forty dollars of it minus the two with which you purchased this latest affront. So—oh, joy!—is your Visa gold card. For that matter, so is the altered tarot card, which you'd brought along to show to Belford in the event he proved receptive: he did not. The way things have been going, it would not have astonished you had that dumb card been the only item missing.

In a sense, you are greatly relieved, relieved to the point of saying "Thank you, dear God" to an entity whom you have long suspected of the most flagrant indulgence in insider trading. On the other hand, you feel shortchanged in some perverse fashion, as if you cannot even be properly raped and robbed. You massage the back of your neck, which has commenced to ache: the gutter Galileo must have taken you out with a rabbit punch. How appropriate at Easter. Since your various treasures are intact, the assault must have been motivated by a desire to humiliate you. Such crimes, vented against the haves by the have-nots, are on the rise, you've heard, prompted by envy, resentment, and vengeance movies. If only they knew how near you are to having not.

ELEVEN-FOURTEEN P.M.

You are traveling home by a curiously circuitous route, due to the fact that every time you see in the distance a congregation of street people or a gang of threatening teenagers (black hair plus brown eyes equals threat, eh, Gwen?), you turn so that you won't have to drive past them. Perhaps you worry that should you spot the astronomer you could not resist swerving onto the sidewalk and sending him to the moon with the front end of the Lincoln. Or maybe you are afraid that a well-groomed woman alone behind the wheel of a luxury automobile will be perceived as an opportunity, and at a traffic signal or stop sign, lightning could strike twice. Affluence has its downside.

In any event, still shaking and sobbing a little, you are now on Second Avenue, a one-way artery running south; which is to say, you are heading away from Queen Anne Hill rather than toward it, a problem in navigation that will have to be corrected. As you slow to investigate the advisability of the next cross-street, a sudden surge of music smacks the car with a force that makes you jump. You swivel to see zigzags of festive neon and a marquee that reads, LIVE FRIDAY! BETTY SPAGHETTI & THE MEATBALLS. Ah-ha: the Werewolf Club. If only you had consented to go there tonight, maybe Q-Jo would have come home on time, and none of this would have happened. On the other hand, had Q-Jo better taste in music, the Werewolf would not have been an issue. For that matter, you could not agree on a movie, either. You had wanted to attend a Cary Grant double feature at a revival house, Q-Jo was excited about a transcendentalist porno film entitled *Deep Thoreau*. Good grief! Yours is a futile friendship—but you sure hope she has finally come home.

As you are wheeling onto the side street, you notice a throng

105

in the middle of the block. Immediately, you brake and shift into reverse, considering a retreat back onto Second. But, no, that won't be necessary. You can make out that the people are dressed in trendy leathers and are lined up, more or less, before a velvet rope. You ease forward. Neither marquee nor neon here. A discreet brass plaque identifies the place as Club Woman Ray. The Marcel Duchamp robot, a fuming cigarette in its rubberized lips, is admitting would-be guests only after careful scrutiny of their bearing and attire. The dorky, the insolvent, and the overanxious are summarily rejected. You like that. It's like the eighties. Nowadays, most clubs and restaurants are so financially strapped they practically pull in patrons by their collars. Marcel—how, you wonder, did they program him to be so discriminating?—opens the door to admit a couple in matching outfits of pink snakeskin. For a fleeting moment, you see all the way to the stage. There, in Filipino guerrilla garb, squats your father with his bongo drums, as you have seen him squat a thousand times. Before the heavy steel door can swing shut, you catch a few familiar lines.

> *"With gaunt teddy bear won*
> *at love's cheat-o carnival*
> *tucked under my tendrilous*
> *armpit,*
> *I climb into the pickup truck*
> *with Death,*
> *lured by his hypnotic kitchie-koo,*
> *by the everlasting licorice*
> *of his lollipops."*

Right. You remember. That one was called "All-Day Sucker." She wrote it just before she threw herself off the Aurora Bridge. You linger to catch another glimpse of your dad, but a stretch limo pulls up behind you and blasts its horn. You drive away.

106

HALF ASLEEP *in* FROG PAJAMAS

ELEVEN TWENTY-TWO P.M.

Should you choose, in your moment of parental reverie, you could motor to Queen Anne by way of the Aurora Bridge, ascending the hill from the north, but it is the long way home, and besides, you are not really certain the bridge is where your mother took her life. The truth is, you don't know what method she used to liquidate her mortal assets. What you do recall, and recall vividly, is that in the June of your twelfth year, your mom, emulating her poetic idol, Sylvia somebody, turned the oven on and stuck her head in it. Unfortunately or fortunately, as the case might be, she was guilty of an embarrassing oversight. Your family had an *electric* stove.

Instead of gassing herself into sweet oblivion, all she did was get unbearably hot and set her hair on fire. An awful odor filled the flat. When you crawled out of bed to see what the smell was about, she was kneeling in the middle of the kitchen, smoking like a smudge pot, while your father emptied a jug of red wine on her head. That was your last sight of her. She was overnight in the hospital for treatment of scalp burns, and the next morning you and your brother were dispatched to Oakland to spend the rest of the summer with Grandma Mati. Sometime in August, your mother was successful at suicide. They decided to spare little Squeak the details.

ELEVEN THIRTY-FIVE P.M.

You park the Lincoln outside your own building. If Belford thinks for one minute that you're going to comb Queen Anne for that god-damned monkey, he's lost his mind. Even had you not been brutally attacked, you wouldn't look for André. Not tonight, at any rate. Tomorrow is another day.

Before going inside, you steal an impulsive peek at Sirius. Sirius A. Sirius B is invisible to the naked eye. If, indeed, there is any such thing as Sirius B. The guy could have been leading you on. "Psst, little girl, wanna come up and see my white dwarf?" You will have to ask the Huff about it. Q-Jo told you once that all of the heavy elements in the universe, including those in the human body, were created by the terrible death throes of iron in the stars. This knowledge made her feel a kinship, she said, with the most distant galaxies. All it did for you was remind you that you hadn't taken your vitamins.

Well, looking up at Sirius (which is bright, all right) isn't helping your sore neck any. You climb the stairs and bang on Q-Jo's door. No response. You scoot down the hall and check the messages on your machine. There is only one, and it is from Belford, calling from the airport to tell you he misses you already. *Belford's an unmitigated dweeb,* you think, but in a way you miss him, too. You desperately need somebody to talk to.

On a whim, you go back down the hall and let yourself into Q-Jo's place. Nothing has changed. She has not been home. The cards are still spread on the table, her appointment book is still lying open on the rickety old chiffonier. Hey! The appointment book! Good thinking, Gwendolyn. Alas, the lone entry for Friday after the noon session with the garden buff is a hastily scribbled reminder: "Call L.D." That's the extent of it. Call, obviously, Larry Diamond. But no uckingfay number, excuse your Pig Latin. You take a chance and look him up in the directory. Naturally, he's not listed. Posner might possibly have Diamond's number, and Posner is a night owl, but you are feeling just too vulnerable to ring him up. Before you speak with Posner again, you have got to recalcify your shell.

You sit down at the cherrywood table where, by the low-wattage shine of a tasseled lamp, you, first slowly, absentmindedly, then with rapid purpose, turn over the tarot cards. It is reassuring to find that no other card has been tampered with, although it makes the mystery of the Nommo card seem all the more befuddling. You rummage through the disarray of your purse and retrieve the card in question to return it to the deck. Let somebody else deal with it. You've got enough on your mind without pondering web-footed star girls. As the card slides through your fingers, however, you feel an electrical fizz in your nerves—and for no logical reason you get up and take another look at Q-Jo's appointment book.

There it is, lying on the page like a jellyfish on a beach: imperceptible until you are about to step on it, but then, oh my, how it looms. "Friday morning, nine-thirty, Larry Diamond, Thunder House, 783-0190."

ELEVEN FIFTY-FIVE P.M.

What will you say when he answers? Wouldn't it be wise to disguise your voice? Can you ask for Q-Jo Huffington without quaking or squeaking? An hour ago, you were assaulted on the street, why aren't you in bed? In the shower? At your doctor's? On the phone to the police? You are shaking again as you touch 7, touch 8, touch 3. . . .

There's a hole in God's ether where all the ringing goes. One burble after another passes through your brain on its way to the nirvana of noise, where it will either join eternity's choir or reincarnate as, say, the sizzle of a patty or the mew of a cub. One more ring. You'll give it one more ring, and then you're hanging up. Okay, one for good measure and that's all. The last ring is interrupted between the *bur* and the *ble*. There is a second or two of canned silence, so easy to distinguish from good old-fashioned farm-fresh organic silence. Then, holding your breath, you hear these recorded words:

"You're wasting your time calling here. Unless, of course, you've gotten your hands on the appropriate libretto."

Aside from the shock of its content, two things strike you about the message: One, while the man is speaking, there are huge rumbling and crashing noises in the background. Two, his is the voice from your dream.

Saturday
Morning
April 7

Cheeseball Thunder

Six A.M.

Once, in a spasm of sappiness, you asked Q-Jo if she thought your dreams would ever come true. "You aren't talking about dreams," she corrected you, "you're referring to your pathetic bourgeoisie ambitions. Dreams don't come true. Dreams *are* true."

You thought about that as you tossed and rolled—sleepless, dreamless—through the night, but there were so many thoughts playing bumper cars in your brain that you hadn't more than a few seconds to spend with any particular one before it was rear-ended or broadsided by a different thought—that then took *its* brief turn leading the pack. You tried to stay focused on the market, on your chances for survival if there wasn't a major rebound on Monday, but there were simply too many other cars careening and caroming in your cerebral motordrome. For example, even though a squeamish examination of your vagina convinced you that you had escaped sexual molestation during your downtown ordeal, you could not help but worry if you should not be tested for AIDS. With the disease rampant these days, a test might be prudent, and only moderately embarrassing. Certainly less embarrassing than taking your pants-down story to the police. And speaking of the police, maybe you should. . . . No, no, Q-Jo would be home in the morning, just forget about her, the oracular hussy. Yet, you could not forget about her for very long. Thrice during the awful night, you got up to give her a call, and following the third unsuccessful attempt, you redialed Larry Diamond's number, as well. You were almost relieved when you got the same pompous message as before, but it set you to thinking about your libretto dream. And about that dumb word,

Bozo. Apparently, Diamond had been Q-Jo's Friday morning tarot client, in addition to hiring her to look at his Timbuktu souvenirs on Friday afternoon, so it was probably him, Diamond, you'd bet a hundred shares of Microsoft on it, who had messed with the Huff's Star card. To what end? She must have permitted him. To what end? Assisted him. To what end? Tossing on the pillow, you felt a pain in your neck, a welcome pain because it *ka-whammed* the Diamond car against the rail of the arena, allowing yet another thought—*ooga-ooga,* blink-blink—to scoot triumphant out of traffic.

Now, at six a.m., your eyelids as heavy as rubber bumpers but your transmission too jarred and jangled (and conditioned by the brokerage business) to let you rest, you bounce out of bed and patter to the window, through which you notice with mild surprise that the rains have returned.

SIX-FIFTEEN A.M.

The rains have returned. The runaway sky, as though connected by a bungee cord, has been yanked back to earth, where peaks are perforating its bladder and ridges are wringing out its glands. Your building is surrounded by the soft, the gray, and the moist, as if it is being digested by an oyster.

This is Seattle, the brief, bright spring has stalled, and the rains have returned. They have stolen down from the Sasquatch slopes. They have risen with the geese from the marshes. It rains a chattering of totem teeth. It rains a sweat lodge of ancient vapors. The city, with its office towers and electricity, has been somehow primitivized by the rain: every hue darkened, every wheel slowed, every view foreshortened, every modern, commercial mind-set turned in on itself, forced to rub shoulders with the old salamander who sleeps in the soul. Hour after hour, the rain will fall; apartments, decorated to be showplaces, will take on the character of burrows or nests; and espresso carts, the little pumping stations of Seattle's lifeblood, will glow beneath their umbrellas like the huts of shamans. Drops spiral

114

from every cornice, every antenna, every awning. Drops glisten on each plate-glass window, each tailgate, each inch of neon that sizzles in the mist. Dense, penetrating, and modifying, the rain narrows the gap between nature and civilization. Forgotten longings stir in the crack.

You read somewhere that in Botswana, the word *pula* means both money and hello. You like that arrangement. Whenever you meet somebody, you say "money," and they say "money" back. What a happy greeting! How honest and to the point! You read, further, that *pula* also may be translated as "rain." That's nice, too. Pennies from heaven, so to speak. Old Botswanans knowing it's going to rain because their wallets get stiff. And never a need to save for a rainy day. Staring into the sheet music of precipitation, you try to think of it as cascading cash, yet you remain at least partially aware that somewhere out there, not many blocks away, failed businessmen and their families are taking refuge from the weather beneath freeway ramps and in cardboard shacks. Maybe money would be better expressed by *aloha* than by *pula*. In each hello an implied good-bye.

As for the rain, it manifests all of *aloha*'s ambiguity and then some. Rain is protective in ways that the seemingly more affectionate sunshine can never match. It dims the monster's glare, dampens the dragon's fire. But like the pockets of a drowned sailor, it can conceal disintegrating packets of forbidden opiates and any number of rusty knives.

You brew a latte, pull on a robe—with the wetness there has come a chill—and return to the window to stare some more. *André's aquaphobic,* you think. *Maybe the downpour will send that darn beast home.* All that comes home to you, however, are those strange old longings. The ones you thought your financial goals had long ago replaced.

"Sears, Philip Morris, Merck, General Electric," you commence to chant. But the magic words have little power against the rain.

Nine-Ten A.M.

Q-Jo Huffington loves the rain. She considers Seattle's prevailing meteorological mode a refreshment, a benediction. It blesses the brows of those who brave it and makes the little mushrooms grow. She persists in her belief that the Northwest rains not only nurture and renew, but consecrate and sanctify, even though she is privy to reports of withering acids in the raindrops. You regard the contradiction as one more example of her proclivity for self-delusion, although you must admit that even the holy water sprinkled on christened infants is teeming with microbial life that, when magnified, is as fierce-looking as wolverines, yet does less harm than good.

A resumption of rainy weather after a dry spell is one of the few things that can pull Q-Jo out of bed before nine in the morning, and you are hoping that it has roused her today, that it has piped her from the sordid sheets in which she undoubtedly has been wallowing. So firmly do you expect her within the hour that moving to the computer, you are able to concentrate with reasonably pellucid focus on ammonias that might jolt the money gods from their swoon.

The rich, from whose scroll your name is inconceivably and infuriatingly missing, maintain that a nice, forceful slashing of the capital gains tax is the tonic the comatose economy requires, although Sol Finkelstein et al. contend that such a move would serve only to widen the moats around the palaces. There was a time when a cut in interest rates by the Federal Reserve could be counted on to stimulate borrowing and thus increase consumption, but like the flourishes of an aging arthritic magician, that sleight-of-hand has become so creakily obvious that only the myopic in the audience are fooled anymore.

There are those—largely the marginal and uninformed—who blame the budget deficit for everything, but insiders such as you know full well that the Treasury could simply print stacks of fresh new money—a vision of such loveliness that it wets your eyes—and wipe out the deficit overnight. The fly in that green ink is that the good old worn money would no longer be worth as much, and the palace moats would constrict, perhaps to a width that could be vaulted by the more spring-loaded in the middle class (among whom you, so taut of calf, would have to be counted), and since the Mint is in the julep of the wealthy, you will not hold your breath until it cranks up the presses.

A far bigger problem is America's short end of the trade stick. Many are the steps that Congress and the President could take to restore the balance of trade, but every single one of them would rub turpentine into the rectum of some sector or another of the voting public, and by now, all but the terminally naive are aware that politicians, almost without exception, are more interested in reelection than in a daring rescue of the nation. Truly powerful "Americans" are multinational anyhow, and have been for decades, so what do they care? You can't blame them. You just wish *you* had a villa in Tuscany to which to repair. The Bahamas. Anywhere. Short of Timbuktu. What had taken a financial professional to that distant outpost? you wonder. For a second. Jesus, your mind must be a morbid thing to bring *him* up again. As if to exorcise Mr. Diamond, you shake your head until a single hair, decidedly gray, breaks loose and flutters to a landing on the computer keyboard, where it lies like a strand of Medusa vermicelli across the A, the S, the D, and the F.

Well, girl, you cannot afford a haven in a foreign paradise, and lots of luck convincing Belford Dunn to desert his native land in its hour of need. None of the aforementioned remedies are likely to be applied, and if they were, they probably would be too little, too late, the ladder to the moon having already toppled. So what is the solution? *The solution*, you think, *is war.*

Yes, why not? You type in "war" (knocking the errant hair aside as you strike the A), and watch the word shimmer like a line of phosphorescent battle dust on the PC screen. As you understand it, the United States has been operating under a wartime economy since 1941. With the end of World War II, there were those who feared a resumption of the Great Depression, and some who reasoned that an ongoing military state was an excellent way to control both the American populace and foreign competitors, so instead of beating our swords into plowshares, we invented a new enemy—the downtrodden, depleted, but "godless" Soviet Union—and devoted our capability to making bigger and better swords. This history lesson came to you, you must confess, by way of your dad and his radical pothead pals and thus should be totally discredited, except that this morning you are finding a hempseed of truth in it. Nobody can deny that in our national security society, with a defense industry smoking around the clock, we prospered. For a while. But a wartime economy, sucking up tax dollars like a thousand-foot teenager sucking up sugar and grease, can flourish for only so long in peacetime. Eventually, growth in productivity dropped, the competitiveness of industry declined, wages stagnated, the once-steady rise in living standards turned tail, and underfunded non-military priorities such as education, health care, and environmental protection went to hell. Meanwhile, the defeated nations of Germany and Japan, by ignoring the military and concentrating on the manufacturing of civilian goods, began kicking our butts from factory gate to bank door; and, despite a few financial setbacks of their own in the early nineties, are kicking them still. Nobody can deny that, either. Someday, perhaps, by shifting emphasis we can revitalize our peacetime industries to the point where we can skin cats with the best, but that is long-term. Short-term, the stock market is lying in a pool of blood, and your Porsche is hiding in the bushes from the repo man. Short-term, the only way to stimulate a pulse in this flatline victim is to crack another vial of war under its nostrils.

Is it so far-fetched? Certainly, the President would have no moral qualms about it. Wartime presidents are more popular than Santa Claus, and this one is aching to be reelected. As for an enemy, there is hardly a shortage of attractive candidates. Now that the U.S.S.R. is gone, most of them are rather fish in a barrel, but they might hold out against us long enough to raise significantly the juice level in our pitcher; and, who knows, one of them could prove as worthy an opponent as North Vietnam. To do *you* much good, however, war, or the imminent threat of war, would have to materialize with giddy haste. By Monday morning, to be exact.

Okay, you realize that that prospect is about as likely as one of your clients phoning to thank you for the tireless effort you put into separating them from their life savings, but nevertheless, in a move characteristic of your girlish optimism, in a move that frankly is several kilometers south of rational, you sort of absentmindedly switch on the shortwave band of your radio—just to check, casually to be sure, hope against hope, if there are any ominous growlings on the international scene.

What you receive is a great deal of static, an indication that the solar flares—or whatever has been responsible for the cosmic interferences of the past few days—are still raging. At one point on the band, you momentarily intercept a clear transmission, but it turns out to be the scores from the East Indian Basketball Association. The Bengal Tigers have defeated the Singapore Slings, the Bombay Gin and the Black Holes of Calcutta are tied in overtime, and the Madras Shorts have moved out in front of the Kashmir Sweaters. The Poona Tang did not play.

Ten-Fifteen A.M.

Standing at the window again, still in your robe, you watch raindrops wriggle like daydreaming tadpoles down the pane. They seem perfectly healthy, perfectly formed to you. One round head. One tapered tail. Translucent as you please. Standard issue. Right out of the manual. If they are mutated by contamination, they wear it well. Besides, you would venture that acid rain is good for the environment. Isn't industry part of the environment?

In waves, orchestrated by the wind, drops dash themselves against the window, where they surrender their antic wildness, their whiplash abandon, their sea-bullet roulette, to join the *zendo* of day-dreamers sliding in a slow, soft, wriggly meditation toward the puddle of being, the watery nimbus around the soul. The rain produces a sound that is somewhere between finger-drumming (your father at the lunch table, impatient for his adobo?) and the mumbly marriage bed conversation that every child in the house strains to catch. Is there meaning in its nuances, is it what remains of an Ur language once spoken by the common ancestor of humans and dolphins, or are the raindrops no more than extras mouthing "rutabaga, rutabaga" on the set of a movie whose script they haven't been privileged to read? You are listening to the rain more carefully than you ever have, harder than someone in your position and with your goals ought, when the mood is shattered, thank goodness, by the loose-hubcap-on-a-UFO sound of the telephone.

Q-Jo at last! You feel it. You know it. No doubt about it. She may be calling from her unit down the hall, from the pay phone at the Dog House after a pork chop breakfast, or from the quarters of that broken-down ex-broker who quite likely has taken advantage of her Winnebago silhouette, her voluminous unappeal to the normal male, to visit his most disgusting urges upon her. The source of the call is inconsequential. What matters is that it is she, and that that portion of your mind given over to anger and concern about her can now be cleared for more productive activity. Moreover, once she has endured your tongue-lashing, she can satisfy that itsy-bitsy twinge of curiosity you have concerning the altered tarot card and the other oddities that have afflicted your orderly life of late. At the very least, Q-Jo will lend a sympathetic ear to an account of your humiliating attack downtown last night, and she may well lead you to accept it with a kind of fatalistic grace. Though she cares little about the tragic accidents disabling your career, cynical as she is regarding profit and profiteers, she will prove fiercely protective of your physical health and vindictive toward whatever or whomever has endangered it.

You are feeling almost sisterly as you lift the receiver, the embarrassment of your association with her displaced momentarily by a geyser of relief. But it isn't her. It isn't her! You can hardly believe it. You are beside yourself. It isn't Q-Jo, it's Belford.

"Hi, honeykins. Sorry I didn't phone earlier but I've been trying to track down the French consul general. I found out he's gone to the Napa Valley for the weekend, to some winery or something, and I was getting ready to rent a car and drive up there, and then it occurred to me that my little rascal could possibly have come home." He pauses expectantly. The expectant pause is so large that were it a house, Christ and all twelve disciples could live there, although Judas Iscariot would probably have to sleep on the sun porch. The expectancy, though silent, is so tremendous and insistent that you refuse out of spite to respond to it, and when Belford finally speaks again, panic, like an opera of termites, has undermined his voice. He squeaks worse than you, his beloved, when he asks, "There isn't bad news, is there?"

"Good grief, Belford! Are you kidding? There isn't anything *but* bad news. Are you living in a pumpkin or something?" You fumble for the rheostat to dim your vexation. "If you're talking about André, and I assume you are since that's the only damn thing that makes any difference to you, no, there's no bad news. No good news, either. Everything's the same as when you left, at least it is where your ape's concerned."

"You sound upset."

"Me? Upset? Where did you get that idea? Have you been puffing on one of those San Francisco dope sticks? I bet you have. I bet. . . ."

"Gwen! Honey. What is it?"

"What's what? Everything's perfectly hunky-dory. Just 'another day in the life of a fool,' to quote from the wisdom of the East. So. Why don't you go sober up, and if I run into André, I'll have him call your hotel. Bye."

As you slam the receiver down, you mutter, "Bozo!" And for some inexplicable reason, it makes you laugh out loud.

121

Tom Robbins

Ten-Thirty A.M.

Something has changed. You have changed. Your dad told you once that Dizzy Gillespie sat on his trumpet and bent it, accidentally creating an instrument that transformed his career. Change can occur that fast. *Snap!* Ouch! And the next thing one knows, one is blowing a whole new tune. Something about the telephone call, the disappointment of the call, the "Bozo" that slipped out at the end of the call, the last straw of it, as it were—something ordinary yet indefinite, mundane yet mysterious, silly yet profound, something tiny but very, very pure, has happened, and you may never be the same.

Nature, supposedly, rewards energy and aggression. Well, you have been energetic and aggressive enough for five, and where has it gotten you? Perhaps it was a matter of improper alignment. Your horn was always pointed dead ahead when it ought to have been crimped a little toward the ceiling. And now. . . . This is idle speculation, mind you, this is fancy. Should anyone doubt, however, that you are in an unusual mood, they need only to observe the manner in which you tear off your robe and pajamas and pull a tight black dress on over your unwashed body—not even any underwear! —the spontaneity with which you paint your lids and lips, and the steady gleeful arrogance with which you punch in Larry Diamond's number.

"If you're calling to whine about the market," his recorded voice responds, rumblings and crashes in the background, "you're not going to get any sympathy here. Did you really expect that a culture that believes the Second Coming is right around the corner, sucking on a breath mint and straightening its tie, could have the long-range vision or the long-term will to sustain a superpower economy? You guys are truly amusing." He cackles like a mechanical magpie laying a barbed-wire egg.

You gulp once and blink twice, surprised both by the content of the recording and that there is a fresh recording at all, but your nerve holds, and after the beep you say, "Listen up. This is

122

Gwendolyn Mati. I want to speak with Q-Jo Huffington, and I want to speak with her pronto. If she's not in touch with me in ten minutes, I'm contacting the police." Your voice is sawtoothed with determination, although to be perfectly frank, you are still an octave or two away from sounding quite adult.

While you wait, you select a pair of black pumps and the handbag du jour. Into the latter, you pour the contents of yesterday's bag, minus the stupid Nommo card, of course, which is now back in Q-Jo's deck where it belongs. You flick on CNN, and sure enough, the news pertains to the financial crisis. "News" is probably too strong a word for it. It is primarily conjecture about how the market might behave on Monday, assuming the SEC allows it to open on Monday. "If it doesn't open Monday, then when *will* it open?" one expert asks. "If we wait until conditions significantly improve, it might not reopen in our lifetime." The tone is less than merry. But at least no one on CNN is blaming the crash on Christian dogma.

TEN FORTY-FIVE A.M.

Ten minutes pass. In fact, fifteen minutes pass: you want to be fair. When, at ten forty-five, Q-Jo has yet to call, you don your Burberry raincoat, seize a pretty polka-dot umbrella as if it were a pig-sticker, and march out the door. Downstairs, you decide to drive Belford's Lincoln, reasoning that if by some miracle André should appear in the drizzle along your route, he might consent to come aboard. Driving the Porsche, you would deny him a ride even if he were standing in an intersection flagging you with an SOS banana and a broken arm. You cannot forget the time you agreed to take André to the vet's for his annual flu shot. (Belford was closing a big sale.) Riding home, the cute little fellow ripped off every button and knob in your Porsche, bit holes in the leather upholstery, and swung from the rearview mirror. As you pulled into Belford's driveway, he tore open his jar of purple monkey vitamins, stuffed his mouth with them, then, screeching at their foul flavor, spit them out, permanently staining the seats, the floor mats, and your new Armani pantsuit. Belford made the brute get down on his hairy knees and pray for God's forgiveness, which is touching, you suppose, but to this day your nine-hundred-dollar Hermès attaché case bears embarrassing purple spots.

The choice of car proves academic, however. You encounter no stray animals and few pedestrian humans on your way to police headquarters. The relentless rain has taken its toll on that minute portion of the citizenry still brave enough, affluent enough to shop. From the occasional doorway or cardboard lean-to, arms can be seen thrusting soggy candy boxes into the gloom, hoping to attract a coin or a cigarette. Aside from that, little moves on Seattle's sidewalks except rivulets of rainwater. When, between the U-Park and the Public Safety Building, a wild, wet gust turns your umbrella into a scarecrow chest X ray, you begin to regret that *you* have ventured out.

In terms of your reception, the weather is no balmier indoors. You might have anticipated it. Put yourself in their place. You step up to the window in that fifth-floor lobby decorated by Kafka's proctologist and announce, "I want to report a missing person." And the woman with a face like a slab of Cro-Magnon bacon regards you with a ripple of recognition on the flat yellow surface of her ox-bile eyes and says, "You mean a missing monkey."

"No. Person."

" 'Person' as in 'human being'?"

"Exactly."

" 'Person' as in your gentleman friend, who went looking for his chimp and got lost his own self?"

"Negative. May I speak with the detective, please." Holding your temper is not unlike containing a pit bull in a pillowcase.

"The detective ain't here. He's off on a real situation."

"Are you insinuating that this is not a real situation?"

"I'm not insinuating nothing, lady."

"Can I make a report or not?"

"That depends."

"On what?"

"Situation."

So, you try to explain the situation, but she keeps interrupting. "The individual's name is *what*?" "She weighs *how* much?" "She's been missing since *when*?"

Eventually, the carrion-faced clerk goes to a phone at a desk out of earshot and makes a call, doubtless to the detective who is alleged to be absent from the premises, although you suppose it could be to the nut squad at Harborview. As she talks, her eyes never leave you. Her co-workers watch you, as well. Such wariness, such suspicion! You are suddenly keenly aware that you aren't wearing underpants. After she hangs up, she returns to the window, intent on sending you away. The police, she explains, will not investigate the whereabouts of a person missing less than twenty-four hours unless there are mitigating circumstances.

"Well, damn it, there *are*!"

"Well, damn it, there *aren't*! You said yourself that the individual has been known to stay out nights with male individuals. The fact that this particular male individual has a tattoo on his hand and talked smutty to you in a bar don't make him a suspect. If your individual don't turn up by seven tonight, you can come back and an officer'll take a statement. I'm obliged to tell you that. Myself, *I* think. . . ." She bites her suety tongue and with a cross between a smirk and a glare, leaves the window.

"Thanks for the help!" you yell after her. You are boiling—but can you really blame the cops? One day you waltz in with a soiled swain begging for assistance in locating a born-again French monkey jewel thief, and the next day you are here claiming that a three-hundred-pound queerly named woman in a turban may have been abducted by a man who was paying her to look at pictures of Timbuktu. They must think you've got a six-ring circus for a fantasy life. Okay, they can choke on powdered doughnuts for all you care. You are going to go find Q-Jo Huffington. Dead or alive.

Tom Robbins

ELEVEN THIRTY-TWO A.M.

The rain has increased in volume, and inexplicably, so has traffic. Cars hiss along with their lights on and spray water on one another. (Pity the poor windshield wiper, for its Sisyphean labors will never attain the status of myth.) For years now, most automobiles have been designed to roughly resemble eggs. Manufacturers claim the ovoid shape maximizes aerodynamic efficiency, but if that is true, how come a bird has to break *out* of the egg before it can fly?

At Grandpa Mati's funeral mass, you asked why men were made to remove their hats in church and women were not, to which your mother replied, "In the Middle Ages, it was decided that only men should have to remove their hats because women are *already* eggs." Your understanding of that decision remains incomplete. And this unintended meditation on eggs is making you nervous. More than once in the past, you have entertained horrific visions of Belford's sperm: so steadfast, so patient, so annoyingly persevering in their attempts to hoist their little sacks of fertilizer over the barricades you have erected at the portals of your womb. Good grief! You shudder and switch on the Lincoln's radio.

A Zen nightmare of clapping hands roars out of the speakers. You assume the applause is for the President, who must be outlining to the nation his plan of action in the wake of Thursday's crash. Better late than never, you suppose. Alas, what follows, rather than a presidential proclamation, is just another fillip of flapdoodle from Dr. Motofusa Yamaguchi. The governor of Washington State has just asked Yamaguchi if his cancer cure will usher in a better age for all mankind. "When one thing get better," the good doctor replies with the hint of a giggle, "some other thing have to get worse. A big front has a big back."

"Right. You tell 'em, Doc." Jesus! For some reason, you always expected the breakthrough in cancer research would come from a very sober, very earnest team of white-smocked, sharp-featured, metallically clean, handsomely paid Swiss chemists in the employ of

one of those giant drug companies of whose alleged net worth you,

126

in your time, have peddled oodles and oodles of shares. Life *is* full of surprises, most of which we could well do without. "Wuf," you bark at the radio as you turn it off. Better to listen to the curses of unseen street people—"Drive me to the hospital in yo' Lincoln, bitch!"— and the rat-a-tat of the rain.

A womanish figure in a red turban ducks into the doorway of a burnt-out building. Instinctively, you touch the brakes, although you know from a glance the person could not possibly be Q-Jo, who, as if living proof of Yamaguchi's law, is equally big, front and back. This woman was way too narrow, and besides, it was probably a bloody bandage wound 'round her head. Once when you told your large psychic friend that her turban made her look like some kind of cartoon swami, she responded, "It may be a cliché to a tight-ass titmouse like you, but to regular human beings, my turban is like the dome of a cathedral or the steeple of a church. It identifies what they can expect to find underneath it and guides them to a particular variety of assistance." Right or wrong, her towelhead has remained an embarrassment to you, although you'd pay a pretty penny—had you a pretty penny left—for a glimpse of it this morning.

Only the rain fills the void of Q-Jo's parking space, however, and only silence greets your knock at her door. The lone message on your machine is from Belford, moreover, apologizing that he had been insensitive earlier to your PMS. PMS? *What* PMS? Normally, this would have taxed your sweet disposition, and, indeed, you are on the threshold of fury, but hey, your horn is tipped now ever so slightly toward the stars, and there is a fresh melodic line, reckless and vaguely self-amusing, that you seem destined to pursue.

ELEVEN FIFTY-FIVE A.M.

From the Posner residence, Barbara Posner, a gracious blue-haired matron whom you have met socially on several occasions, takes a moment to register your name. "Oh, yes, of course, Miss Mati," she says at last, and she excuses herself to fetch her husband. But it is her voice, not his, that next comes over the line. "Very sorry, it would be inconvenient for Mr. Posner to speak with you right now, but he says he is looking forward to a conference with you in his office on Monday. He had already penciled it in."

"Tell him it's not work related."

"Oh? If it's a personal matter, Miss Mati, perhaps that could be broached at your conference, as well."

"Look, all I want from your husband is an address. Larry Diamond's address."

"Who, please? I'm not sure we're acquainted with this person."

"Would you ask? Larry Diamond. It's vital."

When she picks up the phone again, Barbara Posner says, "Yes, oh yes. We do remember. Mr. Diamond. Rather a character. Left Dean Witter under somewhat of a cloud, I think, though he's said to have recently returned from the wilds of Africa, heavy with wisdom."

"That's the guy," you declare, although privately you are unwilling to concede the "wisdom" part.

"Sorry. Mr. Posner has no idea where Mr. Diamond resides."

You swallow hard. "He doesn't?"

"Happy Easter, dear."

Neither Phil Craddock nor Sol Finkelstein is at home, and Ann Louise is too recent on the scene to have successfully offered Diamond her ass. Where to turn? What to do? You prepare a small salad, using the mizuna and patsoi that you had the Thriftway produce manager order especially for you. The store hasn't stocked greens like those since the eighties. They are bitter enough to turn a bunny rabbit into a carnivore, but you are too lost in thought to notice.

Midway through the salad, mizuna leaves virtually sawing on your tongue, you spring up from the table and punch Diamond's number again. The message hasn't changed, but it isn't his message that interests you now. Those rumbles, those crashes in the background! They are familiar somehow. You hang up and call again. And again. On the fifth call, there is a sudden synaptic click, and the hall light flickers on in your brain. On the sixth call, a heavy marble-ized ball rolls down the hall.

Excited, you drop the receiver and dash to the bookcase, from which you snatch the slender sheath of your mother's poetry. There it is. On page fourteen. "Homage to the Chinese Master, Bo Ling."

> *Fingers dipping like rat fangs*
> *into the round black cheese*
> *—O moon that orbits Milwaukee!—*
> *you heave it onto the path,*
> *the wayless Way,*
> *the long and slippery road*
> *at whose end there await,*
> *amidst thunder,*
> *the ten buddhas.*

Bo Ling, indeed. Your mom wrote that poem after she had reluctantly accompanied your father and his friends to an Asian-American ten-pin tournament—you wish now you could remember at which lanes. Never mind. You're on to something. The noises on Larry Diamond's phone. Thunder House. Yes, by Jesus, in an embroidered shirt! For whatever reason, goofy or corrupt, Larry Diamond is conducting his life from a bowling alley.

Whither the Amphibians?

Twelve-Twenty P.M.

Fourteen bowling alleys are listed in the yellow pages of the Seattle telephone directory. As you might have expected, there is not a Thunder House among them. There is, however, a Thunderbird Bowl in the Ballard district, and that strikes you as as good a place as any to begin.

Tarrying only long enough to step into a pair of panties—you most certainly are not about to risk encountering Larry Diamond with your little clam on the half-shell, so to speak—you grab your extra umbrella and the keys to the Porsche and set out. For about five seconds, you consider taking the Lincoln but reject the notion on the grounds that wherever Belford's little rascal might be, he would not be in Ballard. A jewel thief in Ballard? Don't make you laugh. A lutefisk thief, perhaps.

Ballard is known as Little Norway or Little Sweden, depending upon which side of the Skagerrak one's sentiments lie. The irreverent call it Snoose Junction, referring to the snuff some residents dip. "It ain't hip to dip," your dad said once, refusing to move the Mati family to a cozy cottage in Ballard, even though rents in that area were among the lowest in the city. Odd that Ballard's bowling alley would be named for Thunderbird, rather than, say, for Thor. But then, Indians lived on the site long before Scandinavians, so it may be fair. *Ethnically, everything is all mixed up now anyway*, you think. Cultures strewn and scattered among other cultures like shingles after a tornado. Japanese tourists in German cars stopping off at the South Seas Motel in Moscow, Idaho. Your Filipino father beating Caribbean drums and talking like he was raised in the streets of

Tom Robbins

Harlem. You wonder if this multiculturalism of which Belford Dunn and his ilk are so admiring isn't at least partially responsible for the nation's economic fizzle. In point of fact, America has *always* been multicultural, but until fairly recently the nation was a symbolic pot in which various peoples were metaphorically melted, blending into one rich alloy; and it was that fusion of talents, philosophies, attributes, and inclinations—renewable and adaptable—that gave the U.S. its zip and its zest. Nowadays, however, it seems few immigrants are inclined to assimilate. They bring their native cultures with them, virtually intact, and cling to them, refusing even to learn to speak English and getting angry when the social institutions of their adopted land fail to address them in their indigenous tongues. Which keeps them out of the work force, naturally, and in a state of victimization; a selfish, self-pitying, self-perpetuating state insidiously exploited by leftists for their own political ends. Thus, instead of a strong, nutritious broth, pungent with the aromatic spices of labor and success, America has become a plop of separate little lumps of undigested stuff. Kind of like—vomit. Good-bye, melting pot, hello, chamber pot.

Ah, yes, Gwen, but what if there was some way to take advantage of *your* minority status when the hatchets start to swing on Monday? You cannot deny that it has occurred to you that you might charge Posner Lampart McEvoy and Jacobsen with racial discrimination or sexual harassment, or both. Get a settlement, at the very least, and maybe collect damages or preserve your job. That occurred to you yesterday. It occurred to you during the night. Today, though, you feel strangely disassociated from the idea, as if you have somehow risen above it.

Good grief! Will this rain never stop?

Ballard is the home port of Seattle's fishing fleet, and as the Porsche plows through standing water onto the long bridge that connects Snoose Junction with lower Queen Anne, you can gaze down through the business-page format of the mist (endless columns of minuscule gray symbols furnished by some atmospheric equivalent of the New York Stock Exchange) and see work boats of various lengths and tonnage, from bantamweight purse seiners to monstrous floating canneries, hitched to the docks, twiddling their antennae, waiting for the salmon runs of summer. One might never guess the salmon were dwindling—the crab and halibut, too—from the plenitude of boats in the harbor. "Fish," you say aloud, with a squeaky and altogether mirthless chuckle. You could be thinking that it is quite amazing how much we human beings—evolved, civilized, sophisticated, created in God's own image—depend on those cold-blooded, elongated, squamous vertebrates (slippery, pop-eyed, and pornographically scented) that hide from us in un-known numbers beneath the waters, deep or shallow, broad or nar-row, fresh or briny, rough or placid, of the world. Heaven forbid you are thinking of the Nommo card.

Having traversed the bridge now, you turn the Porsche to the right and travel for a couple of blocks through an industrial neigh-borhood with direct links to commercial fishing. Then you turn north again, away from the docks, and motor very slowly up a street lined with the modest clapboard cottages your father had been too cool to inhabit, until you spot, at an intersection with a busy com-mercial avenue, an excrementally brown, draconically oversized, windowless hellbox of a building that could only be an Albanian mental hospital, a Midwestern schoolhouse, or a bowling alley; and although its neon sign is not illuminated—like many local establish-ments, it must be trying to conserve on its utility bills—you are confident it is the last. Shifting gears, you speed up and fairly squeal into the parking lot. It's the Thunderbird Bowl, all right. You fix upon a nylon-jacketed man carrying a round satchel into which a human head would fit perfectly, even a chubby-cheeked head bound in a turban. When he pulls open the wide front door, you can hear rumblings and crashes inside. The next thing you hear are your tires, squealing back into the street again.

Tom Robbins

Twelve Forty-Five P.M.

Four times you drive around the block, the Porsche weaving in and out of the rain-slowed traffic like the essence of a Henry James sentence weaving in and out of prepositional phrases, dependent clauses, and parenthetical asides (periodically hitting the brakes to avoid misplacing a modifier). You are telling yourself, all the while, that the prudent thing to do, the wise thing, the safe thing, the simple thing would be to go home—or downtown to the disco if you can gain admittance—and concentrate on repairing your career: there's got to be a way to blow some smoke in Posner's eyes when he summons you to his teakwood desk on Monday. You can think of plenty of reasons to flee Ballard, not the least of which is the unlikelihood of coming across Belford's precious monkey here, and hardly a single reason to remain. In the end, however, you return to the Thunderbird Bowl, park, and get out of the car. What is it that that irksome Yamaguchi said? Another day in the life of a fool.

And as if you hadn't enough to feel foolish about, you allow your capitulating bumbershoot to expose its soft white underbelly to the fangs of the wind so that seconds after opening, it has gone from concave to convex and joined its polka-dotted counterpart in umbrella Valhalla. By the time you reach the door, the hairs of your head, black and gray alike, are pearled with raindrops that jiggle and vibrate with each rumble, each crash.

Twelve Fifty-Five P.M.

Bowling, how doth Gwendolyn Mati despise thee? Let you count the ways. One, bowling is a marginal sport (precious little athletic ability is required of its practitioners, most of whom seem more interested in drinking beer and chit-chatting than in the finer points —if there *are* finer points—of the game). Two, bowlers are marginal people (in the hive that is America, only the drones go bowling). Three, bowling alleys are marginal places (there's hardly a one that

136

could not have been designed by Mussolini, built by his brother-in-law, and decorated by his teenage mistress). Four, bowling is popular with the masses (enough said).

The instant you enter the Thunderbird, you are overcome with an edacious distaste and a puncturing depression. In the totalitarian glare of its half-hectare of fluorescent tubing, you suddenly are rubbing shoulders with working stiffs and blowzy babes, the sort of blue-collar rabble that habitually you have gone to great lengths to avoid. You fancy you hear them belching and farting, quoting Clint Eastwood, exchanging off-color punch lines, and making all the other uncouth and threatening noises with which the rabble customarily express themselves, but soon you are forced to admit that most of it is in your imagination. In the lounge area, a selection of louts grin at you and beckon you to their various tables, but active bowlers by and large ignore you, and minute by minute, your fear, if not your aversion, diminishes. At least nobody is barking.

Trying your hardest to appear inconspicuous, you stroll around, searching in vain every nook and cranny for Larry Diamond or someone who looks as if he might in some way be associated or acquainted with Mr. Diamond. In particular, you scrutinize the area around the pair of pay phones bolted to the wall near the entrance, scarcely more than a bowling ball's throw from the first of the Thunderbird's sixteen lanes. Nothing out of the ordinary, as far as you can tell. Fishing a quarter from your bag, you decide to make a call. The equipment behaves exactly as any other public telephone, you attract no undue attention from patrons or staff—and Q-Jo Huffington doesn't answer at home. "Drat!" you exclaim, oblivious to the fact that no Filipina has ever, in the history of the world, said "drat" before you.

Could it even be possible, you wonder, that Diamond lives in the neighborhood, in one of those dreadfully déclassé little snoose-stained houses, and slips into the Thunderbird to use its pay phones? Of course not, dummy! He couldn't attach his answering machine to a public phone. And neither of the numbers on the pay phones here matches his number. Even their prefix is different. Undoubtedly, this is a wild-goose chase of governmental proportions. The relationship between Thunderbird Bowl and Thunder House seems about as close as that between toilet bowl and toilet water. Okay, but hold on a second. What *about* the prefix? You could ring up the telephone company, give them Diamond's prefix, and they would tell you what part of town he's in. Good grief! It has taken you this long to think of that? You are to detective work what Grandma Moses is to German Expressionism.

The directory assistance operator seems to have been waiting all morning to honor your request. "Seven eight three," she says quickly and cheerfully, "is one of the prefixes for Ballard."

As you hang up, you glance over both shoulders, while something cold and bristly, like Nanook of the North's toothbrush, runs up and down your spine.

ONE OH-NINE **P.M.**

The Thunderbird's office is located in a loft area above the cocktail lounge. As you climb the stairs, you are both pleased and alarmed that you may be homing in on your target. You remove your index finger from your lips, where you have been gnawing on its nail, and press the buzzer. On the other side of the door, there is a scampering sound, causing visions of gerbils, hamsters, field mice, deer mice, voles, muskrats, wood rats, lemmings, and all things cricetid to scurry past your eyes. "Whatta you need?" somebody asks. And you think *your* voice is squeaky. The door is opened by a woman not a whole lot taller than a bowling pin. And you think *you* are petite.

"Uh, is the, uh, manager here?"

"Not today. It's Saturday."

As the woman answers, you are furtively looking past her—which is simple to do: one can look around her and over her as easily as if she were a garden ornament; why, one could wind her entire body in one of Q-Jo's turbans and have enough fabric left over to wrap King Tut's biscuits. Speaking of which, Q-Jo read in one of her esoteric magazines that genetic scientists, using dried blood scraped off mummy bandages, may someday be able to clone the pharaohs. "That's nice," you told her, "but I wouldn't buy any stock in the company, considering that the demand for resurrected pharaohs is likely to be weak." "Yeah," she agreed, "but there're other applications for the technology, and I suggest you and I squirrel away a few used tampons, just in case."

Remembering that conversation makes you blush. The midget, probably believing her appearance the source of your embarrassment, commences to fidget and shuffle her feet. Visions of gerbils, hamsters, field mice, voles, etc., scurry past your eyes. You hasten to speak. "I'll . . . I'd like to call the manager next week then," you say. "Would you mind giving me the number here?" The office, cramped, cluttered, and entirely banal, lacks a single element that might connect it to Larry Diamond, yet you are sure he is somewhere in Ballard, either in a bowling alley or with bowling alley sound effects on his telephone tape, so you must turn this stone.

"Seven . . ." gerbils the tiny clerk.

Uh-huh.

"Eight . . ." she field mouses.

Yes? Yes?

"One . . ." she voles.

And before she can hamster another numeral, you are swiveling to leave, disappointment and relief lying in a lover's braid upon the unmade bed of your heart.

ONE-FOURTEEN P.M.

Because bowling, on the whole, is not a particularly strenuous activity, the clothing of the bowler is seldom soppy with the moisture secreted by a body in a state of exertion. A body playing basketball or tennis, for example. (The attire of the bowler is at risk from spilled beer, but that is a different matter.) If there is anything that you might mark in bowling's favor, it is its relative aridity. Whenever possible, you avoid any but the most distant association with sweating persons. Except in the abstract, you find the term "honest sweat" regrettable. On the other hand, "no sweat" is a phrase coined in Paradise with you in mind, although it is unlikely that your mouth would pronounce the phrase, "sweat" being one of those words that thicken the tongue. Your mother did not perspire. Ever. So she boasted. As for you, you are uncertain whether or not you are guilty of the act of perspiration. You would be inclined to contend that you have inherited your mother's glandular immaculacy, except that there are times when your breasts and belly are so wet you have to wonder if that much wetness could be entirely the output of the pores of Belford Dunn. In any case, you shower immediately following sex.

When a person is fastidious, to the point of being very nearly squeamish or prim, odds are forty to one in Vegas that that person's secret inner sanctum is a mess. One needn't be a riverboat gambler, a psychiatrist, or a sage from the Orient to figure that out. Through the rackety basilica of the Thunderbird, your shortish but shapely legs transport the unmade bed of your heart. Happily, if that isn't too strong a word, none of the bowlers whom you pass en route are visibly sweating (as has been noted, bowling is not ranked among the arduous sports), but many look to have the *potential* to perspire, to sweat like hogs, in fact; and that is quite enough to spur you to quicken your pace.

So, you quicken your pace. But where, Gwen, are you going? Well, your first stop is back at the public phones, where, by consulting the directory, you learn that there is one other bowling alley—Sunset Bowl & Recreation, by name—in Ballard, but the Sunset's prefix is 782, rather than 783. Still, you will have to check it out, you suppose, although for some reason you are disinclined to abandon the Thunderbird right away. While the jukebox vocals of Bruce Springsteen and Waylon Jennings fill the spaces between rumblings and crashes; while the fluid levels in glasses, bottles, and bladders rise and fall; while chicken wings flap their last in the deep-fat fryer, as if waving to the memory of henhouse companions they will never fan again, while spares engender whoops and splits give rise to groans; while tobacco smoke, steadily accumulating, attacks your sinuses and the hungry eyes of the lounge lizards attack your derriere, you stride over to the bulletin board area purposefully, giving the impression that you are expecting a message there.

League standings have been recently posted. The Swedish Pancakes, you discover, are leading in their division, easily outdistancing the Danish Moderns and the Norwegian Wood. In the Tuesday night league, it's the Troll Patrol out in front of . . . oh, who cares? Elsewhere on the board, there is a history lesson. Bowling, it seems, is a very old game. "The ancient Egyptians enjoyed outdoor bowling about seven thousand years ago." How about that? If mummy-wrap cloning proves successful, the pharaohs could form a bowling team.

Flyers on the bulletin board also alert you to the existence of a Bowling Hall of Fame. Honored therein are champions with names such as Marion Ladewig, Andy Veripapa, and Ed Lubanski, hailing from burgs such as Grand Rapids, Milwaukee—your mother's poem was on the money—and Akron. Your mom's verse was also correct in establishing a link between bowling and religion, although the connection is not to Buddhists but to Protestants. No less a Protestant than Martin Luther, who took it upon himself to fix the number of pins officially at nine. Prior to Luther's edict—nailed, perhaps to the door of a sixteenth-century bowling alley—there had been considerable argument among German churchmen concerning the correct number of pins. Surprised? You shouldn't be. Did you think theologians were referring to something other than bowling when they argued over how many angels could dance on the head of a pin? Today, of course, there are ten pins in the game. Maybe the Dead Sea Scrolls proved Luther wrong.

According to the fascinating literature at hand—and this item is more down your alley, so to speak—bowling emporiums flourish in hard times, financially troubled populations tending to gravitate toward cheap, wholesome recreation. But of course. When the going gets pinched, the pinched go bowling. Hmmm. What conclusions about the depth and potential length of the current economic trough might an analyst draw from the fact that early upon a Saturday afternoon, the Thunderbird is packed like a tin of Norwegian sardines?

A party of white-haired, ruddy, snoose-dipping septuagenarians has assumed responsibility for feeding the jukebox. As a result, Bruce Springsteen and Waylon Jennings have been supplanted by Lawrence Welk. Nobody in the Thunderbird seems to mind, least of all you. One form of blue-collar music is as unfortunate as another, in your opinion. It is not a Lawrence Welk polka, then, but the grudging admission that you really ought to be investigating economic indicators over at the Sunset Bowl (might it be crowded, as well?) that propels you at last from this particular cacophonic cavern of cretinous keglers and out into the torrent.

Despite the lack of a functional umbrella, you stop midway between the exit and your car. The unmade bed of your heart stops with you. Are you certain, Gwendolyn, absolutely certain, that you haven't overlooked something here? God knows, you wouldn't want to have to come back.

ONE-THIRTY P.M.

Like a rice farmer in an upside-down paddy, you stand amidst the self-harvesting stalks of the rain. Thin as chopsticks and chopstick-straight, greenish-gray as the strings of the ocean's zither, the stalks hang from the clouds by their roots and shake free their bursting grains. The rice bowl of your collar is soon overflowing. When you hunch your shoulders, they make rain sushi.

In the parking lot, three-quarters of the stalls are occupied. Is this indicative of a recessionary economy, whereas full occupancy would signify an out-and-out depression? That the vehicles in the lot are mostly battered pickup trucks and aging Japanese minicars is probably meaningless: you suspect that avid bowlers drive clunkers even in the best of times. Your Porsche stands out like an orchid in a septic tank. And speaking of the Porsche, it's going to be just grand getting in it and driving away. First, however, you had better walk over a wee bit closer to the ramp—the ramp that, as you have just discovered, descends to what apparently is a lower level, a sort of daylight basement, of the Thunderbird. Hmmm? At the bottom of the incline, there is a handsome wooden door that, in substance and design, seems incongruously juxtaposed with the cheesy Dead Zone aesthetic of the rest of the building. If this is a service entrance, it is an unusually fine one. There looks to be a sign of some sort on the door. With raindrops bouncing off your astigmatic eyeballs, it's difficult to tell. Yes—you are nearer now—it is a sign, or, rather, a plaque: one of those handcrafted redwood plaques, the kind that say "The Schicklgrubers" or "Bob & Mary Ann" or "Loafing 'R' Us" in an awkward, chiseled script. You are more than halfway down the ramp before your tremulous suspicions are confirmed. The plaque reads "Thunder House."

ONE THIRTY-SIX P.M.

The clouds are throwing shoes, as well as rice. You feel like the bride at some elemental wedding. Somalia could wring out your hair and end its drought. Still, you stand in the deluge for another minute or two, weighing alternatives, plumping your nerve. The smart thing to do at this point would be to scour the parking lot and adjacent streets for Q-Jo's car. Yet, what would you learn, really, from its presence or absence? This business has gone on long enough. You may have to wait until Monday to find out how many spoonfuls are left in your honeypot or what sharp bees may be circling its rim, but here is a mystery that can be solved. Now.

You rush down the ramp and pound on the door.

It's a hefty door, with strong iron hinges; its central panel embellished with low-relief carvings of cumulus spitting zigzags of lightning. The wood is dark, the carvings discreet and hard to see.

That the door requires study is fortunate, in that it gives you something to do while you wait.

You are hardly surprised that Larry Diamond would keep you waiting. You have the impression that he is the sort of person who might not answer his door at all. Larry Diamond might not answer his door even if he didn't have your best friend, Q-Jo, bound to his round water bed with leather thongs and rubber goods. Which he probably does not, but still, this business has gone on long enough. Don't they understand? The U.S. stock market is swirling down the drain, threatening to suck foreign markets into the vortex, unraveling world economic order and creating chaos and despair. Don't they get it? Chaos and despair. A great unraveling (which means the same thing as "raveling," an etymological fact that you find wholly irksome). You haven't time for this nonsense. Q-Jo! Diamond! As your tight little fist strikes the door another blow, you make a mental note that the stylized thundercloud against which your knuckles are rapping is an American Indian motif. That realization should have lessened your astonishment when the door is opened by a rather large American Indian. It should have, but it does not.

Muscular, more stocky than tall, the man is dressed in clean, pressed denim and a beaded headband that holds in place hair as black as yours was once, before occupational pressures, bad luck, and life's annoyances took their toll. His age is indeterminable, as it often is with you non-European types. He has a narrow brow, a nose more broken than hooked, a mouth with thin, straight lips, and heavy eyebrows curved like elk-hide canopies over a pair of serene, though slightly protruding, brown eyes. Coldly returning your own rude regard, the man is motionless, silent. His entire being, especially his eyes, suggests an interruption of an inward gaze. Feeling as if you have intruded upon an arcane reverie, you cannot help sounding apologetic when you stammer, "Uh, hi. Hello. I'm, uh, I'm-I'm looking for a guy called, uh, Larry Diamond."

The Indian's smile is so slight, so shy, it reminds you of Dr. Yamaguchi's. Such a contrast to the grins of the bowlers upstairs, grins as loose as bar rags and wide enough to put the cat out through. "Larry's not here," he says softly. There is a syncopated cadence to his speech.

"Uh, well, where is he?" You almost blurt it out, forgetting the manners your mother managed to teach you even as your father was deriding good manners as a tactic designed to camouflage the insidious motives of the bourgeoisie.

Again, the hairline smile like the first chalk-scratch of daylight on the blackboard of the little red schoolhouse of dawn. "Larry went to see the amphibians," he says. At that, his smile widens. But the door closes.

As if trying to be helpful—or maybe they're just rubbing it in —raindrops repeat the Indian's parting words in your ear. "Larry went to see the amphibians."

Good grief!

ONE FORTY-ONE P.M.

This is the scene: you are standing in the wind and rain, beating on the basement door of a bowling alley in Snoose Junction, shrieking in your twinkie-tone falsetto, "Where? Where? Where are the amphibians?" And the bowlers, those entering the Thunderbird and those leaving, are looking at you as if you are a lunatic. They are laughing at you and hooting, and one woman yells, "Get a life!" as if you don't have more of a life in your toilet than that blowzy bimbo has in her entire . . . her entire . . . *life.* These are bowlers ridiculing you—low-life *bowlers,* for God's sake; and you are red all the way to your bones. Yet, neither embarrassment nor fury stops you from pounding, or from shrieking "Where are the amphibians?" although you do tone things down a bit when a couple of bon vivants in thin nylon jackets and baseball caps commence in unison to croak like frogs.

You are in such a state that it is slow to dawn on you that you might not really want to know the whereabouts of "the amphibians." There is information that is not in one's best interest (although one

145

must decide that for oneself; the decision should never be the pre-rogative of the government, the networks, or the medical profes-sion). Moreover, until one possesses the information, it is nearly impossible to judge its effect. At any rate, a vision of the Nommo card, or rather the disfigured Star card, begins now to flicker in your consciousness. You recall the young woman with the green scales and the flippered feet. Green scales and webbed toes are hardly normal attributes of a healthy human female but may be regarded as commonplace, if not definitive, in the amphibian sector. Listen! Is activity of an occult nature being dabbled in here? The very fact of Q-Jo Huffington's involvement infers an affirmative.

Ice cubes clink against the swizzle stick of your spinal column, and you start to wonder if this would not be the ideal moment to go home, take a hot shower, and curl up with a glass of chardonnay in front of a friendly computer. However, when one is playing with a tipped trumpet, one does not retreat so easily into the tried and true. You square your shoulders and give the Thunder House door an-other rap. As you strike it, it creaks open again, and there stands the big Indian with that look of someone who has been reading the Book of the Dead with his eyes closed. Once more, you have the guilty feeling that you are tracking mud onto a prayer rug. "Let me explain," you say, making an effort to lubricate the conspiratorial syrinx that you reserve for clients on whom you are trying to push a particularly risky investment. The Indian has scant interest in your spiel. He treats you to a faint, almost pitying smile; hands you a piece of paper, and with the confidence and ease of somebody who is growing accustomed to the act, shuts the door in your face.

Two P.M.

Built for the Seattle World's Fair in 1962, the Pacific Science Center remains one of the most handsome structures in the city. Perhaps "handsome" is too masculine. With its reflecting pools and soaring freestanding arches of swan-white filigree, the Science Center resembles the Taj Mahal if the Taj Mahal had been eaten away from inside by trillions of marble-eating termites so that only a lacy shell remained to blind itself with its own reflection, a snowy honeycomb secreted by angels, and as gleamingly bright in rainy weather as in sunshine. No, the Science Center is more beautiful than handsome, especially when compared to the beige Kleenex boxes that stand on their monolithic and monotonous ends downtown, buildings that would appeal not to the taste of delicate insects but to sewer worms and ogres.

Architecturally, the Science Center is decidedly feminine, although the human enterprise it was erected to honor seems at times to have been rather thoroughly usurped by the very worst facets of the male sensibility. On this rainy Easter Eve, however, activities inside the center have scant connection with profit, property, or power. The focus here today promises to be a small, quiet focus, having more to do with curiosity about small, quiet things than with breakthroughs along yet another path to pay dirt. Not that you wouldn't prefer the latter. But you were directed here by the flyer the Thunder House Indian shoved at you, and, for better or for worse, you have a general idea what to expect.

The flyer announces the annual Reptile & Amphibian Fair, sponsored by the Pacific Northwest Herpetological Society. "Are toads really slimy? Do boas actually crush their prey? Have all your questions about reptiles and amphibians answered." Gee, Gwen, what *are* your questions about reptiles and amphibians? Only one comes to mind. What's the best way to go through life without ever having to encounter such things? "On display: more than 100 live non-venomous reptiles and amphibians, from the common to the exotic." You like the "non-venomous" part. Moreover, an event that lists among its attractions "brown-bag puppet-making, featuring turtles and frogs" has got to be reasonably innocuous. On the other hand, kiddies adore the creepy and the disgusting. Your worst nightmare has you popping out a little Belford Dunn Junior and watching it play with garden slugs and the contents of its diapers.

The wind has gone on break, and the rain has nozzled itself

down to a mizzle—a bit late, as far as your hair and eye shadow are concerned. For some totally illogical and annoying reason, you are feeling self-conscious about the possibility of meeting Larry Diamond in your present bedraggled condition, and you walk slowly, even cautiously, across the Science Center's spacious open-air atrium. Pausing beneath one of the Easter-white arches, you think, *If there's a McDonald's franchise in Heaven, this is what it looks like.* Then you wonder if, considering Heaven's entrance requirements, there are enough customers there to *support* a McDonald's. And would fast foods not be irrelevant in eternity?

The concept of eternity has always, since you were a child, made you queasy. You can understand how life in the hereafter might go on for an extremely long time. Millions of years. Heck, even billions—or trillions—of years. But to never stop. Never, ever, *ever* stop! How can there not, sooner or later, be an end? Some people might take comfort in the notion of eternity, but to you it is confounding, overwhelming, even horrific. *Forever,* in the literal sense, is a shock to the system.

You are about to continue your march to the ticket booth, where with great misgiving you will shell out five dear dollars to go wander among tanks of crawlers and slinkers, among clouded salamanders and Illinois chorus frogs, among river cooters, diamondback terrapins, red milk snakes, island night lizards, hellbenders, mud puppies, and rough-skinned newts, you are about to dip into your endangered capital to finance an excursion into the realm of the relentlessly repulsive when a voice close to your ear says, "Time doesn't exist in eternity."

You nearly jump out of your rain-ruined pumps. And when you see his face, so close to yours, you jump again. "Eternity is timeless," he continues. "It's by definition outside of time. So terms like 'beginning' and 'end' are meaningless."

Your first response is, How dare you sneak up on me before I've had a chance to go to the women's room and repair myself! But what you actually say is, "How did you know what I was thinking?"

To which he replies, "A little trick I picked up in Timbuktu."

HALF ASLEEP *in* FROG PAJAMAS

"What are you doing here?" you ask. It is almost an accusation.

"The real question is, what are *you* doing here? First you refer to the Bozo, then you show up at the amphibian exhibit. Leads me to conclude that you could be on the pad."

"*What* pad?" If this is some crude, masculine reference to menstruation, you'll be sorry you asked.

"The alien pad."

"I don't have the foggiest idea what you're talking about. I'm a native-born American citizen whose father happens to be from the Philippine Islands. And if you can read my mind, Mr. Diamond, then you ought to know what I'm doing here."

He laughs his jungle-movie laugh. If Belford were listening, he'd think you'd found André. "I can't read your mind," Diamond says. "The nature of consciousness being what it is, anybody can pick up on other people's thoughts occasionally, if the thoughts are strong and the person receiving them is open enough. Since I've been on the pad, I've found that I can sometimes get into other people's heads, or into their dreams." He puts his hands on his hips and gives you that leer that could peel the velvet wallpaper off the walls of virtue. "But what I'd really like to get into is your pants."

You pivot and walk away at a swift clip. If he follows you, you'll scream bloody murder. Several families are crossing the atrium, parents blowing the weekly entertainment budget so that their kids can participate in "brown-bag puppet-making, featuring turtles and frogs." Surely, some stalwart dad would rescue you from him. The degenerate! The wet willie!

Your soggy pumps have covered less than ten yards, however, when it occurs to you why you came looking for him here in the first place. You stop and spin around. For at least a year you have needed glasses—vanity has blocked your path to the optometrist—but Diamond's ripsaw smile stands out quite clearly in the mist. "Where is she?" you yell at him. "Where's Q-Jo Huffington?"

"You mean you don't know?"

149

"Hell no, I don't know! What have you done with her?"

He starts toward you. You prepare to scream. But the leer—the vulgar comic—has been hooked offstage, and in its place stands a trustworthy and concerned expression, the Hamlet look of a TV anchorman during yet another national crisis. "I think you and I should sit down and talk," he says quietly. When you hesitate, he adds, "About Q-Jo. Not romance. To tell you the truth, I don't think getting in your pants is a very good idea."

You could not agree more. But all the way to the coffee shop, you can't help wondering what made him change his mind.

TWO-TEN P.M.

You walk in silence, although Diamond seems to be humming under his breath. As much as possible, you avoid looking at him directly, but you observe him sufficiently to note that his eyes have lost much of their savage redness; it must have been the alcohol and the smoke that colored them on Thursday. A coarse rye stubble still Ben Day's the gaunt plains of his chin and cheeks, however; his long hair still swings like the tail of an Arabian stallion swaying languorously home from stud. He has neglected to change his leather jacket, which seems old and oily, like the skin of a goat; or to remove his golden earring (the drizzle has set gem chips in it); and light passes effortlessly through the frayed areas of his jeans. His snakeskin boots strike you somehow as inappropriate footwear for a visit to a Reptile & Amphibian Fair—with each step, would not a wave of dread echo through the vivariums?—and his tattoo makes you cringe from the uncouthness and immaturity of it, although you don't get a clear look at his tattoo until you are seated across from him in a booth at Pony Espresso.

While he is placing his order—and flirting shamelessly with the waitress who is taking it—you sneak a glance at the back of his left hand, the hand that is rattling a pair of sugar cubes as though they were dice, but where you expect to see a death's head, a rearing cobra, or a grass-skirted hula slut, there is instead a weird configuration of celestial symbols. Since Diamond's attention remains elsewhere (what's so darned interesting about that floozoid waitress?), you help yourself to a longer look. The tattoo depicts three circles, stacked, one above the other. They are a lot like sun symbols, or, rather, variations on sun symbols, for each one is different: the top circle is broken in four places, and its rays are broken also; the middle symbol, the most conventional, resembles a sun drawn by any child with a neat and steady hand, the kind *you* might have drawn in kindergarten; while the bottom "sun," the one closest to his bony wrist, is more elaborate, consisting of two concentric circles emitting double, closed rays that are a lot like petals.

"Admiring my skin art, I see."

You flinch, and then, it goes without mentioning, you blush. "Not really," you say, trying to sound casual and disinterested.

"Would you like to hear about it?"

"Uh, no. No, I wouldn't. I want to hear about Q-Jo. And that is *all* I want to hear about, thank you." It is not lost on your central nervous system that it might be sharing a booth with a dangerous maniac. Your hands are all atremble, and you wonder how you will handle your tall vanilla latte without betraying your fear. So far, you have resisted the urge to go to the ladies' room to reapply makeup and brush your drenched hair, reasoning that any improvement in your appearance might encourage predatory tendencies. You have, however, removed your sodden raincoat, revealing your reasonably dry, relentlessly tight, black dress.

"Q-Jo is your friend?"

"Yes," you bark. Then it dawns on you that this is the second time, ever, that you have owned up to that friendship. The first time was earlier today at police headquarters. An extra stratum of strawberry surfaces in your blush.

"And as far as you know, she hasn't been home."

"That's right."

"You have no idea where she is?"

"No, I don't. The last I heard, she was with you." You muster the courage to stare him in the eye. Now that their capillaries are no longer rupturing, his eyes are deep blue and would be rather nice were they not as mocking as crows and as lecherous as fleas.

"Yesterday."

"Beg your pardon."

"Yesterday. She was 'with me,' as you put it, yesterday afternoon. Q-Jo came to my place to look at slides of a trip I recently made. It was a business arrangement."

"Right. And after the business was dispensed with, she decided to stay on. It got, shall we say, 'social' in nature."

Diamond smiles. It is a raw, stinging smile, like a cat scratch. Oddly, there is something forgivable, even likable about it, as if the scratch were made by your favorite kitty and you are convinced it was only playing. "Quite the opposite," he corrects you. "She left before the business was completed."

"Oh, really?" You envision him coming on to her in such a gross, twisted manner that even Q-Jo, who is not averse to a pinch of kink, was driven to bolt for the door. "So you scared her off."

He smiles again. You feel the claw rake your brow. "If she was frightened, which I sincerely doubt, it wasn't by me. Not personally. I wasn't even in the room."

"What do you mean?"

The waitress arrives with your latte and his almond soda, but you both ignore her.

"I mean, Gwendolyn"—the way he pronounces your name, like William S. Burroughs ordering a root beer float, sends a shudder through your lungs—"your friend and I were looking at slides of Timbuktu, and I excused myself. To go to the bathroom. When I came back, she was gone."

TWO-TWENTY P.M.

"Gone?"

"Gone."

The waitress has set your beverages before you but has not left the table. She is hovering, in fact. You regard her with annoyance— and with pity, recalling the attraction that naive young victims were said to have had to certain serial killers. Diamond regards her as well, which should come as no surprise, but then the way she is hovering, neither of you has much choice.

"Hope you guys don't mind," she says apologetically, "but the boss is gonna turn off the ball game now." She lifts a shoulder toward the television set on a shelf high above the counter, and you notice for the first time that a Mariners game is in progress on the nineteen-inch screen. "I guess the President's gonna make an important speech or something."

You scowl at her for confusing you with one of those Cheeto heads who short their potential and downside their IQ's watching televised sports. For his part, Diamond winks and says, "Go for it, darling. Tune in the ol' pufftoad. I could use a laugh."

From his tiptoes atop a bar stool, the manager manually changes channels. A pitcher dematerializes in the middle of a windup and is replaced, not by an angel-headed reliefer from the twilight bullpen, nor by Dr. Yamaguchi, as you half expect, but by the man to whom journalists who ought to know better still refer as "the leader of the free world." Having cleared his throat and fine-tuned his countenance, the President is poised to address that ever-shrinking portion of the population that isn't actively engaged in panhandling, smoking crack cocaine, or bowling.

"So, Gwendolyn, as I was saying, when I came out of *la toilette*, your friend had . . ."

"Shhh," you shush him. "I want to hear this."

Diamond cocks his head and shoots you a look that could give sarcasm a bad name, a look that, in its every cynical nuance, questions the sincerity of your concern for Q-Jo. "Listen," you say, "I have a job, I have clients to protect. This could be jumbo."

"Be my guest," he says, and lifts his Italian soda. Until now, you thought it impossible that one could drink and smirk at the same time.

Meanwhile, the President is saying how he doesn't wish to minimalize recent disturbing events in our great land. Then, he proceeds to downplay every item on the hellish list: bank failures, credit revulsion, municipal bond defaults, rising national deficit, declining property values, falling oil prices, mortgage foreclosures, unaffordable health care, personal and corporate bankruptcies, water shortages, racial tensions, poverty riots, street crime, the legionary exodus from New York City, and attempts by Hawaii and Vermont to secede from the union. The black cherry atop the cyanide sundae, of course, is the stock market tumble on Thursday. Each of these pesky gophers in the broad green lawns of the American dream can be routed, the President assures his constituents. The grass will sprout sweet and high—though not *too* high—at the base of our family flagpoles again. Alas, the rebuilding of financial America is going to require belt-tightening, is going to require lower living standards, is going to require (groan!) personal sacrifice. The President has been meeting with his staff of experts day and night, it seems, and they have come up with some brilliant measures to assist us in sacrificing, just in case we cannot sacrifice sufficiently on our own.

"Uh-oh," says the coffee shop manager. "Get ready to duck."

You would nod in agreement, except that you wouldn't want to be seen nodding in agreement with a man of his low station. You refrain from nodding, but in your mind's eye you picture a federal-green tow truck hauling away your Porsche, picture yourself living next door to Q-Jo Huffington until the cows come home. Assuming, of course, that Q-Jo is living. You glance guiltily at Diamond, who grins back at you like an unripe jack-o'-lantern carved with a nail file.

"The pufftoad's going to ask Congress to hike taxes," says Diamond matter-of-factly. "He's going to ask the Fed to increase M-Two. He's going to press to impose restrictions on foreign investments and blocks on currency exchange. He might even demand that a portion of Social Security reserves and regulated pension plans be appropriated to finance the deficit. Then he's going to do away with the civil service system and fire a whole gang of government employees. And you can kiss the welfare state sayonara." He puckers and makes a loud smacking noise, which elicits a titter from the waitress and a scowl from you.

At this point, the President commences to enumerate his measures, and they are exactly as Diamond predicted, except that the President soft-pedals them until they seem almost benign. He says, for example, that he will "suspend," not do away with, the civil service system, and that rather than being fired, the targeted bureaucrats will be "temporarily disemployed." Moreover, he suggests that many of these measures need not be enacted if world financial markets put on a happy face come Monday.

You might have looked at Diamond admiringly were not the little strumpet of a waitress already doing that. "Was this leaked in advance?" you ask. "Or can you read his mind, too?"

He scoffs. "Any dimwit could've figured it out. I mean what else *could* he do? Problem is, it's too late for a lot of these steps, they should've been taken years ago; and doubling the M-Two money supply should never be done at all. It'll drive interest rates over the rainbow. Hope you weren't planning to buy any real estate."

Yes, by God, there goes the new condo, passing the Porsche in its haste to get out of your life. Not that you would have a life. Come Monday.

TWO THIRTY-FIVE P.M.

The President closes by imploring Americans to be thrifty and brave.

"Two-twelfths of a Boy Scout," says Diamond.

"Twelve-twelfths of a disaster," says you. "Jesus, everything's an ugly mess!"

"Ugly? I think it's rather grand."

"The fun is just beginning."

"Yeah. Absolutely. From the vantage point of the pad."

The manager switches the channel back to the baseball game, nearly toppling off the stool in the process. The waitress wiggles up to see if Diamond wants another almond soda. You can sense the humidity thickening under her skirt as she talks to him. It's like Miami under there. "Here!" you snap, shoving your untouched latte at her. "This needs to be reheated." She could probably bring it to a boil between her thighs. If you would go to the ladies' room and attend to your grooming, you doubtlessly could wilt this irksome flirtation on the vine—but you'll be damned if you will stoop that low. Or assume that risk.

"Pardon my bluntness, Mr. Diamond," you say when the girl has torn herself away, "but I think you're sucking on about a vine-yard and a half of sour grapes."

"Do you, now?"

"I think you're taking a childish pleasure in this crisis because . . . because you can't be involved in it anymore. In the market, I mean. You screwed up and got kicked out of the business, and now you're happy the business is in trouble. It's a vengeance thing, if you ask me. Pure spite. If you could get your job back, you'd be singing a different tune."

Diamond's irritating grin grows irritatingly brighter. "I'd be suffering along with the rest of you?"

"Yes. That's one way to put it."

When he laughs, the waitress looks at you enviously from across the room, jealous, no doubt, that he finds you so entertaining. "Oh, Gwendolyn," he sighs. "Such naiveté in these times might be refreshing if it wasn't actually pathetic." You turn as red as a cardinal's beanie and rise from your cushion, but Diamond doesn't seem to notice. "NASD never got around to banning me," he goes on, "and even if it had, there're entire firms on Wall Street comprised exclusively of brokers who've been banned from the business."

Hmmm. This is interesting. You settle back down.

"Within three months of the day I was sacked, I could've gone to work for any disco in the country, with the possible, I emphasize *possible*, exception of the one that canned me. And I burned my employers as well as my clients."

Yes, indeed, this is getting very interesting.

"Seriously?"

"Of course. There's only one rule in the investment business: squeeze juice. You know that. And as long as you obey that rule, it doesn't much matter what other rules you break. Wall Street loves guys like me the way a pimp loves a tight-twatted hooker with a habit."

You are so intrigued you ignore the indelicacy of his analogy. "Uh, let me ask you something," you say. "In confidence. If Posner should let me go on Monday, if I'm accused of churning and stuff— and I'm not saying I will be—you think I could catch on with another firm? In due time, I mean? A relatively short time?"

The way Diamond chuckles, the waitress must think you're Dorothy Parker's granddaughter. In one rainy Saturday afternoon, you've transformed Pony Espresso into the Algonquin. "Oh, proba- bly," he says. "You can sell, so I hear, and there're chop houses that'll hire *anybody* who can sell. So, if you want to run for dwarfs, they'll run you. But, frankly, I can't see you running for a jumbo, not even if you were clean, because you don't squeeze that kind of juice."

"I very well could."

"Doubtful, Gwendolyn. It's doubtful. You've got the drive, all right, but you lack the talent. The truth is, you've chosen a profes- sion in which you'll never be more than a marginal success."

Marginal! How dare he! You are so outraged you lose all fear of him. "Why? Because I made a few mistakes? The same damn mis- takes you made, only not as bad. Because I'm a woman? Is that it? Because I'm Filipino? I have an MBA! How would *you* know what my abilities are?" The more your voice rises, the more boopsie-woopsie it sounds. The waitress is looking at you in a new light, now. As they say in sports, Mr. Momentum has moved to her side of the field.

"Calm down. Calm down. It's no big deal. If it was a crime collecting pay for a job you're not good at, half the country'd be eating jail chow—including that evil pufftoad who just spoke to us from the Oval Office. Anyway, I'm not saying you're incompetent. You're probably an average bookie. But why diminish your soul being run-of-the-mill at something? Mediocrity: now *there* is ugliness for you. Mediocrity's a hairball coughed up on the Persian carpet of Creation." He takes a gulp of his soda. "But how do I know you'll never be a major player? Simple. Day before yesterday, after the bell, after the crash, I watched the bookies stream into the Bull and Bear, rattled, shaken, unnerved. They were wringing their hands and sniveling—and you were right there sniveling with the rest of them. Now, if you had what it takes to be a major player, you would've been at your desk calmly pinpointing buying opportunities, tracking down bargains. Believe me, that's where the all-stars were."

You protest. "I couldn't buy. Not even on the bargain table. I didn't have the liquidity."

"You had a computer, didn't you? If you know how to bulldog a computer, it doesn't matter if you've got cash in the drawer or not. Hey, right now you could cowgirl into your desktop and probably save your ass, no matter how much butter you've churned. If you were good enough."

Extremely interesting. "Are you good enough?"

He shrugs. "I used to be."

"But you didn't save *your* . . . job."

"Didn't want to. And I can't imagine why you would want to, either." He grins. "Now that you've met me and are starting to have an inkling that there're things transpiring in this universe that make the equities market seem like a cross between a gang-bang and a Tupperware party."

To what Diamond may be referring, you neither know nor care. You decide to play on his sympathy. "Well, you probably come from a wealthy family," you say. "For me, it's first and foremost a matter of security. I know what it's like not to have money."

"To go through life feeling up when the market's up, feeling down when the market's down: that's your idea of security? And don't try to play on my sympathy. I was an autistic child, and I'm still narcissistic enough to be virtually immune to hard-luck stories. Everybody's got one. Except the people on the pad."

Okay, you have underestimated him. Perhaps because he's more than a smidgen crazed. To take advantage of his disco skills, you may have to resort to more unseemly, and perilous, tactics. You excuse yourself and head for the women's room, your bag with its cargo of cosmetics clutched in your hand.

Two Fifty-Nine P.M.

The waitress is mewing to Diamond when you return to the table. She is so engorged with hormones her eyes are bulging. But it doesn't matter. One look at you—spiffy now, vivacious, confident, smiling (with good reason, for you have had good news)—and the screen door is slammed on her eager little clitoris. "Try eating asparagus," you advise, woman to woman, as you push past her into the booth.

Diamond is approving, you can tell, but though the red lanterns of lust blink continually from the marquee of his personality, he is not given to slicky boy flattery or Latin Lover lines. As a matter of fact, he mentions nothing about your appearance, electing instead to turn the spotlight back on Q-Jo. "I guess what you're telling me is that your friend has been incommunicado since she left for Thunder House yesterday afternoon. I'm afraid I can't help you much, but I'll . . ."

"It's okay," you say through a smile of such width and wattage an observer might confuse you with one of those uninhibited sprites who swill soda pop on TV commercials. ("Gurus and philosophers might as well give up," the Huff herself said once. "Apparently, all it takes to send human beings into ecstatic bliss is the right combination of sugar, carbonated water, caramel coloring, phosphoric acid, potassium benzoate, caffeine, citric acid, and natural flavorings." To

159

which you replied, "Coke was up one and an eighth today, Pepsi up a quarter. *I'm* happy.")

"What do you mean it's okay?" The viperous way Diamond's eyes narrow, the switchblade spring of his voice, warn you anew that this is not a man to be trifled with. But you are not trifling.

"I mean she's home. Q-Jo's back. From wherever she's been." He looks incredulous. "I called when I went to the restroom," you explain.

"Well, Jesus, what did she say?"

"I didn't speak with her. Her line was busy."

"Gwendolyn, that doesn't mean she's home. It could've been incoming on her machine."

"No, I waited for over two minutes and tried again. Still busy. She's home, all right. This whole thing must seem bizarre to you, but, look, she was gone all night and most of today, and I truly did believe something awful had happened. I'm sorry I involved you in it, I really am. But Q-Jo's safe, and that's what matters. She's safe."

THREE-TEN **P.M.**

Larry Diamond had taken a bus to the amphibian show, so you offer him a ride home. He is thrifty, you are brave. The President must be very proud. Yet, what else could you do? Had you simply gone off and left him at the espresso bar, he and that scruffy little server would soon be copulating like alley cats. It was written in the steam. For reasons that remain less than clear, you harbor objections to that union. "No, no, I insist," you insist. "It's practically on my way."

"As the Thunderbird flies," he mutters, because even someone as unfamiliar with the local terrain as the average Seattle taxi driver (is that Bengali they are speaking?) knows Ballard is beyond your mark.

Diamond is uncharacteristically quiet, even sullen, on the way home. Perhaps he is hypnotized by the thin, steady rain. Or else the

purring of the Porsche is reminding him of the companionship he
has forfeited by leaving the coffee shop. Well, you certainly have no
intention of making it up to him, but in case he is suspicious that
your Q-Jo story is a ruse, you swing into a service station a block
before the bridge, where you suggest that the two of you try her
number from the telephone booth.

"What's the matter with the car phone?"

"Doesn't work."

"It looks mangled."

"Yeah. Sort of does." How can you explain that your boyfriend's pet monkey mistook it for a gymnastic device?

You let Diamond dial—the pair of you dangerously close in
the booth—and when he gets a busy signal, he seems satisfied. Back
in the Porsche, he is talkative again. "So you came to the amphibian
fair actually looking for Q-Jo?"

"Well, yes. Why else?"

"Wishful thinking, I suppose."

Does he mean that he wishes you'd been looking for *him*? Or
that he wishes you were 'on the pad'? You decide not to pursue it.
"Aren't you curious how I tracked you there?"

"Nothing surprises me anymore. But how did you track me
there?"

"The Indian told me."

"Oh. So you've met Twister."

" 'Met' may be an overstatement. Tell me, Mr. Diamond . . ."

"Larry."

"Larry. Are you really in such straits that you have to live in the
basement of a bowling alley?"

He lacerates you with that terrible smile again. "Gwendolyn, I
lived there when I was still in the business. I've lived there since
eighty-six." Your ill-concealed perplexity amuses him further. "You,
you work in the financial markets for the material rewards. That's
okay. I suppose the market is as good a place as any to chase after
that mirage of security that spellbinds this race of primates into

161

which we erstwhile amphibians have devolved. But the money was never that important to me."

Oh, Jesus, you think. *Don't tell me this guy's just some hipper, weirder version of Belford Dunn?* "Way I hear it," you say, "you cooked your career and just about cooked your disco going after bigger and bigger scores."

He chuckles—somewhat like a demon and somewhat like a little boy. "If I'd been interested in the jumbo juice, I'd have gone into investment banking," he says. "But I did push the envelope of equity brokering about as far as it could go. Yes. Yes, indeed. It was a game to me. And for a few years, it held the drama and romance of any well-played game. Then, it got boring. It was too easy. I was too good. Here I was in Seattle, Washington, putting Michael Jordan moves on the aces of Wall Street. That was part of the challenge, part of the charm. But it got dreary. Because no matter how sweet the scores, they never added up to anything. You know what I mean?" He sighs. "I suspect you don't."

You don't.

"When legal squeezing ceased to be fun, I squeezed illegally. That restored the thrill, the romance. For a while. Then I guess that got boring, too. I set myself up so that if there was a crash, I'd be naked. On October 19, 1987, the crash came. It was a huge relief."

"What about the people you burned?"

"First, I never burned any small fry. No old folks, no struggling young couples, no boat people seduced by immigrant dreams. As for the bigger investors, I felt a twinge of remorse for them, I suppose. But, hey, they were playing a game, too, even if they were too blind or too hypocritical to admit it. Did they really think Mother Teresa was dealing the cards? How sympathetic can you be toward people who buy into the Lie, who cozy up to it, eat from its plate, kiss its ass, and then whine and snivel when the Lie betrays them? As sooner or later it always will."

You are not quite sure, but you think you like the tenor of these remarks. The defiant part, at any rate. As you pull into the

Thunderbird parking lot, you ask, "So in the end, you allowed your-self to be caught? That's fascinating. You wanted out. But suppose somebody wanted to stay in?" You fight to keep your mind a blur, lest he "get into" your thoughts.

"You, for example?"

"Okay. Me. You realistically think I can arrange to stay in the business?"

"Yeah. Sure. If there *is* a business."

"What do you mean?"

"I mean, this could be the Big One. The end of the Lie. It probably isn't, but it could be. We may be hearing the death rattle of financial America."

Your heart sinks like a roll of quarters in a wishing well. The pitch of your voice is that of a cartoon bunny who has just spotted Rodney Rabbit Hound between herself and the carrot patch. "You really think so?"

Here comes that grin. "Could be," he says. "Isn't it grand?"

Three Twenty-Five P.M.

You stop the car at the top of the ramp. For several minutes, you sit in silence. You are unable to speak, Diamond chooses not to. The rain taps its cereal fingers against the windshield. Whenever the door to the Thunderbird is opened, rumblings and crashes spill out.

Eventually, he grasps the door handle. The peripheral vision you have perfected in office politics tells you this. "Thanks for the lift," he says. "When you finish scolding Miss Huffington for the worry she's caused you, ask her why she ran out on me. I'd like to know."

Then, just before he slides out into the weather, he leans over with mongoose speed—and ever so briefly, but with electrifying pressure, kisses you on the mouth.

163

Three Thirty-Five P.M.

George Washington's teeth: were they hardwood or soft? Mahogany for strength or spruce for warmth and luster? Painted, varnished, or raw lumber? Carved from a single block or an assemblage of various small pieces? If the latter, were they glued, nailed, or simply notched and fitted together? Rot? Splinters? Woodworms? Did cherries stain them red, mustard turn them yellow? In use, would they clack and knock aesthetically like the clacking and knocking in traditional Japanese music, or would they have sounded more like a woodpecker in a sycamore? Accidentally dropped while crossing the Delaware, would they have sunk, or floated like a toy boat? During lovemaking, were they in or out? What marks might they have left on Martha's nape? By candleshine in an eighteenth-century dining room, what shadows did they cast upon the walls?

All the way home, you think about George Washington's teeth. Your mother told you that whenever a person is confused and overwrought and not thinking straight, they should pause for a few moments and contemplate something from history. You have tried this many times, but the only thing from your history classes that seems to have stuck in your mind, aside from the Great Depression, which you simply refuse to ponder, is George Washington's teeth.

Whatever calming effect, if any, the image of the heroic dentures might have on your mind, it does not carry over into your driving, which is erratic, to put it mildly. You go very fast—too fast for the wet streets—and then you go very slow. Fast and slow, fast and slow. An Italian automobile might understand mood swings of this magnitude, but the Germanic sensibility of the Porsche is sorely tested. It's probably going to require a tune-up.

On the one hand, you are frantic to get back and find out what has been going on with Q-Jo. On the other, you want to drift along, allowing the waves of conflicting emotions that Larry Diamond has precipitated to break over you. You have fresh optimism, you have new fears. You have an electrifying tingle that surely ought to be unplugged.

So you drive too fast. You drive too slow. And you think: *Were the Father of our Country a careless smoker, might he have set his teeth on fire?*

Three Fifty-Nine P.M.

"Q-Jo! Hello. Q-Jo?"

When Q-Jo did not answer her door, you let yourself into her apartment. It was instantly apparent that she—or someone—had recently been there. The place hadn't exactly been ransacked, as though by thieves or cops, but it was in a state of mild disarray. Now, an eerie sensation climbs your spine as you move warily from living room to bedroom to bathroom, calling her name. "Q-Jo?" There is no response. The unit is empty.

In vain, you search for signs that might indicate that she had come home and left again. Her multicolored shawl is not in the closet, her oversized handbag is not on the dresser, there is no evidence of newly purchased groceries (rarely does the Huff come home without food), the tarot deck is still spread on the table. You turn the cards over rapidly, holding your breath until the doctored Star card shows up. You forgot to ask Larry Diamond about that card. There were several things you forgot to ask Larry Diamond.

It is while picking up scattered sprigs of dried larkspur from the nubby sofa and returning them to their dime-store vase that you notice that the telephone receiver is off its cradle. The eerie sensation intensifies, although indications are that the receiver was carelessly knocked askew rather than deliberately removed. In any event, you replace it, then hurry down the hall to your own apartment.

Somebody has been in your flat, too!

Jesus Dow Jones Christ! You very nearly turn and sprint. As you are backing out the door, however, the mystery abruptly clears. It is not so much the overturned Dale Chihuly fruit bowl (the scattered pieces of orange peel, the bits of apple) as it is the open freezer door that identifies the intruder. Oh, yes. The logic is plain.

There was a time when that freezing compartment had been a treasure chest of banana Popsicles.

Four-Fifteen P.M.

It is only after you have left your Burberry and your shoes to dry in the shower stall, cleaned up the mess André has made, poured yourself a glass of chardonnay, and retrieved the messages from your machine that you collapse on the bed and ask yourself, silently but emphatically, *What's next?!*

Three of the four messages were from Belford, naturally. He has been racing around the Napa Valley, vineyard to vineyard, but the French consul general and his party are managing to stay one wine-tasting ahead of him. Since you have not been home nor left any word at his San Francisco hotel, he can only assume that you are fully, and, so far, futilely occupied with the dragnet for André. He appreciates your dedication and, again, is sorry that he was callous to the psychological rigors of your monthly infirmity. Or ex-logger's words to that effect. Good grief! What kind of lover can't remember that his alleged girlfriend had her period just a week ago? The fourth message began, "Hey, Squeak! Las' night at Woman Ray! *Mas* cool, man. How come you . . ." At which point you cut it off.

Okay. Have a sip of wine. Unzip your dress (for it is constricting your rump). Clear your mind (without the aid, one hopes, of George Washington's choppers). And consider the possibilities.

First, you suppose you ought to get yourself over to Belford's to see if André is there. Yet, had the little rascal found what he was looking for at his master's house, it is highly doubtful that he would have come pillaging in your place or Q-Jo's. The truth is, André does not especially care for you, probably because you see through his born-again act. No, there's no telling where he might be at the moment, where he might strike next. Now that the rain has given itself a haircut, he's likely roaming far and wide. At the very least, you should send word to Belford that his beloved beast is alive and well and looting. Of course, were he to receive such word, your prospective husband would be on the next flight to Seattle—and that is a homecoming you might prefer, rightly or wrongly, to delay.

Regarding Q-Jo's continued absence, the correct course of action has become increasingly problematic. Suppose that Larry Diamond is responsible for her disappearance, after all. That would mean that he is a far more sinister, far more dangerous psychopath than you had originally imagined. Conversely, if Diamond is as innocent as you, in the past hour, have slowly, begrudgingly come to think, he, being the last person known to have seen her before she, all three-hundred-plus pounds of her, went *poof,* he could offer valuable assistance in your efforts to find her, not to mention the boost he might give your efforts to preserve your career, a prospect you cannot afford to ignore. The question: Is Diamond useful or deadly—or both?

Between the horns of that dilemma you swing so fast and long you get sick to your stomach. It is at the bathroom sink, gagging down two tablespoonsful of Pepto-Bismol ("stockbroker's champagne"), that you finally decide which card to play.

FIVE THIRTY-EIGHT P.M.

Like pigeon racing, telephone tag is a sport with no spectators, and although you have participated numerous times in the past, on this day, under these circumstances, you simply refuse. When Diamond's recorded voice comes over the line (you smile now at the rumblings and crashes, break out in goose bumps at his wickedly dry intonations) to say, "If you're calling about the President's speech, my advice is, go out in the backyard and plant some potatoes. Better plant some in the front yard, too. While you're at it, dig yourself a frog pond. And don't forget to feed your head. *Ahhh-ha-ha-ha-ha*"; you respond, after the customary beep, "Goddamnit, Larry, this is Gwen Mati. I need to talk to you, and I'm not hanging up until we have a conversation."

You had expected a lengthy, perhaps indefinite, wait, but hardly forty seconds pass before he pipes up, "Gwendolyn, what took you so long?"

Naturally, his presumptuousness annoys you. "You were expecting me to call?"

"Well, Q-Jo's not back at the ranch. Is she?"

"How did you know?"

"Just a hunch."

Yeah? Maybe it is his keen intuition, or maybe it is because he knows where she really is. Maybe he has spent the two hours since he kissed you good-bye feeding her body parts to a sausage grinder. A gorge of Pepto-Bismol rises like flamingo diarrhea in your throat.

"I'm sorry," he says, "that I've not been answering the phone, but I can't waste my time commiserating with frazzled bookies. Even your man Posner called me earlier. Can you picture Posner digging up his lawn? *Ahhh-ha-ha-ha.*"

"Posner phoned you, eh? Tell me, has Posner ever been to Thunder House?" It is a loaded question, but you successfully filter suspicion from your voice.

"Hardly," he says. "Posner knows me mainly by reputation. Why? Has he been dropping my name?"

You partially sigh with partial relief. "No, no. I've never heard him mention you—although his *wife* believes you've come back from Africa heavy with wisdom."

"Well, she's wrong about that. People do not get 'heavy' with wisdom. They get light. The wiser you become, the lighter you become. This is an unsolicited testimonial for lightheartedness, Gwendolyn. I suggest you pay attention."

"Sure. Okay. But what about Q-Jo? I'm not feeling overly bubbly about *that* situation." Nor any one of a dozen others, you might have added.

"Why don't you come over to Thunder House, then, and we can—"

"No!" you snap, a bit too quickly and a bit too strongly. You have sworn on your mother's book of verse that you will never permit the spider to coax you into that noisy web. What, are you supposed to feel safe because some character named "Twisted" is roaming the premises? That zonked-out Indian isn't exactly the chaperon most guardians of health and decency have in mind. "No." You say it softer this time. "How about this? I need to go downtown." That is a lie, but meeting Diamond in a familiar, and public, place is essential to the compromise at which you have arrived. "Could we meet at, oh, let's say the Bull and Bear? In half an hour?"

"Sorry."

"Oh."

"No Bull and Bear. I don't think I can take. . . . Aw, all right. We won't be allowed a lot of privacy, but this economic catastrophe is so endlessly entertaining, it'll be worth the interruptions just to hear what lemmings say to one another as they go over the cliff. But I can't make it in thirty minutes. My scooter's torn apart. . . ."

"Your scooter?"

"You know. My bike. Unlike some things I could name, it doesn't perform well when wet." You wince. *Is he talking about amphibians or about . . . ?* "Been working on it off and on all day. I'll have it together in an hour, but I could still be held up. I'm expecting a call. Let's say we meet at seven-fifteen. But don't blow your little gasket if I'm late."

"The call can't wait?" For some reason, you are positive it is to be from that hotsy pants at the espresso bar. Animals! Haven't these people heard of AIDS?

"Afraid not. Getting Motofusa Yamaguchi on the line is no piece of cake."

Saturday
Night
April 7

The Queen's Wino

Seven-Fifteen P.M.

By six-fifteen, the sky has gone as bald as a bottle of hair tonic. Not a strand of rain dangles from its smooth gray pate. By seven-fifteen, the streets downtown are once again teeming with the dispossessed, almost catatonically passive in some cases, menacingly aggressive in others. You pass hurriedly among them, careful not to make eye contact.

The sigh of relief you expect to release upon reaching the safety of the Bull & Bear dies, stillborn, in your sternum. The Bull & Bear is closed!

Your initial reaction is that the restaurant has gone in the bucket along with the market. Then you come to your senses. This is Saturday. Of course the Bull & Bear is closed! The Bull & Bear is *never* open on weekends. You've known that for years.

Come on, don't berate yourself. You are not a helium head. You have had a lot on your mind lately, more than the usual ration of stress; and this workweek, due to Good Friday, ended early. It is understandable that you might lose track of time. But what about Larry Diamond? Did he, too, forget what day it was? Or did he let you proceed to the Bull & Bear knowing full well that you would find it shut? Diamond might be capable of that. Even if he is not physically dangerous, he strikes you as the sort of man who likes to test people, likes to play with their minds. He probably would find it humorous, in his dry, sardonic way, to see you cringing in the restaurant doorway, constricting to make yourself invisible to the riffraff in the street—some of whom might remember you, pants down, from the previous night.

173

You must decide whether to tarry here awhile—it is still light out, thank goodness—or whether to retreat to your car. You suppose you could just drive around the block until Diamond arrives. While you are debating your next move, a bum lunges up. So closely does he resemble a teller who used to wait on you at SeaFirst Bank that you are hesitant to shoo him away. "I know my body language is bad," says the man slurringly but politely, "but I need five dollars."

You just stare at him. He looks so familiar! He begins again. "I realize my breath is possibly objectionable . . ."

"Didn't you . . ."

". . . but I require five dollars."

". . . used to work at . . ."

"In small, unmarked bills."

Good grief! You never should have made eye contact. How can you get rid of him without shelling out the five bucks you saved by avoiding the amphibian fair? He won't believe you if you tell him you're broke. You are all decked out in a darling, snugly cut wool suit in bold tribal print by Ellen Tracy; not to impress Diamond, perish the thought, but in the event some broker of note happened to be investing in Johnnie Walker in the Bull & Bear lounge. Big mistake. Oh, and now a second bum, a short, ragged claw of a fellow in a derby hat, is joining you in the doorway.

"If you was to eat dog shit," says the newcomer, "and then shit it out, would you 'ave dog shit or human shit?"

You are ripe with revulsion, faint with disgust. In your tummy, the cry rings out for more Pepto-Bismol. The teller bum, though, is studying the query. After a moment, during which he vigorously scratches his rib cage, he says, "We used to have a hound that would eat its own. . . ." You jam your fingers in your ears. When you remove them, the second derelict is saying, "Righto, and that is precisely why the hound dog was no friend of Mr. Presley's. But it begs my question, bloke."

"Use five dollars?" the ex-teller asks him, jerking a thumb in your direction. It almost pokes you in the eye.

"In my native England," says the other with some dignity, "I was, by special appointment, wino to Her Majesty the Queen."

"Use five pounds, then?"

"The Queen's wino."

"Dollar's weak against most major currencies, but at Gary's Mini-Mart, it's good as gold."

Good grief! You feel a wave of nostalgia for the days when bums rarely spoke a word beyond, "Spare change?" Fumbling with the latch on your purse, you are about to slip them each a buck just to buy your way out of torment—when across Sixth Avenue, in front of a fancy florist shop, whom should you spot setting up his telescope but astronomy's Jack the Ripper, the sex-offender stargazer who showed the world your moon.

Seven-Twenty P.M.

You shove the vagrants aside with such force that the one loses his derby, the other his balance. Forcing a Mercedes-Benz luxury sedan and a smoke-spewing old Japanese minicar to slow for you, you dash across the avenue.

"I'm not open, lady. Waiting for a break in the overcast."

"I'll break your damn overcast."

"Oh, it's you."

"Yes, it's me, scumbag. And in a minute it'll be the police. Did you really expect you could get away with that?"

"I didn't do it, missy."

There is such sincerity, such feeling in his voice that you are momentarily hushed. Under your gaze, he commences to clear his throat, prompting you to step back a few paces in case he launches one of his mucoid projectiles. "What do you mean you didn't do it? You were standing right next to me!"

"It was the rich boys. I didn't see 'em till it was too late. If I hadn't grabbed my 'scope and run, they'd a popped me, too."

"Are you lying to me?" You have heard of the rich boys, actu-

175

ally. Young men from wealthy Eastside families who ride around and terrorize street people, much as some street people have been terrorizing the well-to-do.

"No. I'm telling you. It was a carful of 'em. In a new BMW. Stoned on something or other. They just jumped out and let you have it. Having fun, you know. They were gonna take your clothes and leave you naked, it's a joke they play on homeless women, but somebody was screaming for the cops and they got spooked and drove off."

"But . . . but, I'm not homeless."

The astronomer hacks. Before he spits, he smiles. "Not yet, anyway."

Seven Twenty-Four P.M.

One of the bums has followed you across the street. "I remember you," he says accusingly, in his slow, slurry voice. "You're the one tried to get me fired at the bank."

"You shortchanged me."

"She blames other people because she can't count money," he says to the astronomer. "And she shoves people."

"There'll be an excellent view of Sirius tonight, if we get some clearing."

"You bitch, you shoved me."

"The Bozo tribe in Mali describes Sirius as sitting down."

"What did you say?"

"You think you're hot stuff."

"Not you! Get lost!" You address the astronomer. "About the Bozo?"

"Seated, they say it is. How could a star be perceived as sitting down on something? Unless . . ."

The bum is shoving *you*, now, shoving you away from the astronomer, whose words you are straining to hear.

". . . it was sitting . . ." *Snort.*

"You think you're better than other people, but you can't fool me." He pushes you against the marble facade of an upscale travel agency.

". . . like a frog, maybe . . ." *Hack.*

"Your account was always overdrawn!"

". . . on top of a big ol' . . ." *Splat.*

"Now, it's my turn, mama. I wanna withdraw five smackers."

Because you are occupied with blushing—how dare anyone discuss your bank balance in public!—and with slapping the disaffili-ated teller's hands away from your purse, you cannot be sure you hear the disaffiliated astronomer correctly, but unless your ears and your imagination are ganging up on you, he uses the word, "pad." He says, "like a frog sitting on top of a big ol' pad."

SEVEN TWENTY-SEVEN P.M.

The bum's face is in yours, and his breath is, indeed, objectionable. Apparently, he is no longer self-conscious about his body language. Well, enough is enough. You kick him forcefully in the shin with the pointy toe of your new Kenneth Cole sling-backs. While he is howling, like an alarm at the bank, you break away. As you dart past the astronomer, you sing out, "I'll be back!"

"Forget it, lady. You'll never pin anything on the rich boys." Darting back across Sixth Avenue, you hear him add, "Sirius gave you your two bucks worth."

Your head is spinning, your heart is playing a tape of one of your father's bongo parties. Adrenaline is propelling you toward your car, although what you will do, where you will go once you get there, is not something you've thought about yet. A grape-colored Vespa pulls alongside you—driving on the sidewalk, for God's sake —and you instinctively reach in your purse for the can of Mace that you nearly used on the mad bank clerk. "What's your hurry?" asks a voice that sounds as if it were strained through a bowl of cheap dog food. "Making a sudden career move?"

Although it is most certainly a passing, situational, emotion, you are relieved—happy, even—to see Larry Diamond. As decorously as you are able—it is incumbent upon you, you think, to maintain some semblance of propriety at this particularly barbaric moment of our cultural history—you endeavor to swing one leg over the comically putt-putting Vespa. (Somehow, you had envisioned him roaring around on a big black Harley.) You manage to climb aboard—but for a very short ride. Instead of whisking you off into the night and the wind, a prospect that adds three sets of bongos to your heartbeat, Diamond circles and brings the motor scooter to a stop a few yards away, directly in front of the Bull & Bear.

"They're closed," you remind him, clinging ever so lightly to the back of his leather jacket.

"Only to amateurs," he says, and he dismounts and limps toward the entrance.

Seven Forty-Five P.M.

You are so humiliated you could crawl into the peanut dish and cover yourself with salted goobers. The Bull & Bear, it seems, operates as a private club on Saturday nights. Its doors are locked to the public, its blinds are drawn, but "members" gain access by punching in a code on a key pad. And who are the "members"? Why, everybody who is anybody in Seattle's brokerage community. Larry Diamond is a member, and he hasn't been in the business for years. Ann Louise, a newcomer, is apparently a member; you recognize her well-traveled rump at the bar. You, however, weren't even aware of the club's existence. In some respects, that is a more lacerating blow to you than the stock-market crash.

"Something wrong?" Diamond asks.

Your eyelids are pushing back tears like security guards holding back fans at a rock concert. "Oh, Jesus," you say, biting your lip.
"I swear, this has been the worst weekend of my life."

"It's not over yet."

"Yeah. That's what scares me." You drain a third of your wine
spritzer and dab your lips and your eyes with a cocktail napkin.
"Every single thing in my life has gone totally haywire."

"That's a good sign. Disaster's always best when it's on a grand
scale. As Yamaguchi puts it, 'A big back has a big front.'"

"Uh-huh. Well, it's all back and no front from where I sit.
Where's the flip side, Mr. Diamond? And while we're at it, where's
all this damn fun you claim is just beginning?"

"It's all around us, Gwendolyn. We only have to have the eyes
to see it."

You are under the impression that Diamond's idea of fun en-
compasses events and activities that a normal human being might
regard as catastrophes. But you say, "Your eyes are obviously better
than mine. If they can see fun which is to the rest of us invisible, just
think how clearly they'd see something the size of Q-Jo Huffington." You pause and take a sip of your drink. "Where the hell is
she?"

Lighting in the Bull & Bear is fuzzier than usual, the music
softer, the patrons, of which there are less than a dozen, more
subdued. The ambiance borders on the romantic, although you perceive the absence of commotion as a reflection of economic trauma.
Still, you are grateful for a quiet, safe place in which to pick this
warped brain. You are safe from rich boys and poor boys in the
street, and as for the perils of Diamond himself, well, Ann Louise
has been shooting curious glances at your table: should he wax
amorous, you can always foist him off on her.

Your companion has removed his jacket. Beneath it he is wearing a collarless cotton shirt, fancifully stitched about the neck and
cuffs. You would guess it to be African in origin, and while it is not
much of a fashion statement, its motif blends reasonably well with

179

your own more expensive, more elegant "tribal print" suit. He is drinking a tequila sour, but with less reckless gusto than you might have expected.

"Everything I know about Q-Jo Huffington could fit in this peanut dish" (there goes your hiding place) "and have enough room left over for a balanced meal. You seem to think her vanishing act has something to do with me, so I'm going to walk us through my two meetings with her, as brief as they were. I'm going to include everything I remember because some tiny thing I barely noticed at the time could turn out to be a clue. Okay? Goethe said, and some famous architect built a career on it, 'God is in the details.' Maybe Q-Jo's there, as well."

SEVEN-FIFTY P.M.

"I'd like to ask you one thing first?"

He subjects you to his cynical smile, the one that suggests that Q-Jo might not be at the tippy-top of your personal agenda. "Does your question concern business trends or gainful employment?"

You shake your head.

"Then fire away."

You might safely conclude that as a subject for conversation your job status fails to entrance him—not a favorable omen, Gwen, not a favorable omen. Yet, given the right circumstances, you can always change his mind. Meanwhile, you do have a question of a different order. "Well," you begin, "you got us in here tonight by punching a key pad. And I've been thinking: there must be lots of clubs in Seattle and around the country which a person can only access if they have the entry code. So, does being 'on the pad' mean you're a member of an elite social group that knows the codes to punch in on all the right key pads? Or"—you hold your breath for a beat or two—"does it refer in some way to Sirius, Sirius A, that is, and how the Bozo say it's sitting like a frog on a lily pad?"

You haven't the remotest idea what you're talking about, of

course. Just a couple of stabs in the dark. For the effect it has on Diamond, however, you might have been wielding a pitchfork at high noon. Impaled, he regards you with astonishment and grudging respect. And he regards you at considerable length before replying, "You're playing games with Uncle Larry, sweetheart. That's okay, Uncle Larry enjoys a nice game—providing the stakes are high. Uncle Larry's instincts tell him you're bluffing: he doesn't think you know jackshit about Sirius and the Bozo. But somehow you know enough to connect the two, and to recognize that the subject interests him, which indicates you've got a *smear* of jam on your toast. So he's going to take your question at face value and answer it honestly, even though he finds the first half of it insulting and the second half fiddle-fucked."

Well, gee, Uncle Larry, there's no reason to mince words.

"What kind of low-IQ, low-blood-sugar, pathetically insecure, socially desperate cockroach would hallucinate that there was something more meaningful than a chicken poot in the fact that he or she has the entry code to an exclusive club? The whole idea of being 'on the pad' is a conceit, I admit, but it's not a *shallow* conceit. At least, I hope it isn't. As for the Bozo, their name for Sirius A is *sima kayne*, which translates literally as 'sitting trouser.' Yeah, that's correct, heh-heh, 'sitting trouser.' Even the animal outfitters at Disney don't put pants on frogs, so I don't know where you dug up that piece of misinformation. But there *is* a link between Sirius and amphibians, you're warm on that one, and you may be getting warmer. Some of this stuff will leak out as we talk, whether we want it to or not, so I suggest we just push forward. Unless you've got another fascinating question that won't wait until Q-Jo. . . . I can tell that you do."

"No, no. Forget it."

"Go ahead. I insist."

"Well. Were you raised in the Midwest by any chance?"

"Why would you think a thing like that?"

"Your accent. The way you speak. You kind of sound like W. C. Fields."

"W. C. Fields was from Philadelphia."

Tom Robbins

SEVEN FIFTY-THREE P.M.

So far, the other customers in the Bull & Bear are leaving you and Diamond alone, although some of them, particularly Ann Louise, cannot resist looking your way. The waiter takes your order for another spritzer. Diamond stands pat. "I went to see Q-Jo Huffington because I couldn't eat mushrooms," he says.

"Whoa. Wait a second. You scheduled a tarot reading to help you overcome a food allergy?"

"Sorry. Forgot who I was talking to. In the future, I'll try to gear down to your speed."

"Don't slow down, just make sense."

"If you insist. Here's the story. I've recently had my brain redone. A little cognitive redecorating. Started in Timbuktu and continued after I got back; remodeling always takes twice as long as it's supposed to, you know how that goes. It's turned out real nice, but some days I wake up and look around at the new furniture, the new carpets and draperies and paint, and it's a minute or two before I know where I am; it just doesn't feel like home. Ever had that sensation?"

"No."

"I wasn't fully integrated into my new cerebral space, you might say. Well, when it comes to reorientation, nothing aligns the old ontological gyroscope like fifteen or twenty milligrams of psilocybic fungi. However . . ."

"You're talking about drugs!"

"*Plants,* Gwendolyn. God's own sweet baby plants. However, I've, uh, I've had some medical problems, physical problems, lately, and the fellow who's treating me advised against mushrooms. They're like squirrels, he said: you can learn a lot from them but they chatter too much. Wearing on the immune system, I think is what he's getting at. At any rate, I was in the market for a nonchemical alignment process, and when I heard that your friend Q-Jo was the Northwest's most gifted psychic, I decided to give her a whirl."

"You've hardly touched your drink. Are you actually ill or something?"

"Ut, ut, Gwendolyn. No hard-luck stories, remember. If your misery's craving company, go talk to one of those bookies at the bar."

"All right, Mr. Difficult. Suit yourself. How did you get along with her?"

"With Q-Jo? Famously. Famously. Although the reading itself wasn't exactly Nostradamus on ice. For example, she said the Lovers card in the seventh position was indicative of impending romance, but since I'd already met you the previous evening, that came as no great surprise."

"Ha!" You are so busy blushing, "Ha!" is all you can say, but you are thinking, *Mister, when you redecorated your brain room, you hung the pictures upside down.*

"The Five of Pentacles popped up, indicating poor health, as if I needed a reminder. I got the Tower in the fifth position, which signals upheaval or major change in my past. Hey, the Tower's been my permanent address. I wouldn't live anywhere else. So, there wasn't much headline news, but I was entertained when right next to the Lovers, the Fool appeared. Big as life. Position number three, the current-influence position. Q-Jo wasn't sure if the Fool in that spot was me or if it was the new woman in my life. Me or you, Gwen? What do you think?"

"It's painfully obvious."

"Yeah, I think it's you, too. Didn't you pull the Bozo and Sirius out of that sack you're carrying? There's some amazing stuff in that Fool bag. If you'd just take it out and examine it, maybe this relationship of ours could evolve beyond the level of mere physical attraction."

"What relationship? Would you just get on with it! Jesus, Larry!" At the Exasperation Olympics, this guy would win all the gold medals.

"On the other hand, the Fool might be Dr. Yamaguchi. Except he never returned my call."

183

"Sorry to hear that. Would you please get on with it." If Diamond had any idea how often you had drawn the Fool card in recent months, you fear he would dive across the table to embrace you or else run for cover.

"As I've indicated, it was a routine reading. No clouds parting, no veils dropping, no urgent faxes arriving from the Other Side. However, if we aren't learning something from a new experience, it's usually because we aren't paying attention. Or we're following the wrong libretto. So I shifted my perspective on the cards, and the first thing that hit me was how much water they contained."

"Water?"

"H-two-O. At least a third of the cards in the deck have got some image of water on them. An ocean, a lake, a pool, a river, a creek, a fountain: the whole aquatic repertoire. The Ace of Cups has got a nice crop of water lilies. You've expressed an interest in pads, if I'm not mistaken. There're fish, too, including a lobster that could scare the steak off of every surf-and-turf platter in the city. The Page of Cups . . ."

"Dear ol' Dad," you mumble under your breath.

". . . features a guy holding an ornate sort of golden chalice, and there's a fish in the chalice or goblet or whatever the hell it is, there's a live fish that looks like it's talking to the guy, like it's trying to tell him something. In addition to all this aquatic stuff, there's the celestial stuff, the moons and suns and stars; and the place where the aquatic intersects with the celestial is where I've been hanging out this season, intellectually speaking. I know that the tarot pictures represent an ancient, highly evolved symbol system of apparently European origin, and the fact that these pictures, this system, contains images that suggest the same themes, *some* of the same themes, as the Bozo in Africa, as the people 'on the pad,' if you don't object to my conceit, this gave me a little buzz, which I shared with Q-Jo."

"And I'll bet she told you to back off and quit analyzing."

"You know her well. Yeah, she reminded me that the tarot's like our dreams, it comes to us from a level beyond the reach of reason. 'The tarot figures are creatures of the imagination,' she said. 'The

184

cold light of intellect will send 'em scurrying back underground.' Since I'm convinced imagination creates reality and not the other way around, I could accept that, although 'underwater' might have been a better word. But my buzz persisted, and when I began elaborating on my enthusiasms, she tuned in with both ears: I'm assuming she has ears underneath that turban. She fished a key out of her bosom—how she found something as small as a key in there I'll never know: talk about cleavage! I could've parked my scooter in the slot between her tits."

"Please!"

"She fished a key out of her—where does one buy undies to cover the Andes? . . ."

"Please!"

". . . and unlocked an ebony box and showed me a Fool card from a French deck that's four or five centuries old. In the lower left corner there was an alligator, or rather, a crocodile. Are you aware that the Bible refers to crocodiles as 'the eyelids of dawn'? No? Anyway, there it was, a full-fledged amphibian in the tarot. Both of us are excited now—"

"Physically excited?"

"Please!"

You blush and urge him to continue.

"We have an animated conversation, during the course of which I grab her marking pens and impulsively mark up the Star card, to show her how things might be if. . . . Never mind that now. We could have flapped our jaws for another hour, but she had a previous engagement to look at somebody's travel photos for a fee, she said, and when I heard that, I offered to hire her to peruse my slides of Timbuktu; I thought she might provide another viewpoint, you know what I mean. She wasn't sure she could make it before next week; she said she'd phone later and confirm, but less than an hour later, she called from an ice cream parlor and announced she'd stop by Thunder House at three. Guess I'd aroused her curiosity."

"Was that the only thing you aroused?"

Diamond pulls himself to his feet. "Gwendolyn, I'm going to

185

the men's room to give you an opportunity to wrest your mind out of the gutter. If you fail, you can always follow along and join me. I assure you, it wouldn't be the first time a couple ever consummated their love in one of the Bull and Bear's stalls."

Leaving you to boil in your own isochronous juices, he limps off to the restroom, from which he does not emerge for fifteen minutes.

Eight Twenty-Nine P.M.

You think: *He must have run into a former colleague, and they're chewing over the market.*

You think: *He's doing drugs in there.*

You think: *He may have slipped out through the kitchen, which is fine with me.*

You think: *If he doesn't come back, what in God's name will I do?*

You think: *Did Washington's choppers contract in the bitter cold at Valley Forge?*

You think: *Here he comes! The bookies are waving, but he won't acknowledge them. He never limped that much before.*

"Are you okay? You never limped this much before."

"It's because I've been riding the scooter. The vibrations aggravate it."

"Aggravate *what?*"

"Old wound. Pork Chop Hill. Battle of the Bulge. Dien Bien Phu. I can't remember which. I don't like to talk about my war experiences. As a woman, you wouldn't understand."

You think: *He's putting me on. But he knows that I know he's putting me on. So in terms of his overall veracity, I guess it's acceptable.*

"I want to address," he says, "what appears to be a concern of yours. The world is a very different place than ninety-eight percent of its inhabitants think it is. Q-Jo and I understand and appreciate that. If there was any bond between us, that was it. Not one mote of sex pollen was released in the atmosphere around us. How could there be, Gwendolyn, when I only pollinate for you?"

"Yeah? So what was that pixie dust you were sprinkling around the coffee shop this afternoon?"

He beams at you in the most infuriating way. "Ah, yes—Natalie. What was I to do? The little pussy willow has an outgoing personality."

You think: *How does he know her name is Natalie?*

EIGHT-THIRTY P.M.

"Q-Jo showed up at Thunder House about twenty minutes late. She'd stopped on the way for a meatball sub."

"Sounds right."

"I gave her a brief tour of the flat, like any genial host, and then I dimmed the lights and commenced to project the slides. You do understand, do you not, that the dimming of the lights was intended to enhance the definition of visual images on the screen, and not for—"

"Larry, let me make myself clear. I do not care in the slightest how you might express your basic urges with any consenting adult. I've only inquired about . . . things of that nature—because—because I'm trying to establish motives for what may or may not have happened to my . . . to Q-Jo."

"That's perfectly understood."

"I just don't want you to get any wrong ideas."

"My ideas are pristine, I assure you."

"Well—all right."

"Well, all right, then."

"So why are you grinning like that?"

"I'm smiling because I'm merry and bright. In the circles you travel in, you've probably never met a man who was merry and bright." Gradually, his fractured smile rearranges itself into a frac-

187

tured frown. "Gwendolyn, are you by chance anxious about some upcoming dental work?"

You shake your head. "I'm not even due for a checkup until July."

"Mmmm. Interesting. Well, I suppose I ought to leave the telepathy to Q-Jo." He rakes his nails over the stubble on his chin. "You know, if her mojo was up to speed, she'd most likely be aware that we've been sitting around discussing her. At the very least, she'd be cognizant that you're worried." Yes, you had wondered about that yourself, but you refused to consider that it indicated that she was dead, unconscious, or even incompetent. Q-Jo is a complex, difficult individual, not unlike present company. Why, oh why, is it that Fate gets a kick out of throwing you in with such people? "Of course," Diamond continues, "if the only thing she's picking up from you is a set of false teeth. . . ."

"Would you get on with it!" You glare at your Rolex, as if you had somewhere else to be besides watching television news or scouring the back streets for a monkey.

EIGHT THIRTY-THREE P.M.

"First off, I projected the slides I'd taken in Bozo and Dogon villages. We talked some more about the Nommo phenomena that we'd discussed at her apartment after the tarot reading. She seemed to be enthralled and asked lots of questions. I served her a plate of chocolate chip cookies and put on the slides from Timbuktu. I think she may have been surprised by how desolate it looks. Anyhow, she didn't have much to say after that. Could have been the desolation, could have been the cookies. I baked them myself and they were a wee bit charred. Come to think of it, they went very well with the desolation. About two-thirds of the way through the slides, pictures of the university—University of Timbuktu—started hitting the screen. She made me linger over each one, while she kind of mumbled through the carbon she was masticating. I had to go to the toilet then, I couldn't delay it any longer, so I left her staring at a group shot of the faculty. And when I came back, she was gone. No note, no nothing. There were two and a half cookies left on the plate, and she hadn't collected her fee."

You are ready for another wine spritzer, but since Diamond has not finished his first drink, you feel it might be unseemly to order a third. "Running out on food and money," you say. "Doesn't sound like Q-Jo. Let me ask you something, if I may. Let's see, how can I put this? Uh, just now, when you went to the washroom? You, uh, were in there quite a long time."

"Relative to what?"

"Relative to how long it takes a normal human being to go to the damn bathroom."

"Are you referring to number one or number—"

"I don't want to talk about it! Okay? Jesus! I just want to find out, I would like to know if you were in your bathroom as long as you were in the men's room here at the Bull and Bear."

"Approximately, yes. I was—"

"No, stop. I don't *care* what you were doing in there. But can we safely say that Q-Jo was alone in your apartment for ten minutes or more?"

"Yes, but it didn't trouble me. Unlike the average American, she has an attention span longer than a Mormon's orgasm."

"What about the Indian?"

"You mean Twister? Oh, Twister has an extraordinary attention span."

"Twister, Twisted, whatever his name is. Where was he during this time?"

"Twister was in his wigwam contemplating his investment."

"His wigwam?"

"Maybe 'tipi' is the preferred word."

"*What* are you talking about?"

"Twister refers to his flat as his tipi. This could be irony, or it could be corn. Hard to tell with an Indian. Thunder House consists of two flats. His and mine."

"Adjoining? Does he have access to yours?"

"Affirmative on both counts." Diamond is smiling like the Ma in "Look, Ma, no hands": pleased but apprehensive. "You know, Gwendolyn, you have a natural talent for interrogation. With a couple of bad breaks, you could end up a Republican lawyer."

You shrug. That would certainly be preferable to nursing. "How well do you know this Native American?"

Diamond signals the waiter, orders you a drink. In the process, he attracts the attention of one of the men at the bar—a broker from PaineWebber if you're not mistaken—who trundles toward your table with a question, about the ability of oil companies to unload industry-specific assets if the credit crisis worsens, forming like a petroleum bubble on his lips. Diamond waves him away. "Oil!" he snorts. "How quaintly old-fashioned."

Since you personally own a hundred shares of Exxon, worth approximately a third what you paid for them, you are anxious to pursue the subject. "Obviously, if the dollar continues to decline as the world's reserve currency, there'll be even greater reductions in U.S. oil imports, but—"

"Let me tell you about Twister," Diamond interrupts. "Speaking of oil. His Comanche name is Tornado Warning. For business purposes, he went by the name of Tory Warren, but one of his associates, it might've been me, nicknamed him Twister. In the eighties, he sold drilling rights in Oklahoma to some paleface outfit and moved to Seattle with a half a mil in his jeans. His father's a famous Comanche medicine man, and this change of venue didn't sit too well with papa. But the young buck did okay in the big city. Quite fortuitously, I became his investment adviser, and I made him a ton of wampum in the market. A ton of wampum. He was homesick, though, he missed Oklahoma, and one of the things he missed most was the thunderstorms. Driving back from the Ballard Locks one day, where he'd gone to watch the annual salmon migration, he noticed the sign for the Thunderbird Bowl and stopped in on a whim. Turns out the bowling noises actually did remind him of thunder, and he took to hanging out there, although he never bowled a frame. And one day, he up and bought the place."

"Twister owns the bowling alley?"

"He owns the bowling alley and one other thing. That's what I'm getting at. He converted the basement into living quarters so he could lie in bed and listen to 'thunder' in the 'sky,' the way he used to do on the Plains. At the price, I didn't think it was much of an investment, but joy's always more important than juice. Or do you disagree? There was space in Thunder House for two large apartments, and when he offered to rent one of them to me, I felt like that guy in the movies, you know, the 'only white man the natives trust.' I was residing in a motel room on Aurora Avenue at the time, so any way you sliced it, Thunder House was a step up. When they introduced all-night bowling, however, my Z's turned into X's. Lost a fair amount of beauty sleep before I adapted. I used to be considered dashingly good-looking."

By whom, you think, *biker chicks whose boyfriends were all in prison?* But your drink arrives, and with it a fresh saucer of peanuts, so you make no response beyond rolling your eyes.

"Couple of years after Thunder House became my primary domicile, Twister got seduced by the art market. Fell in with the wrong crowd and started attending parties where guests stripped naked and watched Sotheby auctions via satellite. To be fair, the art scene was generating jumbo juice in those days, prices were doubling literally overnight; every paint-spattered cockroach in SoHo was riding around in a stretch limo, and if you were a dead European artist, every time the auctioneer's gavel came down, you'd twirl again in your coffin. So, I was only half-shocked when Twister shelled out three million clams for a drawing by Van Gogh."

"Wow! Three million for a Van Gogh drawing?"

"Yeah, but it was by *Vincent* Van Gogh, Gwendolyn, not his brother, Elmer. The price wasn't out of line at the time. The problem was, three mil was the sum total of Twister's assets, aside from the bowling alley. And a few years later, while he was waiting for his

191

smeary little drawing to quadruple in value, the Japanese collectors came to their senses, and the bottom fell out of the art market. A Dutch industrialist offered him eight hundred grand for the piece, but I guess Twister's got a genetic memory of the Manhattan Island deal. He wouldn't sell. Eventually, Twister's daddy got wind of his boy's art folly, and he flew into a shamanic tizzy. He showed up at Thunder House one night in his buffalo robes and demanded to see the drawing. Well, the Van Gogh had been stored in a bank vault ever since its purchase, and that drove the old man nuts. 'You waste big fortune on picture you not even look at?' He forced Twister to bring the Van Gogh home and hang it on his wall. 'Now we look at picture,' he said, and the two of them sat on the sofa and stared at it —we're talking about a murky, dark sketch of some peasants peeling turnips—for about a week. Then the old man went back to Oklahoma. Meanwhile, though, Twister had gotten hooked on the drawing. He couldn't stop looking at it. He didn't want to stop looking at it. It became a meditation for him. It brought him peace and understanding. He still stares at it—all day every day. The Dutchman raises his offer every few months, but Twister won't listen."

"What was the latest bid?"

"Oh, fuck, Gwendolyn, I don't know! That's not the point. The point is, Twister sits on his duff all day lost in contemplation of the compositional and spatial flatness with which the expressive, antinaturalist Van Gogh turned ordinary daily experience into a vehicle for a new set of meanings that defied the history of Renaissance perspective. The point is, Twister's blissed out over his fucking turnip peelers, and there's not a chance in hell he would've harmed Q-Jo, even if he was the type to abduct grossly overweight white women, which he's not."

"All right," you say. "I was only asking."

EIGHT FORTY-FIVE P.M.

"Waiter," you call as your server passes by. You are aware his name is Brian, but you are reluctant to get on a first-name basis with the help. "Waiter, this spritzer tastes different from the last one. In fact, the second one didn't taste like the first."

"You noticed! Oh, good! The bartender's trying out the new line of Walt Disney wines tonight. He made your first spritzer, if I'm not terribly mistaken, with the Donald Duck chardonnay. The next one was with the Minnie Mouse liebfraumilch, and this one's got the Goofy pinot blanc. Aren't they fun?"

"The fun is just beginning," you grumble, pushing the spritzer aside. It is all you can do to keep from burying your head in your arms.

EIGHT FORTY-SIX P.M.

"Gwendolyn, I've been automatically assuming that you've long since telephoned Q-Jo's friends, lovers, relatives, et cetera, to inquire if she might be with one of them. Now I'm forced to ask: is this a false assumption?"

"I would've called if I'd known where to call. I mean, her family lives in Ohio somewhere, I could've gotten their number out of her book, but I didn't want to worry them. Anyway, she wouldn't have just run out of your place and gone to Ohio. Q-Jo hates Ohio."

"She's not alone in that, I'd venture. How about friends?"

"There're a couple of astrologers she's chummy with, but she certainly wouldn't stay overnight with them. I can't remember their names."

"Lovers?"

"Nobody steady. She free-lances. When she can. Her size, you know."

"Yeah. And yet you thought *I* might have found her irresistible. . . ."

"Well, you're—sort of unusual."

"Not when you know me better." Diamond lays his hand, the one with the mystical tattoo, on top of your own. You freeze. Then, ever so slowly, casually, fraudulently, you slip free, on the pretext of requiring a sip of your spritzer, for which you've actually lost all taste now that you've learned it was concocted with *vin de Goofy*. The freed hand vibrates for a full forty seconds.

"Any suggestions?" you ask.

"Absolutely." He reaches again for your hand. You pull it just out of reach.

"I meant about . . ."

"Q-Jo?"

"Yes, her, naturally. But also about my situation at—work." Ever so slowly, casually, fraudulently, you slide your hand back within his range.

He shakes his head from side to side and looks at you with pity and dismay, exactly as your father used to look at you after your singing lessons. When you were about fourteen, Freddy Mati was struck by the notion that you could turn the tables on your funny little voice, make it work to your advantage. Freddy entertained a vision of your becoming a jazz singer in the mold of Blossom Dearie. Twice a week for a month, he made you bus after school to the Central District, where you were coached by a black woman only nominally slimmer than Q-Jo. Toward the end of each lesson, your dad would show up and listen with his eyes closed as your voice jumped from key to key like a tonality squirrel at harvest time. "Ah, Squeak," he would sigh when it was over, and he'd shake his head the way Larry Diamond is shaking his now.

"Smarten up," Diamond says.

"Sorry?"

"Smarten up." He resumes his W. C. Fields cadence. "Just because you've got the cutest ass west of Chicago and north of L.A. doesn't mean you have to go around with your head up it. Leaves no room for me." Before you can do more than sputter, he says, "Rise above this job fixation, Gwendolyn, rise above it or resign yourself to life with the toads."

"Life with what toads?"

"Most toads can swim if they're forced to, but unlike frogs, they rarely enter the water. Since the planet is two-thirds water, where would you say the limitations lie: with the frogs or the toads? Frogs are smooth and sleek and moist; toads are rough and dry and warty." He scratches his jaw. "There's one other problem with toads."

"Oh, do tell me quickly, I beg of you."

"They can't mate with frogs."

You drain the remainder of your stupid spritzer and fake pushing your chair from the table. "Rise above this mating fixation, Diamond, rise above it or resign yourself to an evening without my company."

"Touché. Touché. And forgive me the resumption of my amphibian fancies. I'll try in the future to keep a lid on them." Acknowledging with his eyes that you are half out of your chair, he says, "If I help you with your job, will you stay?"

EIGHT-FIFTY P.M.

Naturally, it is too good to be true. Diamond's idea of helping you with your job is to lecture you on the obsolete and retrograde nature of salaried employment. He goes on at length, in his constricted nasal manner, about how, in our social history, jobs are an aberration, a flash in the pan. Human beings have been on earth for a million years, he claims (you think he's mistaken about that), but have only had jobs for the past five hundred years (that doesn't sound right, either), an inconsequential period, relatively speaking. People have always worked, he explains, but they have only held jobs—with wages and employers and vacations and pink slips—for a very short time. And now, with the proliferation of cybernetics and robotics and automation of all types and degrees, jobs are on the way out again. In the context of history, jobs have been but a passing fancy.

Nowadays, he would have you believe, the state uses jobs, or rather the illusion of jobs, as a mechanism for control. When there is a public outcry about some particularly vile instance of deforestation, wreckage, or pollution, the "pufftoads" hasten to justify the environmental assault by trumpeting the jobs it allegedly will save or create—and then the protests fade like the rustle of a worn dollar bill. Foreign policy decisions, including illegal and immoral acts of armed intervention, likewise are made acceptable, even popular, on the grounds that such actions are necessary to protect American jobs. Virtually every candidate for public office in the past seventy years has campaigned with the rubber worm of "more jobs" dangling from his or her rusty hook, and the angler with the most lifelike worm snags the votes, even though all voters except the cerebrally paralyzed must recognize that there are going to be fewer and fewer jobs as time—and technology—progresses.

"Would you say then, Larry, that those of us who're concerned with jobs are reading the wrong libretto?"

He beams at you so magnificently that the infrared sensor in your groin is involuntarily activated, and you have to gaze off in the direction of Ann Louise in order to curtail the annoying warm tide that is negotiating the locks of your perineal Panama. "There's hope for you yet," he declares.

"I wouldn't count on it."

The waiter, who had assumed your look was meant for him, minces up to take your order. "I'll have a martini," you say recklessly, "and if there's a cartoon character on the gin bottle, I'm going to remove a can of Mace from this handbag and bring both you and the bartender to your knees."

Diamond beams even brighter, and you can't help but grin yourself. You have to bite your lip, in fact, to regain a sober demeanor. Interesting how the bent trumpet summons levity.

"We already had double-digit unemployment before Black

Thursday," Diamond resumes. "In the weeks to come, if there's not a magical turnaround, it could exceed twenty percent. But even that's a union-made paradise. In two or three decades, eighty percent of the able-bodied may well be out of jobs. You notice I said 'out of jobs,' not 'out of work.' The problem is, we've forgotten how to work unless we're on the job. We're job junkies, and not one of our institutions is prepared or qualified to help us kick the habit."

"Because the toads are too busy grinding out irrelevant librettos."

"Factitious and profoundly accurate in the same breath, my dear. Not bad for an amateur. Here's your cocktail. I hope for Brian's sake it's a martini and not a martooni."

"Oh, it's made with Tanqueray, Mr. D., I promise. Can I bring you another tequila sour?"

"Just a club soda, Brian. Twist of the ol' citrus peel. Now, Gwendolyn, wipe that unattractive smirk off your face and tell me who's better equipped to escape obsolescence, the toads of industrial fundamentalism—lost and hysterical in a world without jobs—or the transformative frogs who—"

"If they can't pay their grocery bills, one's just as dead as the other."

"No jobee, no eatee, eh? They must've used a harsh detergent when they washed your brain. On the roof of Thunder House, we could grow enough food to feed everybody in a six-block radius, year-round. You could do almost that well on top of your apartment building. You wouldn't need to haul a lot of heavy soil up there, either. Tomatoes'll grow like weeds in shredded wet newspaper."

"I can't make Porsche payments with tomatoes."

"True, and you can't drive a Porsche underwater."

"What is this underwater stuff? My accounts are underwater, that's all I care about." His club soda arrives. "You expecting a great flood or something? If I'm not mistaken, the Bible says it'll be fire next time." The martini is tasty, but this conversation seems to be constantly veering off track.

"So it does. And so it shall. But fire is the flip side of water—and a big back has a . . ."

"Big front. Yeah, I know." Still, it beguiles you in ways that most of the conversations you have had in the Bull & Bear have not.

"Listen, my little hoptoad, I'm about to make you a proposition."

"I thought you already had."

"I'm going to the men's room . . ."

"Not with me you're not."

"I'm going to the restroom . . ."

"You just got back."

". . . and in my absence, I'd like you to do two things. First, order us some dinner. The kitchen'll be closing soon, and we can't live on love alone. Then, I want you to make a decision. When I come back, I'll talk with you about your ill-chosen and ill-fated career, I'll pass along any and every tedious tidbit at my disposal that might be of use to a desperate soul who's screwed up royally in a profession that's screwed up royally. Or—*or*—I'll expend the same amount of time and energy to tell you a few things that are really interesting. And really important. Knowledge that may turn out to be considerably more empowering to you than an MBA. Or maybe not. In any case, it's your choice. One or the other. It's up to you."

With that, he rises and long hair swinging, hobbles, lurches, and weaves away, like an animal who's been stung in the hams with a tranquilizer dart.

NINE OH-FOUR P.M.

"I'll have the vegetable stir-fry. But without asparagus. Repeat: *no asparagus.*"

"I get the picture," says Brian, a bit too snippishly for an underling. "And what will Mr. D. be having this evening?"

"Uh, Mr. D. will have . . . I think Mr. D. would like. . . ."

This is wicked but you can't help yourself. "Bring Mr. D. the frog legs."

NINE OH-FIVE P.M.

There is an exaltation about the Bull & Bear that is due not only to its decor—darkly warm, weighty, polished, aged—and its clientele —well-groomed, smartly tailored, educated, savvy—but also to its function as a refuge from chaos: the controlled chaos of the financial markets and, increasingly, the far less predictable chaos of the streets. In the outside world, civilization is frequently and perhaps accurately perceived as a thin veneer over the rant and scrabble of an essentially savage species. In the Bull & Bear, conversely, the slosh and bluster seems a thin veneer of atavism over a bedrock of refinement and order. That part of America that remains affluent, that is neither on fire nor on sale, neither shot full of holes nor rusting away, that affluent part appears many places to be tricky and dazed. Here in this citadel, however, no matter how noisy, smoky, or unruly it may at certain hours of the day become, the stability and calm traditionally bestowed by Buddha the Banker somehow has prevailed. Ever since you discovered the establishment while on lunch break from the ski department at Nordstrom a half-dozen years ago, the Bull & Bear's mystique has had a powerful hold on you.

Tonight, you feel it slipping away.

You sense an odd, almost poignant, alienation from the knot of brokers across the lounge. They are unusually restrained this evening, their concentration focused on their anesthetic beakers of booze and on the screen of the bar TV. There is a silent communion among them, however, in which you suspect you would not share, even were you to press your taut little belly to the bar. They are watching the financial channel, no doubt, and you wonder if you might be missing something of import. All you can see from your table is a dancing miasma of red and green, like an atomized Christmas wreath. You simply must get your eyes examined. Stock quotations, like the Scriptures, are a common source of optic erosion. Those tiny names and numbers: So difficult to read, so fraught with secret salvations, if only the eye muscles could pry them loose!

Some portion of the poignancy that is seizing you may be attributed to the fact that your bladder is brimming. You hadn't wished to go to the bathroom at the same time as Larry Diamond, lest he perceive—and celebrate—a repulsive intimacy in the synchronized discharge of wastes. But you can delay no longer. Passing the bar as unobtrusively as possible, you steal a look at the TV screen. What your colleagues are watching, it turns out, is a Latino horror movie about a vampire mariachi band. No wonder there is an excess of green and red. When these musicians stroll through the plazas of nighttime Tijuana, they give a whole new dimension to *"Besame Mucho."*

NINE OH-EIGHT P.M.

There is an electrical problem in the women's room. It is as black as outer space in there, and the light switch flips up and down uselessly, like the lips of the President. Oh, well, pity the woman who cannot pee in the dark. Having grown up in a household where the power was routinely shut off due to nonpayment, you are practiced in the art of locating toilet seats by touch and feel. Once the target has been locked in, the compact urinary jet of the female, unlike the helter-skelter garden hose of its male counterpart, can fire with almost pinpoint precision.

It is appropriate, you are forced to admit, to be sitting in literal darkness since, after all, you have been in the figurative dark for about three days. Were it not for its overtones of outsider ignorance (it is the masses who usually are left in the dark), a certain cheery comfort might be derived from the blackout. Darkness can protect as well as threaten. Of course, there is a limit to how long you can enjoy asylum in the ladies' room. And when at last you leave, you must take a decision with you—not that there is really much to decide. Or is there?

When the last note of water music has subsided, you dab your little valve with tissue and still seated, lean against the right panel of the stall. Of the many batlike rumors circling the ruins of the market, the one that seems to want to hang upside down from the rafters of your cranium is the scenario that has the Arabs reducing the ruins to rubble by further raising the price of oil. Then, when the market has sustained all the damage it can endure without being obliterated, the sheiks will come in with the vault loads of petro dollars they've been hoarding and buy out the store. Then, they will lower oil prices to today's levels or below and stand at the top of the stairs to watch the indexes climb to greet them, oozing megabucks from every pore. It makes sense. And there has to be a way for a smart cookie like you to grab a little bitty piece of that bonanza. By going long on oil futures, for example. But you would have to buy on margin, and you would probably have to buy in London, preferably late tomorrow night, as soon as trading reopens in Europe. You lack the faculty to buy without resources, you lack the skills to buy abroad on short notice. Larry Diamond, on the other hand, if he is the wizard he is cracked up to be. . . .

Diamond, unfortunately, has a different agenda. He wants to fuck you (were it not for the wine and gin, you could not even think that word, the word that leaves a salty ring around your brain like the scum line in a bathtub), but that's only part of it. He is challenging you in areas that have little or nothing to do with sex.

Your daddy used to tell you bedtime stories, accompanying himself on the bongo drums. His favorite story, though not necessarily yours, was "Jack and the Beanstalk." It was really something the way he could make those drums say *fe fi fo fum.* As you grew older, the bedtime entertainment petered out, but one night when you were nine, or maybe ten, he told "Jack and the Beanstalk" one last time. You listened dutifully, although you were somewhat embarrassed. When he ended the tale with a loud squashed-giant *blop* on a drumhead, he said, "This a smart story, Squeak. This a lesson

201

story. Person learn righteous things from this story, man. You keep it wit you." He slapped you a high five and left the room, off to a club or a party. In the morning, you asked your mother what he might have meant. "I think," she replied, "that he means that you should never hesitate to trade your cow for a handful of magic beans." On the way to school, you considered—and rejected—the fatherly advice. *Why not milk the cow*, you reasoned, *and exchange a pail of milk for just one or two of the beans?* That way you get to keep the cow, and how many magic beans does a person really need?

Well, you have left the barn door unlatched, and a storm has blown it open. Your cow has run away. You want to chase after it, to entice it home or force it home. Larry Diamond is urging you to let it go. Cows are of no consequence, he is saying: here, forget the cow and accept these magic beans. Diamond is daring you to become a part of something totally unfamiliar, to move outside the realm of normal expectations. It intrigues you, primarily because he doesn't want a cow in return. But he obviously *wants*. Is it merely sex he wants, or something other? And how can you be sure his beans will grow? They might be jelly beans or jumping beans—or pellets of poison.

On the toilet seat, you shift your weight from your right to your left buttock. Now your head and shoulder are resting against the left panel of the stall. In your bloodstream, molecules of wine and gin wander, cartwheeling, singing, like a troupe of minstrels. A few more drops dribble out of your urethra. Your challenge, as you see it, is to convince Diamond to lasso your cow plus fork over a bean or two without your having to sleep with him.

An alcohol bubble bumps against your libido and bounces impishly along its unguarded surface. Sleeping with Diamond might be, well . . . a consideration, at least—if you could be assured he wasn't responsible, in some dire way, for Q-Jo's hiatus.

A sudden finger of light juts into the restroom. Two fingers, three fingers. Widening. Four fingers, five. A creak follows, and finger by finger, the hand of illumination balls up with a click into a fist. The door has opened and shut. You sense someone standing just inside the room, perhaps futilely flicking the wall switch. Undoubtedly it is Ann Louise or the single other woman from the group at the bar. You clear your throat and rattle the toilet paper dispenser to signal that the stall is occupied. How awful if Ann Louise were to back in in the dark and plop her wanton fanny down on top of you.

The person walks farther into the room. And you realize, with a chill, that the footsteps—heavy, flat, wide-spaced, spikeless—are those of a man.

NINE-THIRTEEN P.M.

The steps advance to the stall door—latchless and none too snug—and stop. There is no sound beyond breathing. Yours. His.

Slowly, you pull up your panties, realizing, with a shock and a tingle, that were the man to speak, were it Diamond's voice and were that voice tender and reassuring, you might leave them down.

He does not call out. He does not whisper your name. Nor does he move. He only breathes. You can no longer hear your own breath, it is corked, like a ferment of oxygen, like a distilled scream, in the jug of your lungs. *His* breathing is slow and even, and the ordinariness of its rhythms, the absence of rasp or rush or thickness, makes it all the more menacing.

Minutes pass. Panic throbs in you like a gypsy guitar. From the purse at your feet, which are only inches from his feet, you withdraw your canister of Mace. *What kind of world is this?* you think. *What kind of world?*

Then, without a word, he turns, walks leisurely to the door, and exits, leaving behind a faint smell of burnt sugar.

You take several minutes to compose yourself before following him out. Once your eyes have reaccustomed themselves to the light, you scan the lounge. Nothing has changed. The bartender tends bar, the waiter waits, the bookies, absorbed in the movie (mariachi vampires are serenading a honeymoon couple from Brooklyn), don't so much as blink as you wobble by. Larry Diamond is at the table.

"Started without you," he says. "Hope you don't mind."

He is eating the vegetable stir-fry.

Nine Twenty-Three P.M.

Onions with their pearl-skin layers, like the pages of newspapers published by oysters.

Baby carrots, orange and droopy, imitating the mustachios of Yosemite Sam.

Green pea pods: the detached spines of elves.

Broccoli boutonnieres plucked from the mildewed lapels of dandified Swamp Things.

Sliced sweet peppers, yellow and red, vaulted and naved, like cross sections of Caribbean cathedrals.

Zucchini, poor Italian, wearing its envy of eggplant on its sleeve.

Button mushrooms—but what do they button? Dirt's clown suit? The meadow's fly? One thinks of Satan undressing his bride.

Beets as intense as serial killers, celery as stringy as soundtrack orchestras, sesame seeds as blank as the eyes of termite queens.

One by one, Diamond forks vegetable pieces into his mouth, while you avert your gaze from the plate you have inherited, and try to get a grip on yourself. From time to time, Diamond looks at you quizzically, but he doesn't ask for your decision or why you haven't bitten into the leg of a frog. If it was he who terrorized you in the ladies' room, he certainly isn't gloating over it. He forks, he chews, he glances at you quizzically until eventually, because you feel pressured by the silence, you sigh and say, "Larry, do you think George Washington flossed with an awl?"

Diamond doesn't miss a beat. Guiding a broccoli floret toward his chops, he says, "If the father of our country was reduced to such a thing, he had only Christianity to blame."

"Sorry?"

"Christianity," he says, "the enemy of the teeth, as well as the clitoris and the brain."

"Enemy of the *teeth?*" you ask, hoping he will drop the clitoris part.

"Dentistry was already a fairly sophisticated science in ancient Egypt. There're mummies with fillings in their teeth; with root canals and bridgework, for crying out loud." He chews broccoli while you think, *Good news for cloned pharaohs. They can go right from the sarcophagus to a steak house.*

"Jews considered such practices a form of mutilation, and our European Christian ancestors believed it was blasphemous to mess with the Almighty's handiwork, we being created in his own image, overbite and all. Never mind that their molars ached—that was the result of sin, or the mischief of demons. By the time the King James version of the Bible hit the stands in sixteen-whatever-it-was, dentistry in the English-speaking world was a rustic joke, which is why, four thousand years after Imhotep got his cavities filled, the President of the United States was forced to replace *his* troubled teeth with blunt objects carved out of a fallen log. The Christians crucified dental science, just like they nailed up astronomy—you know what happened to Copernicus and Galileo—and the rest of the human race's intellectual and artistic progress. Yes, indeed. It was a bishop of the Church of Rome who burned the great library at Alexandria because he was uncomfortable with the reminder on such a grand scale that there were successful human enterprises that pre-dated Jesus. You have any appreciation of what was lost in that fire? The science, the records, the scholarship, the wisdom, the literature? Our understanding of the past and what it may portend for the future was irreparably sabotaged by arrogant Christian fire-bugs. The second greatest library in the world happened to be in Timbuktu, and *it* was torched by Islamic revisionists for the very same reason. Let history begin with Muhammed! If these religious assholes are really convinced of the power and the truth of their big boohoos, why are they so scared by historical fact, by thought, by knowledge?" He jabs the prongs of his fork into a pea pod. "That's a rhetorical question. Get on with your din-din."

If chickens played basketball, their drumsticks would look like the deep-fried appendages on the platter in front of you. Long, graceful, athletically bent. Good thing the feet are missing. They probably would be sporting a little pair of Nikes. Obviously, Diamond can see that you haven't touched them. "Whether it's about their finances or about their souls," you venture, "most people tend to be a bit insecure. But you have absolutely no sympathy for them, do you? Haven't you ever experienced insecurity?"

"Insecurity? Me?" He forces the words through pea pulp. "Constantly. Every waking moment of every day, and probably when I'm snoozing. There's no such thing as security in this life, sweetheart, and the sooner you accept that fact, the better off you'll be. The person who strives for security will never be free. The person who believes she's found security will never reach paradise. What she mistakes for security is purgatory. You know what purgatory is, Gwendolyn? It's the waiting room, it's the lobby. Not only does she have the wrong libretto, she's stuck in the lobby where she can't see the show."

"That might not be all bad. What if the show's a dog?"

"Jesus, that poor penniless wretch whose failed attempts to reform Judaism, to make it less commercial and corrupt, have been exploited into the biggest, most profitable business in history—how'd you like to have bought Christianity, my dear, when it was selling for a shekel a share?—ol' Jesus said, 'The Kingdom of Heaven is spread upon the Earth, but men do not see it.' Personally, I suspect the Kingdom of Heaven has got to be a pretty hot show, although I admit the reviews have been sketchy. Even if it's a flop, it beats waiting in the lobby. At least you can reach your own conclusions. But first you have to claim your seat and have a look."

"Everybody's waiting for something."

"Yeah, and everybody's got to stop it. It's making 'em crazy. Worse, it's making 'em mediocre. Even the Dogon, the Bozo. They're waiting for the Nommo—and growing more pedestrian with each passing decade—in the same way the other nitwits are waiting for the Messiah." He stabs a carrot. "Which is worse, having a boil lanced or sitting in the doctor's waiting room hour after hour, filling out forms, thumbing through those out-of-date magazines, sneezers and coughers spraying microbic wildlife at you, babies howling, hard-luck stories being traded like baseball cards? Better to be in the examination room learning the boil is actually a cancer than waiting your life away with unhappy companions on plastic-covered furniture. Purgatory's not only inferior to Heaven, it's worse than Hell."

As he shoves the carrot into his thin smile, like a cartridge being shoved into the chamber of an antique rifle, you say, "We both know what *I'm* waiting for . . ."

"Among other things, for me to stop pontificating."

". . . but how about you? Is there nothing you're waiting for, Larry?"

"Among other things, for me to stop pontificating."

"And what else?"

"Well, short-term, I suppose my breath's bated for your decision. Which is it going to be, cocoa eyes? Wisdom or steady employment?"

You sit up straight and push aside the frog-leg platter. "Larry, you're going to be very disappointed in me. However, I—"

You are interrupted by a loud murmuring from the area of the bar. "Oh, shit!" somebody exclaims. "Can you believe it!" exclaims another. Even those customers who had not been watching the movie are fixed now on the television screen, where the picture and sound have changed drastically. Mexican music and coffin-lid creaks have been replaced by the excited but controlled voice of a reporter; the color has gone from gore-red and vampire-green to tints of gray and beige. Blurred by the contracting muscles of your myopia, images are indistinct, although you can tell from the infrequency of flicker that the footage is too static to be yet another gang skirmish or inner-city riot. Impulsively, you rise and glide over to the bar.

NINE-THIRTY P.M.

To your credit, perhaps, your first thoughts are of Q-Jo: what if her decapitated body has been found in a dumpster? But no station would interrupt its Saturday night movie to report on a messy bit of business that has become fairly commonplace in America; and, anyway, the reaction of the bookies indicates news with financial repercussions. This spurs you to move closer yet.

The bulletin, you soon learn, involves Motofusa Yamaguchi. The doctor, it seems, returned from an early dinner a short time ago to find that his hotel suite had been burglarized. Missing in the robbery is a "device" or "instrument," not specifically described, said to be absolutely indispensable to Yamaguchi's cancer cure. Without it, his appearance at the conference on Monday would be pointless, his life's work curtailed, if not ruined.

"There goes the Nikkei," a broker says.

"There goes the Nikkei, the Hang Seng, the DAX, the Crédit Suisse, the Bourse CAC, the Footsie One-Hundred . . ." elaborates another, his voice trailing off in despair.

Repeatedly, the camera pans the crime scene, a crowded, only moderately disarranged, luxury suite, in a corner of which Dr. Yamaguchi can be seen speaking with detectives, shrugging, shyly smiling, tapping his front teeth with a Bic.

"The doc doesn't look all that upset," says Ann Louise. "For a guy whose bird has flown."

"They're inscrutable, you know."

"The whole thing could be a setup. I mean from the get-go. I, for one, was never convinced he had a cancer cure in the first place."

"Oh, come on, Joel. What'd be the point of a hoax?"

"*Wuf,*" barks Joel.

The movie resumes, but the brokers have lost interest in fangs and frijoles. There is a hubbub about the bar, everyone—except you —talking at once.

"I'd enjoy hearing Larry Diamond's take on this," Ann Louise says rather loudly. "But apparently, Ms. Mati here has screwed his brains out." Everyone, including you, follows her gesture. Diamond is leaning back in his chair with his eyes shut, looking pale and insensate. Ann Louise lowers her voice to a stage whisper. "Did you see him earlier? The poor stud could barely walk."

There is a round of dirty laughter, but by the time you have tossed your head, gray strands and all, and stalked half the distance to your table, the talk has returned to the Yamaguchi robbery. "There'll be no shortage of suspects," you hear a bookie say. "Pharmaceutical houses. The National Cancer Institute. Any number of terrorist organizations, including the AMA."

"Larry? Are you all right?"

The beads of sweat on his forehead are bigger than bugs. Some of them scatter when he opens his eyes. "Fit as a fiddle," he says weakly. Then, in a stronger voice, "Let's get out of here." From his chewed-up jeans he pulls a roll of bills one could open a Texas S & L with, peels off three fifties, drops them on the bread basket, and throws his leather jacket about his shoulders like a cape. You can tell he is struggling to walk normally.

"Larry. Got a second?"

"Larry, can I ask you . . ."

A chorus of "Larry this" and "Larry that" rings out as the two of you approach the bar. Again he pulls out that beautiful tumbleweed of cash, wads another fifty, and tosses it to the bartender. "Poorer of some hopes but freer of some illusions," he says cheerfully. "Drinks are on me."

"But, Larry, do you believe . . ."

"I believe that Buddha was a frog. And the frog is Buddha. Look at frogs meditating on their pads and tell me they aren't monks." A hush falls over the bookies. They step aside to let him pass. "Mother Mary may have been a frog, as well. That would explain the Immaculate Conception."

Diamond starts toward the door, you on his heels. As you brush by Ann Louise, your hand shoots out and grabs her nose. You twist it until it feels like a gum wrapper between your fingers, and she yeows with pain.

It would have been a great exit, a potential candidate for the Exit Hall of Fame, except that TV spoils it, as TV has spoiled so much. Diamond, mumbling something about Baby Jesus being a tadpole, has taken only three or four steps, you have barely let go of Ann Louise's crumpled snout, when another news bulletin snuffs a sombreroed bloodsucker in mid-bite. With a mixture of relief, amusement, and annoyance, the reporter comes on camera to announce that Yamaguchi's anticancer device has been recovered. It was in his room all along. Under the bed. "Unofficially, police are saying Dr. Yamaguchi consumed a couple too many cups of sake at dinner, and when he came back to his hotel, he knocked over a table with his attaché case on it, and the instrument rolled under the bed."

Looking rather sheepish, Yamaguchi is shown holding up an object that resembles a translucent twig. The brokers shush Ann Louise, who is hysterical, so they may hear more clearly what the doctor has to say for himself, but Yamaguchi just sways from side to side and giggles.

"The guy's *fried*, for God's sake," the bookie from PaineWebber says with disgust.

"So? We're well on the way ourselves."

"Yeah, but we're not famous scientists. We're not some genius who's supposed to have the cure for cancer."

"The guy the world's counting on."

"Precisely. I don't trust that flaky Nip."

"If we get a strong opening in the foreign markets tomorrow night, you'll smooch him where the rising sun don't rise."

"Did you see what that little slut did?" Ann Louise is sobbing and rubbing her nose, but nobody is paying attention.

210   "The Father's a frog, the Son's a tadpole, the Holy Ghost is

swamp gas," announces Larry Diamond. He grabs your hand, and with him tugging you along, you complete your exit.

NINE FORTY-TWO P.M.

Out on the street, Diamond is beaming again. He pitches a coin to an armless woman, who catches it in her cleavage. It drops through and rolls south on Sixth Avenue. "The rich boys stole my brassiere," she explains. She chases the coin down and snatches it up with her teeth. Diamond's face, which at times can be frighteningly fierce, is radiant now with an unearthly joy. The way things keep changing, back and forth, back and forth, you feel like Alice in Wonderland.

He has your hand in his. A waning but still yeasty moon bumps its golden beer belly against the more ascetic solar plexus of cityshine. Although the cool, dry air ripples with siren and shriek and car alarm, you can hear somewhere a Jew's harp playing "Strangers in the Night." Diamond is either drawing you into his embrace or your feet have become toy trucks, wound up tight and pointed in his direction. You close your eyes as your face nears his.

"If you was to eat dog shit and then shit it out, would you 'ave dog shit or human shit?"

Good grief! You reach in your purse, fully intent on treating the royally appointed vagrant to a taste of good American Mace, but Diamond looks the Queen's wino in the eye and says sincerely, "I believe it would depend upon the sauce."

The little man tilts his derby in salute. "And the wine as well? Hmmm. An interesting solution, guvner, to a perplexing problem."

With a wince of pain, Diamond straddles the Vespa. "Climb aboard," he says. "I'll give you a lift to your car." The Queen's wino snares the coin that he flips.

"You're going, then?"

"Appears I'm waiting for something, after all," he says. "I'm waiting to make contact with Dr. Yamaguchi—and I can't wait a whole lot longer."

"What is it, Larry?" You are talking to the back of his head as the motor scooter bounces over the curb and into traffic—what there is of traffic in the financial district after business hours.

"Just another hard-luck story. And, unfortunately, one of the more unromantic ones."

"You have cancer. Don't you?"

"I was the guy who went in to get the boil lanced."

"Of the colon?"

"Of the rectum."

"Oh, Larry."

"I warned you it held a minimum of romance."

"Larry. I'm so sorry."

"Oh, if it isn't one thing it's another. Something's always trying to knock us off the pad. Twister's father, Wide Place in the Road, has been treating me, and up to now the tumor's been under control. This evening, however, the little dickens let its hair down and decided to rock and roll."

He parks the scooter alongside your Porsche, but you stay aboard. "Why didn't you tell me? That's awful. What can you do?"

"Yamaguchi holds the trump card. I have to wait for him to play it. Meanwhile"—he lowers his lids lasciviously—"would you like to come over to Thunder House and see my slides of Timbuktu?"

For better or for worse; out of career ambition, passion, compassion, or general confusion, you have every intention of saying *yes*, but when he turns and leans his face into yours, as you brace for his kiss, his breath envelops you in an effluvium of burnt sugar, the exact confectionery aroma the intruder brought into the ladies' room.

You pull away and dismount.

"I've, uh, ah, got to check on Q-Jo," you stammer. "Got to notify the police if she's not back. Call around the hospitals. Stuff like that." Although you do not mention it, you also need to call a certain party in San Francisco. Belford is probably eating his knuckles by now.

Diamond smiles. "Doubtlessly a wise decision. I wish you luck." He guns the Vespa. "Thanks for a lovely evening. Too bad you didn't partake of the frog legs, though." As he speeds away, still talking, you catch the words "Easter," "Host," and "Holy Communion."

TEN P.M.

It is indicative of your state of mind that you drive past Continental Place without bothering to gaze up at the ninth-floor windows of the luxury condominium that you have so coveted and for which you must deliver a down payment within a week or else lose it and your "earnest money," to boot. You feel as if your brain, which only a few days ago sat like a well-fed hen on a nest of warm numbers, hatching schemes and clucking in waltz time, has been painted with radium and smacked with a flyswatter. It is a wonder you find your way home.

After ascertaining that Q-Jo remains at large, you telephone the missing persons bureau at police headquarters and are left on hold so long three more of your hairs turn gray. Eventually, you are permitted to file a preliminary report, although you must appear in person on Monday before it can officially become a "case."

You reach Belford Dunn in his room, almost out of breath from pacing the carpet. In an effort to tint a black lie a whiter shade of pale, you relate that while there has been no real sign of André, you think you might have heard him in the maple tree outside your window. When Belford gets excited and threatens to fly home at once, you backtrack and say it could have been a raccoon or your imagination. You urge him to stay on for the interdenominational sunrise service in Golden Gate Park and for the meeting with a French consulate flunky, whom the consul general, distracted and rather inebriated when Belford finally intercepted him in Sonoma, promised to send by the hotel on Sunday afternoon.

"Are you tired, Gwen? You sound—I don't know—*funny.*"

213

"Must be this PMS."

The sarcasm eludes him. "Oh, dear. I should have remembered. Poor baby. I'm sorry."

Good grief!

You kick off your shoes and flop onto the bed—landing, of course, among millions of mites. Had you any inkling that your bedding was alive with arthropodic crablets, chomping away on flakes of your dead skin, you would be so disgusted you would probably choose to lie on the floor. Yet every one of us, including the rich, the pious, and the royal of blood, sleeps each night in colonies of such mites. The ultimate witnesses, the most intimate voyeurs, these mites. What books they might author, what tales they could tell! Imagine the memoirs of a multitude of minuscule malcolm lowrys, expatriates in a martex mexico, soused on dandruff tequila, living and writing under the volcano of love. Jolted by mattress-quakes, buried by thigh-slides, swept away by flash floods of seminal lava, they cling to the linen with their petite pincers, recording with literary objectivity our orgasms, our fevers, our pillow talk, our dreams. Who knows more of our secrets? Who? Nightly, and often by day, they sail with us in the lunar barge, their flake steaks marinated in our tearwater, their breakfast boiled in our sweat, the winds of our farting at play in their hair. They are familiar with wife and mistress, husband and lover, hot-water bottle and fetish, favorite sitcom and favorite drug; have memorized confession, recrimination, prayer, delirium, and that sweet name we cry out in our sleep. Our babies are conceived—and born—in their midst; our parents—and someday we ourselves—die in what passes for their arms. Yes, all this: but the mites do not betray us. If they gossip, it is only among themselves. Perhaps they see an order in our messy bed-lives—our tossings and turnings, moans and nightmares, snacks and snores and trading of partners—that we have not discovered yet. Perhaps they regard us as glorious, even; as agents of the raw miraculous, capable at any moment—not in spite of our folly but because of it—of a transcendence that exceeds transformance. As a rule, we do not sing in our beds. We have no need. The mites sing for us. Sing *of* us. They are our Greek chorus, our geek chorus, choirs of microscopic angels ever ready to dance on the head of a pin. Their appetites are ghoulish, their hunger divine. They are what they eat.

Excerpt from a bedmite tome:

Shortly before eleven on the night before Easter, our hostess, Gwendolyn Mati (fully clothed, unfortunately), lay herself down in our city to gather her wits, to collect her thoughts, to sort things out—things ranging from rectal cancer to sugary aromas, from missing friends to the possible demise of that powerful and enduring conviction that every generation of Americans could and would move beyond the social and economic station of its predecessor. However, being chaotic, overwhelmed, worried, frazzled, exhausted, severely disappointed yet strangely free, her various thoughts coagulated, her mind went to test-pattern, and she slipped rather quickly into slumber. Within minutes, she commenced to dream. A voice spoke to her in her dream, spoke so loudly and distinctly (although it dragged its syllables contemptuously through its proboscis, in the manner of that bulbous old comedian on the late, late show) that we heard it above our traffic and crunching, as clearly as if it were there in the sheets. Startled, Ms. Mati reared up in bed. And in a low, wondering whisper, she repeated the statement we all had overheard.

"The Fool's journey ends on Sirius C."

Sunday
Morning
April 8

Wither the Amphibians

Five-Thirty A.M.

Bandaged in dirty clouds and seeping rabbit milk from a wound in its side, the sun rolls the stone from the tomb of night, to emerge—pale, blinking, but triumphant—into Easter's yard, somewhere between "Coca-Cola" and "IBMmmm." As you become more fully conscious and it dawns on you what day this is, your spirits are both gilded with hopes of resurrection and shaded by fears of sacrificial death; and this in spite of the fact that thanks to Q-Jo Huffington, Easter is a cipher to you now, another round hole into which the square peg of your conditioning cannot fit.

According to Q-Jo, Easter was an ancient pagan festival named for the Saxon goddess Eostre, Eostre being a regional pronunciation of Astarte, the principal creator/destroyer worshipped by Indo-European cultures for tens of thousands of years: Mother Nature in her fundamental, unexpurgated, paradoxical, bud-sprouting, blood-guzzling guise. Well, that old business—gone now and good riddance—is to your taste thoroughly barbaric, not to mention funky. It has the whiff of the atavistically agrarian about it; of wet wool, afterbirth, wood smoke, and dung heap. And sweat, tubs of stinking sweat; sweat of horse, sweat of husband, sweat of brutal labor and crude, unromantic coupling. Furthermore, even if one is not a puppet of the church, as you, much to Belford's chagrin, clearly are not, one would have to be pretty cynical to believe that early Christian spin doctors appropriated the Eostre festival in an effort both to usurp the charm it held for the peasant population and to weigh in with a manufactured miracle.

Oh, it might ring true to Larry Diamond, him with his rants   **219** about dental suppression and torched libraries in Africa somewhere; Diamond and Q-Jo are rather alike in that regard. One thing about Q-Jo, however, she is not one of those ninnies who goes about proclaiming that if we would only force God to submit to a sex-change operation, everything would be cake and pie in the land. Her opposition to latter-day goddess worship is the main reason the Huff has so few friends among others in her field. She contends that the Divine is no more female than male, that it is without gender, beyond gender; that while it may have its male and female aspects, those are merely two facets of the infinitely faceted infinitude it presents to the world, and that any impulse to ascribe gender to the Divine is a foolish display of chauvinism that vainly attempts to place limits on that which is limitless. Or words to that effect.

She makes sense on a certain level, you suppose, but why would people want to agitate themselves with unanswerable questions long out of date—unless, of course, it's their version of Washington's teeth. There's trouble enough these days just eluding violence and servicing one's debt. Concepts of God, celebrations of his and/or her holidays, have evolved over the centuries, have changed profoundly since their primitive beginnings, but the struggle to survive has remained constant. Survival: that's the bottom line, on Easter or any other day. The next line up is genteel survival; survival with authority, comfort, and good taste—a goal far easier to imagine today than in Eostre's time, although, as recent events have demonstrated, still maddeningly elusive.

Q-Jo also said, as long as you are on the subject, that if each of us, in secret, were allowed to ask God one question, absolutely nobody would ask, "Are you a man or a woman?" or "What color's your skin?" proving that issues of gender and race are ultimately trivial. Most likely, we would inquire of God: "Any chance of getting out of here alive?" "Where'll I be when I'm no longer around?" "Will I ever see so-and-so again?" "What's the punch line?" or "Cat got your tongue?"—questions we rarely ask one another because our intellectual betters consider them sophomoric and because we are privately unconvinced that any mortal, including clergy, can provide encouraging answers based upon more than circumstantial evidence.

Well, it's too early in the morning for this nonsense, although you must say you feel surprisingly refreshed. You slept fully clothed, there was a voice in your head louder than any dream, and at some point in the night you woke up and masturbated for the first time in so long even the mites can't remember it—traditionally, you have fantasized about Cary Grant while abusing yourself, but last night, when the white pony rode over the hill, you whispered a name that sounded suspiciously less like "Cary" than "Larry," an aberration you would just as soon forget—yet you are not merely rested but strengthened; prepared, you naively believe, for the events of the day.

You patter to the kitchen to pour yourself a glass of tomato juice. Inside the refrigerator are what are left of the eggs you purchased for Belford's breakfast on Friday. Were there children in your building, you might donate the eggs to their little festivities. Maybe Q-Jo is right about Easter. What could the coloring and hiding of feminine fertility symbols possibly have to do with the drama surrounding the crucifixion of Christ? Unless, perhaps, omelets were served at the Last Supper. Think of it, the most famous meal in history and nobody has a clue what was on the menu. It must drive gourmets wild. You and your brother hunted eggs once in your parents' drafty downtown loft. That unlikely Easter Bunny, Freddy Mati, painted them for you. Each one solidly, uniformly, existentially black.

FIVE-FIFTY A.M.

One thing is as clear as the bathwater in your sunrise soak: you have a choice between submitting to your fate, in which case you will end up either a jobless pauper or a marriage-license whore, or taking the

221

offensive. The latter involves, as you see it, an oil-futures play: betting that the price of crude will rise short-term, decline long-term; and placing that wager with the International Petroleum Exchange shortly after it opens for trading in London at one a.m. tomorrow, Seattle time. Should you elect to roll the petrol dice, there are a couple of possibilities. With Larry Diamond's help, you might be able to buy on margin, although since your credit is as thin as the gold on a pawn shop's balls, an electronic caper of that nature would be risky and a wee bit fraudulent. If it went awry somewhere, it could land you in the steel hotel. Considering your already shaky position, it would seem incumbent upon you to engage in a legitimate cash transaction. Of course, if your back were really to the wall. . . .

Nevertheless, you should investigate, at least, potential sources of cash. You glug an amber oyster of shampoo onto your head, and by the time you have lathered half your black hairs and two-thirds of the gray ones, you have run through the list.

One. Were you to unload, at a loss, every remaining instrument in your personal account, you might raise, at the most, nine or ten grand. Peanuts. Peewee peanuts. Dwarf juice, and you are not referring to some condensation of Sirius B.

Two. Belford, despite his foolhardy philanthropies, must still have funds salted away. He would have to. He is going to need money to live on while he is in school studying to be a stupid social worker. You would guess him to have upwards of a hundred, a hundred and fifty thou in a sweet little bank somewhere. But while he might be persuaded to part with a hunk of it to a threadbare, wild-eyed Lutheran missionary who recites Bible stories in a Midwestern monotone to the uninterested in, say, Timbuktu, fat chance of him lending any to you, although *you* would pay him back—with interest—in a matter of months, guaranteed.

Three. Lastly, there is Diamond himself. That was quite a wad he was flashing last night. The thing is, although he certainly is not ostentatious on any other level, it could have been a show roll. It could have been every cent he has in the world. With a loose cannon such as Diamond, one never knows. Like Milken and many of the other naughty boys of the eighties, the gifted bookies who were punished for being too good at capitalism for capitalism's own good, Diamond doubtlessly had many a fine sparkler concealed in his lunch bucket when he was bounced out of the emerald mine. True, he apparently has not worked in nearly a decade, he putts about on a rusty scooter, dresses like a grunge rocker, and lives under a bowling alley, but one could scarcely say conclusively or with conviction that he hasn't got a pretty pile of rubles in the cookie jar. Question is, would he be willing to do a deal with you? It is hard to imagine an old fire horse not responding to one last bell. Yet, Diamond seems totally and genuinely absorbed with other interests, strange matters that bespeak a loss of practical faculties, the festerings of an infirm mind. He might even be dangerous. To you, personally. He is so . . . so sexual! And not in a responsible or judicious way. Furthermore, he is—or is pretending to be—seriously ill: yet another complication.

Face it, Belford is the safer bet all around. You have never actually approached Belford about a loan before, so you cannot automatically assume he would refuse. Besides, there are ways to soften him up. Conversation about your alleged future together, for example, never mind if the promises are vague. And something that might *really* throw open every duct in his oozing heart would be your delivery to him, safe and sound, of his AWOL macaque. To that end, you decide—as with a soapy sponge you flush a tiny tumbleweed of lint from your belly button (a side effect of sleeping in one's clothes)—that you must hasten to a store where you might make a substantial investment in Popsicles of the banana-flavored ilk.

Yes, you will load your freezer, and your friends' freezers as well. You will reopen the transoms, yours and Q-Jo's, that you closed after yesterday's unlawful entries, and upon each transom you will deposit a Popsicle as lure. You will position banana Popsicles on

223

window ledges, where they will glisten like the teeth of heavy smokers; sow banana Popsicles about balconies, where they will glow like bug lights on a southern porch. Melting, they will perfume the neighborhood like one giant Harry Belafonte belch, and a certain little rascal, no more able to resist the musaceous nose-music than any model-building boy, will tarantella, yellow-lipped and sticky-furred, into your waiting trap.

With a final swipe of the sponge, you seal the self-addressed envelope between your legs. Then, toweled, powdered, creamed; dressed in gold-colored Christian Dior underwear, black medium-length wool skirt from Perry Ellis, and a navy blue Ralph Lauren sweater over a white silk shirt, you trot downstairs, only to be met at the front door by two very serious-looking uniformed policemen.

SIX-THIRTY A.M.

The first thing that crosses your mind is that the cops are here about Q-Jo: that she's in the hospital, in the morgue, in jail, in— Liar! Tell the truth, Gwendolyn. The first thing that crosses your mind is that there has been an audit at the disco, that Posner has jumped to conclusions, that without giving you an opportunity to explain, he has notified the SEC and called in the police. Only after those fears have jumped rope with your heart do you consider that there could be dire news about Q-Jo. In fairness, however, you utter no silent prayer that the authorities are here about her and not you. As it turns out, they are here about the Safe Sex Rapist.

The Safe Sex Rapist, so called because he wears a condom during every attack, has claimed twenty victims in the past thirty days. The pace of his raping is such that some Seattleites suspect it the work of more than one man (forgetting, perhaps, when they were young). The rich boys are frequently mentioned. Although the victims have been by no means exclusively homeless or poor, the rich boys have been mentioned by just about everybody except the mayor, city councilmen, and newspaper editors, who golf with

224

the rich boys' dads. At any rate, according to the cops at the door, the Safe Sex Rapist struck again last night, or rather early this morning, assaulting a late-shift nurse after she got off a bus on her way home from work. The rape, it seems, was interrupted in progress by a taxi driver, who gave chase in his cab when the attacker fled. Police joined in, and the rapist is believed to be cornered and hiding in your neighborhood.

"We're asking everyone in the area, especially women, to stay inside with their doors locked until we flush this partridge," one of the officers says.

"But it's light out now," you protest, "and I'm just going to the store. I'm just going to drive over to Queen Anne Thriftway."

"Sorry," says the cop. "Can't let you do that. This guy's still around here, and he's dangerous."

"Believe it, lady," says the other officer. "Hell, the Thriftway parking lot's where he abandoned his motor scooter."

Six Thirty-Three A.M.

Your heart trips on the jump rope and skins its elbows. "Oh, Jesus, oh no," you mutter.

"There a problem?"

"No. Yes. I mean, I know who it is."

"What say?"

"The rapist. I know who he is."

"Are you sure? How do you know him? He live here?"

"Look, it's a long story. But it's got to be him. It must be him. If I saw his vehicle I could say positively."

"Cecil," the senior of the two officers says, "why don't you flag Smokey and get him to drive you and her over to where the scooter is. I'll find the manager and have him warn the rest of the tenants here."

"Owners," you correct him.

"What?"

"We're owners in this building, not tenants."

"Yeah, okay, lady," says Cecil. "Come with me."

SIX THIRTY-NINE A.M.

The abandoned scooter, being loaded now into a police department van, is one of those fancy new sparkle and glitter Hondas, in a candy-apple color that your blush matches exactly, although without the metal flakes. "I'm sorry," you say. It doesn't take a detective to tell that you are less contrite than relieved, less relieved than embarrassed.

"It's okay. We all make mistakes." Smokey produces a pad and pen. "What's the suspect's name and address?"

"*What* suspect?"

"The guy you thought was the rapist."

"But it isn't him."

"You can't be certain of that. He coulda changed scooters."

From the patrol car radio, a voice slips the words, "Car Forty-seven," between two slices of static.

"Forty-seven."

"Forty-seven, we got a report there's a monkey running loose, disrupting the sunrise service at Kinnear Park. You respond?"

"Negative," replies Smokey. "No can do. You're aware we got a ten-sixty in progress. Call animal control, for Christ's sake."

"Roger, Forty-seven."

"Can you believe that? Taking us off a ten-sixty for a damn monkey?"

"I know who it is!"

"The rapist?"

"The monkey. I know that monkey."

The police officers look at each other and roll their eyes.

"You don't understand. It's a friend. I mean, it belongs to a friend of—"

226

"Lady," says Cecil, "I want you to get outta the car."

"But, really, I—"

"Out! Right now. You bug anybody around here, I'm running you into Harborview where you belong. I'd run you in right now if I had the frigging time." He taps his partner. "Let's roll, Smoke."

Barely have you slammed the door than Car 47, sirens ban-sheeing, lights star-spangled bannering, tears out of the Thriftway lot toward your once-thought-to-be-temporary neighborhood, leaving you to boil and bubble in a cioppino of outrage, humiliation, remorse, and one or two other all-too-familiar emotions.

Six Fifty-One A.M.

When the cashier invites you to have a nice day, you give her a look that leaves her wondering how a woman who just bought two dozen banana Popsicles could be in such a shitty mood.

Part of your foul disposition is due to the fact that now that you are in possession of a fair amount of monkey fodder, you are unsure how to distribute it. Apparently, André has been amusing himself at the expense of the pious in Kinnear Park, but by the time you walked over there, both he and the worshippers would probably be gone, for the sun is shinnying up the eastern quadrant faster than a Peeping Tom up a sorority house drainpipe. Even were the Easter service still in progress, you hardly could stroll into its midst wagging yellow ice on a stick without attracting the wrong kind of attention, the kind that might bring Cecil and Smokey back into your life. Anyhow, rather than go chasing after André, a proposition designed for futility and slapstick, it would be wiser to let him come to you. The problem here is that you cannot at this time return to your building, albeit a scant ten-minute walk, because your block is sealed off, two or more squad cars at every intersection. The path to Belford's is clear, however, and it soon becomes equally clear that

227

since you had planned all along to seed his place with Popsicle bait, hoofing to Belford's is your only logical option.

On your way there, shivering ever so slightly in the morning chill, although the temperature is actually several degrees too warm for the optimum health of your cargo, you cannot help but puzzle over André's reported presence at the sunrise service. Coincidence? An act of rebellion? Or was he drawn there because there is some validity to this "born again" . . . ? No, no, no. Ridiculous. Animals, even intelligent animals—perhaps most especially intelligent animals—do not share man's pathetic need to socialize bliss, codify awe, pigeonhole the Mystery, and tame the Divine. For an ape, born twice is entirely redundant, since an ape gets it right the first time. At least, that is how Q-Jo has put it. Personally, you haven't a clue in spiritual matters, but you do know, or deeply suspect, that a monkey who once mingled with aristocrats in Swiss ski resorts and movie stars on the French Riviera, would find the company of Seattle Lutherans drab, dour, and dorky beyond all belief.

Seven-Ten A.M.

As evidenced by an overturned cookie jar and an open freezer door, André has stopped by home at least once in Belford's absence. Encouraged, you place three or four Popsicles in the freezer, and with the remainder of the first box, Hansel and Gretel a trail leading from the garage roof to the balcony to a broom closet in which, with a swift slamming of a door, a greedy little macaque could be surprised and contained. Satisfied, although scarcely overconfident—you are all too aware that the infamous simian jewel thief is nobody's fool—you take a seat in Belford's favorite armchair. Using a remote, you switch on the radio and tune it to KIRO so that you will be immediately informed when the manhunt in your neighborhood has ended. On the seven-fifteen report, you learn that the rapist remains at large somewhere in your quarantined block. You also learn, a moment later, that Dr. Yamaguchi has called a press conference for ten o'clock, presumably, the announcer speculates, to explain his behavior last evening. As well he might. Good grief!

Thoughts of the sake-sodden scientist lead, like an abbreviated trail of synaptic Popsicles, to thoughts of Larry Diamond. Soon you yourself are shut in a closet, a closet of guilt. How close you came to officially accusing Diamond of serial rape, how eager you were to name his name! If those suspicions were unjustified, even irresponsible, could the same not be said for your willingness to lay Q-Jo's disappearance at his feet? To some extent, it is his own fault for allowing lewd impulses to rule him, for forsaking decorum, for behaving like a nut and a goat. Nevertheless, he is ill and in pain— dying, for all you know—and you have wronged him. You have borne him false witness.

How badly do you feel about it? Not badly enough to confess and apologize. What the oversexed lunatic doesn't know won't hurt him. Yeah, but what if on some level he does know? Ever since he's been "on the pad," whatever in marginal hell *that* is, he's had the ability to highjack dreams and burglarize thoughts. It seems to you, slumped in Belford's monkey-soiled chair, the second box of Popsicles thawing on your lap, that you ought either to have a talk with Diamond soon or else avoid him like the IRS for the rest of your life.

In less than nine minutes, a radio-dispatched taxi arrives at Belford's building. The driver looks bewildered and mutters in Sanskrit or Aramaic or Urdu when you say, "Thunder House, please," but you straighten it out, and when, after no more than the usual amount of wrong turns and near collisions, he deposits you at the Thunderbird Bowl, you hand him, in lieu of a tip, the carton that is now rather soggy with a flowery yellow sweat. "For your children," you say generously, thinking all the while that these undisciplined Third World types invariably have stockpiles of progeny.

To fair Natalie, who sashays out of Thunder House just as you approach its door, you—so olive of skin and iodine of eye—probably look like the cabdriver's wife.

229

Seven Fifty-Seven A.M.

For several tense seconds, you and Natalie fire tracers into each other's orbs, you thinking, *espresso bimbo!* Natalie thinking, *prissy witch!* —then you spin around and start back up the ramp.

"Gwendolyn! Wait!"

You slow down and glance over your shoulder, but you don't actually halt your retreat until you hear Diamond say, "Natalie, I want you to meet Gwen Mati, the woman I inexplicably yet inescapably love."

Midway up the ramp, a trifle stunned, you stand with your hands on your hips, defiant but intrigued, curious whether the lecher and his tramp are sharing a joke at your expense, whether Diamond is toying with both you *and* Natalie, or whether he is sincere; and if he is sincere, whether he is in or out of his mind.

"I guess that explains it," Natalie says.

A sharp twitch fishhooks the left corner of Diamond's appeasing smile.

"Well," adds Natalie, "at least now I know it wasn't *me.*"

"Distracted," says Diamond meekly.

"For sure." Natalie sighs.

"Don't let me interrupt anything," you say, your sarcasm an inch thicker than hers.

"You already did," says Natalie. "Hours ago." With a toss of her blond head, she propels herself up the incline. As she brushes past you, reeking, you think, like a cat-food casserole, she says, "I hope you guys live happily ever after."

"We promise," calls Larry cheerfully. "You can count on us."

"Look, I only wanted to give Mr. Diamond a brief message," you say, but the waitress proceeds expediently to a Japanese minicar that looks as if it has been kicked at least once by Godzilla, leaving you to face that philandering bastard at the foot of the ramp, who is now petitioning you with a grin that a sheep could use as a paperweight.

HALF ASLEEP in FROG PAJAMAS

"Timbuktu. The end of everybody's road. The capital of Nowhere. Geography's perennial avant-garde and the armchair traveler's inevitable cul-de-sac. Timbuktu. Hometown of mystery, fugitivity's final refuge, remote crossroads where Obscurity runs into Exotica, and Daydream and Exile intersect. Timbuktu. The far of which there is no farther. Out there. Gone. Closer to the moon than to New Jersey. Rivaled by only Katmandu as the planet's most musical city-poem. Tim-buk-tu. One of the phonetic wonders of the world. Great place to pronounce but you wouldn't want to live there."

No, indeed, you certainly *wouldn't* want to live there. You wouldn't want to spend a minute and a half in Timbuktu. You hadn't planned to spend much more than a minute and a half in Thunder House, for that matter—"I was in the neighborhood, so I just stopped by to tell you that Yamaguchi's holding a press conference at ten o'clock"—but Diamond had coaxed you inside (on the round heels of that coffee house strumpet) after finally convincing you that if you looked at his slides of Timbuktu, they might offer some insight into Q-Jo's disappearance. He had led you into a spacious, dimly lit room, unfurnished except for a cushy butterscotch leather sofa but whose floors were covered with the richest, most gorgeous, and probably expensive Oriental carpets you had ever seen and whose walls were adorned with African masks, several presumably meant to represent frogs. He had set you on the sofa (which you sniffed for traces of Natalie), served you mint tea (drugged? you wondered), switched on the slide projector, and now has you thoroughly and unwillingly hypnotized—yes, *hypnotized*, there is no other word for it—by his strange manner of speaking.

"Timbuktu. The last pure place. Isolation being the mother of purity. All men are jealous of Timbuktu because Timbuktu is removed from men, it's the wholeness men have fractured, the sacred extreme they've traded away. Like Hell, like Heaven, Timbuktu is a place in the brain, a place whose existence may be often doubted

231

but never dismissed. Timbuktu. A constellation by which the imagination can navigate, the joker that haunts the map-maker's deck."

EIGHT THIRTY-THREE A.M.

You may be hypnotized, but you aren't gregarious. You maintain an aloof distance from your host, not even bothering to ask how he is feeling—he felt well enough to spend the night with Natalie, didn't he?—and when he illuminates the first slide and it appears to be an empty, limitless ocean formed by the melting of trillions of banana Popsicles, you snort, "Huh. No wonder Timbuktu's so hard to find," implying that there's no there there.

"That, my dear, is the Sahara. Empty, yes; barren, yes; fierce and deceptively featureless, but, I assure you, unforgettable."

"Yeah, I suppose. If you like beige."

Diamond moves on to the next slide, which is virtually the same. "As vast as it looks in this picture, this is merely a sample. You could fit the entire United States, including Alaska, into the Sahara and have room left over for Q-Jo's groceries."

"All that sand. What a waste of real estate."

"It's as much stone as it is sand, believe it or not. And twice in its history it was covered by water. Frogs and fishes used to swim in there, Gwendolyn. Turtles and crocodiles. Their skeletons are all over the place."

"How nice."

"When the great deserts and the great oceans get bored, they just switch places. Fortunately for us, it doesn't happen every Saturday night. They have a lot in common, the deserts and the seas. For our purposes, short-term and long-term, the sea is more important, but I do have a fondness for the desert. It shows us how beautiful the Earth would be if men weren't on it. The Sahara may be the only place left that we haven't fucked up. When you look at it, you get an idea what the planet was like before our ancestors hopped out of the

232

soup, and what it'll look like when we've hopped back in. Metaphorically or literally. More tea?"

"Thank you, no. Timbuktu, is it in that desert somewhere?"
Subconsciously, you are wishing he would revive the hypnosis.

"Not yet. It will be." He brings up yet a third view of parched
basins, cinder cones, yellow dunes.

"Timbuktu is moving?"

"It's the Sahara that's moving. Going south like a homesick
bluesman. Even as we speak, the desert's sucking the toes of Timbuktu, although hardly as adoringly as I'd suck yours. The fact is, the
Sahara's gradually swallowing Timbuktu. As delectable as you are,
pussy cakes, I'd never eat you alive."

"You're a gentleman, Larry. I admire your restraint. Can we
please get on with it?"

"You're always wanting to get on with it. Are you aware that
rushing toward a goal is a sublimated death wish? It's no coincidence
we call them 'deadlines.' The Sahara'd be good for a hustler like you.
If the sea teaches us humility, the desert teaches us patience. Timbuktu's never in a hurry. And you and I aren't going to rush into
Timbuktu. We agreed, I believe, that I'd show you the slides in the
exact sequence that I showed them to Q-Jo. Which means, I'm
afraid, our entry into Timbuktu is at least a quarter hour away. First
we have to spend some time with . . ."

Snickersnee. Diamond changes slides, and a broad, shallow river
comes into view.

". . . the Bozo."

Eight Forty-Four A.M.

Mali, not to be confused with Bali, and certainly not with Malibu or
Maui, is a largish, generally arid, landlocked nation in northwestern
Africa. For six centuries, roughly from 1000 until 1600, Timbuktu
was Mali's richest, most powerful city; one of the richest, most
powerful—and learned—cities outside of the well-traveled, "civi-

lized" world. The success of this remote oasis was entirely due to its position at the southern terminus of the trans-Saharan caravan routes combined with its proximity to the Niger River. Upon the Niger, salt, spices, slaves, cloth, and manuscripts that the camel caravans exchanged for gold in Timbuktu could be transported by riverboat all the way to the Atlantic.

"The Niger," intones Diamond, "the mighty Niger looks like a question mark drawn by a left-handed octogenarian dipsomaniac, a most fitting shape since European geographers went batty questioning its source, its mouth, and its course. The Niger is eccentrically shaped and flows in the opposite direction from what a knowledgeable person might expect. I assure you, many an explorer landed in an early grave trying to make sense of the Niger. Their efforts weren't helped by the fact that this baby is twenty-six hundred miles long and there was a fresh disease and a new hostility waiting around every bend. What we're seeing are views along the five-hundred-mile stretch that runs from Bamako, the capital, northeastward to near Timbuktu. This is Bozo water."

"Bozo water," you mutter under your breath. A perfect name for that artificially carbonated tap water many U.S. bottlers pass off as *eau minérale*. As Diamond advances the slides, you are treated to picturesque scenes of natives in long, low dugout canoes, each one poled, rather than paddled, by a solitary poler who stands in the stern. Some of the pirogues appear to be means of public conveyance, others are cargo vessels, and others, perhaps the majority, fishing boats. There is much casting and drawing of nets.

"They're Egyptians originally, the Bozo are. For some reason, they gave up on the Nile and migrated all the way to the Niger about five thousand years ago. A tiny nation of riverine folk who brought with them an Egyptian language that they continue to speak and a complex animistic, highly ritualized religion that despite Islamic inroads they continue to practice. The hub of this religion is the Dog Star, Sirius."

"Sitting trouser."

"Yes. Ha-ha. Sitting trouser." He regards you with genuine admiration. "Lately, though, I've started to wonder if that wasn't a mistranslation. Maybe the Bozo called Sirius 'sitting bowser.'"

"Wuf," you bark, prompting Diamond to reward you with a smile that could paint a doghouse.

Up close, the Bozo are nothing if not disappointing. Apparently, you were expecting a race of displaced Tuts and Cleopatras, but with the exception of their relatively fine features, they more closely resemble Mississippi sharecroppers than mystic Egyptians. The men are in dirty T-shirts, plastic sandals, and cotton pants that might have been plucked off a bargain counter at Kmart and run through a shredder. Although the women wear the traditional, long, brightly patterned dresses of West Africa, the garments are wrinkled and torn. Sacred robes and celestial adornments are nowhere to be seen, and if there are temples, they are indistinguishable from the poor huts that cluster on the riverbanks, awash in a secondary river of naked children, skinny chickens, and mud.

"I can see you're less than knocked sockless," Diamond says. "Soon we'll be moving along to the Dogon, whom I suspect you'll find more impressive. Almost everyone does."

The Dogon are cliff dwellers who reside in secluded pueblos, caves, and strange clay towers along a mammoth escarpment that rears out of the sunbaked savanna some hard, harsh miles from the Niger. Their ancestors fled to this forbidding natural barrier to escape foreign influences, and the Dogon have proven fiercely resistant to modern mores, pan-Malian assimilation, and Islamic conversion. It strikes you, from Diamond's pictures, that the Dogon dress with no more flair than the Bozo, and, frankly, you had rather be laid out stiff in any well-maintained American cemetery than be alive and salubrious in a milieu so devoid of comfort and chic. You agree, however, that the Dogon's masks and wooden figures, their elaborately carved doorposts and altars, and their bizarre booga-booga dance costumes are more impressive, in a cultural sense, than the muddy fundamentals of the Bozo.

"Were these people originally Egyptians, too?" you ask, motivated less by curiosity than an attempt to make polite conversation. Diamond's slide show reminds you of an ethnological documentary on public television, and, to be honest, you have always preferred to watch those old movies in which nimble dandies soft-shoe in top hat and tails and everybody sips champagne.

"No, as a matter of fact, the Dogon migrated down from Libya, where they might have been descended from shipwrecked Greeks. There's a theory that they were the lost crew of the *Argo*, who, when they couldn't get home to Greece, intermarried with black Libyans."

"You don't say?"

"Gwendolyn?"

"Yes?"

"Are you by any chance thinking of Fred Astaire?"

"Why, no. Where would you get an idea like that?"

"Never mind. The Argonauts, before they wrecked, were searching for the Golden Fleece. Right? You know all this, you're an educated woman. It's rumored you have an MBA. At any rate, the Golden Fleece is a celestial symbol. It refers to the stars in the constellation Canis Major—the hair of the dog, so to speak—which was directly above the oracular center of Colchis when the golden meadow colchicum, or false saffron, an important medicinal plant in the ancient Mediterranean, came annually into bloom there. Sirius A is the big box-office boffo celebrity star in Canis Major, of course, but it's Sirius B that's important to the Dogon. And the Bozo. They share the same mythologies, the Dogon and Bozo. Among the Dogon, the rituals are more perfectly preserved, and the ritualistic objects more plentiful and aesthetically refined, but my heart ticks louder for the Bozo for the simple reason that they've remained so loyal to the water world. They're consummate river folk. The first toys a Bozo child are given are fish bones and fish heads. They eat what swims and are themselves strong swimmers. A Bozo believes the crocodile is his father, and he claims to have a blood pact with the crocs: a Bozo doesn't hunt crocodiles, and crocodiles don't hunt Bozo. Witnesses swear it's true. From that alone, it's obvious Bozos have maintained closer bonds with the Nommo than the Dogon have, but I don't suppose you want to get into that."

The Nommo, huh? Well, as a matter of fact, you do have a mild interest in that subject after the fright that ridiculous card gave you and all, but what you truly want is for Diamond to complete his presentation—which so far has afforded not the softest hint of why Q-Jo might have fled Thunder House—so that you can solicit his advice on an oil futures play. Naturally, he will insist that any market play is trivial and a waste of time and consciousness, but he could be quite helpful with the mechanics of the deal. Also, you need to get back to Belford's to check if there has been a nibble on your monkey line. Whether there has or has not, you wish now to turn your own apartment into Rancho Popsicle because of the stronger impact it possibly will have on Belford should you impound André in your place instead of his.

"No?" says Diamond. "No Nommo? A pity. Well, okay, you can lead a toad to water, but you can't make her think. Let's move along then to Timbuktu."

"Good," you say curtly. You would bet your last battered share of Union Carbide that thinking about Bozo Nommo mumbo jumbo was not something he required of Natalie.

NINE A.M.

"Timbuktu. A town made of pastry dough and starlight. A mirage you can walk around in—if you can stand the heat. Solitary, sealed, and shuttered, it wears a mask beneath a mask behind a veil. Timbuktu. A dehydrated Venice, crumbling into a plexus of dust canals. Conceived when the sphinx lay down with the goldbug at a campsite half as old as time. The Sahara crackles in every bite of its bread, the ashes of dead books blow through its streets; the lost wisdom of a dozen races is buried under its drifts, never to be jiggled by the archaeologist's spade. Timbuktu. A city only an adventurer would risk, only a romantic would forgive, only a nomad would find inviting, only a camel could love."

Babble, hypnotic crackpot babble. But Diamond is right about one thing: Timbuktu *does* look as if it's made of cookie dough and starlight. Which is not to say it is sweet or radiant or even slightly appealing. It has a definite mystique, all right, due primarily to the audacity with which it occupies the void, boldly existing where no city ought to be; and to the sheer exoticness of its architecture, the oddly organic jumble of boxlike clay houses, stacked atop and against one another like something a compulsive child might construct, a child who could not imagine spires, arches, or domes, yet is imbued with enough childish whimsy to paint every third or fourth door a brilliant blue. But undercutting that mystique is the sheer empty starkness of the place, the tan monochrome relieved only occasionally by a winking blue door, the stillness so still that even the slides convey it: had Diamond employed a movie camera the effect would have been the same—a ghost town that will not quite give up the ghost, a place where people spend their lives listening to the wind blow.

"You're not the first to be disappointed," says Diamond, as if reading your mind again. "All through the Middle Ages, Timbuktu signified to Europeans some kind of tantalizing out-of-reach magnificence, a magical but entirely tangible city of wealth, sophistication, intrigue, and learning; a dreamy shopping mall, as it were, where you could buy salt, pepper, unicorn horns, tarot cards, books, virgins, eunuchs, dwarfs, and carpetbags of unrefined ore; where you could cavort in luxuriant roof gardens with your newly purchased slave girl and speak with scholars or holy men on every street corner. Ah, yes. But when the first white men began to actually zero in on the place in the nineteenth century, it was at least three hundred years past its prime. The palaces had crumbled, the bazaars had closed, the library and university had been torched. Fully expecting to be rolling in gold dust, the honkies got a faceful of hot sand instead. The African Eldorado. Yes, indeed. Are you aware, my dear, that Marlon Brando called the inside of a camel's mouth the ugliest thing in the world?"

"Why?"

"Why? Peel back their lips and you'll soon enough. . . ."

"No, no, Larry. For Christ's sake. I mean, Timbuktu, if it was so rich and glamorous, why did it turn into this, this—boneyard?"

"You might ask the same thing about Wall Street. Things run their course in the material world. Specifically, if you must know, Timbuktu started to decline after European traders landed on the west coast of Africa in the fifteenth century and provided an alternative to the trans-Saharan caravan routes; and then the town got its brains knocked out, literally, when it was overrun by Moroccan mercenaries and fundamentalist bushwhackers in 1591. But events such as those are just the vehicles change likes to ride around in. Evolution drives a bulldozer disguised as a stationary bike. With history, it's the other way around."

Could it be, you wonder, Diamond's non sequiturs aside, that you are, indeed, like those European explorers? That you set out optimistically to partake of the wealth of a fabled land, only to arrive, after much hardship, when your destination was well past its prime? Obviously, the days of giddy prosperity are over, but is the decline by any chance permanent? Are America's once-powerful financial centers destined to sink deeper and deeper into a spreading economic Sahara until one day, ten, twenty years from now, they are, relatively speaking, mud-ball villages whose inhabitants, including you, have nothing better to do than contemplate their obsolescence and listen to the wind blow?

"Or watch the stars."

"Pardon?"

"Listen to the wind blow—I'm reading you like an ad in the personals today, aren't I—or watch the stars." Diamond refills your teacup. "You know, even these days travelers arrive in Timbuktu expecting, I don't know, something epiphanic, phantasmagorical, and leave feeling cheated, bitching that there's nothing there. But maybe it isn't a matter of there being nothing there. Maybe they just don't know what to look for."

"Everybody's not a mind reader like you, Larry. What could they realistically look for? Where could they look?"

"Oh, they might begin with the university. Timbuktu does have a university again, and I can assure you, it's in a class by itself. Taught me a thing or two. Yes, indeed. A genuine thing or two." *Snickersnee, snickersnee.* He advances the slides rapidly in a staccato blur, finally pausing at a scene of a high, dun-colored wall. Timbuktu is not a walled city, a fact that surprises you, considering its legendary mysteriousness, but on the outskirts of town, there are several walled compounds, one of which, evidently, is some kind of school. A subsequent scene depicts an elaborate wrought-iron gate, opening on a courtyard resplendent with banana plants, flowering trees, and, believe it or not . . .

"A pond?"

"Yes. Did you think in a place where the moon looms so large, there wouldn't be frogs to praise it? Timbuktu is, after all, an oasis."

The next slide reveals a largish, squarish, two-story building, made of clay in the Sudanese style and sporting blue shutters (closed) on the second floor. With its shady green courtyard, it is somewhat of a retreat, you would imagine, from the bleak alleyways and sun-fried sandpile surrounding it (an oasis within an oasis), but it's a poor excuse for a university. You are about to say as much when, *snickersnee,* Diamond pushes the button and brings up another view of the gate, this time with a group of a dozen or more Westerners posing formally in front of it.

"The faculty?" you ask.

"Yes and no. Yes and no. That's Robert Anton Wilson, front row, left end; and on *his* left is Terence McKenna, Diane di Prima, and, I believe, John Lilly. You can recognize Timothy Leary in the back row next to Carlos Castaneda—only extant picture of him, by the way—and there's Andrei Codrescu, Ted Joans, uh, Rupert Sheldrake, Fritjof Capra, R. D. Laing, and, well, several mathematicians, quantum physicists, and artists you probably never heard of."

"I never heard of the others, either," you say, somewhat un-
truthfully, because you seem to recall Q-Jo—or was it your parents?
—mentioning a few of those names.

"Needless to say, these luminaries aren't in residence full-time.
The non-Africans come and go virtually at random. And always in
secret. They do lecture now and then, they present papers, and
seldom hesitate to speak out in class—if one could call them 'classes'
—but they seem to be there to study as much as to teach. Teachers
or students, it's hard to draw the line. But they aren't faculty per se.
Here . . ."

Snickersnee.

". . . is the faculty."

Same gate, same pose, same number of people, give or take
one or two, but this group is pigmented in various shades of cinna-
mon and asphalt and dressed in various examples of African fashion,
from white robes and turbans to white linen suits, from jazzy two-
piece patterned ensembles to loincloths, from flowing dashikis to
animal skins.

"Shamans, soothsayers, griots, and big boohoos," says Diamond. "Tell me, how do you suppose this faculty would rate your
MBA?"

You don't answer because you aren't listening. Ever since you
thought of Q-Jo, you have been refocusing on the reasons you are
attending this stupid Easter morning show-and-tell in the first place.
"Larry," you say, "a few minutes ago you mentioned that tarot cards
were sold in Timbuktu in the, uh, Middle Ages, I believe it was. Did
you mention that to Q-Jo, as well? I'm just wondering if that
might've sparked something, if there's a clue there or. . . ."

In the semidarkness, you can detect cocktail onions of sweat
popping out on Diamond's brow, you can actually feel his sudden
fever. "I . . . I can't remember right offhand." He shudders. "You'll
have to excuse me. I've got to go to the bathroom, as denatured
Americans insist on saying, although their particular mission rarely
involves the act of bathing."

He lurches away and vanishes in the gloom.

241

Nine Twenty-Eight A.M.

Face it, Gwen, you are slow. You are slower than zombies playing Monopoly, a nursing home sack race, Christmas in Saudi Arabia. You are so slow that if you jumped out of a plane, the plane would land before you did. You are so slow that a full five minutes pass before—before what should have been immediately, horrifyingly obvious finally occurs to you. When it does, it sloshes the tea out of your cup and the adrenaline out of your adrenals.

Spell it out, Sherlock, lay it on the table: less than forty-eight hours ago, Q-Jo Huffington was seated on this very same couch looking at this identical slide when Larry Diamond excused himself to visit the toilet, as he has done once again as if on cue, and in his exactly similar absence, something happened to Q-Jo, something drastic, something that caused her to vanish from the face of the earth. This is more than coincidence, beyond déjà vu, this is history deliberately repeating itself, with one terrible step left to go.

Nine-Thirty A.M.

For a long moment, you just sit, hands trying to steady the teacup on its quaking saucer, eyes wide and fused to the screen, as if some member of the faculty of the University of Timbuktu might call out and advise you what to do. Then, abruptly, you spring to your feet, dashing the carpet with tea, and like a t'ai chi novice with both feet in a bear trap, whirl awkwardly around. No one had been creeping up on you. The room is empty. And, except for the faint, nervous hum of the slide projector, quiet. Dead quiet.

You stand there, on guard, fighting to clear the panic and gather your thoughts. Like some instant creepy cream of cholesterol, some cellular duck fat clotted by epinephrine, fear has clogged your mental conduits. All you can think of is that whatever happened to Q-Jo Huffington, you must not allow it to happen to you.

It occurs to you, naturally, to make a run for the door, but you automatically reject the notion of running, on the grounds that to be caught running would be an embarrassment. (Better dead than red, eh, Gwen?) Setting the cup and saucer on the sofa, you commence to *stroll* toward the door, just strolling nonchalantly, *dum-dum-di-dum*, trying not to interpret every awful shadow, thrown by every African mask, as a lunatic with a knife. Separating the huge living room from the front door is a small vestibule, and as you stroll into the vestibule, arms innocently swinging, *dum-dum-di-dum*, you notice that an interior door opens into it, and light is seeping over the doorsill. It's the bathroom! Which you must pass to reach the exit.

You hesitate. What if this is a trap? Whether an insidious trap with harmful consequences or one of Diamond's ostensibly instructive practical jokes, in either case the very notion of it infuriates you. Cold globs of fear start to dissolve in a hot acid bath of anger. As you rummage in your purse for your trusty can of Mace, you can sense your trumpet bending upward at an angle that would have made Gillespie dizzy.

NINE THIRTY-FOUR A.M.

Tiptoeing now, Mace at the ready, you steal past the bathroom. Just let him try something! Your heart is pounding against your sternum like a landlord's fist against your daddy's jambs, but so great is your fury and defiance that you are almost sorry when you reach the exit without interference.

You pause. Are you absolutely sure you want to vamoose? Yes. Yes, you are. You aren't merely fleeing a disagreeable situation, you may well be escaping with your life. Go on. Get out of here!

Alas, the handle will not turn. In any direction. You yank, you twist, you pull, you push, all for naught, because the door is locked tighter than a prude's lips. In vain, you search for a latch of some sort. Apparently, you have been locked in with a key.

Slowly, you release the frozen handle and turn around. Nothing has changed. Thunder House remains empty, dim, and quiet.

Around the corner, in the living room, the slide projector buzzes like a bug in a jar. On your left, six feet away, a hem of light continues to show beneath the bathroom door.

Your options, it strikes you, are limited. You could look for a phone and play 911 roulette. (These days, the calls for help are myriad, the responses few.) You could seek assistance from that Native American, that Twister character, assuming Twister is on the premises and is not a party to whatever it is that is happening here. You could simply stand in the vestibule and await Diamond's next move, allowing him to determine your fate. Or you could take the initiative, go on the offensive, become a boiler room broker in the bucket shop of life. In your current state of exasperation, the last choice seems inevitable.

With a toss of your rapidly graying hair, and with a squeaky, kittenish version of a battle cry forming in your throat, you charge the bathroom door and throw it open, ready to Mace the bastard from here to Timbuktu.

NINE THIRTY-SEVEN A.M.

Nothing in your experience, not even Bosch's *Temptation of Saint Anthony*, a reproduction of which your mother tacked to your nursery wall and whose inexhaustible grotesqueries in your earliest years you were obliged to watch in lieu of television (until Grandma Mati, crossing herself like a motorized bandoleer, ripped it down), no, nothing, not even the pit at the Chicago Board of Trade, has prepared you for the tableau you have now intruded upon in Larry Diamond's toilet.

Naked below the waist, Diamond is on his hand and knees on a handsome, and probably expensive, Afghani kilim, busily stuffing green leaves up his rectum.

"Jesus!" you gasp. The erstwhile genius of the Pacific Northwest equities market looks like an incomplete mutant, an alien life-form from a homemade sci-fi movie, a kind of cut-rate half-man, half-plant crawling to a garden-store Bethlehem to be born. Either that or he's acting out a nightmare in which he gives live birth to a Caesar salad. "Jesus!"

"I don't believe I rang for the maid," says Diamond matter of factly, cocking his head to one side and gazing up at you.

Thoroughly mortified, you commence to retreat, walking backward, geisha-style: steps tiny, mincing and close together, punctuated by meek, apprehensive bows; and all the while conceal-ing the Mace canister behind your back like a bottle of inferior sake. Diamond signals you to stay, although the process by which he signals is somewhat fuzzy, considering that he is busily impersonat-ing a three-legged dog trying to free its haunches from an azalea bush. "Forgive my primitive presentation," he appeals, but it is not easy to summarily absolve a pantsless man who wears a wicked grin on one end and skunk cabbage on the other.

"It's my therapy," he explains. "Big medicine." He releases the wad of leaves he was applying to his rump, letting it fall to the floor, and picks up a fresh batch from a sheet of damp newspaper. "Here," he says, sensing that you are about to Madame Butterfly toward the vestibule again. He hands you the soppy bouquet for your reluctant scrutiny. "Twister's daddy sends me these specimens of Oklahoma's finest flora. Big medicine."

"This is what you're using to treat your—your . . ."

"My cancer? Yes. Yes, indeed. Wide Place in the Road is a celebrated healer, although I'm forced to say his herbal prescription seems to be losing its effectiveness where my particular infirmity is concerned. Maybe I should try smoking the stuff."

Jesus, you say to yourself. *The poor, poor guy. How could I ever have thought . . . ?*

Your heart, which is already going out to him, receives both a prod and a caution when, lifting the leaves closer to your face, you detect that they release an aroma like burnt sugar, caramel, or tinned fruit cocktail.

Nine Forty-One A.M.

"You-you-you must be in pain," you stammer, feeling that you should probably wipe his brow or something, but you've got the wet leaves in one fist and the Mace in the other, and you are a trifle uncertain, in any case, whether you want to lay a comforting hand on him or excuse yourself on a permanent basis.

"Oh, it's a bit like camping on a blowtorch, but everybody's got a hard-luck story. They warn us when we're kids that we're going to have to suffer, but they neglect to mention the indignity. What self-respecting fetus, if shown its future as a proctology patient, boot-camp recruit, or game-show contestant, would still elect to be born?" He looks away, and you seize the opportunity to drop the Mace into a laundry basket. "Of course," he continues, "a big front *does* have a big back. Yamaguchi, that old rascal, could turn out to be my hero if he plays his cards right. Meanwhile, it seems, I'm on my knees."

"How-how bad is it?" You inch a geisha step closer to him.

"It only hurts when I don't laugh," he says. With that, he raises up on his knees, whereupon you find yourself looking directly at his —his what-do-you-call-it. And with its single epicanthic eye, it is looking back at you! Immediately, you are struck by how, how altogether *elegant* it appears. When compared with Belford's, that is. Belford's penis, while probably exceeding Diamond's in length and breadth, is a wrinkly, crooked, blood-gorged thing that so reminds you of a boiled turkey neck that you scarcely can bear to look at it. Diamond's shaft, on the other hand, is like an alabaster gun barrel— smooth, straight, and lunar white—while its crown resembles a satin apple, a rosy cross between a virgin pincushion, a tulip bulb, and the head of a bubble gum cobra. And if it is a cobra, you are the charmer's flute, for wherever you move, in your nervous shuffling, it follows, swaying, dancing, holding you in hazardous regard.

Blushing as violently as you have ever blushed in your life, you are nevertheless fascinated, mesmerized by the grace and polish of his stalwart member every bit as much as you were mesmerized by

246

his feverish monologues. Furthermore, your knees feel like they're made out of helium and chicken broth, and when Diamond reaches up to take you by the wrist, they not only feel weaker yet, one knee seems to want to go east, the other west, as if to provide more space for the patch of moisture that is starting to spread in your underpants, accompanied by a melting sensation akin to that that the banana Popsicles must be experiencing here and there in Belford's apartment.

Diamond draws you closer. The next thing you know, you are on *your* knees. First shyly, then wholeheartedly, your lips collide. When his warm tongue explodes into your mouth, where it darts about like a hooked trout, where it turns your own tongue around and over, and over and around, like a cutlet in the grip of a zealous meat inspector, where it brushes and lathers and frescoes your palate ceiling like a mouse-sized Michelangelo wired on espresso; when that transpires, you fling the mess of leaves—ovate and lanceolate, peltate and perfoliate, orbicular and deltoid—against the wall, the toilet bowl, the side of the tub. Within seconds, you have replaced the vegetable matter with his . . . *O God!* Never have your fingers closed around anything so glossy and stiff and alive. So alive it is almost sonorous, so alive it is all you can do to hold on to it. It is as if you have grabbed a length of cable of such high voltage that it bucks, hisses, and sparks in your grip.

You feel his hand—somehow you sense it's the one with the arcane tattoo—spider up your skirt. This is followed by the unmistakable sound of fabric in distress. Out of the corner of your eye, you see the shreds of your panties go flying by. It is the last thing you see, for like a teenager so blinded by those squirmy red winds of lust and longing (the ones that sirocco out of the chlorine pots of the soul) that concepts such as "disease," "pregnancy," or "humiliation" fade to black, you redundantly squeeze your eyes shut and roll slowly onto your spine, emitting little whimpering noises like a puppy in a snowbank.

What is he waiting for? Oh, yes, of course: the condom. How irresponsible of you to forget. But what is he saying? Down between your legs, you hear him growling, grunting, aahing, oohing, muttering. "This is more than a vagina, this is a *monstre sacré*! This is the pothole in which empires break their axles. These are the gates Samson couldn't pull down. The grin of the mollusk. The anthill of the miraculous!" And so forth.

Good grief! You open your eyes, only to snap them shut again when you feel his long tongue swab you from your anus to your belly button. O God! What is he doing? You have heard about this from that filthy-minded Q-Jo, but never in your life . . . ! Your entire body quivers as he licks your vulva, you cry aloud when his tongue snakes in and out of you; and when, ever so tenderly, he takes your clitoris between his teeth—O God!

A moment later, his face—glistening with the brine of the portable tide pool—is above your face, kissing your eyelids open, and you feel his stiffness, slowly, slowly, inch by impudent inch, sliding into you, pushing rapture ahead of it like an embolus.

It is then that the whole building shakes, causing a toothbrush to fall off a shelf and bounce on the kilim beside your head; and your ears are filled with a series of rumblings and crashes, like the sounds of distant battle, and you think, *It's true, the earth does move!*

But wait a second. That noise. That noise. It sounds familiar. . . . Diamond smiles fatalistically, brakes his locomotive just short of your womb, and nodding in the direction of the ceiling, whispers, "Ten o'clock. They're bowling."

TEN A.M.

The carnal embrace is self-insulating. With efficient ease, it stifles all other biological urges, dissolves the intellect, and obliterates the conscience. If, while it endures, it can edit out hunger, fatigue, pain, time, reason, responsibility, and guilt, surely it can muffle the banal booms of bowling. And quickly enough, it does. Soon the ten-pin thunder is obscured by the softer slip-slap of his belly against yours

—your skirt is up around your neck—and you are holding on for dear life to keep from plunging into the bottomless though narrow-walled pit of the fuck.

As your vaginal muscles contract around his phallus, the larger muscle of the fuck contracts around your being, and you feel as if you are being compressed into a single drop of musky fat, a dollop of electrified lard sizzling in a skillet upon a stove of silk. Your Bartholin's glands are bobbing in their juices, and when, every now and again, his scrotum bangs against them, the white pony rears on the ridge. Let bones buckle! Let gristle grind! Let spit fly! Let . . .

Good grief. What now?

Diamond smiles fatalistically again, his rhythmic thrust sliding to a jerky halt. *What is it, darling?* you want to say. *Please don't stop. Don't ever stop.* No word leaves your mouth, however, and over your lover's shoulder, you glimpse the figure who has arrested his motion and chased the white pony off the back forty and into the mesquite.

It's Twister, for the sake of humble Jesus! Twister. The big Native American is standing in the bathroom doorway, impassive, nonplussed, so distracted he seems not to realize that *he* is the ultimate distraction, the personification of what is, next to death and call-waiting, the most unforgivable intrusion in the human universe: coitus interruptus. And as the blood rushes into your face with the speed of a bowling ball—you can almost hear it rumble—he says in a quiet voice that seems to come from very deep inside, "Excuse me, Larry, but you told me to let you know when that Japanese doctor is on TV."

Ten Oh-Five A.M.

Twister withdraws. Diamond doesn't—but you can feel him shrinking inside you. "Bad timing," he says.

"Uh-huh."

"Success in life and love depends always on timing."

"In the market, as well."

"Totally. Good timing versus bad timing. This was bad."

"Uh-huh."

"Inopportune."

"Yes." You feel him withering away. Where does it go when it goes?

"But there'll be other opportunities."

You can't tell if he's making a statement or asking a question, so you say, "We should get up. He may come back."

"No, Twister's in his tipi. However. . . ." In one swift motion, he lifts his hips, pulling free of you, and lowers his head, kissing you sweetly. Then, backing up on his hands and knees, he plants a forceful kiss right at ground zero between your thighs. Licking his lips like a Bubba at a barbecue, he stands. Feeling suddenly very exposed and very shy, you scramble to *your* feet. "As long as we're up . . ." he says.

"What?"

"Well, I'd rather like to have a peek at Yamaguchi. Would you mind?"

"I . . . uh. . . ." You find your panties on the floor in a heap of foliage. Tattered and moist, they resemble what would have been left of Little Red Riding Hood if the woodsman hadn't shown up in time. "I ought to freshen up."

Diamond takes the panties from you, holds them to his face, and inhales. "A fresher peach than you, my dear, would still be on the bough."

You are about to protest when an aroma, not of your ruined underpants but of the scattered leaves, reminds you of his illness, of the hope that that goofy Yamaguchi might hold for a cure, and you allow him, after he puts his jeans on, to take your hand and lead you from the room. In leaving, you glance back, half smiling, half frowning, as if your confused brain is straining to comprehend. Did the most thrilling thing to ever happen to you, outside of the confines of Posner Lampard McEvoy and Jacobsen, actually just transpire on that bathroom floor?

HALF ASLEEP in FROG PAJAMAS

TEN OH-SIX A.M.

Twister's flat, entered through an inconspicuous door on the right side of the vestibule, is furnished with Heritage House Early American pieces that to a Comanche, you suppose, must seem Late American and then some. To you, they just seem tacky, although definitely superior to Q-Jo's thrift-shop heirlooms. His living room is equally as voluminous as Diamond's, but most of the furniture has been herded into one end of it, the far end, where it gathers dust and vibrates in harmony with the clattering ten-pins. At the near end, against the east wall, is a bulky old television cabinet. Facing it, in the middle of the room—the Indian must have better vision than you—is an uncomfortable-looking settee in a folksy calico print. Closer to the west wall, its back to the sofa, is a wooden colonial rocking chair, which you know to be a reproduction and imagine to be hard on the buns. Twister occupies the rocker, though he is not rocking. He is, in fact, so motionless he might be perched on a rock. He is staring at the wall or, rather, at a small picture on the wall. That must be the famous Van Gogh. Naturally, you are anxious to examine it, but Diamond leads you directly to the sofa and bids you to sit down beside him.

"Don't *you* have a TV?" you whisper in his ear, the unfortunate one with the ring through it.

"Threw it in the dumpster," he says. "When I got back from Timbuktu." He fixes on the screen with the same attention that Twister devotes to the Van Gogh drawing, although he is flexible enough to run a hand up your skirt and squeeze your bare, sticky thigh. You flinch but neglect to resist. *It must be because the market has crashed,* you tell yourself. *The fact that I seem to have lost all shame.*

TEN OH-SEVEN A.M.

Apparently, Motofusa Yamaguchi has devoted the first few minutes of his press conference to an elaborate, rambling apology to Seattle and all of its men, women, and children; indeed, to humanity at large, for permitting strong drink to alter his rational responses, fog his judgment, and precipitate the farcical incident that occurred last evening, undermining, perhaps, public confidence in him and his medical methods. If the good doctor has lost face, however, if he is contemplating hara-kiri to avoid further disgrace, it is not blatantly evident in his demeanor. There is, in fact, an amused twinkle in his eye as he sits alone at a small, spotlit table in a hotel meeting room, tapping his considerable teeth with a Bic lighter, while a more somber spokesman, someone from the staff of the Hutchinson Cancer Research Center, announces that Dr. Yamaguchi has decided to make public immediately certain details of his treatment that heretofore he had planned to reveal at tomorrow's international conference. Presumably, this is an effort to restore faith. At any rate, an excited buzzing can be heard among the roomful of reporters, and Larry Diamond increases ever so slightly the pressure on your thigh. You glance at him, trying to comprehend what he must be going through. Empathize as you might, you remain undecided about whether the fact of his cancer increases or lessens your feeling of squalor.

> Yamaguchi: First, there any question?
> Reporter: Yes. Doctor. Do you have an alcohol problem?
> Yamaguchi: Of course. Every person who drink alcohol have problem. That why alcohol so popular. Make new problem for our entertainment.

The scientist emits a shy chuckle, the reporter looks perplexed, Diamond grins and slaps the sofa with his free hand, the one that isn't fondling you. "Got to get this guy to the University of Timbuktu," he says.

> Reporter (a different one):   Can you tell us about that device of yours? The one that—

Yamaguchi: Ah! Happy you ask. One moment, please.

The doctor lays down the Bic, opens his case, removes a smaller case, opens that one, removes a slender object, about five inches long, an object identical, as far as you can tell, to the one whose temporary disappearance caused all the commotion last night. He holds it aloft.

Reporters (several, in unison):   What is it?
Yamaguchi: I believe in English you call "nozzle." Nozzle for enema.

A riptide of murmuring cuts through the room. Photographers and cameramen crowd in for tighter angles.

Reporter (cautiously):   Is there something special about this enema? Nozzle?
Yamaguchi (shrugging):   Oh, little bit special. Is very old, for one thing. Is made of jade, for 'nother thing. Jade and mineral crystal. You see? (Holds it higher, rotates it in his fingers. It has a faint mint-green glow.)
Reporter (from back of room):   What's the function of this nozzle?
Yamaguchi: Function is to regulate and facilitate flow of solution into bowels.
Reporter (yet another one):   Right, we understand, but what's so special about it?
Yamaguchi: For one thing, is very old. (Regards it admiringly.) Was personal enema nozzle for empress of China, two, three hundred year ago. For 'nother thing, is made of—
Reporter (exasperated):   Yeah, but does it do something other ordinary nozzles can't do?
Yamaguchi: Of course. Yes. (Pauses.) It chew the rice.

253

You turn to Diamond. "Did he say it chews the rice?" The reporters are looking at one another, asking the same question. The representative from Hutchinson, inadequately trying to conceal his panic and preserve what remains of the ostensibly soteriological nature of the occasion, speaks up. "Dr. Yamaguchi, could you please inform our guests. . . . Could you explain exactly what you're getting at here." To the press, he says, "Remember, ladies and gentlemen, English is not Dr. Yamaguchi's native tongue."

"Gwendolyn, my love, would you say that I have a native tongue?"

Naturally, you blush, yet try as you might, you cannot refrain from smiling.

Yamaguchi: Secret of good health is chew. Person have nutritious diet, no matter if not well chewed. Many many persons in industrial nations have secret malnutrition because don't chew food 'nuff. You want long, healthy life, you chew, chew, chew. Okay? Now. Enema solution I give patients is make of—made of— rice, beta-carotene, one, two more things. Rice—unrefined, what you call *brown* rice—restore normal condition, good health to MCC gene. MCC start produce good protein. This allow tumor or polyp to go small. To shrink. Is simple, no? Ah, but one thing missing. Where chew? Must have chew for rice solution. Teeth (he retrieves Bic, plays his overbite like a xylophone) are in mouth, not rectum. Is so? No teeth in bowel, so nozzle must do all chewing. (Pauses.) How come nobody chew 'round here?

Reporter (which one doesn't matter): How does this nozzle of yours "chew" the rice and beta-carotene solution?

Yamaguchi: As say down in Houston, Texas, "Beat the hell out of me."

0

Reporter: You mean to say you don't have any idea how it works?

Yamaguchi: I have idea. I think refraction of light by jade and crystal allow nozzle to do chewing. Of course, as say down in Houston, we put enema nozzle where sun don't shine, so I am not refer to literal light, I am refer to poetic light, to energy.

Never have you seen a media mob so tongue-tied. Even those whose expressions indicate they believe they have uncovered a monumental quackery, even they are verbally unable to move in for the kill. Diamond seems thoroughly enthralled by the doctor's performance, so much so he has momentarily lost interest in making slow, maddening passes at the periphery of your pubis.

Reporter (finally): So, Dr. Yamaguchi, administering brown-rice enemas through a jade and crystalline nozzle is going to enable us to destroy tumors? To conquer cancer?

Yamaguchi: What you mean, "conquer"? What you mean, "destroy"? Western medicine all a time think in terms of destruction. In West, person get virus, he wish kill it. Get tumor, wish fire magic bullet at it. Not a healing but a gunfight. O.K. Corral, *ne*? (Points nozzle at press corps, fires imaginary shot.) My method not warfare. My method is pacify. Make friend with tumor. Friendship with cancer. Change friend's diet, teach friend good manners.

General muttering.

Reporter: Last night, you were very upset when you thought your nozzle had been stolen. Don't you have backup nozzles, or is this the only one in existence?

Yamaguchi: Behind every star in sky is 'nother star. But they are long way apart.

Reporter: Doctor, you must appreciate that some of us
are having trouble taking you seriously.
Yamaguchi (shrugs):   As Popeye say, I sweet potato
what I sweet potato.

At this point, the visibly shaken spokesman from Hutchinson
stands and gestures that the press conference is concluded. "Ladies
and gentlemen, thank you for coming. More information will be
made available to you after tomorrow's presentation. Meanwhile, let
me remind you that while communication in these East-West areas
can sometimes be problematic, Dr. Yamaguchi's successes in arrest-
ing colonic malignancies are impressive and verifiable. Thank you
once again."

Having returned the nozzle to its case, Yamaguchi rises to
leave. Suddenly, Diamond slides forward on the settee and yells at
the TV screen, "Hey? Can your enemas cure rectal cancers, too?"

Poor guy, you think. Underneath his quirky savoir-faire, he's
desperate. What he must be going through!

Yamaguchi (looking into camera):   Treatment may also
work for malignancy of rectum.

He waves.

TEN-TWENTY A.M.

"Jesus, Larry! How, how did you *do* that?"

"As they say down in Houston, Texas, 'Beats the hell out of
me.' I just started imitating some of the stuff I witnessed at Timbuk
U. Sometimes it works for me, usually it doesn't."

"Well, it's scary. Don't you think it's scary?"

"Oh, it's no scarier than the Bozo's familiarity with Sirius B.
Most people are scared of those things that don't sit still and pose
for our official portrait of reality—which means they have a hell of a

lot to be scared about. I suppose that's why they're careful not to look very far in any direction."

Speaking of sitting still, Twister has not budged. Yamaguchi's press conference, Diamond's outcry, the virtual *fingering* of you—can you believe it?—a few feet behind his back, all passed unnoticed, as near as you can determine. You squint to attain a clearer view of the valuable drawing—you have simply got to relent and get contact lenses—that holds him so, but it remains a murky little rectangle on a big shaky wall (upstairs in the bowling alley, activity has gradually increased).

As Diamond leads you to the door, you impulsively call out, "How much is the Dutchman offering these days?" What the heck. After the in flagrante delicto, the two of you should be on somewhat intimate terms. ·

Twister neither moves nor speaks. Well, okay, it's not the first time you've been snubbed. Can't fault a girl for asking.

Following Diamond into the vestibule, you hear a voice behind you, one of those folded-upon-itself tortilla voices that seems to have sifted through centuries of cornmeal and ashes, you hear that voice say, "Two million and . . ."

Rumble. Crash.

My goodness. Even before the Brunswick lightning struck, Twister was talking some jumbo juice.

Ten Twenty-Five A.M.

"Enemas," says Diamond, as much to himself as to you. "Irrigation. Timbuktu is in want of irrigation and apparently so am I. A ritzy little irrigator, that nozzle. Tip translucent, carved out of some sort of colorless crystal; stem carved out of green jade." He shivers. "I bet it's cold, don't you? She must've been a real dragon lady, that Chinese empress, shoving an icicle like that up her behind. The jade or the crystal or both interact molecularly somehow with Yamaguchi's home remedy—you notice the old fox withheld a couple of ingredients—and alter it so that it becomes electrochemically active on a subcellular level. If there's a carcinogenic virus involved, it would make sense, I guess. Viruses thrive on fats and sugars. Stuff like brown rice and broccoli, even when it's not been electrochemically mutated, pisses them off. They'd rather die than eat it. Come to think of it, we humans are a lot like that, ourselves. Remember that, Gwendolyn, the next time you order deep-fried frog legs. If there's a virus in you, it'll be egging you on. 'Come on, lady, go for it! Send me down some fat! And how about chocolate mousse for dessert? Mmm!' Of course, there's probably not a virus anywhere in your cute little system. Your little system's too cute for that." He runs his fingers through his long, stringy hair and treats you to one of his Halloween cackles. "Well, enough of this, my precious hoptoad. Let's see. Where were we?"

Diamond means to resume something, although whether it is the slide show or the sex you cannot be sure. You are sitting meekly on the leather sofa while he paces back and forth between you and the projected image of the T.U. faculty, your ripped panties hanging out of his back pocket like a referee's penalty flag, waiting to be thrown. The truth is, you do not really have a lot of time for either slides or sex. After all, Belford is due home at ten this evening, the London exchange opens a few hours later, and at six tomorrow morning, O God, you will be back at the disco to face Posner, your clients, what's left of the market, and the fates who have mocked you throughout your whole damn career. Meanwhile, there is a deal to set in motion, a monkey to be outwitted—and Q-Jo. Poor Q-Jo. You should try calling her again right now.

You stand up and are looking about for a phone when Diamond slips an arm around your waist and draws you into an embrace. Oh, well, it's doubtful if you would be able to concentrate on the tasks ahead anyway until you get *this* out of the way. *If Larry'll just take me to bed and make love to me—okay: fuck me—for twenty minutes—okay: an hour—I'm certain I'll be able to think a lot more clearly. And so will he. Poor fellow.*

You snuggle up against the lump in his groin. When you kiss, you stick *your* tongue in *his* mouth. It's kind of exciting in there. Of course, you are disgusted with yourself. Never have you felt like such a mare. Sure, you have been aroused before. For better or for worse, arousal is a feature of the human condition, and even nuns, even female CEO's, so you are told, do not wholly transcend it. It is the curse of the meat, and a woman must learn to live with it. No, a woman must learn to leverage it, to hedge it, to manage it, to make it work for her; to politely sample its undeniable if shoddy pleasures when it announces itself and to refrain from either stressful fasts or mindless binges. She must familiarize herself with it, exploit it when it is exploitable, but never ever get careless around it. Otherwise, it will turn on her like the lean and famished wolf that the maiden, in her innocence, invites to sleep on the hearth, and she will become its supper or its slave or, worse, its rival: a famished she-wolf who eats herself out of emotional house and independent home. She will fuck her dreams away and settle for lesser goals.

No, the wolf is no stranger to you, but you cannot recall a time when its howl was so melodious, its pelt so downy, its carnivore's breath so sweet. For once, you do not mind that sex is gooey or smells like Cupid's socks. You find yourself wanting Diamond to do dirty, nasty, unspeakable things to you, although you have scant notion what those things might be. They are beyond your powers of imagination. For all you know, they might be painful or overly strenuous. And certainly they would be time-consuming; they would cut into your day.

I sure picked a fine time to get horny, you think. You make a face, inasmuch as one can make a face while kissing. "Horny" is a proletarian expression. A cartoonish word. A word for clowns, galoots, and adolescents. *My desires may be crude, but they aren't frivolous. It would take a far more complicated and heartfelt word than "horny" to measure the dimensions of my wet itch.*

You reach behind you and undo buttons. The sound your skirt makes when it cascades to the floor, a sound so muted and brief, yet so emphatic, bold and rife with liberation—the *fru-fru-froomph* of a sail unfurling on a blockade-runner's sloop—that sound sends a delicious tingle up your spine.

Diamond reacts by slowly twisting free of your tongue. Giving your bare bottom a baby pinch, he says, "Gwendolyn, I'm hesitant to suggest such a thing, but I wonder if you would object to . . ."

Yes? Yes? What is it, Larry? What dirty, nasty, unspeakable thing does he want to do to you? Or want you (gasp!) to do to him? What filth and degradation has he in mind? (You are palpitating like a gospel singer in a church fire.) What kinky slinky licky sticky sucky . . . what revolting and forbidden practices will be forced upon you, what accoutrements might be required, and how many of your major orifices will they involve? *Yes, Larry? Yes?*

". . . I wonder if you would object to accompanying me to a lecture on frogs?"

Ten Forty-Seven A.M.

Thus it is that you find yourself—frustrated, demeaned, yet oddly buoyant—on the back of Diamond's scooter (he grinned at you knowingly in his most irritating fashion when you explained that you had arrived by taxi), backfiring across the Ballard Bridge, leaving Thunder House, its faux tempest, its Timbuktuan poetics, its dark and dinky Van Gogh drawing (worth two million and change in Amsterdam), its draconic shadows and love-stained kilim behind; headed, by way of Queen Anne Hill, to the Pacific Science Center, where, as part of the final day's activities at the Reptile & Amphibian Fair, there is scheduled at eleven-thirty a lecture entitled, "A Silence in the Swamps."

You had insisted on going by way of Queen Anne in order that you might stop off at your building. "To check for news of Q-Jo," you told Diamond, although news of André is just as eagerly sought, and to that end, you will direct Diamond to stop off first at Belford's place and then, if warranted by events, at a grocery store.

The burial cloths and egg whites through which the rising sun had surfaced are still present in much of the sky. The air is mild enough when one is afoot in it, but as it breaks about the scooter, it takes on a bit of a chill. You cling to Diamond for protection, protection from wind, protection from detection. It is unlikely, but what if someone with whom you do business should spot you aboard this ridiculous machine with this unkempt companion upon an Easter morn? They wouldn't even have to know that your bottom is bare—and sticky and cold—against the ratty leather seat.

Diamond reeks: of deteriorating leather, of sugary foliage, of you; a contradictory combination that provokes in you a certain tenderness. You slip your arms around his waist and bury your face in his back. Then, your downcast eyes spot your ravaged undies blooming like a magician's handkerchief in his back pocket. You yank them out, resist the temptation to swing them above your head for the benefit of passing motorists, and as the scooter pulls off Elliott Avenue to begin its laborious ascent of the hill, you sling them over a hedge bordering a modest lawn. "Fly away! Be free!" you sing, then instantly admonish yourself for your light-minded behavior. *Someone will probably discover those panties and turn them over to the police.* A memento from the Safe Sex Rapist, they might suspect, or a souvenir of a rich-boy prank, although few if any women whom the rich boys disrobe have ever stepped into knickers as stylish as these.

ELEVEN TWENTY-THREE A.M.

Got him!

You got him! Let economies lose their wheels and minds their reason, let hormones go ballistic and prayers go unanswered, let daddies box bongos and employers box ears, let hairs turn gray and inks crimson; let the fates break off in mid-chortle, for sooner or later, Gwendolyn Maria Mati was bound to outwit them. You got André! You got the mad monk.

Only a cursory survey of Belford's apartment (you are feeling

261

pretty guilty about Belford, but you mustn't think of that now) was required to determine that André had feasted there on the sweet baits of the morning. The freezer door again hung open, and naked Popsicle sticks were strewn about like yarrow stalks after an *I Ching* typhoon. One needn't be a primatologist or an Interpol sleuth to predict that the macaque would move on to your place, Belford's former residence, looking for more treats once these were digested. You had had Diamond swing by Thriftway—he putted right up to the entrance, practically driving the scooter inside the store, embarrassing you painfully—where you purchased another carton of banana ice and avoided the cashier's stare. To Diamond's credit—nothing seems to surprise him—he did not question your errand, but drove you and your plastic bag to your building, where he was content, again, to wait in the parking lot. A kiss, with a flicker of tongue, assured him you would not be long.

Your freezer door was also open, and a package of baby bok choy lay defrosting in the middle of the living room floor, next to your mother's poems. People do sometimes conceal jewelry inside hollowed-out books, but if he supposes anybody would hide a Popsicle in a volume of verse, this monkey is not as smart as he is cracked up to be. Anyway, you had missed him, but odds were highly favorable that he would return, so you left a Popsicle on each of several different windowsills and put the rest in the freezer. *I hope this stupid lecturer doesn't peep and croak all day*, you thought, as you wriggled into a fresh pair of underpants. You listened to your phone messages, all from Belford and mostly pitiful, and left without locking up, although locks had seldom been challenging to André in the years before he accepted the Lord as his Savior.

There was no response to your hopeful depression of Q-Jo's buzzer, and you were about to hurry on down the hall when your nostrils contracted, and your incongruously narrow proboscis began to behave as if it were packed with jumping beans and gunpowder. The aroma that drifted through the seams around the door was that of Q-Jo's tobacco! There was no mistaking that smell. Q-Jo's was the tobacco Satan would smoke, if smoking in Hell was not redundant, and only your father's marijuana was more familiar and more offensive to your nose.

Maceless now but brazen, you let yourself in, expecting who knows what, Q-Jo maybe, gone insane from her trifling with supernatural forces, crouched in a corner, drooling, smoking, staring into space through rubbery eyes. What you found instead was André. The monkey, a pouty expression on his face, was bouncing up and down in an overstuffed chair, looking like a pygmy Elvis impersonator from the Congolese club circuit, and he was puffing on a cigarette he had rolled himself. The cigarette was a splayed, shaggy, droopy mess, but, then, Q-Jo didn't roll them much better, and she had fully opposable thumbs.

Faking nonchalance, you spoke in your most gentle storybook voice. "Hi, André. Hi, honey. Nice to see you. Hi. You sit right there, and Auntie Gwen'll bring you something delicious. Okay, dear? Okay?" Slowly, softly, you pulled the door shut. Then you sprinted down the hall like Jackie Joyner-Kersee with a wasp in her shorts. You snatched the box of Popsicles from the freezer and tore back to Q-Jo's at top speed, praying all the while that he hadn't fled.

"Here, honey. Look here. Look at what I have for you." As he ripped the offering out of your hand, he blew a river of acrid smoke in your face, causing you to choke and very nearly retch. You almost gave yourself a hiatal hernia trying to suppress a cough, but you held your ground and presented the rest of the Popsicles. While André busied himself removing the paper wrappers and trying to figure out how to eat and smoke at the same time, a trick he could have learned in any redneck restaurant, you got a hammer and nails from the pantry and, as unobtrusively as possible, nailed each and every window shut, including the transom. You filled a bowl with water and canned fruit punch and emptied what was left of your last Valium prescription into the liquid to dissolve. You set the bowl on the floor by his chair—"Here, honey, in case you get thirsty"— stamped out the fire that was beginning to smolder on the carpet, for he finally had jettisoned the cigarette, and backed geishalike— you are getting good at this—to the door. "Bye-bye. Bye-bye, now.

You enjoy yourself, and Gwendolyn will be back in a little while. Okay? Bye-bye. Happy Easter." You engaged both locks and drove in a few nails for good measure. "There. That ought to hold you, you little bastard. I've got you."

ELEVEN TWENTY-FOUR **A.M.**

"Got him!"

There are a half-dozen residents gathered in the downstairs lobby, and one of them says to you, "Got him!"

"Beg your pardon?" How the hell did they know? These people are as nosy as they are unsophisticated. You have simply got to move into a higher-class building.

"They got him."

"Who?"

"Why, the rapist. They missed him earlier, but they got him now."

Oh, my God!

"Mrs. Kudahl spotted him in the parking lot and called the cops."

Good grief!

Shoving neighbors aside, you rush outdoors, where you spend the next ten minutes persuading the police that the man they have up against the wall is a friend of yours—you, an owner here!—and, despite his appearance, a law-abiding citizen. There is generous scoffing and eye-rolling on the part of Smokey and Cecil, who are of a mind to put you up against the wall, as well—on top of everything else, you are absentmindedly brandishing a hammer; but eventually, due as much to lack of evidence as to your brokerage-honed skills at salesmanship, they are forced to release him. There is one last thing. In patting down the suspect—looking for weapons or condoms or what?—Smokey had found a large roll of currency, and they want to know why Diamond is packing this cash.

264

"Surely, officer," says Diamond, "it has not escaped one as

observant as you that I am also in possession of airline tickets. I'm going away tomorrow to visit my dear parents, missionaries spreading the Gospel in a distant and heathen land. And surely someone as informed as you is aware of the sad and disgraceful fact that American credit cards are not as enthusiastically welcomed abroad as they once were. This may seem a sizable amount of moola, but with the dollar in its present weakened condition, godless foreign hustlers will consider it chicken feed."

So, they let him go. Cecil's parting words to you are, "Lady, I don't know what your story is, but I don't ever want to run into you again, and I mean never."

"Don't worry, officer." As they climb into their squad car, you turn to Diamond. "Where are you going, Larry?"

"The Reptile and Amphibian Fair is my announced destination."

"I mean tomorrow." Is that a catch in your throat?

"I'll explain later, pussy dumpling. The lecture started five minutes ago, and I'm afraid my scooter's given up the ghost."

"All right. Let's take the Porsche."

ELEVEN-FIFTY A.M.

Where have all the froggies gone? That is the subject of the talk at the Pacific Science Center's lecture hall. You must confess that you had not missed them in the slightest, but obviously some folks noticed, because the speaker, a mild, bearded, thirty-fiveish herpetologist in jeans, blue work shirt (why do people who can afford better choose to marginalize themselves in the garb of the field hand?) and tweed jacket is reeling off statistics when you and Diamond join the surprisingly large audience—you would guess eighty to a hundred people—and apparently he has been doing so for some time. These figures are the results of various independent surveys conducted by scientists worldwide, and they strongly indicate that there has been a sudden, baffling, and alarming decline in the planet's frog population. As he reads the findings of each survey, the herpetologist chalks the name of yet another disappearing species on his blackboard. There were more than a dozen listed when you arrived, and to these he adds "golden toad," "Bufo boreas," "harlequin frog," "yellow-legged mountain frog," and "Canadian chorus frog." My goodness. You hope the chef at the Bull & Bear had not placed the lower extremities of one of these particular creatures on your dinner plate last evening.

On the other hand, what does it matter? The last whole frog you recall seeing was the one you were forced to dismember (yuck!) in high-school biology class, and in all honesty, you have not felt in the least deprived. If these nerds were as concerned about the decline in the crisp green dollar as in the slimy green frog, maybe you would be closing on your new condominium next week.

"For two-hundred million years, frogs have survived floods, droughts, glaciers, meteorites, volcanic eruptions, and whatever else killed off the dinosaurs; for two-hundred million springs, through ice ages and fiery cataclysms, they serenaded Mother Earth. Now, their song is almost done. Without some miraculous recovery, we estimate that half of the world's thirty-eight hundred known species of frogs and toads will be extinct within twenty years."

Gee, you think, *that still leaves nineteen hundred species. How many varieties of creepy little peepers does one planet need?* You glance at Diamond. He winks.

As if in answer to your question, the speaker explains that for every creepy little peeper who succumbs, an untold number of bugs will thrive. "The decline in frogs creates a field day for insects," he says, and he cites the rise in crop destruction, mosquitoes, and malaria in parts of Asia where native frogs have all but bought the ranch. (Is this good news for your shares in Union Carbide?) And as frogs dwindle, birds, fish, lizards, snakes, and small mammals dwindle, too, for many, many creatures lunch regularly if not exclusively on amphibians. They are a vital link in the food chain. (Q-Jo told you that when she stayed home sick from school, her mother would feed her alphabet soup. Every time she threw up, Q-Jo would check the puddle to see if the little pasta letters spelled out anything. For the psychic, omens are everywhere, you suppose, but for some reason you can never hear the term "food chain" without thinking of Q-Jo's story—and feeling a twinge of nausea.)

"It isn't simply a matter of saving frogs."

Oh?

"There's a kind of domino effect operating here, and the frog is just the first domino in line. The more biological diversity we lose, the less flexibility we have to create new food sources that can tolerate the new environmental conditions that progress is spawning. Today, the frog; tomorrow the bird; the day after that, who knows? As Dr. Richard L. Wyman of the State University of New York has said, 'We don't know how many species can be lost before the system as a whole ceases to function. In the past, life responded to change through evolution, and that process depends on genetic diversity. If everything's the same, evolution stops.' Now, isn't that a scary thought?"

Throughout the small auditorium, there is a low hum of concern. Looking around at the audience, you are struck by *its* lack of diversity. Virtually everyone, regardless of age or gender, is wearing a down-filled nylon vest over a plaid flannel shirt. For decades, this expression of backpacker chic has been the unofficial uniform of Seattle's white middle class, and now you have to wonder if uniformity might not be partially at fault for the demise of the bourgeoisie? But is there less standardization among the poor, whose numbers are escalating, or the rich, who are holding their own (and successfully resisting efforts by you and others like you to infiltrate them)? This line of thought leads directly to an introspective examination of your present situation, financial and personal, and you are only half listening as the speaker explores possible causes of the dramatic and mysterious amphibian decimation.

"If it were human encroachment and habitat destruction alone, it wouldn't be quite so problematic. Pesticides and herbicides have been devastating, clearly, and a lot of people point fingers at acid rain, but fifty miles from here frogs are vanishing from pristine

Cascade Mountain lakes where repeated measurements reveal no acidification, nor, for that matter, pollutants of any kind. This suggests that what may be responsible is an increase in ultraviolet radiation, but since, thanks to governmental and corporate opposition, we lack the data that might show whether UV radiation is actually increasing or not, we can only speculate. Most likely, what's killing off our frogs is a complex mixture of global environmental changes.

"Because in the course of their lives they live both underwater and on land, eat both vegetation and insects, and are covered by a permeable skin that offers little protection from the external world, frogs are the ideal barometers of planetary health. Frogs are telling us something about the general condition of earth's environment, and the news is not reassuring. For tens of millions of years, they've been such hardy survivors that it makes the fact that they're now all of a sudden hurtling toward extinction all the more of a dire warning. Frogs may be the proverbial canary in the coal mine—except that when the canary keeled over, workers could evacuate the mine. We can't leave the planet. We shouldn't have to." He takes a breather, and the silence snaps you out of your introspection. "Are there any questions?"

You lean into Diamond. "I have questions," you whisper. "Are you really going away tomorrow, and if so, where are you going? What do you intend to do about connecting with Dr. Yamaguchi so that you can arrange to get treatments? Was Q-Jo locked in at Thunder House the way I was? Why are you attracted to someone like me when we're such opposites: is it sheer animal appetite, and did you know all along that I'd be an easy conquest? And is there actually a Sirius C?"

It is plain to Diamond that you have not been paying attention to the lecture, and he glares at you accusingly. "Sorry, pussy sugar," he says, "but all queries must address the topic at hand." He grins at you in that disturbing, maniacal manner of his, and then he stands and grins at the herpetologist and the audience in the very same fashion.

"Since the sole function of the majority of the human race," he begins in his elongated nasal drawl, "is to eat, shit, procreate, and watch television . . ."

Oh, good grief!

". . . and since those few who aren't outright larcenous and violent are fearful, ignorant, and, most of all, insensitive . . ."

There is a shuffling of Birkenstocks and Rockports—the audience is not thrilled with the comments of this wild-looking individual, and neither, frankly, are you.

". . . and since their collective greed and imbecility has shoved the entire biosphere to the brink of oblivion . . ."

Now, there are random nods of agreement.

". . . and since our so-called leaders—political, commercial, and religious—deserve to be mashed to jelly and sandwiched between hunks of ripe Limburger . . ."

"Careful, mister!" you hear someone exclaim.

". . . and since the newspapers and magazines that support these shysters are fit for nothing but outhouse bung fodder . . ."

Won't he please sit down and shut up?

". . . and since everybody has a hard-luck story, including the frogs . . ."

"Excuse me, sir," says the herpetologist. "Excuse me. Do you have a question?"

". . . I'm reluctant to propose that the depletion of our amphibian population might be due to something other than the foul and feckless follies of our fellows or that what seems like a biospheric catastrophe might actually be a positive and hopeful sign. I'm hesitant to propose these possibilities, but I must."

Abruptly, everyone is on the edge of his or her seat; and the herpetologist, who had been politely trying to silence him, guardedly bids Diamond continue. Diamond is, as he would put it, merry and bright. It would appear that you alone are cringing.

"As you erudite people well know, the word *amphibian* comes from the Greek *amphi* and *bios*, meaning to live a double life. This refers, needless to say, to an ability to live both in water and on land. In that regard, amphibians are the most adaptable creatures in the world, the ones, ironically, best suited for residence here. But as those of you who've read spy stories or had extramarital affairs are aware, a double life implies a clandestine life, a life of secret behaviors. Now, a frog is a little dumb animal with a poot-sized brain. It probably isn't the custodian of a hell of a lot of covert information. No, indeed. But rather than possessing secrets, suppose a frog *is* a secret. A secret link."

This would be a prudent time to head for the ladies' room, if not the Porsche, except that Diamond, the man who everyone in the auditorium knows is *your* escort, is blocking the aisle.

"The amphibian is the bridge between the terrestrial and the aquatic. I invite you to consider that it may also be a bridge between our water planet and the largely arid galaxy. A bridge between earth and the stars. A bridge, most importantly, between the mind of man and the cosmic overmind. And, of course, it's the biological bridge between the fishes, which many identify with Jesus Christ, and the reptiles, which many identify with Satan."

Members of the audience, some amused, others uneasy or anxious, are regarding him as if he could be a nutcase, after all. You, your face as stinging red as a freshly skinned knee, refuse even to glance in his direction. To think, a few short minutes ago, you were entertaining the girlish notion that you could be developing a romantic attachment to him!

In fairness to Diamond, granted an opportunity to elucidate, he might oxidize a patina of credibility on his screwball postulates. Alas, when he says, "I'm going to ask you to consider that hyperintelligent entities—agents of the overmind; aliens, if you will—could be abducting our frogs as part of a benign scheme to free us from the tyranny of the historical continuum and reunite our souls with the other-dimensional," you spoil his chances by shooting to your feet, pushing past him, and hustling from the auditorium.

You pray that he won't follow, but as you hurry between the

reflecting pools and salt-white arches, virtually sobbing from embarrassment and remorse—how could you have permitted unruly bodily cravings to temporarily blind you to his dementia?—you hear him shout, "Wait, pussy pudding! Hold up! Wait for me! You haven't heard the punch line!"

Sunday
Afternoon
April 8

Starting Out As Seafood

Twelve-Seventeen P.M.

The creature is the size of a standard poodle. It has a body of crunchy armor, several more legs than good taste dictates; long, wiggly antennae that seem to be sorting through atmospheric molecules like old women buying tomatoes; and eyes that are all pupil and no expression, yet follow your every move as if heat-seeking scanners had been implanted in a pair of black golf balls. It's a repulsive, willy-giving thing—but it's the monster beside it that scares you.

After your mother threw herself in front of a cement truck, Grandma Mati, with sewing shears, snipped her image out of every photograph in the family album, whether from Filipino superstition or ordinary malice you could not say. In any case, you wish you had a pair of scissors capable of cutting Larry Diamond out of the reflection the two of you are casting in this plate-glass window. On second thought, maybe you ought to snip out your own image and leave his there. The window, in a storefront alongside which your Porsche is parked, belongs to a pest-control business and is occupied by a holographic cockroach as large as an ocelot. It is the roach that is out of place, for roaches are fairly rare intruders in the northerly clime of Seattle, whereas Diamond, from your point of view, would be a plague at any latitude.

"My, my," says Diamond, ignoring the fact that you have been trying to ignore *him*, "it would take a frog of considerable girth to lunch on this entomological entrée. Makes me curious about what the Nommo might eat."

"Listen, Larry," you say, doing your best to coat your singsong

275

with a husky phlegm, "it just isn't going to work out with you and me."

"Work out?" He seems genuinely puzzled.

"Yes, you know, isn't going to lead anywhere."

"Oh, you'd be surprised where it might lead."

"I bet I would. But it isn't. I mean, as a relationship, it has zero future."

"Future? Oh, I get it. You mean you don't foresee a pot of gold at the end of our juicy rainbow. You mean that our intimacy isn't likely to yield a dividend. You disappoint me, Gwendolyn. I hoped you might have a watt or two more light in your bulb than those poor toads who look on romance as an investment, like waterfront property or municipal bonds. Would you complain because a beautiful sunset doesn't have a future or a shooting star a payoff? And why should romance 'lead anywhere'? Passion isn't a path through the woods. Passion *is* the woods. It's the deepest, wildest part of the forest; the grove where the fairies still dance and obscene old vipers snooze in the boughs. Everybody but the most dried up and dysfunctional is drawn to the grove and enchanted by its mysteries, but then they just can't wait to call in the chain saws and bulldozers and replace it with a family-style restaurant or a new S and L. That's the payoff, I guess. Safety. Security. Certainty. Yes, indeed. Well, remember this, pussy latte: we're not involved in a 'relationship,' you and I, we're involved in a collision. Collisions don't much lend themselves to secure futures, but the act of colliding is hard to beat for interest. Correct me if I'm wrong."

You can't argue that your encounter with Diamond hasn't been interesting. And no matter what he might presume, you, of all women, do not regard every male you meet as a potential partner in a domestic compromise. But fairies? First, he makes fools—fools!—of you both by raving in public about frognappers from outer space, and now he's talking fairies. Please! If it's all a joke, let him share it with the cockroach. You have other chores.

"It's disappointing because I was rather hoping we could have done some business together; I've got a plan. . . . But it's probably best I do it on my own. As for the, uh, sex part, those things happen. No regrets. As long as you're disease-free. You *are*, aren't you?" He merely grins, and the reflected grin looks by no means out of place next to the vermin in the window. "See? You're impossible." (The irony of asking a cancer victim if he is disease-free is lost on you.) "And I absolutely cannot deal with those public displays of yours. Your scenes."

"Really? I thought you were quite a sport at the Bull and Bear last night."

"Okay, damn it, I've been a little out of control lately. I've been flighty at times. This is not an easy time for me. But that's not who I am."

"Who are you, Gwendolyn?"

You sigh, bite the kiss-sack you call your lower lip, and turn away from the window. "I'm a blackballed jockey on a lame horse in a fixed race. But I'm not a quitter. I'll ride to the finish. And I'll ride alone. Now. If you want, I'm willing to drive you back to the bowling alley. But that's the extent of it. I've got moves to make."

As you rummage for your car keys, he taps the plate glass next to the giant roach. "Gwendolyn," he says, "if our child should turn out like this, would you love it anyway?"

Twelve Twenty-Two P.M.

Diamond accepts a lift, but not to Thunder House. He requests to be driven to the Sorrento, the aging but still graceful hotel on First Hill, where Dr. Yamaguchi is reportedly staying. "I've got moves of my own," he says. He lays a hand on your thigh. You slap it away.

"No, Larry! Please. It's after the bell. Okay? My life's hectic enough right now. I'm not sure I could even handle a normal relationship, but certainly the last thing in the world I need is some kind of 'collision.' "

"*Au contraire.* A collision is exactly what you *do* need, because collisions are transformative. A relationship can occasionally fulfill a

277

person, but only a collision can transform them. It's the same for cultures as it is for individuals. Shall I cite historical examples?"

"What makes you think, Mr. Arrogant, that I need to be transformed?"

"Because that's what we're here for. It's obvious. Or do you think we're here to service our debt?"

"I'm a growing person. I've grown a lot. How would you know whether I've grown or not?"

"I'm not talking about growth. Little tadpoles don't just grow into big tadpoles and call themselves frogs, the way little children grow into big children and call themselves adults. Tadpoles are *transformed* into something entirely other."

You are about to shriek, "Who gives a hoot what tadpoles do?!" when you are forced to slam on the brakes to avoid plowing into a shopping-cart train that is crossing the intersection of First and Denny against the light. Around six months ago, several of those homeless individuals who push all of their earthly belongings—and often the day's pickings from refuse cans—along the streets in appropriated supermarket carts got the bright idea to start convoying. It quickly caught on. Nowadays there are convoys or "trains," as they are called, thirty or forty carts long, and they have attained a certain amount of protection—from cops, the rich boys, and bullying peers—and a certain amount of power, especially over motorists, for downtown traffic is frequently at the mercy of these squeaky-wheeled, slow-moving, irreverent caravans of detritus and desperation.

You are both vexed by the delay and rattled by its source, but Diamond surveys the scene with an expression of wonder. "Can you picture them trasversing the Sahara," he asks, "on their way to Timbuktu?" And his wonderment only increases when, a few blocks farther, you see a toolless burglar smash a car windshield with his head, a procession of hysterical half-naked Christians flagellating themselves with strips of steel-belted radials, and a cadre of neo-Marxists extolling the joys and benefits of bloody revolution to

clusters of purple-lipped winos, hip-hopping crack runners, and a few dazed couples newly exiled from suburbs that no Jacuzzi sales-man will ever cruise again. Lining the curbs, like storks on a rail, and sometimes executing disjointed veronicas in traffic, as if bullfighting were an event in the Special Olympics, panhandlers of all ages, races, social backgrounds, and degrees of mental health screech, mumble, warble, and whine their pleas for alms; and as you pass the corner of First and Stewart, you can swear you hear the strains of a familiar theme being played on a Jew's harp.

Diamond must have noticed your grimace because he says, "Yes, yes, I agree: it's much too early for 'Strangers in the Night.' If the guy had his wits about him, he'd ply us with a diurnal tune." With that, he throws his head back and launches into "Zip-A-Dee-Doo-Dah."

"I really don't understand how you can be amused by this degradation."

"Congratulations, hoptoad. Once again you've hit upon the wrong word. The theater of man is not always 'amusing,' but it *is* always theater, and theater can be marveled at even when its con-tent is somber and harsh. You're acquainted with Greek tragedy?"

The next thing you know, you are sounding like Belford Dunn. "These people aren't performing, for God's sake. Their misery is real."

"Everybody's performing. We only think it's real."

"Oh? Is that another nugget of wisdom you dug up in Tim-buktu? I hope you make it in to see Yamagoofy. He'll give you a free enema just to hear you yak." You swerve to miss one jaywalking wino and then another. If the *Titanic* had been a Porsche, it would still be afloat. Of course, if winos were icebergs, scabs would wear snowshoes, and fleas would need picks. "I have a friend," you say, "who believes that it's our fault these people are in the streets and our duty to shelter and feed them. That may have made sense at one time, but now there're so *many* of them."

"Yes, isn't it grand? A bum or two on a corner is a bittersweet vignette, but this, this is spectacle! Numbers aside, your friend is a presumptuous twit to be assigning blame and delegating duty. Your friend insults the homeless by giving them no credit for having made the decisions that shaped their lives, and demeans them further by declaring them powerless to alter their situations. There're many ways, my dear, to victimize people. The most insidious way is to persuade them that they're victims."

"Now wait a minute, Larry." You try, quite hypocritically, to approach it from Belford's point of view. "I doubt very much if anybody chose this as a way of life. I mean, can you see the kids hanging out at the video parlor after school, one says he wants to be an engineer someday, a couple want to be lawyers, a girl's ambition is to study veterinary medicine, and then this other kid says, 'Gee, I think I'll be a homeless person—or else a stinking toothless wino who sleeps on cold cement'? I don't buy that."

"Nor do I. And yet, except for the legitimately, congenitally insane, each and every one of them is where they are because of choices they made. Dumb choices. At some point, the gods placed two sealed bags in their vicinity and said 'Choose.' One bag had a pepperoni in it, and one had a turd. Now, if they had bothered to examine the bags, to squeeze or shake or smell them—pepperoni having a decidedly different feel, bounce, and fragrance from its excremental counterpart—well, you get the picture. But because the turd bag was closer at hand and they didn't have to exert themselves to retrieve it or because it looked to be lighter and thus easier to carry, or larger and thus promised more of something for nothing, or because they were distracted by television—actually, if they're watching a lot of TV, they may already have selected the shit—or because the turd bag was decorated in the colors of their favorite team . . ."

"Maybe somebody else chose for them."

"That's very often the case. But we can choose to make our own choices."

"Easier said than done."

"What isn't? If you're going to complain because there frequently are extenuating circumstances or because we're forced to choose bags when we're too young or uninformed to know what we're doing, you'll have to take it up with the gods. Uncle Larry didn't invent the system. All Uncle Larry is saying is that individuals have to accept responsibility for their own bad choices. If every time we choose a turd, society, at great expense, simply allows us to redeem it for a pepperoni, then not only will we never learn to make smart choices, we will also surrender the freedom to choose, because a choice without consequences is no choice at all. Maybe it boils down to the premium we want to place on liberty. It's *numero uno* in Uncle Larry's book, far out in front of food and shelter, though only a clam whisker ahead of your little—"

"Stop it!"

If the Porsche had rather be racing on the Autobahn at 120 mph than idling through a stream of vaguely hostile pedestrians at First and Pike, gateway to the fabled Pike Place Market and center of the wino universe, it doesn't let on. The throttled-back Porsche behaves as if it is sipping brandy and puffing a cigar in the library of a Bavarian hunting lodge. If only you were as equanimous. For years, the down-and-out have secretly annoyed you, and for years, Belford's teary-eyed concern for them has made you feel guilty. Now, here is a guy suggesting that both annoyance and concern may be misplaced, that the homeless are simply players in one great pageant and may be essential, even intrinsic, to the plot. At least, you think that is what he is saying. Resisting, more out of fear than kindness, the urge to honk your horn at the "actors" who are clotting the crosswalk, you say, "The fact is, Larry, there're people out there who *did* choose your pepperoni, who grabbed it and ran with it, who didn't quit school or flunk out, who didn't rob a convenience store or steal a car or get pregnant, get married too young or get hooked on booze or crack, people who made the most of a happy childhood or transcended a rotten one, who worked hard and made a success of themselves in business, only to have the rug yanked out from under them when the economy went south. What about them? Aren't they victims?"

"They are if they think they are. Everybody's got . . ."

"A hard-luck story. That's all you have to say?" A temporary

281

break in the procession allows you to gun the Porsche through the intersection.

"I apologize if my incipient boredom is a millstone around the neck of this conversation, but as far as I'm concerned, these matters are all sociology and noise. Noise and sociology. I should remind you, however, that authority—and fate—can be outwitted and that for every actual victim in our culture, there're a hundred who victimize—and trivialize—themselves by indulging their anger and nursing their bitterness. 'Zip-A-Dee-Doo-Dah.' "

"And that's all you have to say?"

"I wouldn't have said that much if you weren't such a little mango-bruiser. Come on, pussy butter . . ."

"Don't call me that!"

"Apparently, you want me to chirp a lament for our brothers and sisters in the financial sector, but the Ice Capades will be touring Hell before your doomed colleagues inflate a gas bubble of sympathy in my dirty breast. Ruined investors and bankrupt bookies alike, most of them set themselves up for whatever's happened to them by buying into the Lie."

"Did they, now? And what lie is that?"

"The Lie of progress. The Lie of unlimited expansion. The Lie of 'grow-or-perish.' Listen. We built ourselves a fine commercial bonfire, but then instead of basking in its warmth, toasting marshmallows over it, and reading the classics by its light, we became obsessed with making it bigger and hotter, bigger and hotter, until if the flames didn't leap higher from one quarter to the next, it was cause for great worry and dissatisfaction. Well, any Bozo on the riverbank could have told us that if you keep feeding and feeding and feeding a bonfire, sooner or later you burn up all the fuel and the fire goes cold; or else the fire gets too huge to manage and eventually engulfs the countryside and chars its inhabitants. Nature has always set limits on growth: limits on the physical size of individual species, limits on the size of populations. Did we really believe capitalism was exempt from the laws of nature? Did we really confuse endless consumption with endless progress? Benjamin De-

Casseres, a Frenchman who lectured at Timbuk U., defined progress as 'the victory of laughter over dogma.' Now *there's* a victory worth celebrating."

In English, there is a quaint expression, "making good time," a colloquialism that if taken literally implies that time is something that can be crafted or manufactured, and either poorly so or else expertly, a notion every bit as fanciful and illogical as naming a star "sitting trouser"—until one becomes acquainted with quantum physics, whereupon one learns that time, as measured by clocks on earth, is, indeed, a contrivance, a thing we have conveniently made up. Moreover, the "better" time we make, which is to say, the faster we go, the less time there is, so that "by the time" we reach the speed of light, there is no time at all, indicating, perhaps, that the only good time is a dead time. Something else to ponder is that if higher science has justified the figure of speech, "making good time," might not it someday validate the name, "sitting trouser," as well? For the moment, however, it is enough to say that you are fairly flying along First Avenue, "making good time" at last on your trip to the Hotel Sorrento.

You downshift, turn eastward up Marion, and within a few steep blocks leave the last remnants of the "spectacle" behind. Soon, shopping-cart convoys will have been replaced by luxury automobiles, derelicts eclipsed by folk in Easter finery. This lifts your spirits, and there is barely an accusatory burr in your voice when you say to Diamond, "You're a man who's turned against money."

He emits half a cackle. The bottom half. "That's like saying I've turned against the crowbar or the hoe."

"But . . ."

"Like saying I've turned against the stunt double."

"The what?"

"The surrogate who stands in for principals and does their stunts for them."

"Oh," you say, but you don't quite get it.

"Surely, my dear, I'm not so obtuse that you've mistaken me for an ascetic. One of those self-destructive poverty snobs. Have you ever seen an ascetic who was merry and bright? Have you ever heard of a saint who was creative, brilliant, attractive, or anything besides a masochistic, sexually dysfunctional, unnatural egotist who thinks he or she's spiritually superior to you because he or she revels in misery and you don't? People who've bought into poverty are just as shallow and exploitative as those who've bought into wealth. Both have been stultified by their lack of imagination."

"Well, that's certainly not your problem."

"I'll accept that as a compliment. Especially since, as an autistic child, I began life with no imagination whatsoever. Why, when I was six years old, I was as prosaic as a bean-counter in a bureau."

"Honest? I remember you saying you'd been autistic, but I thought it was one of your jokes."

"As seen from the pad, it's *all* a joke, even autism—but there're good jokes and bad jokes, and autism, on its own terms, is worse than that chicken that keeps crossing that road."

"I'm afraid I don't know much about it, but I guess the doctors don't, either."

"My theory, and few if any doctors subscribe to it, is that unlike ordinary emotional disorders, which, as Papa Freud taught us, are usually the result of childhood trauma, autism is the result of fetal trauma, something that disturbs us while we're still in the waters of the womb. While we're in our minnow stage. I mean 'minnow stage' literally, by the way. We all start out as seafood."

Not wishing to test those waters, you ask, "How were you able to overcome it? The autism?"

"Dolphins cured me."

Good grief! You give him a look that prompts him to say, "Don't give me that look. Save that look for the apologists at your disco tomorrow. When I was eight, my parents took my sisters and me to a place in Florida where we could swim with dolphins. After an hour, I came out of the water and asked for a peanut butter sandwich. Up to that point, I'd never spoken. Not one word. The next day, we did it again. This time, I emerged from the water and

hugged my father. It was the first time I'd voluntarily touched another human being. My dad took a leave of absence from his job,
and we stayed at Grassy Key for several months. I swam every day
with the dolphins, and by the time I was nine, I was a so-called
'normal' boy. A very naughty boy, but, by psychiatric standards,
normal."

"But how . . . ?"

"Autistic children are disappeared into themselves. The dolphins broke through, went in there, and brought me back. How?
We could communicate, the dolphins and I, because we were on the
same level. The self-contained, intrauterine level. The submarine
level. Emotionally, autistic children are still in the womb. Underwater. They can't relate to land animals. To life in the air. Somehow,
the dolphins showed me how to make the transition from a liquid to
a gaseous environment. It seems perfectly logical. It's well known
that depression and hypertension can be reduced by simply observing fish in a tank."

"Maybe that explains . . ."

"Why I'm a Nommophile? Not entirely. However, it's safe to
say that I am more disposed than most to drawing major conclusions
from the arcane aquatic traditions of the Bozo. But you don't want to
talk about that. You want to talk about money."

"That's unfair. Money's not the only thing I'm—"

"Don't be defensive. It'd be a bad sign if you weren't inclined
toward abundance. Abundance in all things—material, emotional,
intellectual, spiritual—is the goal of any first-rate soul. But into
which of those categories does money fit? Automatically, you say
'material.' Uncle Larry disagrees. Uncle Larry says 'spiritual.' Money
may be our greatest spiritual teacher. More edifying than a stadium
full of swamis. Nothing can knock a pilgrim off the path as fast as
money. That's the job of a spiritual teacher, you know. Not to hold
us on the path, but to knock us off of it. Until we can stay on the
path without ever being knocked—or tempted—off, until we can
resist the teacher's carrot and withstand his rod, our transformative

journey can be little more than fits and starts. When it comes to illuminating the inner structure of consciousness and highlighting its weaknesses and flaws, nothing, not even love, casts as bright a beam as money. The things we're willing to do to obtain it, to protect it, to express our guilt over having it, are incomparably revealing. There's a thin line between charity and greed: at bottom, they're both expressions of insecurity and manifestations of ego. If you want to know how insecure you are, how swollen and stiff your ego is, what your chances are of staying on the path, just examine your attitudes toward the juice. Money's a terrible servant but a wonderful master. Far be it from Uncle Larry, my dear, to come between a seeker and her guru."

Jeez! What are you supposed to make of that? You are still trying to interpret the nuances of Diamond's latest pedagoguery— could this be a veiled invitation for you to enlist his aid in your oil futures play?—when you arrive at the barricades around the Sorrento Hotel.

TWELVE FORTY-FIVE P.M.

First Hill has neither physical nor thematic connection to First Avenue. The two are separated by nearly a dozen blocks. Moreover, many Seattleites are disposed to refer to First Hill as Pill Hill, a tribute to its high concentration of hospitals, clinics, medical offices, and pharmacies. Harborview, in whose public mental wards that rude Cecil and Smokey would confine you, is on Pill Hill, as is the Hutchinson Cancer Research Center. And on the extreme northwestern rim of the hilltop, high above downtown and Puget Sound, so is the Sorrento, a lovely, smallish, turn-of-the-century, Mediterranean-style hotel favored by guests seeking privacy, calm, and refinement in an urban setting. Perhaps those are the very qualities Motofusa Yamaguchi looks for in lodging, but more than likely his hosts booked him into the Sorrento because of its proximity to the

Hutchinson laboratories. In any case, although many a show biz celebrity has successfully hidden away at the Sorrento, Dr. Yamaguchi's residence there has shattered any pretense of privacy or calm.

A crowd quadruple the size of the audience at the frog lecture is milling around in front of the hotel, and while four hundred people is hardly a multitude, they are more than enough to overrun the Sorrento's serene little garden entrance, with its fountain, spiked iron fence, and hardy palms. Whether seeking last-ditch medical attention, business association, or merely curiosity, the visitors have clogged the courtyard and spilled over onto Madison Street, as well as onto Terry around the corner. An overworked and depleted police department has erected barriers about the hotel proper, and two cops are directing and deflecting traffic, concentrating on keeping Terry Avenue clear, for Terry is the direct ambulance route to the Swedish Hospital emergency room, only a block away.

You nose the Porsche into a parking lot off Terry. Every stall is occupied, but you only require space to stop long enough to discharge your passenger. Diamond powers down his window and asks a passerby what is going on. The frail, elderly woman replies that Yamaguchi has been whisked off to lunch somewhere but is expected back around three.

"What will you do?" You can't help but notice that opals of perspiration are studding his brow once again, and as anxious as you are to get rid of him, you are not without mercy.

"First, I'll battle my way into the lobby. If management refuses access to a toilet, I'll come back out here and squat between parked cars." He pulls a Ziploc bag of Comanche leaves from the inside pocket of his leather jacket. "It isn't the pain that bothers me so much as it is the banality."

"I'm sorry, Larry." You don't have cancer, but you know what he means.

"Then I'll wait around with these other needy nonentities to see if I can't steal a word with Yamaguchi-san."

287

"I hope he'll talk to you."

"It'll be good theater, in any case." He turns to face you. "Before I take my leave, however, let me attempt very briefly to answer your other questions, though probably not in the order that you asked them." You must look bewildered because he explains. "The questions you posed in the lecture hall."

"Oh. Those."

"Nobody except the Bozo and the Dogon postulate that there's a Sirius C. But the Bozo and the Dogon have unique credibility in that area. If they're correct, if Sirius has a second sister that astronomers don't know about, if there is a Sirius C, then the quaking custard we call reality is a very quaky custard, indeed.

"In that regard, and in answer to another question, I have to inform you that the way the automatic lock works at Thunder House, nobody can exit without a key. I haven't the foggiest idea how Q-Jo Huffington was able to get out. I didn't want to tell you earlier, for fear of scaring you off."

You stall the car on that one and are slow to restart the engine.

"Now, as for attraction, the instant I first saw you, my dear, I wanted to open your legs like a checking account at a bank that doesn't charge for overdrafts. And believe it or not, I wanted to open your mind, as well. I said to myself, 'Larry, wouldn't it be a fine thing, a swell thing, a boon to the community of man and to all creatures great and small, if this girl's soul was as ripe and stunning as her ass.' It isn't, of course, but maybe it could be. Gwendolyn, you're like a handsome, expensive television set that can only bring in two or three channels. I want to hook you up to cable, sweetheart. I want to be your satellite dish."

While you are trying to decide whether to be flattered or insulted, he removes from his breast pocket a packet of tickets. Green stains, a result of the packet's having been carried next to the medicinal herbs, almost blot out the name of the airline. "Tomorrow," he says, answering your remaining question, "I'm going back to Timbuktu."

HALF ASLEEP *in* FROG PAJAMAS

TWELVE FIFTY-TWO P.M.

"Timbuktu? Tomorrow?" You gulp and endeavor to conceal the gulping.

"Yes. On the morn. Ere the cock crows thrice. I realize this is heartbreaking news, but you needn't despair. I'm confident we can devise a strategy that'll render it a joy instead of a calamity. Obviously, we can devise nothing of consequence with that conga line of cretins caterwauling behind us"—several cars whose futile circlings of the lot you are blocking have begun to honk impatiently—"so I'll bail out knowing that love will find a way and we'll solve everything next time we meet."

Don't count on any next time, you start to say, but then he kisses you, and the kiss is so like a Mexican wedding dress, with layers of lace and tiers of frills, with flounces, embroidery, rows of pearl buttons and loops of bright ribbon, that the angry traffic turns into a fiesta and the parking-lot attendant waving his arms at you becomes a drunken priest bestowing a blessing. By the time Diamond slides away, trailing a thread of saliva, your gonads are riding hard toward Durango.

ONE P.M.

Solid ground. That's what you long for. To stand for a while on solid ground. Bedrock. Terra firma. Reinforced concrete. O Gravity, where is thy hook, thy line, thy sinker?

You choose a circuitous route home, studiously circumnavigating the denser populations of street people, thereby avoiding pedestrian gridlock, possible acts of vandalism and violence, and the temptation to look at the homeless hordes through Diamond's eyes. (If they are, indeed, extras—and, at the same time, stars—in a humongous and vibrant spectacle, you would like a word with the producer, casting couch and all.)

289

You arrive at your building without incident, which is a triumph of sorts, although hardly a harbinger of stability, since you must now look in on André, an assignment that precludes any illusion of firmness beneath the feet. Fortunately, because it is an old building, woefully *démodé,* its doors are punctured by keyholes, and it is with your eye to a worn brass aperture that you are able to peer into Q-Jo's domicile and ascertain that the macaque is present, conspicuously present; is, in fact, sprawled atop the Huff's cherry-wood table, tarot spread and all, like the sacrificial victim of a toupee cult. Due to your cursed myopia, you are quite unable to say for sure if André is breathing, and the awful thought occurs to you that you may have killed him. Who knows how much Valium a twenty-pound monkey can tolerate?

You squint, you blink, you press so far into the keyhole that your eyeball is like a grape being forced into a peashooter. Alas, you are still unable to detect any rise or fall of hairy chest. If you have carelessly murdered Belford's little rascal—well, the consequences are too dire to consider! As you pry loose with your nail file the doornails so that you might tiptoe inside to hold a mirror to monkey nostrils, to feel for monkey pulse, your mind is already scanning for alibis, ways to pin the fatal misdeed on someone else.

Barely have you crept over the threshold, however, than André startles you by grabbing at his rump in an irritated manner, a gesture that culminates in his pulling a tarot card from under him, as if it had been pinching his tight little scrotum, and casting it aside. Although he has not opened his eyes and he stirs no further, you are satisfied that he is okay (you don't consider coma or brain damage) and are greatly relieved. The longer he sleeps, the easier it will be to contain him. At least one thing is going well. You are about to slip out of the apartment when your eye falls on the card that André yanked from the spread. It has landed facedown on the floor, and you are seized by a sudden, sharp curiosity. A card picked so forcefully yet so somnambulistically must have special significance, and you wonder which card it might be. You wonder, too, if the card would pertain specifically to the monkey's subconscious, assuming that a monkey has a subconscious, or might its message be aimed at you? Might it, for example, reflect on the scheme whereby you would exploit the return of the prodigal primate to extract money—in the form of a short-term loan, of course—from Belford Dunn? The next thing you know, you are down on all fours crawling stealthily toward the fallen card.

You are halfway to the card when it occurs to you that this is hardly appropriate behavior for someone who has been yearning to plant her feet on the unyielding crust of routine and reason. You pause to consider your actions and during the freeze-frame of your hesitation, hear someone clear their throat behind you.

Essie Kudahl, the retired florist who lives across the hall, is standing in the doorway, eyes wide, mouth agape. It is a measure of your will, perhaps, that even in the midst of blushing violently, you have the presence to hold a finger to your lips, forestalling any exclamation from the widow Kudahl that could awaken the sleeping prince.

Two-Forty P.M.

As the afternoon passes, your mind strays several times to the unexamined tarot card, but having exhausted your powers of persuasion selling Mrs. Kudahl on the idea that the little scene upon which she stumbled was not as depraved as it seemed, you have no intention of reentering Q-Jo's unit unless André awakens and creates a ruckus. Every quarter hour or so, you do tiptoe down the hall and spy on your prisoner, but not without the distinct sensation that Mrs. Kudahl is peering out her keyhole at you peering in Q-Jo's.

Even more frequently, your mind strays to Larry Diamond. To wit:

One. Having not eaten all day, you reheat some lobster bisque —and while spooning it in, wonder if Diamond has bothered to take nourishment or if the cancer has eaten his appetite as cancers are said to sometimes do.

291

Two. Having run out of other ideas, you call around to the hospitals to inquire if they have admitted anyone fitting Q-Jo's description—and while awaiting their inevitable denials, try to picture where on Pill Hill each particular hospital is located in relation to Diamond and the Sorrento.

Three. Having owed Grandma Mati a letter ever since she left Oakland in February and moved back to the Philippines, you take out your Mont Blanc to pen her a note—and as the ink is soaking into the wood pulp, imagine the old lady throwing up her hands at the sight of Diamond and exclaiming, "He look big crazy, same as you papa!"

Four. Having had minimal experience in the commodities market, you remove a college textbook from the shelf—and while reviewing the chapter on futures investing, rekindle the hope that Diamond might assist you in your desperate ploy.

Five. Having reached the point where guilt and common decency will no longer allow you to ignore Belford's pathetic calls, you dial his hotel—and while the phone rings in San Francisco, find yourself wishing begrudgingly and altogether unreasonably that Diamond and not Dunn would pick up the receiver.

Two Forty-Two P.M.

Belford sounds so low he would have to stand on a ladder to change the bulb in a flashlight. His meeting with the French official has just ended on a pessimistic note, and he cannot fathom why you've not returned his calls. "Where've you been?" he asks, straining his larynx to the cracking point in his effort not to whine or accuse.

"Why, searching for André, of course," you reply so innocently that no turtledove would hesitate to build its nest among the quince blossoms of your inflection. "And I have some good news."

"You do?!"

"Well, sort of good news. I've seen him."

"You have?!"

"Uh, I *think* I have."

"What do you mean?"

"I'm pretty sure I've spotted him in the trees near the school. Twice. And I have a plan to entice him into my car."

"Oh, praise Jesus! I hope you're right. I'd rush back immediately, but every flight's booked solid because of the holiday. Happy Easter, by the way."

"Yeah. Happy Easter, Belford."

"There's no way I can get to Seattle before ten tonight."

"Good."

"What do you mean?"

"I'm sorry, I meant, that'll be good enough because it could take me awhile to, uh, corral him, but I may well have him for you when you arrive."

"But how'll you do it?"

"Never mind. Don't worry about it. I've got a scenario. Trust me."

"Oh, I do trust you, hon, I trust you explicitly, but I have to mention—and I'm not saying this to hurt you—I have to mention that, well, André, you know, he's not always inclined to, uh, respond to you."

"André and I have had our differences in the past, but I have the feeling we're going to get along just fine from now on."

"I'll be praying nonstop for both of you. You know, Gwen, if it's really him, one thing that might help is a banana Popsicle."

"Gee, yeah. Good idea, Belford. Maybe I'll try it."

TWO FIFTY-FIVE P.M.

You stare out the window for several minutes before it dawns on you that it's raining again. The last time you glanced at the sky, it was still largely blue. Well, that's Seattle for you. From lapis to tin in the blink of a lash. Blink once more and your espresso's diluted. Quick to wet and slow to dry, the city is resigned to sudden overcast and

293

prolonged spillage. Newcomers wring their damp mitts and fret about rot; old-timers curse and get on with business, aware that the next sunny day, although it may be weeks away, will trot out such a mountainous array of pagodas, sundaes, hero chins, and God fingers; such a sunset palette of Jell-O, Kool-Aid, Vegas strip, and carrot oil; such a sea-vista display of broad waters, firred islands, whale spouts, and sailboats thicker than triangles in a geometry book, that any and all memories of rain will fizz and implode in a blaze of bedazzled amnesia.

You have long ago grown accustomed to the witch measles of persistent drizzle, and although the assault on your makeup and hairdo never ceases to annoy you, you tend to take it in your snide. This afternoon, however, an unfamiliar ingot has been tonged onto the anvil of the gloom. You wonder if the rain has caught Larry Diamond still waiting outside the Sorrento Hotel. You picture him soaked, lonely and forlorn, risking a pneumonia that might severely complicate his malignancy and lower his resistance to its blows. Of course, Diamond is an amoral seducer and reckless weirdo who means little or nothing to you, and, besides, he is leaving tomorrow for some Timbukstupidtu, where a person would be lucky to find an unused Band-Aid, let alone chemotherapy, so how sick or how smart can he be? Nevertheless, it doesn't seem quite right just to leave him there in the rain without shelter or transportation, not in his condition. Would it hurt to give him a ride back to Thunder House? You ought to search the neighborhood around the bowling alley anyway, to see if Q-Jo's car might be there. You simply refuse to believe that she passed through a deadbolted door without a key.

THREE OH-SIX P.M.

"What are you gawking at?" you demand of the Thriftway cashier. It is obvious what she is staring at—it is the third time on a particular Easter Sunday that you have come in and purchased unusually large amounts of banana Popsicles—but it is none of her business, and you will be darned if you will let her get away with impertinence.

"Excuse me," she says, avoiding your glare while she bags your purchase. It's nice to see somebody else blush for a change.

You seize the bag. "These are the only known cure for stigmata," you say sternly. "If you were more than a jewelry-store Christian"—you nod at the little gold crucifix around her neck—"you'd know that."

"Yes, ma'am."

"And next time remember to ask if I want paper or plastic."

There. That makes you feel better. You smile all the way to Belford's place to pick up the pet harness.

Three-Sixteen **P.M.**

Essie Kudahl, who had seen you drive off but missed your return, is on her knees in the hallway squinting through Q-Jo's keyhole. Now it is your turn to clear your throat. My, oh my, how quickly a sallow face can redden! This is great fun for you, this spate of reverse embarrassment.

Wobbling to her fuzzy-slippered feet and gathering her bathrobe about her chest, as if she feared you were the Safe Sex Rapist, Mrs. Kudahl says, "It's doing something. It's doing something funny."

Brushing her aside and pressing your own chocolate eye to the keyhole, you soon figure out that what the macaque is doing is attempting to roll another cigarette. A bit groggy, he is less successful than he was earlier, and impatient fistfuls of tobacco are spilling off the cigarette paper onto his lap and the nubby old sofa on which he sits.

Ignoring Mrs. Kudahl, although you would love to make her blush some more, you pry loose the nails and unlock the door. "Hi, André. Hi, honey. Did you have a good rest?" You approach him cautiously, but despite his frustration with the cigarette, he seems rather docile. "Look, Auntie Gwen's gone and brought you another treat."

While the monkey slurps the Popsicle, you slip the harness over him and buckle it tight. "Good boy. Good monkey. Here, have another one. You and Gwendolyn are going to go for a little ride. And if you're nice, you can have lots of Popsicles. *Beaucoup.* Okay?"

Leading the happily dazed animal out of the room, you pause by the tarot table. Most of the deck has been knocked onto the floor by now, making it impossible, alas, to isolate from the scatter the card that André had impulsively snatched. You do glimpse a corner of the Nommo card, however, and it spurs you to hasten your departure. To Mrs. Kudahl, whose curlered head is hanging out of her doorway as if on a string, you call, "Happy Easter. The Father's a frog, the Son's a tadpole, the Holy Ghost is swamp gas."

THREE TWENTY-SEVEN P.M.

You anticipated difficulty in stashing André in the trunk of the Porsche, but as soon as you toss in the carton of Popsicles, he bounds right in behind it. He does screech a bit when you slam the lid, but the racket gradually subsides. It is only when you pat the trunk with satisfaction and turn away that you notice the squad car parked across the alley. *Drat,* you think. *Drat to the sixteenth power!*

"It's a Barbary ape," you call. "It hates the rain."

Smokey is rolling his eyes and shaking his head. "I didn't see nothing. Did you, Cecil?"

Cecil will not even look in your direction. Cecil, in fact, is staring at a row of overflowing garbage cans as intently as if he had a grant to study the effects of acid rain on used kitty litter. "I didn't see a goddamned thing," he growls. It is the voice of a defeated man.

All the way down Queen Anne Hill you keep checking your rearview mirror for flashing blue lights, but none appear and you proceed swiftly. Through downtown, the brisk pace continues, for the rain has driven the majority of the homeless and the criminal off the streets and into doorways and various makeshift shelters, where their trash fires hiss at the weather. Nevertheless, you select Third Avenue over the usually more teeming First, a route that carries you close to the Werewolf Club, where the coming attractions, you note, are the Drunk Drivers and the Tijuana Diaper Service. Naturally, the club reminds you of your last conversation with Q-Jo, but it would take more than that memory to tar your current glad mood.

Rain, that thin gray sheriff, has also served its coldhearted eviction notices to the crowd outside the Sorrento. Those who have not sardined into the lobby have returned to their cars or their homes. Scarcely a dozen still stand in the open courtyard, but among them is Diamond. He is soaked, to be sure, but hardly lonely or forlorn. Engaged in animated conversation with an attractive middle-aged Asian woman, his match-strike of a grin sulfurs the soggy air.

Fortuitously, a minivan has just vacated one of the limited parking spaces on Terry Avenue, and you nose right into it, beeping your horn to attract Diamond's attention. Eventually, he notices you and strides blithely over to the Porsche, his long hair, heavy with moisture, swinging to and fro, batting raindrops aside right and left.

"I was in the neighborhood," you say, powering down the window.

"Yes. Yes, indeed. Me, too." For some reason, you don't mind the mockery in his smile.

"I'm surprised you're still here. What's going on?"

"Well, the good doctor came back about twenty minutes ago. Not a very imposing figure, less so in person than on TV, and apparently he'd been sucking the sake cork again. He spoke with us briefly, though none too coherently. Showed us a plastic jar full of something that looked like the spinal fluid of a scarecrow. The enema elixir. The anal ambrosia. He indicated that aside from spring water, boiled brown rice, and beta-carotene, there's nothing in it except a pinch of coffee. Anybody could produce it if they were cognizant of the precise proportions."

"That's too bad."

"Why do you say that?"

"If the word gets around that there really isn't any secret formula that can be patented and protected, then the Nikkei's waterwings are going to pop tomorrow; and if Tokyo joins us in the octopus's garden, who's left to play lifeguard? We're pacing the bottom in cast-iron shoes."

"You're forgetting the nozzle. Without Yamaguchi's special nozzle, the formula's just so much dirty dishwater."

"One little enema nozzle can't prop up a world economy." It is only the second time you have ever used the word "enema" in mixed company, but you are too distracted to blush. "Drat! Well, anyway, would you like a lift home?"

"Sweet of you to inquire, pussy nougat, but I think I'll hang around here awhile longer. Yamaguchi inferred that he might come back and talk to us about the possibility of treatments after he changes suites. The hotel's moving him up to the seventh floor penthouse. For security reasons. It's not likely to do me much good in Timbuktu, but I feel I should be cognizant of available alternatives."

"You can't just wait out in the rain. You're drenched. Get in the car for a minute. I'll turn the heater on."

" 'Zip-A-Dee-Doo-Dah,' " sings Diamond. " 'Zip-A-Dee-Ay.' "

Four P.M.

In the beginning was the thing. And one thing led to another.

The simple but enduring truth of that abridged version of the first chapter of Genesis is demonstrated once again in the cockpit of the Porsche, a space in which you, the general public, and the vast majority of German automotive engineers would have deemed it impossible to have full-fledged sexual intercourse—but you remove your Exxon sweatshirt with which to dry his hair, he slips his tattooed hand inside your silk shirt, the windows conveniently fog over, and one thing leads to another.

Still, for the rest of your life, it will remain a mystery to you how the two of you managed it. But manage it you do, with vigor and tenderness and at considerable length. Snorting and whinnying, the white pony comes over the hill, trotting at first, then at a gallop, and just keeps coming and coming, until it reaches your front yard, where it kicks up its heels a few times and then lies down lazily and rolls in the clover. (Q-Jo was right: those other occasions had been false alarms, processed cheese, laugh tracks, and placebos.) The condensation on the windows gives you an exaggerated sense of privacy, but the way the Porsche was rocking at the apogee of your ardor, everyone in the neighborhood—thank goodness the cops have gone—must have guessed that something untoward was transpiring in that little sports car, and poor André must have felt as if he were going over Niagara Falls in a barrel.

"What's so funny, Gwendolyn?"

"Mmm. Nothing." No point spoiling a perfectly good post-coital reverie by informing Diamond there is a monkey aboard. Even after she has given her body, a girl must keep some secrets. You snuggle up to him. "Larry," you say dreamily.

"Yes?"

"Tell me about the good ol' days. Tell me about the eighties."

He sighs. "Ah, hoptoad." So, what did he expect? By now he surely must know you are not the type to inquire of a partner if it was good for him, too? He sighs again.

You sigh, as well. "If you won't tell me about the boat I missed, then tell me about one I stand a chance of catching."

"Well, there's always the nature boat, the art boat, the sex boat, the intoxication boat. They're bobbing at the end of nearly every pier, just waiting to ferry us across our personal doldrums, societal whirlpools, and institutional sewage lagoons. Why, the best of them can even cut the tides of mediocrity."

The "sex boat" had provided a more rewarding voyage than you ever thought possible, but you are ashore now, you have got your land legs back, and never at any time have you had art or nature or intoxication in mind. You untangle your panties from the gearshift. They prove so difficult to acrobat into that you can scarcely believe how easily they came off. When you have gotten yourself somewhat back together, you look Diamond in the eye. And then you spill your beans. You outline for him your oil futures play.

"As you might well imagine," you say when you are done, "I can't begin to meet the exchange minimums for buying marginal securities in a lot large enough to be worthwhile. But as you suggested yesterday—was it only yesterday?—there may be a way to journal around it. There's got to be. Larry?" You kiss him on both stubbled cheeks and then on the mouth. "Do you suppose you might . . . ?"

"Maybe. Perhaps. Let me think about it. Frankly, the prospect strikes me as less unethical than irrelevant. It's about as enticing as a cup of cold coffee and a stale croissant. But I'll lapidate it for a while in the old cerebral gem tumbler. Fair enough? In return, Uncle Larry's going to insist you do some lapidating of your own. Some lapidating and some laps. As in swimming. Because every one of those boats I mentioned is leaky, to one degree or another, and the boat *you're* waiting for may have already sunk. So much the better. It could be time to abandon ship and get back in the water. Or at least onto the pad. So, wipe that manipulative, avaricious entreaty off your chops and listen up to a tale or two."

Okay, Uncle Larry. As long as you put it that way.

FOUR FORTY-FIVE **P.M.**

"I noticed," says Diamond, "that you were admiring the bloom of my manhood."

"I was not!"

"Even an inadvertent peek would have informed you that I've been circumcised."

"So? You're Jewish, aren't you?"

"I'm precisely as Jewish as you are Welsh. Anyhow, it's amusing how we associate circumcision with the Jews. The practice was originated by the Egyptians. Moses, who, of course, was raised in the Egyptian court, commanded the Israelites to circumcise their sons, either because he'd become convinced that it was good hygiene or because, since he'd had his own wick trimmed, he viewed it as an expression of loyalty to him and solidarity among the rebels. Any way you slice it, benign genital mutilation was a feature of predynastic Egypt—we're talking five thousand years ago—and the traditions, rituals, and body of knowledge based on the Sirius star system originated in the same area at about the same time. Today, certain Bozo and Dogon ceremonies that are centered around Sirius also involve rites of circumcision. To these tribes, the act of circumcision symbolizes the orbit of Sirius B around Sirius A."

"Pardon me, but isn't this maybe another case of males trying to attach cosmic significance to their peepees?"

"Heh! It has to do, smarty-pants, with the elliptical path of the knife. Besides, the 'peepee,' as you so ingloriously label it, already *has* innate cosmic significance, as does your own sweet plumbing, for reasons both ecstatic and procreative. In many, if not most, folk traditions, the peepee *and* the vagina are associated with frogs. Frogs are associated with mushrooms, mushrooms are associated with genitalia, and all three—frogs, mushrooms, and sex organs—have their indirect connection to the stars. I bring this up merely to demonstrate how intertwined these matters are. It's so complex I hardly know where to begin."

"Gee, if it's that complicated, if it's going to, you know, tax your brain, please don't feel obligated to continue on my account."

Diamond starts to reply, then pauses and cocks his head. "Gwendolyn, I'm aware that this is a late-model, luxury automobile, but by any chance do you have mice in the trunk?"

You fake an incredulous and insulted expression, but *your* ears detect the rustling, too; and although the Porsche's cockpit is already heavily perfumed with the comingling of male and female

301

nectars, not to mention the burnt-sugar aroma of Twister's daddy's leaves, your nose is starting to pick up the unmistakable essence of monkey.

Four Forty-Eight P.M.

"I'll be back in a flash," says Diamond. You worry that he is going around to the rear to investigate your cargo, but through the condensation on the window glass, you make out his ghostly silhouette loping across the street toward the hotel. When he returns a few minutes later, he announces, with some relief, that he has not missed anything, that Dr. Yamaguchi is still upstairs, probably sleeping off lunch. "Reiko will yell for me if he shows up." He flicks a drop or two from the chisel of his nose. "I'm going to miss this rain in parched ol' Timbuktu."

"Best reason I've heard yet for going there. Come to think of it, it's the *only* reason I've heard for going there."

"I went there because I thought it was as far as one could go; a value-free, time-free refuge from the shit-storms of commerce and information. However, since the universe is *made* of information, what I ended up doing, under the impetus of a new data base, was shedding one layer of meaning and exposing another. It was an infinitely deeper, more resonant layer, though, and it revealed my naive travel impulses to have been divinely inspired. Gwendolyn, you seem to be familiar with Sirius."

"Isn't everybody? The Dog Star. Brightest star in the sky. Only eight-point-five light-years away."

"Six. Eight-point-six."

You shrug. "That's what they say. Looks more like eight-point-five to me."

Diamond studies you. He cannot tell for sure if you are joshing. "You've scoped it?"

"Why, of course," you say boastfully. "Scoped Sirius B, too."

"Then you must have had a well-made scope. Sirius B is so relatively tiny and so overwhelmed by the light of Sirius A that it's completely invisible to the naked eye and wasn't even discovered by astronomers with telescopes until late in the last century. You're aware of that, I gather?"

"Uh, more or less."

"But are you aware that people in Africa—ancestors of the Bozo and Dogon—knew Sirius B as long as five thousand years ago? Not only knew of the existence, the exact location, of this star that the naked eye can't see, but knew, also, the exact shape of its orbit around A and how long it takes to complete that orbit? Incidentally, it takes approximately fifty years, and contemporary Bozo still have ceremonies that adhere to fifty-year cycles. Furthermore, B, like all white dwarfs, is extremely heavy and dense. The stuff it's made of is so unlike ordinary matter that there's nothing in our solar system to compare it to. The Bozo, who're largely illiterate and never have possessed astronomical instruments of any kind, know that, as well. The knowledge was handed down to them by their ancestors. Needless to say, when I heard about this, it altered the trajectory of my life."

"But why? That's what I don't get. I mean, okay, it's kind of interesting, it's an intriguing mystery, like how did they build the pyramids and who figured out the connection between the human subconscious and those symbols they put on Q-Jo's tarot cards, and which came first, the chicken or the egg—but, hey, what difference does it make? What does it have to *do* with anything? Our family life, our careers, our health and well-being, our personal finances: none of these things are affected in the slightest. Most of us have to concentrate on the realities of everyday existence, Larry. Maybe you have the luxury to become obsessed with some forgotten supermarket tabloid enigma, but the rest of us don't, and frankly, I think you are the worse for it."

"Ah, Gwendolyn, while it may be true that 'everyday existence' is the tirl of dull, repetitive activities that you infer, it's just one layer of a many-layered cake; and if it seems an exercise in pointless mediocrity, maybe that's only because most who live it are too narrowly focused to perceive its underlying kaleidoscopic density."

"Or too darn busy. Besides, I never said it was pointless or mediocre."

"Don't interrupt. I'll concede, however, that there's a dominant consensual reality, and even the broad-minded don't venture too far from it. Yes, I'll concede that. Yet the very fact that certain Africans, thousands of years before the invention of the telescope, could accumulate precise information about an obscure, invisible star, that fact strongly suggests that there's a rip in the fabric of consensual reality, a crack in that rational structure that we'd like to believe holds things together. And that crack calls many of our most fundamental beliefs—historical, scientific, and religious—into question. If Sirius B could be familiarized without telescopes, couldn't molecules or atoms be familiarized without microscopes? And if these feats of perception are possible, what then is impossible? The Dogon and Bozo, by the way, have always claimed that Sirius is a three-star system, that there's also a Sirius C. So far, modern astronomy has found no evidence of it."

"Well, if it's there, they'll find it. And they'll have a logical explanation for it. I'll bet they already have a logical explanation for how the Bozo knew about Sirius B. Now, don't they?"

"Are you kidding? Conventional scientists wouldn't touch that problem with a ten-foot grant. Of course, not a dime of grant juice would ever be made available for such study. There're no apparent commercial or military applications, and, anyway, riddles of this sort scare scientists right out of their lab coats. They're as cowed by the big-time mysteries of the universe as the guy on the street and are only too happy to sweep them under a rug."

"There has to be a logical explanation."

"You're half right. At its macro and micro levels, the universe is no more logical than the stock market. But there *is* an explanation. The few good minds that've addressed the issue have arrived at the same conclusion: the ancestors of the Bozo got their detailed knowledge of Sirius, as well as the content of their complex cosmology, from visiting aliens. Yes, hoptoad. Yes, indeed. They're talking the ol' extraterrestrial contact."

At this moment, as if on cue, André lets loose a barrage of unearthly jabber. You force an extended laugh, pretending that you are ridiculing the suggestion of spacemen in Bozoland, but Diamond is not fooled by your cover-up.

"What in pre-shrunk hell was that?"

"That noise, you mean? Oh, probably a space alien, ha-ha-ha."

"Gwendolyn!"

"Well, how am *I* supposed to know what it was? It's the streets of Seattle out there. These days you're liable to hear just about anything. Could have been the rich boys up to their tricks."

"But of course. The rich boys. They've added impressions of early Tarzan movie soundtracks to their fiendish repertoire." He rakes you with his cat-claw smile. "It sounded like it was right behind our seats."

"Maybe sound carries in the rain. I don't know." André must have polished off all the Popsicles and either has a bellyache or is demanding more. In any case, there's nothing you can do about it now. You just hope Diamond isn't reading your mind. "It's stopped," you say, crossing your fingers. "So, what were you saying about extraterrestrial contact?"

Grumbling like W. C. Fields at a kindergarten picnic, Diamond returns to his narration.

FIVE OH-TWO P.M.

"The argument that the early Bozo couldn't possibly have gotten into the cosmic cookie jar without outside help wouldn't hold quite so much water, so to speak, if there weren't a record of extraterrestrial contact in the oral history of the tribe."

"Seriously? They actually claim they were visited by little green men?"

305

"Green, maybe. Little, no. The Nommo were at least as tall as us."

For some reason, the word "Nommo," like "hostile takeover" or "leverage buyout," sends ripples of nervous excitement through your plasma. You shiver. "Nommo, like on Q-Jo's Star card? That Nommo was supposed to be from outer space?"

"Rather like ol' Jesus, but whereas the Scriptures are vague regarding the exospheric location of Heaven, Bozo tradition doesn't hesitate to list the Nommo's specific address. They came from the system of the star, *sima kayne*. Sirius, to me and thee. Which, by the way, is precisely where modern science expects extraterrestrial contact to come from if e.t. contact is ever made."

"Why there?"

"Proximity. Pure and simple. Sirius is in our neighborhood. Or just outside of it. Still one hell of a long distance from Cincinnati, but within range of a properly engineered spaceship. The mythology of the sub-Sahara relates how an 'ark' landed on the earth . . ."

"So it's only a myth."

"Gwendolyn, Gwendolyn. Surely you're not one of those undereducated boobs who believes a myth to be a set of exaggerated facts. A myth, you ought to know, is a metaphoric method of describing, dramatizing, and condensing historical events and psychological states that are otherwise too complicated to be digested or appreciated by the prevailing society. So, pussy chops, when the Bozo and Dogon say that an interstellar ark once landed on the earth to the northeast of them—and lo! What's to their northeast but Egypt?—they could be referring to an external event, a centuries' long series of events, or a strictly psychological phenomenon, a sort of enchantment. In any case, the Africans say that when the 'ark' touched down, its weight caused its 'blood' to spurt to the sky. The way they describe the reddish rays emanating from the landing craft makes it sound suspiciously like some kind of a rocket ship."

At this point, Diamond flings the back of his hand toward your face with such force that you duck, thinking he is trying to strike you. "A tad jumpy, aren't you, sweetheart? That's said to be the sign

306

of a guilty conscience." You redden. He grins. And André rattles a
tire jack.

Diamond's hand, embarrassingly scented with the oils of your
vagina, remains in your face. He is showing you his tattoo. "This is a
copy of a well-known tribal drawing that depicts three versions of
the Nommo vehicle. It doesn't require much more than the imagination of a state legislator to interpret these circles and rays as various
stages of the firing of rocket engines."

"Okay. Yeah. I can see that, I guess. Kind of a stretch but I can
see it. What I don't see is why you'd have it tattooed on your hand."

Diamond's grin is almost boyish. "Gets me excellent service in
Bozo restaurants," he says.

"How convenient."

You await further explanation but hear nothing beyond the
rain typing its memoirs on the roof of the car and the process of
Popsicle wrappers being turned into monkey confetti in the trunk.
Fearful that Diamond will detect the latter sound as well, you are
relieved when he finally says, "You know, it may be an omen that it's
raining while I'm telling you these things. Aside from being the
'monitors of the universe' and the 'guardians of the soul,' the
Nommo were also called the 'dispensers of rain' and the 'masters of
all water.' Supposedly, the purpose of the Nommo's visit was to
bring spiritual principles to the human race. Sometimes, when my
brain is soft, I think I can almost hear these principles being transmitted by the rain."

"Yeah? Hear voices, do you, Larry?" André uncorks a short
shriek, and you exclaim, "Wow! You're right! There's one now!"

He glares at you so violently that you take his hand and
squeeze his kooky tattoo. "Just kidding," you say. "But tell me something. If these aliens from Sirius, these Nommo, were the masters of
rain and water, why were they hanging out in that part of the world?
Where it's so horribly dry?"

"Five thousand years ago, Africa was a lot wetter than it is
today. Its deserts are a relatively recent phenomena. The Nommo
would probably have found plenty of water. And there would have

307

been large amounts of water aboard their spaceship, too. There would have had to have been."

"And why's that?"

"Because," he says. "The Nommo were amphibians."

FIVE-TWELVE P.M.

While raindrops scurry down the windshield of the parked Porsche like sow bugs rushing to a rotten-wood festival; and the macaque continues to shred Popsicle wrappers in the trunk, as if he were employed in the document room of a Republican president, Larry Diamond, in his astringent drawl, drones on and on about large half-human amphibious creatures with webbed digits and fishtails who, according to the Dogon and Bozo, founded their civilizations. Apparently, they founded other, earlier, more important civilizations as well, for Diamond relates that the Assyrians, Babylonians, and Sumerians each venerated a group of beings who came from reedy, watery regions to bring written language and spiritual values to humankind. In the pictographic and cuneiform fragments from ancient Sumer, which represent the world's oldest extant examples of writing, the half-man, half-fish is referred to as Oannes, and to Oannes is ascribed many of the deeds and functions that the Hebrews later appropriated for their heroes—Noah, for example—in the Old Testament. Jehovah, himself, may have been patterned after the amphibian Oannes, although the Dogon and Bozo insist that the Nommo were not gods but highly developed mortals.

"Nevertheless," Diamond goes on, "there are definite parallels between the accounts of the Nommo and the Christ stories. A French anthropologist was told by a Dogon priest that the Nommo 'divided his body among men to feed them' and that 'the universe had drunk of his body.' Sound familiar? You ever take communion, Gwendolyn? Swallow the leader?"

After you have registered disgust at his pun, he continues. "It is also taught that the alien amphibians will return. Yes, pussy pie. Yes, indeed. Coming soon to a pond near you. The Advent of the Nommo. Will you be ready? Are you prepared? Are you on the pad? You will be, if you stick with Uncle Larry."

You make a face and Diamond laughs. "By the way, the celestial symbol of the Nommo resurrection is *ie pelu tolo*, 'star of the tenth moon.' You can't find this star, not even with a radio telescope, because, according to the Bozo, it'll only be formed when the Nommo's 'ark' descends. So *ie pelu tolo*'s not a star, per se, it's a starship." Again, he shoves his pussy-perfumed paw in your face. "Star of the tenth moon," he says, waving his tattoo. "You'll notice that these orbs also resemble the eyes of a frog."

"Yeah. And the moon does kind of look like green cheese," you mumble. You really don't know how to react to any of this. Is Diamond actually on to something significant, or has his brain been bungee-jumping off a piano stool? You are forced, more or less, to lean toward the former possibility because, otherwise, you have to admit you have just had the crowning coitus of your young life with a crackpot. "I don't know what to say, Larry. I mean, essentially you're asking me to believe that civilization was brought to the human race by a bunch of swamp things from Sirius . . ."

"From a planet in the Sirian system, to be precise. The Egyptian word for the Sirian system, you might like to hear, also meant 'throne.' And what do you do with a throne? You sit on it."

"So that may be where 'sitting trouser' comes from."

"Good girl! Yes, perhaps. Among sub-Saharan peoples today, the phrase to 'keep seated' means to behave in an intelligent, virtuous manner. Obviously, you don't have to look very far in any direction to ascertain that the general population is out of its seat in a major way. Loudmouthed ignorance and criminality abound. It's been a grand show, all these frightened fools and greedy gangsters on their feet, jumping up and down; but it's starting to get a trifle tiresome, and, of course, it's egregiously unfair to other species; to the animals and plants that have had the good sense and the purity all these millennia to keep seated. It could be marvelously refreshing, don't you think, were the Nommo to return and coax us back on our haunches. End all this pushing and shoving, this yammering for attention. Picture us squatting—I'm speaking symbolically—serene and wise, like frogs on a lily pad."

You have to smile. "Yes, Larry, dear, that's a nice idealistic fairy tale. Unfortunately, that's all it is. I mean, come on: to start with, the whole idea of these Nommo mermen is totally far-fetched."

"Before you bet the ranch on that, ponder a few things. It's a mathematical certainty that there're intelligent life-forms in the universe besides us hooligan earthlings. Considering the vast age of many of the other solar systems, it's also highly probable that a number of them have developed technologies more advanced than our own. Since we're an innocuous little planet on the fringes of a mediocre galaxy—a kind of interstellar Timbuktu—any interested parties would likely hail from a relatively close system. The Sirian system's a perfect candidate. For more distant systems, we wouldn't be worth the effort. Well, our sun's a great ball of fire, but it's practically a snowball compared to Sirius A, whose luminosity is twenty-three times brighter than El Sol, even though it's only half again as large. Any planet orbiting Sirius is going to be on the warm side. And probably cloud-covered at all times. Even through the vapor, it would be harmful to one's vision to look up at Sirius. Now, what sort of dominant, sentient life-form would evolve in that hot, brilliant, steamy world? Amphibious mammals, wouldn't you say?"

"Why amphibious *mammals?*"

"Because only mammals possess the brain size necessary to create civilizations and technologies. *Amphibious* mammals because to keep cool and protect their skin and eyes, they would have needed to spend much of their time in and under the water. Long ago, naturally, they would have developed tinted glass and air-conditioning, but since biological evolution lags behind technological innovation by millions of years, these beings, even today, would be as accustomed to, and perhaps dependent on, life in the oceans and lakes as we are to life on land. As mammals, they'd require oxygen periodically, but they'd be quite comfortable underwater. They'd be a lot like dolphins with hands and feet."

310

"You savor that image, I can tell."

"Yes. Yes," he drawls. "It's delectable to contemplate an ambulatory porpoise rocketing in to awaken humanity from its grabby trance, much as the porpoises I swam with in Florida awakened me from the trance of autism." He holds up his hand, but the one without the tattoo. "You're aware, I suppose, that in the fins of dolphins there're the skeletal vestiges of fingers. Yes, indeed. There was a time when dolphins could have performed card tricks or tickled the ivories. Conceivably, our big-brained, playful friends are related in some manner to the space-traveling Nommo."

"Is that true? About vestigial fingers?"

"Cross my heart."

He doesn't add "and hope to die," but then a cancer victim *wouldn't* add that. "Well," you say, "I concede that it's plausible that entities like the Nommo could exist somewhere in the universe, and it may even be plausible that these entities hopped down to Africa and briefed the Bozo on astronomy, but when all's said and done, I can't swallow it. Sorry, but I do not believe that's how the Bozo learned about Sirius B."

You expect him to get huffy and call you "hoptoad," but he smiles and says, "That's good, pussy gravy. Frankly, I don't believe it, either."

Surprise rings your eyes like a pair of goggles. Before Diamond can explain himself, however, there is a rapping at the passenger window.

FIVE TWENTY-FOUR P.M.

Your first fear is that André has jimmied the latch on the trunk and is free and seeking retribution. Your second fear is that someone in the neighborhood has summoned the vice squad: you check to make sure your blouse is buttoned. When Diamond lowers the window, however, the Asian woman with whom he was flirting earlier leans in.

"Excuse me, please," she says shyly. "I'm sorry. I wished to tell you that Dr. Yamaguchi has sent word he will come to the lobby at six o'clock."

"Why, thank you, Reiko," Diamond says. "I'll be there."

"Okay. Excuse me." Her nose is quivering ever so slightly, almost imperceptibly, but Diamond takes notice.

"Smells pretty in here, doesn't it, Reiko? Are you old enough to remember the Beatles? Remember John Lennon and Paul McCartney? When they sang, they'd put their faces together at the microphone in such a way that they'd blend into just one face." He sighs. "It was the most beautiful face I've ever seen. Now, it's the same when a man and a woman put their odors together, don't you think? They blend into the single best odor in the world."

Reiko withdraws gracefully and with dignity, but as she walks away she cannot help shaking her head from side to side. Diamond seems to have that effect on people.

FIVE TWENTY-FIVE P.M.

During the next half hour, cramped in the sex-saturated cockpit of the Porsche, accompanied by the silver whips and molluskan castanets of the rain, and uninterrupted by monkey chatter (André apparently having grown bored and fallen asleep), Larry Diamond serenades you with a medley of unfamiliar and generally unfathomable notions. Here are the several that stick in your mind:

The Bozo received their information about the stars telepathically.

They, or, to be precise, their ancient ancestors, enhanced their telepathic abilities through the ritualistic use of so-called visionary

312

compounds. Hemp derivatives and iboga, a flowering bush with a long history of use as a hallucinogen in West Africa, were certainly employed and enjoyed, but it may have been psilocybic mushrooms, sprouting from the dung plops of migrating herds back when the savannas were blessed with rain, that fostered the early Africans' telepathic powers; that, in fact, provided the expanded awareness that allowed them to evolve to a more complex level than cousin baboon or cousin chimp.

While in a radically sensitized state (among Africans, the state produced by iboga is referred to as "open-heartedness") imbibers, singularly or in groups, may have been able to pick up mental transmissions from the extraterrestrial amphibians whom they were to know as Oannes, or Nommo, and who were never to *physically* travel to our planet. It wouldn't have been necessary.

An even more likely and perhaps more portentous possibility, according to Diamond, is that the transmissions received by early Bozo came not from an advanced amphibian civilization orbiting Sirius but from a dimension of their own consciousness. The temptation is to label that dimension the "higher mind," although it may actually be the lower mind, the aspect that Jung called "the bottom below the bottom." In any case, it is an aspect of consciousness shared, but not easily accessed, by all human beings. It is the overmind (or undermind) of the species.

It is hardly astonishing that the overmind would manifest itself in an amphibious guise, for the simple reason that we land-based primates are essentially, ultimately aquatic.

313

———

Sperm swim in a liquid conveyance. The fetus forms and develops entirely submerged in fluid. Human embryonic development closely parallels the metamorphic stages of the frog. Until the umbilical cord is severed, newborn infants can thrive underwater. In its chemical composition, blood bears a most remarkable resemblance to seawater. Our bodies are more than sixty-five percent water. And our progenitors were marine animals who experimented with dry oxygen and became addicted.

———

In a manner of speaking, human beings are fish out of water.

———

The sea is the cradle we all rocked out of, and it may be the homeplace to which we will someday return.

———

There would be several important advantages in resuming an amphibious way of life. Since, for example, nearly three-quarters of the biosphere's surface is covered by water, and since—thanks to a rampant stupidity compounded by the sinister designs of organized religion—overpopulation is reducing the quality of life, profaning the sanctity of life, and threatening the continuation of life, the oceans and great lakes constitute Earth's final frontier, a vast area for resettlement and refuge. The seas are immeasurably rich in natural resources. Water blocks radiation, providing protection, therefore, both from solar rays streaming unchecked through a depleted ozone layer and from the nuclear fires almost certain to be unleashed sooner or later by any one of a dozen nasty little nations.

————

If global warming melts the polar ice caps, as some predict, we will have little choice in our resumption of an aquatic life-style.

————

Our race has long been titillated by images of a "lost civilization" beneath the sea. Some say it is legend, some say it is genetic memory, a few say there is small difference. Their common mistake is their relegation of this "vanished" utopia to ancient history. Deep consciousness is hardly bound by the constraints of linear time. Atlantis is in our future, not our past.

————

On the other hand, Atlantis may figure both in our future *and* our past. Surely we harbor pleasant cellular memories of dolphinlike romps in warm prehistoric seas, of gentle froggy transformations in the security of a water-filled womb. Lost utopias.

————

Scientists report that no creature on earth dreams as much as the human fetus. If the fetal brain has had no experience, if its newly formed mind is a tabula rasa, what then does it dream about? Do we imagine that the tiny swimmer's dreams are dry? That no Nommo splash therein? That the mood is other than oceanic?

————

315

Oceanic, significantly enough, is a word we choose to describe the immense and ecstatic feeling of oneness—oneness with humanity, with the biosphere, with the Divine—that occasionally overtakes all but the hopelessly insensitive and frequently illuminates the contemplative and astute. In this context, *oceanic* is a spiritual term, and spiritual transformation is what the amphibian-sidereal connection is all about.

———

At some eschatological moment, having at last absorbed the values that the Nommo, literally or figuratively, came here to impart, we may ride the currents to the stars, where, in the dimension of the overmind, we'll experience closure with the godhead, eventually to embark on even higher tides to even stranger destinations requiring even more unimaginable transformations.

———

Meanwhile, at our present level of development, largely oblivious to our origins and our destination, we are half-asleep in frog pajamas.

FIVE FIFTY-FIVE P.M.

Diamond said a lot of other things, but these are the highlights, if that isn't too strong a word. These are the wild ideas with which you might entertain Q-Jo, providing Diamond hadn't already spun them around her turban at their Friday morning session and providing you ever see Q-Jo again. Oh, yeah, and there was the stuff about Buddha: how in almost every picture or statue where Buddha's extremities are shown, he has webbed fingers and toes; and how the seated Buddha's silhouette strongly resembles a bullfrog.

Had you the time or inclination, you suppose you could do some research and ascertain whether the Buddha had webbed feet or if Uncle Larry was pulling your leg. And you might dig out that dog-eared Bible that Grandma Mati sent you before she moved back to the Philippines and check Exodus, Chapter Eight, to see if there really is a passage therein about Egypt being invaded by frogs. Those things you could look up, but what about the Greek business? How there supposedly were fifty sisters called the Danaids who ventured out of the reedy marshes of the Nile delta to bring the gift of water to the most arid region of the Peloponnese. Fifty sisters, mind you, one for each year of Sirius B's orbit around Sirius A. The Danaids were descendants of reed-wielding Io, who in Egypt was known as Isis, a word that referred to "seat" or "throne"—as well as to the Sirius system. "Gee," you had said, "so many crisscrosses, overlaps, and connections."

"Yes," agreed Diamond. "Yes, indeed. And I'm barely skimming the surface. All those ancient marquee cultures were drinking out of the same gourd. Or the same dog dish. 'Dog' as in Dog Star. Virtually everything that sparkled in the Golden Age of Greece was borrowed from the Egyptians, and the Egyptians adapted *their* routines from the royal blacks of Nubia. We moderns overlook Nubia, we forget how proud and fancy and influential it was. Nubia played Professor Longhair and Big Mama Thornton to Egypt's Elvis. The Nubians were lake and river dwellers, and well acquainted with amphibians and stars and mushrooms. I could go on and on."

As far as you're concerned, he *did* go on and on. And now, at the conclusion of his rant, he is bringing up mushrooms again.

"I realize it's cracking your little heart in two, but I've got to get over to the hotel and hear what Yamaguchi has to say. He's not supposed to say *anything* else before the conference tomorrow, but, heh-heh, he gives every indication of being out of control." Diamond slides his hand up your skirt, plucks like a lyre the sex-encrusted crotch line of your panties. You would have stopped him, except that for the past ten or fifteen minutes, he has been squirming in his seat, and it is obvious he is in pain again. Moreover, his plucking is vibrating the lips of your vulva, and it feels, in a vulgar and embarrassing way, rather agreeable. "Before I go, however, well,

I'd be remiss if I neglected to say something else about the mush-room."

"I'll forgive you if you don't. You wouldn't want to miss Yamaguchi."

"No, no, you really must hear this. The Africans often referred to Sirius as the 'seed star.' It may sound quaint today and not very hip, but they believed emanations from the Sirian system were a pouring out of the seed of the soul and that the seed which, um, energized the world came directly from Sirius. Okay? Now, are you aware that it's possible for seeds to drift through space, through outer space? That seeds, over time and on their own, could theoreti-cally travel from one solar system to another?"

"Wouldn't they die out there?"

"Some might, but many are perfectly equipped to survive for millions of years; indefinitely, in fact. Mushroom spores, for exam-ple, aside from being very light in weight, have a particularly lengthy viability."

"This is another tidbit you gleaned in Timbuktu?"

"Well, I sure as hell didn't hear it from Dean Witter. But imag-ine it: the hardy spores of psilocybic mushrooms blowing through darkest space, sifting and sailing, rubbing elbows with particles of cosmic dust for eons before finally entering Earth's atmosphere and eventually falling into bed, so to speak, into the moist soil of some prehistoric meadow. Where they spread their mycelia and display their fruit. Which, someday, inevitably, will be sampled by a hungry or merely curious primate. Bingo!"

"Bingo?"

"Yes. Yes, indeed. A light goes on. The energizing of the world has begun. The awakening of the soul. You see, the Nommo wouldn't have had to voyage to Earth in a starship or even to project telepathically. Everything they had to teach our species, from philo-sophical values to the anatomy of their star system, could have been transmitted through the medium of the mushroom. The mushroom may be the microphone of the overmind."

"And we know, don't we, Larry," you say with just a salt of sarcasm, "that mushrooms are associated with frogs?"

"Good girl."

"And the frogs have started to disappear."

"Yes. Something is afoot. Some force, some program that was set into motion millennia ago, has begun to accelerate. You've mocked, perhaps with justification, my little conceit about the pad, but when I speak of being on the pad, all I mean is being intellectually, emotionally, and spiritually prepared to fully participate in the next breakthrough in evolution. It may occur as a sudden mutative thrust, rather than the microstep by microstep advancement we've come to accept, and ninety percent of the population—those frozen in the ice pack of their bankrupt doctrines and brittle clichés—may be left behind. I'd hate to find you in their company."

"That's sweet of you. But you don't need to worry about me." *If I can ride out this darn market,* you think, *I'll take my chances with evolution; fast, slow, or down the middle.* "Truthfully, I can't understand why you'd want me on the pad."

"Ah, hoptoad! Can't you see? You have potential! You're a mother lode of wit, of spunk, of courage, of adaptability. But it's all repressed and misdirected. You need to cut loose, open up, break free." He snaps your elastic. "And you're *potentially* the best piece of ass in Seattle." You slap his hand away from your groin and push him toward his side of the car. "What's more, I adore your voice."

"Really?" You soften with a suddenness no mutative thrust could ever match. "Really? You *do*?"

Six P.M.

As he limps across the street in the rain, Diamond's good-bye kiss reverberates in your mouth like a firecracker in a silverware drawer. The screwball certainly can kiss. You have to grant him

319

that. But can world-class kissing compensate for. . . . Oh, no! He's turning around and heading back to your car. You hope he isn't going to wax sentimental. He's already tried to extract a promise from you to meet again later in the evening or before his flight tomorrow. You said you would see what you could do. It would influence your decision if there was a chance that you could smuggle him into your disco for an hour or two. Sit him down at your computer.

"Gwendolyn," he says, raindrops glistening on his stubble like champagne on a scouring pad, "I hope you're not going to start thinking of me as your guru."

Good grief! You have to laugh. "Uh, of course not, Larry. Not a chance."

"I can't save your soul . . ."

"How about my job?"

". . . nobody can but you. At this stage of the game, it's every man for himself. Every woman, too."

"I can live with that."

"The Nommo can't save us, either. They may be from Sirius, they may be an extrusion of the overmind, they may be both at the same time. But they aren't going to ride to our rescue, any more than Jesus is or Marx or any cavalry charge yet devised by the sanctimonious pimps who shill for our assorted and voracious ideologies. Mistrust them all, sweetheart."

"Oh, I do."

"The Advent of the Nommo may not necessarily improve our lot. It might even make things worse. Perhaps the best we can hope for is that things will be different. That cycles will be broken. That dogmas will be discredited. Uncle Larry is for change, Gwendolyn. He's for slipping into new skin, sharing information irresponsibly, and belly flopping into those ancient ponds whose still waters we've gone so very long without parting."

"Fine."

"Yes. Well, just thought I ought to mention that."

"Thanks. You're considerate."

"Yes. Yes, indeed. And in return, maybe someday you'll be considerate enough to tell me what you're doing with a fucking monkey in the trunk of your car."

He rips you with his eyes, then hobbles away.

. . .

Sunday
Night
April 8

. . .

"Some People Calls It Madness"

Six Twenty-One P.M.

You fling open the trunk with what amounts to a prayer in your heart, praying that the conspicuously silent André has not perished for lack of oxygen—a detail you should have considered earlier—and are immediately reminded of the Mona Lisa. André and Leonardo's famous model share an ability to look quizzical and curious despite the fact that neither has eyebrows. Ham actors, for whom eyebrows are the banners and billboards of all emotion, could learn a lot about expression from the browless Mona, the browless macaque.

Straighten André's hair, dress him in a Florentine smock and a thin veil, seat him on a loggia with eroded rocks and several miles of bad road behind him, and he could be the Mona Lisa's double. The monkey exhibits the same dainty (and browless) faceful of elusive sentiment, hinting at bewilderment—or is it private amusement? He looks so searching, so poignant, so altogether human as he regards you with unexpected quietness from his nest of Popsicle wrappers and tire chains, that you cannot help but think of Italian art. And evolution.

Primate similarities notwithstanding, you would prefer to avoid the subject of evolution. Not that you doubt Darwin's theory. To the contrary, when you were a schoolgirl you used to argue, as schoolgirls will, evolution with Grandma Mati. Your grandmother did not believe in evolution. She believed in a literal interpretation of the Book of Genesis. She believed in the Bible, in Imelda Marcos, in her homemade octopus adobo, and not much else. Grandma Mati did not accept evolution in Oakland, California, and now that she is back in her ancestral village on the outskirts of Manila, she probably accepts it less. You, on the other hand, have always accepted it as a matter of course. Yet, until you met Larry Diamond, you thoughtlessly presumed that evolution was over with, that it had achieved its goals, then petered out. You, like millions of other arrogant chauvinists, had taken it for granted that the human species was the end product of the evolutionary process, its culminating and crowning glory. How could you have held that notion for an instant?

We, with our propensity for murder, torture, slavery, rape, cannibalism, pillage, advertising jingles, shag carpets, and golf, how could we be seriously considered as the perfection of a four-billion-year-old grandiose experiment? Perhaps as a race, we have evolved as far as we are capable, yet that by no means suggests that evolution has called it quits. In all likelihood, it has something *beyond human* on the drawing board. We tend to refer to our most barbaric and crapulous behavior as "inhuman," whereas, in point of fact, it is exactly human, definitively and quintessentially human, since no other creature habitually indulges in comparable atrocities. This negates neither our occasional virtues nor our aesthetic triumphs, but if a being at least a little bit more than human is not waiting around the bend of time, then evolution has suffered a premature ejaculation.

In any event, André, for all his restrained and reflective Renaissance mien, seems to have endured his imprisonment salubriously. If he is uncharacteristically compliant as you lead him into your building, his motor skills are normal, his eyes bright. The question now is what to do with him until Belford gets home. Hours have passed since you last went to the toilet, and your bladder, repeatedly jostled by Diamond's prow, feels as large as a ripe melon, bursting and bruised; yet, if you are uneasy about leaving André alone, you are doubly uneasy about allowing him to accompany you to the bathroom. What type of woman would let a monkey watch her pee?

In the end, wobbling along with your legs squeezed together, you usher him into the tub, fasten his harness chain to a faucet, and draw the shower curtain closed. By the time you plop down on the toilet seat, your stream is already underway. A close call, but you made it! You have voided only about a cupful, however, before the shower curtain is ripped down like a tyrant's flag, and André, jibbering all the while, is giving you the simian once-over. You attempt to stem the flow, but it's just too painful, so, avoiding his gaze, you blush and squirt away. To the best of your knowledge, André has never enjoyed the companionship of a lady macaque, but you have the distinct sensation that he has a pretty good idea of what it is you are trying to conceal. With that in mind, you are hasty and furtive when the moment comes to dab yourself dry, and you turn obliquely away from him to yank up your underpants.

You smell like midweek at the Biloxi Shrimp Festival, yet a shower and a change of clothes are out of the question until . . . until what? You are uncertain. Maybe you need to sit quietly somewhere and think.

When you go to unhook André's tether from the faucet, his expression is less that of Leonardo's *Mona Lisa* than Frans Hals's *Laughing Cavalier*. You might even describe it as a smirk. Larry Diamond mentioned—God knows you cannot remember why—that frogs, relatively speaking, have unusually large bladders, providing a reserve of water that their bodies make use of on those occasions when they are trapped on dry land. For your own urinary receptacle, you desire Nommo dimensions because there is absolutely no way you will go to the bathroom with this animal again.

SIX FORTY-NINE P.M.

"The Nile will teem with frogs. They will come up into your palace and your bedroom and onto your bed, into the houses of your officials and of your people, and into your ovens and kneading troughs. The frogs will go up on you and your people and all your officials."

327

Thus promised the Lord God in Exodus, Chapter Eight. In what century was that written, you wonder, and what does it mean? It seems the opposite of what is happening nowadays. Nowadays, it's people and officials who are teeming, while frogs are becoming quite scarce.

You read the last line again. "The frogs will go up on you and your people and all your officials." You are reading aloud to André, whom you have tethered to one of the living room radiators (for once you are glad your building has old-fashioned steam heat) and given a loaf of rye bread to mangle and eat. The macaque fancies raisin bread, but you haven't any raisin bread on hand, and you are sick and tired of catering to his tastes. "I don't understand this biblical language, André," you say, "but at least Larry wasn't lying about Egypt being invaded by frogs. I'd almost prefer it if he'd lied. What if *all* that weird stuff he said is true? Maybe we should read some more. Okay?"

Ever since you brought out Grandma Mati's old Bible, the monkey has been so attentive, so respectful, that it actually lends a modicum of credence to the claim that he is a Christian monkey, that he has been "born again." No. Couldn't be. Ridiculous. A coincidence or a con. At any rate, this is the scene: you are sitting rather primly in your favorite Geoffrey Beene Arkitektura chair with an open Bible on your lap, reading the Word of the Lord to a heedful Barbary ape, when through the front door, which you had left ajar on the off chance that Q-Jo Huffington might happen down the hall, there suddenly bursts Belford Dunn.

Six Fifty-Six P.M.

Belford weeps.

He actually weeps. So moved is he by the tableau upon which he has intruded—moved not merely by his abrupt reunion with his beloved pet, but by the unexpected, unprecedented sight of you

sweetly reading from the Holy Scriptures to your erstwhile antago-
nist, that teardrops the size of guppies swim down his cheeks.

And through the tears he is beaming, beaming with such radi-
ance that you would not be surprised if he formed a man-made
rainbow. His smile seems to say, *Here at last, my dream come true: my little
family, my domestic unit, together, all safe and cozy and sweet, savoring each
other's company while pursuing greater knowledge of the splendor of God.*

Once he has pasted your face with trembling kisses and nearly
squeezed the banana-flavored crap out of André, who appears
amused but hardly overjoyed to see his big master, Belford explains,
"I just couldn't stand it, so I went out to the airport and found a sailor
who was willing to trade flights with me for sixty-five dollars. That's
a lot of money for swapping tickets, but he was a Christian, he told
me, so I knew he wouldn't waste it on beer and card games. Speaking of cards, is Q-Jo back, too?"

"Huh! Not only is Q-Jo not back, Belford, she was last heard of
going through a locked door without a key."

"Oh, now, honikins!"

"Either that or. . . ." Or what, Gwendolyn?

"Well, we'll straighten all that out, don't you worry. But first,
you gotta tell me how you found him. My little rascal! Where was
he, what was he doing? Tell me everything."

You concoct a story, a fictional account that puts you in a
favorable light, while Belford paces back and forth between you and
André. Presumably, he fails to detect the fumes that rise from your
sex-soiled body, perhaps because the macaque is likewise a study in
pungency. In any case, he is equally adoring of you and his pet, a
situation you find both endearing and irritating.

"I'm ashamed to admit it, Gwen, but there were moments this
weekend when I lost faith. In André, in you; in Jesus, even."

"That's understandable, Belford, and I'm sure we all forgive
you." You are equally sure that not one of you noticed.

Your alleged swain is feeling amorous toward you, you can tell
by the way he caresses your forearm, by the moony look in his eyes.
He is ripe for a little harmless exploitation, yet you must be cau-

tious, you must proceed slowly. "Listen," you say, "you and André need to spend some time alone together. Why don't you take him over to your place for an hour or two? Then, maybe you and I can visit for a bit. You can secure him later on and come back over here. But only for a while, because I've got a huge, stressful day tomorrow."

"Well, all right. I heard on the radio in the taxi that the market probably won't open in the morning, not because of the crash, they were saying, but because of that atmospheric interference we've been having the past week. I don't know if it's sunspots or what."

"It's going to be a rough day in any case. Here. Here are your car keys." You give him a generic prêt-à-porter smooch and nudge him toward the door. "We'll talk in a couple hours. Bye-bye, André. Have a nice evening." *While I try to repair my shower curtain, you evil beast.*

"Bye, honey. Thank you so very much. I don't know how I can repay you."

Oh, we'll think of something.

Seven-Forty P.M.

Leaving the shower curtain in a heap on the floor, you enjoy a leisurely soak. At one point, smelling the washcloth, you can't help but wonder where into Diamond's speculations fits the fact that human sexuality reeks of cod. An activity so basic, so primal—and so obviously perfumed by the tides. . . . Gosh, you are surprised that the sniff cadet didn't make a big deal of it. Mostly, however, you think about business. It may be to your advantage if the markets do close for a day or two. You'll have more time to put your oil futures play into action, as well as to sweep a few things under the carpet. If it isn't too late. If Posner hasn't already decided to yank your plug.

One of the reasons the market keeled over was the huge increase in margin debt: clients buying stocks on brokerage credit.

Margin buying was a hunky-dory practice in your opinion, until the masses tapped into it. The gates should never have been opened to Sam and Sally Seattle and all of their unsophisticated kin. Marginal people have no business with margins, you have said that all along, and now they have gone and ruined it for you. Or, at least, made it very difficult. On the other hand, they may have unwittingly provided you with a grand opportunity. Larry Diamond, the so-called financial genius, didn't dismiss your scheme as unworkable. Not at all. He simply has other interests. Interests you wish you had never been exposed to, because, darn it all, they've lodged themselves in the back of your mind like one of those catchy, awful, embarrassing pop tunes. Dolphins with fingers, mushrooms with transmitters, Buddhas with webbed feet, starships with frog tanks, people with destinies that cannot be described. Where are George Washington's teeth when you really need them?

Your body is the color of maple butter, and when it glistens with bath lotion, it looks as if it could be spread on the Waffle of the World. You wrap it, instead, in a silk robe and take it to the kitchen to make it a salad. The spinach appears astonished when you dump it out of its plastic bag. You feel almost as though you have interrupted something. A red tomato revolves in your hand like a planet. For some reason, the world around you seems alive in a way it never was before.

You have just forked the last Harpo Marx curl of arugula, jazzy and clownish and dimly electric, into your mouth when the telephone burbles. Diamond is on the line. You hadn't expected to hear from him quite so soon, but you have to confess to a tiny tinge of thrill. And you have to admonish yourself for feeling it.

"Is that something in your mouth, or are you just glad to hear from me?"

"I'm finishing dinner, thank you. I rushed to the phone because I thought it might be Q-Jo."

"Alas, not. But I have a premonition I'm going to hear from her soon."

"*You* are going to hear from her?!"

331

"Yes. Me. That's the premonition—but you know it could be wrong. Anyway, pussy burger, I'm calling from a car phone . . ."

"That explains the static." For a moment, you thought it might be the arugula.

"There's a lot of it tonight. Celestial interference seems to be getting worse. Look, I'm on I-Five, coming back from Sea-Tac. . . ."

"What were you doing at the airport?"

"That's for me to know and you to find out. I have something for you. An Easter present, you could call it. My new friend, Reiko, who's been so kind as to chauffeur me about, will be dropping me off at Thunder House in about, oh, say twenty minutes. Can you meet me there?"

"Oh, uh, I don't know, Larry. I really don't think so."

"Good. You won't regret it. Every little pussy girl likes presents."

"I'm not a little— Don't call me that! I'll meet you in an hour. At nine-thirty. Outside in the lot. Okay? Outside. I'm not coming in."

"Whatever you say. Personally, I've had a lot of fun lately in parked automobiles. Ah-ha-ha-ha-ha. Yes, indeed."

NINE-THIRTY P.M.

The rain clouds have gone. Gambled away their transparent dimes and boxcarred out of town; spent, skinny, ragged, and broke. The moon, always a winner because it knows when to fold, stands on the balcony of the closed casino, looking as though it might light up a cigar. Stars blink at it, as if to say, "As sure as this is Seattle, there'll soon be another batch of big spenders rolling into town from the west." The moon is in no hurry. It wipes its flushed brow with a cirrostratus handkerchief that must have fluttered from some sucker's pocket when he turned it inside out.

You circle the bowling alley twice before parking. The lanes are dark. They must shut down early on Sunday nights. The only light in the building seeps from a narrow row of basement windows on the west side. Twister's "tipi," if you are not mistaken. You picture the burly Comanche meditating on his precious Van Gogh, squinting at one of the vigorously crayoned but lumpy peasants as if the figure were a phantom buffalo.

No sooner have you switched off the engine than a car door slams behind you and Diamond steps out of a late model Volvo. His hair is tangled, his clothing still damp, his limp pronounced, but his grin could paint Liberace's ceiling. "Fun in parked automobiles," eh? What has he been doing with that Madame Butterfly?

He slides into the Porsche and keeps on sliding. Within a second, he has slid his tongue between your lips. Cautiously, as if you might be bitten, you disengage yourself from his osculation. You mustn't get mussed. Belford awaits you.

"How did it go with Dr. Yamaguchi?" you inquire, wiping his saliva from your lips with your sleeve.

"I watched an American western in Paris once. It was in English with French subtitles. A grizzled cowboy walks into a saloon and growls, 'Gimme a shot of red eye!' And the subtitle read, *'Dubonnet, s'il vous plaît.'* Words don strange masks in translation."

"But Yamaguchi speaks English."

"He speaks English subtitles."

"Okay, but do you get a treatment or not?"

"Only if I go to Japan. The FDA hasn't approved his treatment here, and Yamaguchi thinks it could take years."

"Wait a minute. You have to get the government's permission to have an enema?!"

"This may be the land of the free, sweetheart, but you're deluding yourself if you think your ass is your own."

"Well, you're going to Japan, aren't you?"

"No, I'm going to Timbuktu."

"Why, Larry? Why's it so important you go to that stupid place?"

He pauses, drops his head back, and lowers his lids. "I have a date with a frog," he drawls.

333

Tom Robbins

NINE THIRTY-NINE P.M.

You suppose he is speaking of the Nommo. He could have been referring to a French girl, although in that case he probably would have said "frogette." Therefore, it must be the Nommo; some delusional foolishness involving the alleged mermen from outer space. But no, as it turns out, he meant exactly what he said: a frog.

A particular species of frog. A frog whose skin secretes a biochemical agent, a complex nitrogenous peptide, whatever that is, that affects the human nervous system in a most peculiar way.

"It sounds like a *drug*."

"It's a hallucinogenic bufotoxin. *Aspirin* is a drug."

"But it makes you high!"

"On Wall Street, they say, 'Buy low, sell high.' On the pad, we say, 'Buy high, sell high.' Isn't that somehow better?"

"No! It's . . . it's irresponsible and unbusinesslike, and probably dangerous."

"A great deal safer than the streets of Seattle. They're really fairly common, these magic froggies. Everybody who's ever read *National Geographic* knows about their use among the Indians of South America. Well, they're also native to West Africa. There's no evidence of their employment in contemporary religious or hunting practices, such as there is in the Amazon, but it's almost unthinkable, considering the historical relationship between tribal cultures and organic hallucinogens, that the Africans wouldn't have taken advantage of them at some point in the past."

"At least they had the good sense to stop."

"Climate changes, and pressure from Islamic and Christian exploiters had a lot more to do with it than good sense, I'd venture. My theory, the theory that made my reputation at the University of Timbuktu, is that the Bozo and Dogon aquatic cosmology, the legend of the Nommo, was strongly colored, if not wholly inspired, by amphibian hallucinogens."

"I guess that would explain it, all right, if anybody cares. But

334

what's that got to do with you going back to that dried-up camel pit, especially with you being sick and all?"

"As you might imagine, there're no longer any frogs in Timbuktu, but there used to be, the fossils prove that. Inspired by yours truly, a couple of guys from the university recently went into the jungle in Senegal and filled a flour sack with live specimens. Stocked the little pond in the courtyard with them. Imagine them there, pussy gumbo. Sweetening the wind with their erotic prayers, sucking the giant Sahara moon into their pulsating green throats. There's going to be a ceremony this fall sometime. Fifty days after the rising of Sirius. That was when the Greek elite set out for Eleusis, you know, to drink the ergotized sacrament and be initiated into the Mysteries. Ah, but this year, my tumor rose before Sirius, and I may not be in a position to wait for September; so I'm going over early for a sneak preview."

"Of what, exactly?"

"Of the magic frog elixir, exactly. Oh, now, don't look at me with such toady scorn. . . ."

"You're planning to eat one of those poison frogs!"

"Never. I promise. Anyway, a woman who orders frog legs in a downtown restaurant shouldn't be casting stones."

"Well, smoke them, then."

"Smoke a frog? Me, who won't even puff a Havana corona? No, the beauty is, the frogs aren't harmed. What one does is lick their skin for the sweat that's on it. The best spot is right about where the ears would be, if they had ears."

"Sweat?! Ick! Gross!"

"Right out of a fairy-tale romance, darling. Remember those pretty princesses, kissing amphibians? Incidentally, one can't actually get warts from handling frogs, but one could possibly absorb bufotoxin through one's fingers. That's the origin of the superstition. Mustn't have the kiddies blowing their wee minds."

"So why do you want to blow yours? In such a disgusting way?"

"Minds were made for blowing."

335

"Oh, Jesus, Larry!"

"Do you recall why I went to see Q-Jo Huffington?"

"Yeah. Because Twister's father refused to let you blow your mind on mushrooms."

"In terms of strain on the immune system, Wide Place in the Road may have had a point, but I needed to have my cerebral house and lot reappraised, and since Q-Jo, gifted though she is, is not in the same league as the psilocybic elves, I undoubtedly would have consulted the mushrooms anyway, if I hadn't known I had an appointment in Timbuktu. We've established that certain mushrooms may function as Nommo microphones, broadcasting strange non-linear alien information, simultaneously archaic and futuristic . . ."

"You established that, not me."

". . . but if Earth's frogs are directly related to the primary inhabitants of the Sirius system, then the data broadcast by *their* biochemical transmitters might be even more authentic, one step closer to the source. We might compare mushrooms to latter-day missionaries, while frogs are the offspring of the original apostles. At least in terms of the purity of their neurotransmissions. Yes. Yes, indeed."

You clasp your head in your hands. "This is crazy. Insane. I cannot believe you're going off to some African hellhole to lick frogs."

"In the words of Cab Calloway, 'Some people calls it madness, but I calls it hi-di-ho.' It's just part of the process."

You have no idea who Cab Calloway is, although you are sure you have heard your father speak of him, which is not an encouraging sign. "What if you lick too much, or, uh, something goes wrong, you're allergic or something?"

"Risk is part of the process."

"And what are you going to do about cash flow? You're going to be needing medical attention. I bet you don't have a cent of insurance." Jeez! These men! Diamond and Belford. Walking away from a regular paycheck, a big, fat regular paycheck, as if a regular

paycheck were no more than a habit.

Diamond merely grins. "Maybe I should practice on you. Licking, I mean." He allows his tongue to hang over his lower lip like a cold cut hanging out of a squashed sandwich.

"Stop it. Get serious. You look deranged."

"Now, now, be nice, pussy fondue. As advertised, Uncle Larry has a gift for you." Whereupon he digs in the front pocket of the roadkill that serves as his leather jacket, removes a small object, and presses your fingers around it. You open your fist, pleased to discover that in it is nothing mawkish, such as an engagement ring; or embarrassing, such as a sex toy; or creepy, such as a live frog; yet disappointed and perplexed that it is . . .

"A Bic lighter?"

"Not just any Bic lighter. Dr. Yamaguchi's Bic lighter. He gave it to me. A touching gesture. We hit it off. Eye contact, mainly. Hale fellow, well met. Yes. In any case, the lighter's mine, it's not your gift. But fire it up, will you. I'm serious. That's right, go ahead. Flick your Bic."

Gorged with fuel, the little device sprouts an inch-high flame, which Diamond instructs you to hold steady. Then, from the inside pocket of that Paleolithic bathmat he zips about his bony shoulders, he produces a pair of paper envelopes, one about eight inches long, thick, and brightly colored; the other shorter, thinner, plainer. "Actually," he says, "there're two gifts. But you get to keep only one. You have to choose."

"But—what . . . ?"

"In my left hand are airline tickets. First class, you might like to know. To Timbuktu. Not on my flight, unfortunately. Couldn't be arranged. You'd leave on Tuesday. Delta to New York, then Air Afrique to Bamako. I'd meet you there, and we'd enter Timbuktu together. The two of us, hand in hand. Can you imagine what that would be like? Can you even imagine?"

As a matter of fact, you can't. For a slice of a second, maybe, your mind's eye sees a sprawl of crusty sand castles on a vast, sealess beach beneath a gunsmoke sky, you and Diamond standing in a mud arcade looking pale and lost like the Lovers in the tarot deck, while

337

armed nomads in blue veils thunder by on camelback, accusing you in uncivilized tongues of illegally trafficking in frogs; but that image fades as quickly as it comes, leaving you staring blankly at Diamond's right hand.

"In this appendage," he drawls, "I'm holding—keep the flame steady, now—reasonably detailed notes and instructions covering the steps you'd need to take to journal around your disco's data base in such a way that London could read you sitting on a hundred grand or more in your personal account, but without any hint of the phony funds or your trade with them ever showing up in Seattle. Unless, of course, oil prices don't move in the direction you're predicting, in which case, sooner or later, when you can't cover, or you cover out of somebody else's account, some pretty serious gentlemen will come to call. If your hunch is correct, though, you'll end up with bags of free money, and nobody will ever be the wiser. I apologize in advance for the condition of the notes. I wrote them with a ballpoint pen in Reiko's car, part of them while the car was moving. Now . . ."

He moves the envelopes closer to the lighter, which is starting to heat up at an uncomfortable rate. "I want you to set fire to one of these envelopes. One or the other. The tickets or the cheat notes. One of them has to go up in smoke. It's your choice. The pepperoni or the pearl. You can connive to improve your life within the existing boundaries of your life, or you can expand your life; maybe even transform your life. You can risk your freedom for a taste of jumbo juice, or you can risk absolutely everything for something that may be incomprehensible even if you achieve it. Just give one of these babies the torch, Gwendolyn, and we'll both live with the consequences. Come on, don't go numb on me. If you don't choose by the time I count to five, the offer's withdrawn; I'll burn *both* envelopes. *One—two* . . ."

"Wait a minute, Larry." Although the Bic is burning your fingers, you must stall for time. "It's clear out now. Can we see Sirius, do you think? Sirius A. Is it, uh, over my shoulder, maybe?"

"No, it isn't. This time of year, Sirius sets a bit after nine o'clock. *Three—*"

"But I saw it Friday night. Must have been close to eleven."

"Impossible. I'm counting. . . ."

"I did see it. It was the brightest star in the sky. I saw B, too."

"No, you didn't. Not at this latitude, not in April. We're going to run out of lighter fluid."

"Well, I saw something. In the west. An extremely bright star. What else could it have been?"

"Maybe it was *ie pelu tolo*. Now, stop procrastinating. . . ."

"You mean the Nommo spaceship? The ark? The star of the tenth moon? You're not serious. You're kidding me."

"Anything is possible. I'm counting. . . ."

"But, Larry," you say eagerly. "What if you're right? What if it was out there beaming up frogs or something?"

He doesn't go for it. *"Four—"* he says.

Ten-Ten P.M.

So disoriented are you when you weave out of the bowling alley lot that you accidentally turn down a narrow side street that dead-ends at a sheet metal shop. Rather than turning around, once you realize your mistake, you pull over to the curb, shift into neutral, and sit there, idling.

You cannot believe what you have just done. He must have hypnotized you, put you in some kind of African trance. You thought at the moment, if, indeed, you thought anything at all, that you were acting on intuition; but maybe it was something else. A woman is supposed to be able to *trust* her intuition, it's supposed to work in her favor. You couldn't seem to help yourself. And he *does* have strange mental powers.

From the seat beside you, you pick up the envelope, examine it, shake your head. Tickets to Timbuktu. *One-way* tickets to Timbuktu! Good grief! Is this the dumbest, most self-destructive decision you have ever made, or what?

Oddly enough, you are less than overcome with remorse and regret. In fact, for the third or fourth time this weekend, a rare, unjustifiable giddiness has overtaken you. The bell of your trumpet is bent back to the mouthpiece, like a snake swallowing its own tail. You are in a mild state of shock, it is true, yet no sense of grave finality plugs the ducts of your inner workings. Perhaps it just hasn't sunk in yet, perhaps you are in denial, but the cocktail of emotions your heart is guzzling contains a carbonated mixer of unspecified excitement, in addition to the jiggers of fear and disbelief. *Wow,* you think. *Jesus. Wow.*

There is a lump in your chest the size of a cauliflower, which, initially, you identify as a knot of acute anxiety. Gradually, however, it becomes apparent that the lump is a compressed globe of mirth. There is a large laugh inside you—or else a nexus of tiny giggles—petitioning to escape. Under the circumstances, it is embarrassing, this suppressed laughter, and you dare not release it lest it have implications of hysteria. It certainly doesn't feel like hysteria, but just the same. . . .

Again, in the shine of the street lamp, you inspect the packet of airline tickets. *An option,* you think. *Only an option.* As much as you are fascinated by Larry Diamond, as—come on, admit it—susceptible to his sexuality as you have reluctantly become, as concerned as you are about his illness, if he believes for one moment that he has captured you, that you have volunteered to become his Timbuktu love slave, well, he had better not count his frogs before they peep.

Still, what if you did follow him to Timbuktu? What if you thumbed your little Anglo nose at Posner, the disco, the SEC, at the entire economic situation, and took off to the ends of the earth? What if you really did?

With that thought, a laugh breaks loose. It is a short laugh, but rather loud, and since another one is pressing to follow on its heels, you glance around to ascertain that nobody on this inglorious little mixed-up street of Norwegian cottages and marine metal fabricators has overheard you. Instantaneously, the ball of chuckles dissolves— for there, directly across the street from you, parked in front of one of those cheesy Snoose Junction clapboards, is Q-Jo's Geo Storm.

TEN-FIFTEEN P.M.

As noiselessly as a paraplegic cricket, you steal out of your car and over to Q-Jo's. The Geo is empty. Her body is not slumped in its seats, and there is no way she would fit in its trunk, probably not even if she were dismembered. You look up and down the street. The industrial buildings are deserted, and of the half-dozen cottages, two are dark, four faintly aglow with the photonic frost of television. It seems safe enough to try the door.

Not surprisingly, it is unlocked: these days in Seattle, as Q-Jo is well aware, to lock one's car is to issue an invitation to have one's windows smashed. A rush of stale tobacco stink smacks your nostrils. Nothing else. No note, no remnant of clothing, nothing beyond an ashtray overflowing with ill-shaped butts and a wadded-up wrapper from a meatball sub to indicate that the vehicle is not owned and operated by a robot. Maybe Sherlock Holmes might find a clue here, but for you the search is fruitless.

Quietly, you return to the Porsche. When you get home, you will telephone the police and report the whereabouts of the Geo. Meanwhile, its discovery has struck a note of optimism, if for no other reason than it has convinced you once and for all that Diamond is not responsible for Q-Jo's disappearance (maybe "absence" is a better word). Diamond might be eccentric, but he isn't stupid. He would hardly harm a woman and then allow her car to sit a block away from Thunder House.

With that in mind, you drive off for your meeting with Belford Dunn.

TEN THIRTY-FOUR P.M.

"Honikins! Where've you *been?*"

As arranged, Belford is waiting for you at your apartment. He is a trifle agitated.

"I told you I had to run an errand."

"At this hour? On Sunday night? I was worried."

"I was looking for Q-Jo's car. And—I found it."

"No fooling? You did? Where?"

"Oh, over in Ballard."

"But how did you know where to look?"

"Just a hunch. I found André for you, didn't I? I'm a regular detective." You give him a peck on the cheek. "Now, loosen your tie and relax. Put on some music. I'm going to report this to the police, and then I'll be with you."

Easier said than done. You spend more than ten minutes negotiating a bewildering electronic labyrinth before you reach a living human being, only to be told that the "bureau of missing persons" (meaning the white-haired investigator and the iguana woman who fronts for him) is closed and that you should call back after nine tomorrow morning. Your argument that the situation could be serious, the discovery of the car significant, falls on steel ears.

Frustrated and fed-up—could public services be a whole lot worse in Timbuktu?—you slam down the receiver and storm off to the bathroom. There, you wash your face, apply a fresh patina of chic, and analyze the immediate state of affairs. Undoubtedly, Belford will insist on discussing the Q-Jo situation; and once that subject is exhausted, he will have questions about André, about, for example, the methods employed to pacify him, the specific Bible verses read to him (how and why were they selected), and what steps need be taken to insure that he does not fly the coop again (is the monkey completely trustworthy, do you think Belford has failed him, etc.). All this could gobble the better part of an hour, and you simply lack the patience for it. You will, in fact, scream if you have to go through it, and a screaming fit at this juncture would probably not promote your agenda. Thus, with a higher purpose ultimately in mind, you remove your outer garments and return to the living room in your underwear.

Ten Fifty-Two P.M.

"Would you still find me attractive if I hadn't lost my tail?"

Belford has selected the soundtrack from *The Sound of Music*, the closest thing to "Christian entertainment" in your meager collection of CDs, and seated on the plush Paluko sofa, he is absentmindedly humming along with Julie Andrews when you mince into the room in peach lace undies to paralyze him in mid-hum. When he regains the power of speech, he stammers, "What . . . what are you talking about? Tail?"

"I had a tail once. When I was an embryo. I had little flippers. And ridges and grooves alongside my head like the gill slits of a fish." As you say these things, you turn deliberately around and around, as if you were a model on a runway, and with each turn, your hips move closer to Belford's face. "So, suppose I still had a tail?"

"But you don't." Belford's breath is behaving as if his lungs were overweight farmboys trying to squeeze through the strands of a barbed-wire fence; his Adam's apple resembles a squash ball bouncing down the steps of an Aztec temple. "I don't believe it's an actual tail that we have in the womb, but whatever it is that looks like a tail, it goes away long before we're born."

"But if we're created in God's image, how come the human fetus is so much like a fish or a frog? Did Martin Luther address that question? When he wasn't busy addressing the question of how many bowling pins the Lord intended? If there's no such thing as evolution, how come we have tails and gills when we're embryos, and why don't I have any now?"

Taking your question a tad more seriously than you meant it, or perhaps seeking a diversion from the round little bottom that is

343

hovering only about ten inches from his nose, he scratches his large, durable head and after due consideration, says, "We're only in God's image after we're born. If we're, you know, funny-looking, frog-looking, in the early stages of our development, well, it's probably a warning. The Lord is telling us that if it wasn't for his merciful love, we could all be born looking like something that hops around in the slime. See what I mean, hon? That's the way our babies would turn out if Satan was in the driver's seat."

Jeez! You hadn't intended to precipitate a theological discourse. To wrench the subject several degrees to the left of mainstream religion, you peel your panties slowly off your buttocks until your very perineum is exposed. "But you never did answer me. How do you think I'd look with a tail?"

Belford can stand it no longer. He pulls you down on the sofa beside him—practically on top of him, to tell the truth—and commences to kiss and fondle you with an appetite close to frenzy.

"Mmmfff!" This is getting ahead of schedule, if not out of hand. "Unt-unt-unt." You manage to free yourself. "Whoa. Easy."

He looks hurt. "What's wrong? Did I . . . ?"

"Don't you want me to take off my bra? I thought you liked my little Filipina moons."

Belford nods twice, once to indicate that he does wish you to remove your brassiere, a second time to reaffirm his allegiance to your relatively undersized bust. Smiling, you unhook the bra—this model fastens in the front—but draw it back only far enough to reveal the narrow plain of flesh between the mounds. Holding a bra-end in each hand, you pause and look him squarely in the eye. "Belford," you say, "there's a serious matter I need to discuss with you, and . . . I'm sorry about this but until we get it out of the way, it's just going to be weighing on my mind, distracting me." You smile again and saw the bra back and forth, your breasts jiggling like yolks in their poachers of lace. "You don't want me to be distracted, do you?"

He does not. He wants only what you want. Like the gentleman everyone believes him to be, he sits back and listens politely as you deliver a *Reader's Digest* version of your scheme to turn the current financial crisis to your advantage. (Were he truly a gentleman, he probably would not have maintained an erection throughout your speech, although there *are* extenuating circumstances. To wit: you are sitting beside him with your brassiere unhooked and your panties down around your thighs.) Now comes the delicate part, and you strive for composure and an outward display of cheerful confidence. You require a short-term loan. Say, a hundred thousand dollars. More, if possible. To be repaid with interest. And, in the event of matrimony, profits shared. Washington is a community property state.

Attentive, even enthralled, Belford lets you complete your pitch. Then, he takes your small, cute hands sympathetically in his big, rough ones, and, as your bra falls open, he says, "Golly, that's a very interesting idea, sweetie. Kinda risky . . ."

"No, no, Belford. It's a lock. Trust me."

". . . but the fact is, I couldn't help you in any case. I have to tell you what I did." He grins a grin that in certain parts of Montana would attract wolves and coyotes from miles around. "Gwen, I made a promise to God. I promised the Father that if he was to see fit to deliver André back to me, safe and sound, I would donate ninety percent of my savings to the Lutheran homeless shelter. Oh, honey, I'm sorry, I really am. I can't stand to see you disappointed. But, I was desperate, and he heard my plea. He took pity on me in my darkest hour. And, you know, a guy just doesn't break a promise to the Lord."

As your mind plays reruns of the Bic lighter, the envelope of instructions, the fire that illuminated the Porsche cockpit, the ashes that sifted like nuclear snow onto Diamond's jeans, you think, *What about* my *darkest hour? Hey? It was* me *who got your goddamned monkey back!*

For several minutes, neither of you speaks. Your mind races nervously over your list of remaining options like the fingers of a blind espresso drinker reading the Braille menu in a coffee bar. Belford squeezes your hands and sort of coos and moos at you. He

345

sounds like the background noise at a petting zoo. Through it all, however, he never loses his erection, and eventually, like the only tree left standing after a hurricane, it gets your attention. There is a natural desire to touch such a tree, to thump it, to lean against it, perhaps to lunch in its shade. That must be it. Otherwise, why, at this intensely dilemmatic juncture, when so much is at stake and when your romantic relationship with Belford has crossed the threshold of termination, would you reach out and grasp his suited phallus, pulling and bending it as if you were a Sherwood Forest bow-maker testing a sapling?

Misinterpreting your gesture, Belford swoops you up and carries you off to the bedroom. You ought to protest, but, instead, you kick off your underpants en route, while unbuttoning his shirt.

Now, the plunge into the erotic is often a flight from a troublesome reality, yet it can occasionally be a centering device, a furnace in which to burn off all energies except that clear cerebral energy upon whose light an accurate, revelatory focus ultimately depends. In retrospect, you will be able to claim this reckless coupling as a prime example of the latter, but for the moment you are aware of little beyond the keen throb of an incandescent clitoris, a blistered hawthorn aching to be salved.

He lays you down among the grateful mites and steps smartly out of his trousers. Syncopic with a strange impersonal craving, you stare transfixed as he removes his boxer shorts, folds them neatly, and places them on top of the dresser. His member may resemble a turkey neck, but it is very large and very stiff, and you scarcely can restrain yourself from crying out for it. "Hurry, hurry," you mutter, as in the next room a blithe Julie Andrews lists, for anyone who's interested, a few of her favorite things.

Heaving like a garden tractor, Belford busts the sod of your guilt. (Yes, there is a layer of guilt there, but it only makes your submission more frictional, and, therefore, more galvanizing.) You split open for him like a furrow. He plants a root crop, and the root runs deep. You rear, twist, shove, and squirm, so as not to miss an inch of it. His back is a brown paper package, your legs the string. *Take it from the top, Julie.*

Periodically, every three minutes or so, you think that you are finished with this lewd business, that you have had your fill, that you will push him off you and regain your composure if not your dignity, but then he will bump up against some nerve ending that has not been previously massaged, and you lose yourself for another three minutes until you have rubbed every last itch of pleasure out of that spot. "Belford," you say between grunts, "isn't, *uh*, this, *uh*, the best, *uh*, sex we've ever, *uh*, had?" He is so surprised to hear you actually speak during intercourse that he freezes for a moment, as if alarmed. Then he nods in the affirmative—Belford, too, has never spoken during the act of love and he, for one, is apparently not about to spoil his record—and, with his cigar-sized fingers spreading the cheeks of your derriere, he resumes his thrust from a slightly different angle, sending a shock wave rumbling and jerking all the way to your gums.

Now, suddenly, he is lodged against your clitoris, pinning it to the wall, as it were; flattening it against the wall, where he polishes it repeatedly, like an old Greek grocer polishing an eggplant, like Aladdin summoning a reluctant genie; polishes it until you can feel it shine, feel it lighting up your vagina like a Broadway show. *Ta-da!* Down the aisle trots the white pony, proud and frisky. With a swish of its mane, it bounds through the orchestra pit, leaps over the footlights, and lands center stage with a mighty whinny, hooves pawing the boards, mouth foaming, nostrils flaring, eyes popping on and off as if bulbs in a strobe. It brings down the house. And when Belford showers it with a hot tsunami of liquid white roses, it stands on its head for an encore.

Eleven Fifty-Six P.M.

In the breathy aftermath of this show-stopping extravaganza, you feel less satisfied than vindicated, less vindicated than liberated.

Satisfaction is nothing but a temporary anesthetizing of the numinous noogie of existence. Vindication is merely revenge without the mustard. Liberation, on the other hand, liberation is a front so big that the only back that can match it is death, and even death may not be a perfect fit.

Any fear you harbored that Larry Diamond had a hold on you, had put you in some psychosexual trance, completely dissipated in the surf of your orgasm. True, you may not have been able to achieve that orgasm if it hadn't been for Diamond; it was he who showed you how to spur the white pony all the way over the hill, and should there ever come a time when sex plays a more important role in your life than it does at present, a time when an admirer might actually dub you "the best piece of ass in Seattle" and you— God forbid!—feel honored by it, then you suppose you shall be in Diamond's debt. For now, however, having shot the wildest imaginable rapids in a raft launched by the barely competent Belford Dunn, you feel liberated from obligation, from dependency, from awe; feel free from Diamond's potential influence or domination; feel in charge of your own destiny, and not a penny less.

And, washing up at the bathroom sink (while Belford snores), you know *exactly* what action you are going to take!

One thing you do not know, alas, is that Belford, in a rare display of proprietary presumption, unplugged both of your telephones immediately after your futile call to police headquarters. Had your apartment been on line, you would have received an hour ago a message from Larry Diamond, a message urgent in tone if not in substance, a message concerning an alleged sighting of Q-Jo Huffington; an absurd message, frankly, yet one that might have altered the bold course upon which you are about to embark. It might have. And again it might not.

Monday
Morning
April 9

THE FOOL.

Another Day in the Life of a Fool

Twelve Thirty-Three A.M.

An ear being cleaned with a cellophane Q-Tip. A duck eating shredded wheat in an echo chamber. The gods frying ambrosia burgers. The Void gone electric. Termites reading aloud from Kafka.

There is so much static on the line that you barely recognize Sol Finkelstein's voice when he answers the phone at Posner Lampard McEvoy and Jacobsen. He, on the other hand, like an ornithologist who can pick out the chirp of a chickadee in rush-hour traffic, identifies *your* peewee piping instantly. "Where the hell are you, Mati? The fun has stopped. It's time to dance with the dead." He sounds as if he is still slightly drunk, and he offers no apology for his rudeness on Thursday night.

"Uh, listen, Sol . . ."

"Speak up, Mati, I can hardly hear you. Communications are a mess. Posner and I have tried every frigging exchange in Europe—the Yamaguchi bubble is set to burst, and we want to short the whole Japanese index . . ."

Short the Nikkei. Yes! Why hadn't you thought of that?

". . . . but we can't crack the interference. Tried to fax London a minute ago and instead of a fax signal I got Asian sports scores. Ever hear of a basketball team called the Hong Kong Flu?"

"Sol, I've got some personal stuff at the disco. Pictures and stuff. Would you have Judi Mullikin clean out my desk and take everything home with her? I'll send for it later."

"What're you saying, Mati? You're walking? Posner's got a whole bag of bones to pick with you. I'd advise you to come in and face the music. Or don't you have the decency, the guts?"

A cyclone blows a pile of dry leaves through the P.A. system at a high-school pep rally. When the crackling subsides, you say, "Kiss my Third World ass, Sol, and fuck Posner and the cooked books he rode in on." Before you hang up, you add, "If you had a clue, toadbrain, you'd know the fun is just beginning. 'Zip-A-Dee-Doo-Dah!' "

Twelve Thirty-Nine A.M.

Standing over Belford, you watch the rise and fall of his hairy chest. In a pulse of déjà vu, you flash back to André, tranquilized atop Q-Jo's table. Compared to the monkey, though, Belford looks touchingly unworldly. Not that André is actually corrupt, he has just had to be clever in certain unorthodox ways in order to survive. Like you, Gwendolyn? Yes, you suppose you are beginning to feel a modicum of kinship with the exploited macaque.

In any case, Belford isn't free of stain. He unplugged your phones, didn't he? Well, so what? That was easily corrected. In the living room, you simply jacked back in and burned a bridge. A major bridge. Jesus! You hope you won't come to regret it.

You kneel now and reconnect the bedside phone, unaware, of course, that you have missed Diamond's call. Were you a voice-mail subscriber, like nearly everyone else in America who can still afford telephone service, you could retrieve his unique message, but you chose instead one of those state-of-the-art answering machines that are not much larger than a tarot card. You are suspicious of voice mail. Who knows what pirates might hack into one's stored messages? A businesswoman has to be careful these days.

Unlike the typical Filipina who favors long, often fake, brightly painted nails (even Grandma Mati goes in for them), yours are trim and natural (bitten to the quick, frankly), so you do not hesitate to draw them over Belford's smooth, pink cheeks. He stirs. "Mmmmmph."

"Wake up, lover boy. We've got some cliffs to jump off of."

"Huh?"

"Got to make hay while the moon shines."

"What?"

"Belford, you don't by any chance have an enema, do you? The old-fashioned kind?"

Abruptly, he sits up. "Honey, are you sick?"

"Probably. But it's not what you think. Get dressed, now. I need you to run an errand with me."

Twelve Fifty-Nine A.M.

You are all in black. Black jeans, black sneakers, black Jhane Barnes sweater, black beret covering the steadily increasing number of gray strands that violate the blackness of your hair. In your black hand-bag, you have secreted your spare canister of Mace.

"Let's stop by your place first," you say.

"But, hon, I told you I don't have any enema stuff."

"That's okay. I think we should check on André."

"That's so sweet. But I'm sure he's safe and sound."

"Yes, but he may be lonely for us."

Belford regards you adoringly. "Well, all right. He's probably sleeping, though. He and I had a little roughhouse before I locked him up. Boy, is that little rascal strong! I think he got tuckered, though."

"Let's take a peek," you say, and Belford aims the Lincoln toward Queen Anne Avenue.

You have not traveled far before the moon that travels with you (sailing above the dirty sorrows and fortified excesses of the city; an unabashed, charismatic reminder of the primordial magic that the institutionalized, technologized mind has never quite suc-ceeded in repressing), that moon is vulgarly, if temporarily, obfus-cated by a boogie-woogie of cobalt and ruby oscillations. An ambulance and several police cars are blocking the street, emer-gency lamps flashing, and a crowd has gathered outside a modest

353

duplex. When you get closer, you spot Smokey and Cecil—don't those two ever go home to their loved ones?—among the cops who are waving onlookers away from a prone figure being attended to by medics on the lawn.

"Turn around," you order.

"Just a minute."

"No? Turn around. Let's get out of here."

"Honey, that house . . . that's the house where I . . ."

"I *know* what house it is, Belford. You got clobbered there. Wasn't once enough?"

Belford powers down his window. "Excuse me, sir. What's happened?"

"It's the Safe Sex Rapist. Guy who lives in that house captured him. Nearly took his head off with a croquet mallet."

"Oh, dear."

"Come on. Let's leave now." Officer Smokey is looking directly at the Lincoln, gesturing for it to turn around. You lower your head, slump down in the seat. *Good grief.*

"But it's a mistake. That poor fellow isn't the rapist. He's that woman's . . . friend."

"You can't be sure of that, and so what if he is? He got what was coming to him."

"Judge not lest—"

"Screw around not lest somebody screw you around. These people have no morals. Let's go."

"But I can help. I know these people."

"No, you don't! Some nameless lout tries to decapitate you, while his slut of a wife stands there watching with her you-know-what hanging open. You think that makes you boon companions?"

Smokey has started to walk in your direction. You slouch down further, causing Belford to inspect you with a perplexity that borders on suspicion. "If there's a mix-up," you say, "they'll sort it out soon enough. If you don't move us out of here, I'm going to get very angry."

Unhappily, Belford shifts into reverse, backs into a driveway, and wheels the Lincoln around. As it pulls away, you bolt upright and blow a kiss at Smokey. You are uncertain if he recognizes you, but he continues to stare until you turn the corner, and that makes you giggle. Belford is not giggling, however. Puzzled and leery, he pouts all the way to his building. "Here we are," he announces tersely. "You still wanna go up?"

"Listen, I'm sorry I got uptight. I just don't understand why you think you have to hold the hand of every loser who stumbles down the pike."

"It's my Christian duty, Gwen. The weak deserve all the help those of us who're more blessed can give 'em."

"That's very tender of you, but . . . I have a . . . I'm acquainted with a, uh, gentleman who claims that the extent to which a society focuses on the needs of its lowest common denominator is the extent to which that society'll be mired in mediocrity. Whereas, if we would aim the bulk of our support at the brightest, most talented, most virtuous instead, then they would have the wherewithal to solve a lot of our problems, to uplift the whole culture, enlighten it or something, so that eventually there wouldn't *be* so many losers and weaklings impeding evolution and dragging the whole species down. He claims martyrs like you just perpetuate human misery by catering to it. He believes individuals have to take responsibility for their own lives and accept the consequences of their choices."

Belford snorts. "Easy for him to say. Probably some privileged stockbroker who's never had to—"

"He was an autistic child, and now he has cancer."

"Oh, dear me. I'm sorry to hear that."

"Hey, everybody has a hard-luck story. The point is, he's never whined, never given in to fate. He's—"

"Well, that's commendable. It's good to be a fighter."

"He's not really a fighter. He's an adventurer. There's a difference. He doesn't attack, he engages; he doesn't defend, he expands;

he doesn't destroy, he transforms; he doesn't reject, he explores; he doesn't . . . well, you get the picture." (Where, Gwendolyn, is this coming from?)

Belford studies you, his broad, honest face creased with doubt. "Sounds like Mr. Adventure made quite an impression on you. I'd enjoy meeting him."

"He's leaving the country in the morning on a six o'clock flight."

Belford cannot conceal a breath of relief. "Can't blame him, I guess. America certainly can't pretend any longer that it's got the best medical care in the world. But, anyway, with all due respect, I'd have this to say to him: a great many people out there in the ghetto and the street are *incapable* of taking responsibility for their lives. Those who aren't actually incapacitated are suffering from a decay of the spirit. They can't explore options because they aren't aware that options exist. They've never been exposed to ideas like transformation and expansion. Worse than that, honey, they've never been exposed to love. You know? They have zero self-esteem because nobody's ever really loved 'em. That's where 'martyrs' like me come in."

"You can love 'em till your well runs dry, Belford, but you can never love 'em enough, and you know it. No matter how much others might love you, you can't love yourself unless you're in charge of your own actions, and you'll never take charge as long as you can get away with blaming your shortcomings and misfortunes on your family or society or your race or gender or Satan or whatever. Sooner or later, a person . . ."

Patiently, he waits for you to resume, but having become keenly aware of how much you are sounding like Diamond, and dimly aware that in the eyes of some, you yourself are less than a shining example of responsible behavior, you let the matter drop. "I bet the monkey's awake," you say.

It isn't, but when Belford goes to the kitchen for a glass of water, you kick its cage until it stirs. Ordinarily, it would screech in this situation, but tonight (rather, this morning) it gives you the

Mona Lisa look instead. If the fact that there are 550 hairs in the average human eyebrow prompts you to feel superior to the macaque, which is 550 hairs short, you conceal it well. You smile at André conspiratorially, as if to suggest that only he and you are reading the correct libretto. "Wake up, *mon ami*. It's time to get cracking. The moon is out, and it's the color of that big topaz you snitched from the Marquise du What's-her-name in Monte Carlo. You have to see it, *mon ami*. It's as bright as a banana Popsicle."

ONE-FORTY A.M.

The Fleet "ready-to-use" enema (manufactured by the C. B. Fleet Company of Lynchburg, Virginia) costs one dollar and twenty-five cents, is totally disposable, and looks as if it could be used for caulking the planks in a rowboat, filling chinks in a fireplace, or decorating a cake. It consists of a soft, hand-held, plastic dispensary bottle (with a "one-way safety valve" that "controls flow and prevents reflux") containing nineteen grams of monobasic sodium phosphate and seven grams of dibasic sodium phosphate in several ounces of saline solution. The label contains the following caution: "Remove orange protective shield from rectal tip before inserting," which seems straightforward enough until you recall that fifty percent of the American population is semiliterate. "Ouch!" "Fool! That'll teach you to drop out of school."

The disposable squeeze bottle is the only type of enema sold in the only all-night pharmacy in greater Seattle. Belford predicted as much. He said that to obtain an old-fashioned, rubber, bag-and-tube enema apparatus nowadays, you would probably have to go to a hospital supply store. He also said that according to an article in *Nature* magazine, the enema was invented by South American Indians, who sometimes employed the device to administer hallucinogenic mixtures through the rectum. Two days ago, such base and altogether useless information would have filled you with disgust. Now, it brings Larry Diamond luridly to mind and—well, to tell the

357

truth, it still fills you with disgust, all the more so because it was passed along by Belford Dunn, whose tame Lutheran Realtor's brain could scarcely be thought a repository of the grossly weird. Are there no innocents anymore? Could some magazine scanned in a barbershop somewhere also have acquainted Belford with the arcane practice of licking frogs?

Frustrated by the drugstore—although you were hardly looking forward to the embarrassment of purchasing enema equipment —you pick up several items from the vitamin and school-supplies departments, and return to the Lincoln.

"Guess you'll just have to wait till morning, sweetness. I'm sorry. Gee, you know, I think the little rascal wants to eat again."

"I *can't* wait," you say, much to Belford's bewilderment. "And André's just going to have to."

Because he had been feeling guilty about confining him to his old cage again, Belford did not have to be persuaded to bring André along on your trip to the pharmacy, and now monkey and master are staring at you beseechingly, they in the front seat, you in the rear. You stare them down. "Later," you say coldly. "Right now we're heading to Chinatown."

Two Oh-Six A.M.

In other areas of the city, any city, neon is just so much electrified signage, but in Chinatown, neon is song, theme music, the visual soundtrack to the neighborhood. Tourists are yanked into Chinatown by shivering tentacles of unnatural color, to be swallowed up by a radiant carp maw infected with exotica. Among China's many contributions to the world, from gunpowder to pasta, one cannot list neon lighting, yet Chinatown without neon is as unthinkable as the South Seas without palm trees: how else can one be sure that one is there? If food is the Holy Grail of Chinatown, neon is the Grail's aura, its halo, as well as the pendulous lodestone whose swaying luminescence hypnotizes each and every visitor, clouding their minds with illusions of forbidden pleasures and a romantic elsewhere. The neon of Chinatown is a neon of mystery, a neon of joy. FONG, says the neon. FU, it says. Well, all right then! FONG FU it is. Mysterious and joyful FONG FU. The neon can also say IMPERIAL GARDEN or MOON TEMPLE, and while the words are ordinary English, the letters that form the words might have been blown out of a Shanghai opium pipe. Imitating calligraphy like small boys imitating their grandfathers, the letters are ridiculous yet somehow charming; corny yet entirely correct. There is an appropriateness even to those whose elements have been fashioned to resemble stalks of bamboo. And the neon gas that courses through them like a supernatural plasma, pumping life into images of dragons, pagodas, and rice bowls, this gas is the hue of barbecue sauce, the hue of pickled duck feet, the hue of opera. Hue of hibiscus and ginseng, silkworm and firecracker. Neon pushes its embroidery needle in and out of the sky above Chinatown, decorating the canopy that will both protect and advertise it, setting it apart from other parts of town.

The profusion and the nature of its neon signs is the first indication that you and your companions have reached Seattle's Chinatown. The next indications are the deteriorating low-rise buildings, the Buddha-shadows thrown against old brick walls, and the shamble of busted bok choy crates on every corner. The sidewalks of Chinatown are where the outer leaves of green vegetables come to die.

In Seattle, Chinatown is officially referred to as the International District, a polite term that is accurate in one regard and dead wrong in another. Europeans neither reside nor keep businesses in the district, nor do people from Africa, South America, Australia, or the Middle East, so it is hardly "international." On the other hand, the Chinese there have been joined by Japanese, Koreans, Vietnamese, Cambodians, and, yes, Filipinos. A more fitting name might be "Asiatown." In any case, Freddie Mati does not live there in order to rub shoulders with other Asians. Freddie Mati lives in Chinatown because it is close to the clubs, because the police are paid to stay away, and, primarily, because it is cheap.

Your father occupies the fourth and uppermost floor of a small building belonging to the Li Po Trading Company, an importer and wholesaler of convict-made bric-a-brac. His windows are lit, which does not surprise you, for Freddie seldom retires before dawn, and since the clubs are closed for the observance of Easter, he would have nowhere else to go. Belford thinks it is sweet that you are dropping in on your dad, although the hour is rather odd. He insists on accompanying you, due to the fact that the stairs are steep and poorly lit and also because he is eager to foster cordial relations with the prospective in-law.

Freddie is slow to answer your knock, and you can smell marijuana smoke escaping through the jambs. You don't know if Belford is ready for this. On the other hand, you don't know if Freddie is ready for the monkey that is bouncing up and down on its hind legs in the gloom.

"Squeak!" shouts Freddie when he at last cracks the door. "Far out! Hey!"

Although you rarely return your father's calls and visit him no more than once or twice a year, he never complains, and when you do see him, he is invariably grateful and glad. Under the circumstances, his cheerfulness is unsettling. You would almost prefer that he reproach you.

"My Squeak baby. Come in, Squeak baby. Who dat wit you?" He notices André. "Oh, wow! I can't believe I'm seeing dis, man!" Obviously delighted by the sight of the macaque, Freddie begins to giggle and dance around. In fact, his antics and the monkey's are not dissimilar. "Somebody juking me? Wow, man! Dis a true monkey or a robot? Hey, I think dis monkey for real!"

"He sure is, Mr. Mati. Real as you or me. Good evening. My name's Belford Dunn."

If Belford is expecting Freddie to say, "Oh, yes, my daughter has told me so much about you," he is destined to be disappointed.

Even now, you are not inclined to help them get acquainted, although you suppose it no longer matters whether or not Belford learns that your father uses drugs. More than likely, it never would have mattered to Belford, anyway. Belford despises drugs, but Freddie, financially disadvantaged and a member of an ethnic minority, would be the recipient of far more pity than scorn. In any case, they will have to work things out on their own. Barely have you crossed the threshold than you excuse yourself and Druid through a Stonehenge of cardboard boxes, record albums, tapes, compact discs, books, and drums, finding your way to the bathroom.

You don't bother to pull the string that dangles like a strand of spaghetti from the meatball-sized overhead bulb. You know what you are looking for, and the neon gleam sputtering through the window from the signs outside is quite sufficient to illuminate it. In fact, it takes you only a moment to find it. There is an order to Freddie's untidiness, and you are well aware that despite Grandma Mati's complaints, he has never thrown away anything that once belonged to your mother: for example, all those books on the loft floor, stacked, occasionally dusted, used as pedestals for bongos and wine bottles, but no longer read. It is not a book that you drop into your handbag, however, although there are books that are treated with no more dignity.

As a subterfuge, you flush the toilet, quite possibly a mistake since you hear it overflowing as you walk out the door.

Your parents never shared this loft, Freddie having landed it during your freshman year in college when his wife was six years dead, yet signs of your mother are much in evidence. Not only does her old walnut desk occupy a prominent space in the sitting area, but her incense burner, ink bottles, rhyming dictionary, and collection of photographs of Dylan Thomas still sit atop it, as if awaiting her return. Despite your need to get on with the night's precarious enterprise, you pause there for a moment or two before rejoining Belford and Freddie. The men have scarcely advanced beyond the entranceway, but they appear to be enjoying each other's company, quickly establishing one of those relationships based on jocular dis-

361

agreement, common among males and virtually nonexistent among women. They have, in fact, traded propaganda, Freddie pressing a radical anarchist pamphlet upon Belford, who has countered with some sort of Lutheran tract.

"Squeak, you all in black, baby. Looking fine! Make me happy to see you dress so black."

"Yeah, Papa, I guess we've taken to shopping in the same boutiques." He grins at this, although in truth, the belt that holds up your jeans cost more than Freddie's entire ensemble, turtleneck to sandals. (There is a distinct possibility, however, that money is still owed on the belt.)

"Well, hate to hit and run, Papa, but . . ."

"You splitting already?"

"We were passing by and saw your light, just ran up to say hi." Belford shoots you a puzzled, almost accusatory glance. "It's pretty late."

"Night time da right time, Squeak. Course, you gotta go you job in da morning."

"Yeah."

"Okay, but you remember dis, baby: da flute invented before da wheel."

"Really, Mr. Mati?" asks Belford. "I wasn't aware of that."

Freddie is intimating that art is fundamentally more necessary to humankind than commerce or industry, a recurrent theme with him.

"You're the musician, Papa, not me."

"Dat right. I don't forget you singing lessons." You both laugh at that dumb memory. "Anyway, you got you fingers on da frog skins."

You freeze. The look you give your father is not unlike the look you received from Larry Diamond that evening three days ago when you naively called him a Bozo—Bozo as in clown. "What do you mean by that?" you implore warily. "Frog skins." Does the old man know something?

Noticing the shift in your mood, Freddie hastens to explain

that "frog skins" is a slang expression. "Dat street talk," he says. "Street talk for money. Dollar bills." He is pleased—and Belford puzzled—to see that you are relieved.

The three of you are silent for a while. André is mostly silent, as well. Then, you consult your watch and nod in the direction of the door. "Take care of yourself, Papa." Impulsively, you hug him. "I love you," you whisper.

Ah, Gwendolyn, it has been years since you have said those words to your dad. To anyone. Perhaps you say them now because you are going away and are uncertain when, or if, you will return.

"You come back soon," Freddie says. "Bring you Christian friend. I introduce him to God's great gift, Saint Pot. Heh-heh. Bring da monkey wit you. Dat monkey a trip, man." You are a quarter of the way down the stairs when he calls, "Next weekend I be at dat new Vietnamese joint, da Vo Mit Club. Gigging with Electric Baby Moses and His Golden Helicopters. Yeah, and also da Spanish Flies. You don't wanna miss dat one. I leave you name at da door. Dey make dem banana daiquiris, man. Da monkey like dat shit. Heh-heh."

Belford stops and turns, most likely to explain that his monkey is a born-again monkey, but you nudge him on down the steps.

Two Twenty-Nine A.M.

Standing in a lurid cloud of dragon breath, the combined neon exhalations of a half-dozen Chinatown facades, Belford looks confused and a tad leery. "It's time to go home," he says in a flat tone. "I'm tired. It's been an unusual weekend."

Ha! you think. *You don't know the half of it.* "Well, Belford honey, the unusualness is not over yet. But it will be very soon. For you, at any rate."

"I can't understand what you're talking about. I'm wiped out."

"Here, I'll drive. You and André climb in the back."

He does as he is told, and you race eastward on Jackson, wheel

363

to the north on Boren—"This isn't the way home," whines Belford—
and stop at a convenience store on Broadway, where you purchase
two Popsicles and one of those crusty, sugar-frosted little pocket
pies manufactured on the assembly lines of the Hostess company.
You deposit the bag of goodies on the floorboard by your left foot,
whereupon André, smelling the treats, sets up a slobber-jabber.

"Why can't he have 'em now?" asks Belford.

"Because he hasn't earned them yet. We've got enough welfare
gigolos in this town. If André wants to eat, he has to pull his
weight."

Belford looks around. "Where're you taking us, Gwen?"

"To a nice hotel."

"*Hotel?!* We can't . . ."

"Of course we can."

Two Forty-Seven A.M.

Notorious crop-raiders in their native land, Barbary apes are dexter-
ous enough, opposably thumbed enough, to pluck grapes off the
vine or pick up kernels of spilled corn. This species of macaque also
possesses cheek pouches in which it may horde a private stash of
food. André's pouches seem ample, all right—they did once conceal
the entire contents of the Sultana of Brunei's jewel box—yet you
wonder if they can accommodate something as long and inflexible
as the device you have just removed from your purse.

"Will you please tell me," Belford demands, "what in God's dear
name is going on here?"

You have parked the Lincoln on Terry Avenue; across from the
Sorrento Hotel, parked it, in fact, in the exact space where you and
Larry Diamond earlier in the day had enjoyed full-fledged sexual
congress in an automotive enclosure so small that no two circus
clowns, those who fit thirty to a midget car, would so much as
attempt it. Love makes the world go 'round, it's true, but lust stops

the world in its tracks; love renders bearable the passage of time, lust causes time to stand still; lust kills time, which is not to say that it wastes it or whiles it aimlessly away but rather that it annihilates it, cancels it, extirpates it from the continuum; preventing, while it lasts, any lapse into the tense and shabby woes of temporal society; lust is the thousand-pound odometer needle on the dashboard of the absolute. You wish you could invoke some of that carnal de-escalation right now, wish you could reenter the funky cocoon that you and Diamond spun around each other, the sexually generated capsule that so effectively insulated you from the hungers of the clock. If your strategy stands any chance of working, then events are going to have to unfold with scrupulous dispatch, for a time factor is involved, closure imminent, and not a resin-bead of lust left to embalm the minutes or slow the march.

With the lime-green felt-tip marking pen that you bought at the pharmacy, you paint your mother's old white rubber enema nozzle. The result resembles jade to the approximate degree that recent presidents have resembled statesmen, and in this light, color is probably academic, anyhow; but Kongo van den Bos is reported to have trained his simian assistant with visual aids, and considering that this caper is sketchy at best, you want to leave as little as possible to chance.

"*Now* what're you doing?" asks Belford.

Stealthily, you slip out of the car and open the rear door. "Come on, André, come with Auntie Gwen, honey. We're going to have us some fun." You grasp the monkey's paw and draw him outside. His buggy orange eyes are on the goody bag. "Not yet, André. Quiet, now. Belford, you come, too. You told me once how Kongo used to do this, but I'm not sure I have it right."

You lead André across the deserted street. Flabbergasted, Belford hurries after you. He catches up with you at the foot of the fire escape, the last rung of which is a full yard above your head. "What the heck . . . ?"

After showing André the newly decorated nozzle, you point

365

up the fire escape. You remove a Popsicle and the little apple pie from the bag, offer them to André, then when he reaches for them, snatch them back. Again, you point up the fire escape. You press the nozzle into his tiny fingers. How alive they feel, how nimble and strong. "Help me, Belford. We need to get him onto the fire escape."

Belford is dumbfounded. "Are you crazy? What do you think you're doing!"

Your voice is so tinkly and high and sweet, it could be the little pie talking. "I'm sending André up to the penthouse to fetch me something."

"No you're not! Are you out of your mind? Get back in the car!"

"Easy. Take it easy. It's only a prank."

"What kind of prank?"

"A funny, harmless prank. I want André to go up and bring down an enema nozzle." Once more you jiggle the treats under the macaque's nose, draw them away, point toward the penthouse. You are counting on the fact that your alleged fiancé, having been occupied with a wild-goose chase around San Francisco, is unaware of the nature of Motofusa Yamaguchi's cancer cure.

"Why? Why would you want . . . ? Is this some kinda silly scavenger hunt or something?" Visibly shaken, Belford is trying desperately to give you the benefit of the doubt.

"It's a joke."

"On who?"

"Uh, an acquaintance of mine."

"Mr. Adventure?"

"Well, yeah, if that's what you call him. He's leaving the country at six a.m., as I said, and I'm playing a little joke on him."

"Not with my André you're not!"

"Honey . . ."

"If you wanna play some smutty bathroom joke on your . . . your friend, go right ahead, but you leave my André the heck out of it. He doesn't do this."

"Come on, Belford, it's nothing but a little piece of hard rubber." With one of your gnawed nails, you tap the enema nozzle, secure now in the monkey's paw. You point up the fire escape. It follows your gesture.

"No! It doesn't matter if it's an enema nozzle or the Hope diamond, it's stealing either way. It took me years to correct the bad habits that evil criminal taught this innocent animal. I won't have you corrupt him again. I won't! André."

Belford starts to reach out for his pet, but his great padded hands have barely left his side before the monkey leaps up onto your shoulders, giving you an instant crick in your neck, and catapults itself onto the fire escape.

"Stop!" yells Belford. "André, come down here!"

"Hush. You'll wake up the whole damn hotel."

"Yeah. I *will* wake up the whole dang hotel. I'm gonna start yelling for the cops if you don't put a stop to this right now. André!" The monkey stays put. You rub your aching neck. Belford is coming apart like a double-wide in a tornado. "I'm calling somebody."

With the unconscious agility of a gunfighter, you flash your hand into your purse and yank out the canister of Mace. Before your rational mind can get its pants on, you have positioned the spout nine inches from Belford's face. Your finger is on the trigger. "One more sound out of you and I'll blast you into a goddamn amoeba. I'm serious, Belford. I'll turn you to jelly."

The moon has set. Terry Avenue is as dark as a river. So still is the night you can hear your pulse pound, hear the breath stoppered in Belford's lungs. The two of you stand as if transfixed by a clap of psychic thunder. Slowly, the disbelief in Belford's eyes changes to pain and disappointment. Were it not for your pulse, you feel you could hear his heart breaking. He is a strong man who grew up roughly. It occurs to you that he could slap you dead, maybe even before you could fire the Mace. "This stuff can buckle a bear," you warn him. But he isn't going to hit you. His hands hang at his side like disenfranchised puppets. His breathing is as pent as home brew in a crock. He begins shaking his head from side to side, and with

367

each cumbrous vacillation, the hurt in his face widens like an incision.

Gradually, feebly, you relax your grip on the Mace. You let the canister fall to the sidewalk. It clatters there and rolls into the gutter.

You couldn't go through with it. No matter the stakes, you simply couldn't do it. Damn it all! Damn it to marginal hell. What's the matter with you, Squeak? Still an amateur? When the jumbo chips hit the table, you folded like a Mexican road map. What are you going to do now?

Two Fifty-Nine A.M.

Tears are blistering your eyes like some chicken pox of failure, some herpes of rage and capitulation. Before the first sob rocks your sugarbowl titties, however, Belford spins on his heavy heels and walks away. And keeps walking. Walks right across Madison and on down Terry, walks southward, away from the Sorrento Hotel, away from the hospital, walks into the neighborhood occupied by buildings belonging to the Roman Catholic archdiocese of Seattle, a leafy, sedate area even darker and quieter than where you stand now.

Soon he is but a silhouette, a shadow receding into more ponderous shadows. There are no restaurants or service stations down those stodgy blocks, no telephone booths, no private homes, even. Where is he going? Why is he going? Has he snapped? Have you broken him? You feel your sneakers starting to shuffle in his direction.

For whatever reason—and it would be simpleminded to attempt to paste a single label on the emotions involved—you are about to run after him. But then, above the surf of your pulse, through the machinery of your sobs, you hear yourself being paged. It isn't your name that you hear. It isn't even a word, exactly. No, it's more of a cross between a grunt and a chirp, as if the Bluebird of

Happiness were excreting a prune pit. The noise is originating over your head. And it is indisputably intended to get your attention.

THREE OH-TWO A.M.

In the discreet light that seeps from the Sorrento's hallways, you see André poised at a second-story window, an imploring look on his mug, the tip of your mother's enema nozzle protruding from his lips like one of Clint Eastwood's cigarillos. Unless you are terribly mistaken, he is requesting your instruction.

You glance back down Terry Avenue. Belford's sorrowful shadow has merged with the night. You look up again at André. He is growing impatient and commencing to fidget. Suddenly, your pulse changes tempo, your sobs dissolve, the ache in your neck sprouts goose bumps. Okay! Well, all right then!

Making an upward motion with your hands, you direct the monkey to climb higher. It responds immediately. In the bat of a lash, it is at the third-story window, fully prepared to lift it open. So, this *is* how Kongo did it. Okay! All right then! You signal André to continue his ascent, and the next thing you know, he has stationed himself outside the fourth-floor fire exit. Jeez. If monkeys were bellhops, it wouldn't take so long to get room service. This is a breeze. You signal him to keep climbing. Your spirits climb with him.

The macaque is on the sixth level, and you are just raising your hands to wave him on up to the penthouse when you hear the siren. In the sky, you detect the reflected whirl of red lights. It is not your imagination. The siren squawls louder, the lights flash brighter. It's the cops—damn that Belford! damn his treacherous Lutheran soul to hell! They are bearing down on you. And there is no place to hide. This, on top of your tactless lapses at the disco: you, little woman, could end up having to do some very fancy talking to avoid wasting your peak earning years watching the paint peel on a jailhouse wall. You may have been vexed in the past, you may have been embar-

369

rassed, but that was a paler shade of zip compared to the vexation and embarrassment rising in you now.

But it isn't the police. It's an ambulance. It red-balls and waah-bawls right on past you, freighting yet another package of damaged urban meat to the emergency room at Swedish Hospital.

You pull the wooden stake out of your heart and kindle a fire with it to defrost your spine. *Jesus Christos! Cesar Romero!* That was a scare. It wouldn't surprise you to learn that your hair has turned completely gray. But something is protecting you, some guardian spirit: your mother, maybe, who spied you grieving at her desk tonight; or Grandma Mati or Q-Jo Huffington, both of whom are on speaking terms with the spirit world; or Larry Diamond, who has managed to get himself facedown in the saucer of otherness and who can jimmy the lock on your dreams; or maybe it's just that bruised angel who plays goaltender on God's hockey squad. At any rate, kiddo, you are saved and back in business.

Or are you? When you return your attention to the fire escape, André is nowhere to be seen.

THREE OH-SIX A.M.

Nowhere. The monkey is gone. As near as you can ascertain in this dimness, the seventh-floor window is shut. Did André open it, then close it behind him? Could Kongo van den Bos have trained him that thoroughly? You have heard farfetched stories about his skills.

Or did he simply climb on up to the roof? Perhaps he is up there now, scampering about, doing his Freddie Mati dance of life among the ventilation bonnets. Or there is the possibility, definitely not to be dismissed, that he has run off again; that, chasing the melody of his own bent trumpet, he is fleeing across the rooftops of Seattle, consulting the ancient constellations that will guide him back to the wilds of his birth.

Over the years, there have been such frequent, dramatic fluctuations in the Barbary ape population on the Rock of Gibraltar that a legend was spawned about an underground passageway between Gibraltar and North Africa, a hidden tunnel known only to the macaques. Still other Gibraltarians postulated that the monkeys were secretly amphibian and that on moonless nights (such as this one) they would slip into the sea and swim the nine or so miles across the strait. (Is Diamond aware of this tale, you wonder, has he stirred it into his Nommo mix?)

Minutes pass. Your pulse speeds up its drumbeat. In your bladder, there is so much pressure that your legs feel as if they are wrapped in a rug. You glance around for a place to pee, just in case, but no spot looks promising so you stand there in your black clothing, craning your sore neck to keep watch on the penthouse. Between the rich boys and the monkey, your neck has been turned into a bus stop on the Random Violence line.

More minutes go by. You check your Rolex. Nervously, and with the urine damming up in you like a phantom pond, you walk to the corner, near the hospital. Through the budding branches of a maple, you notice a fat star, the same star, you believe, that that gutter astronomer sold to you as Sirius. Sirius A. It seems bigger, hotter than it did a couple of nights ago. No telling where a star such as that might lead a wandering ape.

A car door slams. You nearly jump out of your jeans. At the emergency room loading platform, an engine cranks. You perform a stiff pirouette and start back toward the hotel. The mailbox on the corner is laughing at you. Over your shoulder, you see the ambulance glide away from the receiving dock. You quicken your pace and cross the street. When the ambulance passes, you want to be out of view. You drop to one knee and let the Lincoln shield you from the street. The ambulance rolls by slowly, its lamps and sirens as peaceful as drunks who have finally passed out or hyenas who have howled themselves to sleep. You hear it brake at the Madison Street stop sign, shift gears, and continue on its way.

When at last you stand, André is standing beside you.

371

THREE TWENTY-EIGHT A.M.

So much for "born again." Unless it is another example of thrice born—the sinner who "finds" Jesus, then, due to boredom, embarrassment, education, or need, enthusiastically and without regret resumes his sinful ways. In any event, the manner in which André is clapping his paws together, bobbing his head, and peeling his lips back to exhibit every last molar in a vulgar monkey grin—all this *before* you have awarded him his ices and pie—would indicate that he is thoroughly delighted to be thieving again, and bombastically proud that he has thieved so well.

You are proud and delighted yourself, scarcely believing that you have actually pulled it off. Perhaps your luck is changing, and the second and third phases of your program shall meet with similar success.

All the way down I-5, en route to the airport (having decided against cruising the neighborhood for Belford, on the grounds that the search would impede your progress and nothing positive would result from intercepting him), you pick up the nozzle, replace it on the seat beside you, pick it up again. You twirl it in your fingers, test its weight in your palm, hold it aloft so that the shine of oncoming headlamps simultaneously penetrates its crystalline tip and bounces off of its jadeite stalk. Heavier than it looks, the nozzle is leaden with the ancient weight of idols; as slick as a bloody quill, as haughty as an unpaired chopstick, as elemental as honeycomb, it has the character of molten ritual, cooled through the palpitating centuries into a frozen ray of primal function. Conduit of lotus-scented waters, hard little harpoon for an empress's gastric leviathans, polished root from a chthonian garden, it has, when you hold it against the light, the distant dignity and grave passion of a pale green star.

It is not until you consider more explicitly how and where it has spent the majority of its existence that you lay it down and leave it down. And wipe your hand on your jeans. How chivalrous—and gross—of André to carry such a thing in his mouth!

"Monkey, you're incredible. I'm serious, honey, you're the best. We make quite a team, huh? You and Auntie Gwen are the hottest merger since RJR and Nabisco. Frankly speaking," you intone, imitating Diamond's mannered drawl, "Mr. Dunn doesn't deserve the talents of you and me." André emits a mini-screech, prompting you to glance over your shoulder in a naive attempt to see if he is agreeing, objecting, or merely reacting to his master's name. "Of course, Mr. Dunn does care about us both very much." A wave of emotion precipitates an annoying cramp in your larynx. When you recover, you say, "I'm sorry, but at the airport I'll have to shut you in the trunk again. Now don't get mad. It's a big, roomy trunk this time, and it's for your own good. I won't be long."

Famous last words.

FOUR THIRTY-NINE A.M.

Since higher physics regards time as relative, it might be possible to demonstrate to Einstein's satisfaction that the intervals between your entering the near-empty terminal, taking a long overdue pee, and rousing proper assistance from dozing clerks at two separate ticket counters were actually short intervals (time is relative to the motion of the observer, after all, and as a dead man, Einstein is either in the ultimate stationary position or else has condensed into pure energy traveling at speeds near the limits of light); but from your own more vital perspective, events at the airport proceeded so slowly that you lost all of your temper and most of your mind.

Diamond has a six o'clock flight, which means he must check in at this same airport at about five-fifteen, which means he must leave Thunder House not much later than four forty-five. You had planned to call him on the Lincoln's cellular unit on your way back into town, but now you dare not delay. A public phone in the terminal lobby will have to suffice.

You punch in the number, hold your breath as it rings, and

373

hold your ear when an explosion of static almost blows the receiver out of your fist.

The interference clears, and you catch up with Diamond in mid-sentence. ". . . out behind the barn. Just remember this, chums: the picture doesn't know who painted it, the story doesn't know who's telling it, and the economy has no idea who or what economists are, let alone bookies and bean-counters. What you get is what you bring, and it's all a flying fuck at the moon. Don't bother to leave your name, number, or time that you called, because Uncle Larry is . . ."

"Larry? Larry! Please. Pick up the phone. It's me. You're still home, aren't you? Larry, it's . . ."

Click. "Pussy fricassee. Yes. How genial of you to check in."

Is he being sarcastic? Between the static on the line and his customary menacing intonations, it's difficult to tell. At least you reached him. "Yeah, well, I thought I'd call to say good-bye. I guess you'll be heading out very soon."

"Indeed."

"Uh, is Twister still driving you?"

"Yes, and it should be interesting. I don't believe he's been behind the wheel in a year or more. If my scooter had held together another day, I wouldn't have had to trouble him. I'm not troubling you, am I? What're you doing awake at this hour? Going to the disco? Old firehorse can't resist the ding-dong? Aching to run the gauntlet of crutches? Scour the wreckage for a sign of father tapeworm, gaze one last time into the cash drawer of his eyes?"

Normally, you might have been put off by his verbal excesses, as hypnotic as they can be, but through the crackle and sting of static, you can detect a fever in his voice; something irregular, alien.

His illness must have worsened in the night. "I haven't been to sleep," you say rather weakly.

"Ah, my suspicions confirmed. When I couldn't reach you via the usual telecommunicative hardware, I labored in vain to intrude on your dreams. I'd either lost the knack, or you weren't dreaming. I suppose I should be pleased it was the latter."

"You tried to call me?"

"More times than I care to admit. Are you informing me you were in receipt of none of my bulletins?"

"Er, no. I've, uh, been out driving around. Thinking." Your voice brightens. "But listen, Larry. I have a present for you. A very . . . *good* present. A very, very good present. I took it out to Sea-Tac and left it at the Delta ticket counter with your name on it. Please, please be sure to pick it up. It's important. Okay?"

"Certainly. I wouldn't miss a chance to be surprised, as slight as that chance might be."

"We'll see, won't we? But this surprise, Larry—you must not open it until you get to Africa. You *must not*. Promise."

"Very well, I suppose that's a treaty I can sign."

In your mind's eye, you try to imagine the look on his face when he finds the jade nozzle in his possession. The vision prompts you to blush, although neither at the intrinsic nature of the instrument nor from modesty at the extremity of your generosity. Rather, you are reliving the moment in the ladies' room here at Sea-Tac when you removed your underpants and swaddled the nozzle in them, an exceedingly bold gesture, for you are convinced that, sooner or later, once he has rebounded from the shock of their contents, he will bury his perverted nose in them. That will teach him to question your adventurousness. "How could a woman," he had asked, "be so prim about sex and still be so sexy?" Prim? Ha! Smell these! As for the nozzle itself, once he has made use of it (you included in the panty pack the jar of beta-carotene that you purchased at the all-night pharmacy: the brown rice and coffee he can acquire in Africa), he is certain to mail it back to Dr. Yamaguchi.

375

There is no chance that Diamond will keep it and try to profit from it. The possibility of ransom flittingly crossed *your* mind, you must confess, but, hey, you aren't that kind of girl. Besides, you have other avenues now to financial recovery. Or *one* other avenue.

"So, Larry, I guess you're out of here."

"Pardon?" A ripsaw of static had chewed off the end of your remark.

"I said: Guess you aren't having any second thoughts about Timbuktu."

"Surely you jest. Only a fool wouldn't have second thoughts about Timbuktu. In addition, I'm having second thoughts about deserting America at this particularly pandemoniacal moment."

"But things are a mess."

"Yes. Yes. I believe I just indicated as much. Isn't it grand? A gentleman named Horace Walpole once wrote that "The world is a comedy to those who think, a tragedy to those who feel." Extrapolating, we can say, then, that to the whole person, the person with a balanced view, the world is tragicomedy. Ah, but virtually nobody in America thinks anymore; and nobody feels much either, beyond anger and resentment that they haven't been cut a wider slice of that prodigal pie that they've been deluded into believing not only exists but is rightfully theirs to share, regardless of their talents or virtues. What can you say about a population to whom the world is neither comedy nor tragedy but a sporting match in a seedy and extremely noisy arena, a littered rink where they might score if they're lucky or shrewd or ruthless enough, or go completely numb if they fail? Still, there's the roar. America has a roar, an edge, you won't find in tired old Europe or fatalistic old Asia. Given a choice between our barbarism and their ennui, Uncle Larry'll choose the barbarism every time."

"From what I hear, there's no shortage of barbarism in Africa."

"You hear correctly. The average African today, for any number of regrettable reasons, is as far removed from the complex and glorious metaphysical systems of his or her ancestors as the average Greek hawking souvlaki on a polluted street corner is removed from the Eleusinian Mysteries or the Oracle of Delphi. One difference, though, is that in Africa, for the quester, most of the major stones remain unturned."

"Right. And turns unstoned. Frogs unlicked."

"Now, pussy frangipane, don't try to trivialize my journey."

"I don't think it's trivial. I think it's insane."

Diamond allows a barrage of electrical flatulence to run its course before he responds.

"Yes, 'some people calls it madness,' if I may once again quote Mr. Calloway, but if the majority ignore the rip in the fabric of consensual reality and a few recognize it, ponder it, take it into account, then might I be excused for wondering who's truly mad, the many or the few? Nothing'll do for Uncle Larry but to part that rip. Mind you, he's not boasting that he's going to attempt to squeeze through it. Once he gets a better look into the breach, he may back off like a lecher with heartburn or spring for the hills like an eight-point buck on the first day of hunting season. But at least he'll *know*. My aim, if that's not too precise a term, is to relocate outside the bounds of control and definition. Even when one is on the pad, control and definition labor tirelessly to erect their cast-iron grids around you. The possibility exists that even a periodic peek through the hole in the curtain will be sufficient to ward off their constrictions. Then, I can proceed to the next step. Should it strike my fancy. And if the little monster in my rectum hasn't gobbled up my spark. I'm gladdened to inform you, pussy prosciutto, that I have a strong premonition that somehow I'm going to survive."

Careful, Gwen. You would not want him to pick up anything about the nozzle on his annoying telepathic radar. In an effort to distract him, you go, perhaps, a bit too far. "I hope with all my heart that's the case," you say, "but don't forget, you also had a premonition you were going to see Q-Jo."

A weighty silence hangs on the line. You would figure that atmospheric interference had knocked out the connection, except that you can hear him breathing. You imagine that you can also hear him trembling, feel the heat of his fever through the phone. Did you have to discourage him quite so bluntly? You are searching for the phrases that will restore his hope without revealing the reason why such hope is entirely justified, when he speaks again, but in a voice that sounds as awe-struck and wonder-struck as it is ravaged and frightened.

"I did see Q-Jo."

"What?!"

"I've seen her. That's why I've been calling you all night."

"Where? When? For God's sake, Larry!"

"Easy, Gwendolyn. Easy now. You're going to have to brace yourself for this."

Brace you do, as if in preparation for a devastating punch, but there is nothing in this world that can prepare you for what Larry Diamond has to tell. Speaking as if in a twitch-ridden trance, he relates how, when he left you in the bowling alley parking lot last evening, he went directly to his bathroom inside Thunder House to apply more of the Native American herbs. He had just finished and was washing his hands when there was a flash, followed by a crack and a pop, like a paparazzo having his camera smashed by an irate celebrity, and the lights in Thunder House dimmed, blinked out, and after a few seconds came back on. The atmospheric interference of the past few days had already precipitated several brief power outages, so he gave the matter little thought until he realized that the slide projector in the living room had been on ever since his presentation to you yesterday morning. The projector was buzzing more insistently than usual—like a shipwrecked blow dryer surrounded by hostile cicadas, is how he puts it—so he hastened in to check for damage and to switch it off.

"The machine itself was unharmed," he says, "but when I looked at the screen, there she was."

"Who? What do you mean?"

"Your friend," he whispers, and you can feel him shudder. "Up there. On the screen. In the picture. In the slide. Posing with the faculty. Larger than life, if in Q-Jo's case that's not redundant. I told you that nothing surprises me anymore, but I guess I lied."

FOUR FORTY-FOUR A.M.

"If this is your idea of a joke. . . ." Even as you speak, however, you know he is not kidding.

"Hardly. You're the only person I'd dare tell. I haven't even mentioned it to Twister." Diamond pauses. "You're thinking it was the fever. Or the medicine. That I was hallucinating. Momentarily, I considered that myself. I ran into the kitchen and threw cold water in my face. After collecting my wits, I went back—and there she was! Standing there, in the midst of the shamans and soothsayers. Just beaming, by the way, as if she was in her element and couldn't be happier. I watched the screen for, oh, probably ten minutes. She was definitely there. It was not an illusion."

His sincerity does nothing to temper your incredulity. "I'll have to see it to believe it," you say.

Again, he pauses. "You *can't* see it." There is anguish and regret in his tone.

"Why not? If Q-Jo's really in—"

"Not anymore. There was another power outage. You may have noticed it." (No, you were in bed balling Belford.) "The lights went dark for about five seconds, and when they came back on—she wasn't in the picture anymore. Gone. Completely. I've been observing the slide off and on throughout the night. She hasn't reappeared."

"Larry . . ."

"There's something else of interest, however. I reversed to the previous slide—the group picture of the visiting faculty?—and they're gone, as well. The whole lot of them. There's nothing in the slide now but an empty courtyard. And *that*, Gwendolyn, you *can* see. I'd show you immediately had I time."

379

"Yeah, but it's late. You've got to get to Sea-Tac." *If Diamond isn't joking,* you think, *and if he hasn't been tricked by medicine or drugs, then maybe he really is insane. And if he's crazy, maybe he murdered Q-Jo, after all.* As much as it distresses you, you have to reconsider that possibility.

"Yes. Indeed. Twister's already gone out to start the car. He doesn't want to be away from Thunder House any longer than necessary."

"Well, Larry . . ."

"Listen, darling, I know it's a brainful, but don't worry about it. All right? We'll make sense of it when we're in Africa. And that won't be long. I should warn you, pussy kimchi, that things are a trace raggedy andy in Mali. Infrastructure leaves much to be desired. The Bamako airport is bedlam, night and day, and arrivals and departure schedules are made out of rubber. So if for some reason I fail to meet your flight, grab a taxi to the Hotel l'Amitié. I'll be registered there under the name of Mookie Blaylock."

"I see."

"Very well. Twister's honking. Sirius C is calling. I think I love you. Bye-bye."

"Bye, Larry. I . . . think . . . I care for you, too."

FOUR FIFTY-EIGHT **A.M.**

Did they from the little acorn spring? George Washington's mighty teeth? Or, like much Early American furniture, were they planed from the trunk of a maple tall, after the sap had gone? Red-eyed maple? Slippery elm? Knotty pine? Perhaps they were made of quaking aspen, so as to bring the music of the riverbank to the daily chew. (When he belched, Martha might have heard the wind in the willows. A sycamore serenade.) Consider walnuts cracked by walnut, cherries pulverized by cherry, ash in the mouth before the pipe. Washington eating wood pigeon with wood teeth. Unable to taste the forest for the trees. Every beer would have been a root beer, his bark always worse than his bite.

If Q-Jo was actually in that African slide—which, it goes without saying, she wasn't—you couldn't even begin to think about it. And if Diamond, in some deranged state, only imagined that he saw her, well, you can't think about that, either. You won't allow yourself to think of any of it. There is too little time and too much at stake. You must avoid confusion, assail doubt, and proceed courageously and efficiently with the next phase of your grand strategy.

As the Lincoln purrs northbound up the I-5 corridor at twenty times the speed at which its namesake (condition of teeth unknown) trudged to school through the Illinois sleet, you soothe André with his favorite French nursery song—your baby-doll voice seems to captivate him: Blossom Dearie, eat your heart out!—singing it over and over while you conjure images of balsa dentures that could be sailed around the White House dining room like toy eagles. At some point, Diamond, southbound, will be momentarily parallel with you, but since you haven't a clue what sort of car Twister might own and since Diamond is unfamiliar with the Lincoln, you are destined to pass like ships in the night. Rather, the dawn, for already you can detect a pale yellow thread unraveling (or raveling) in the seam of the horizon.

You take the Mercer Street exit and drive along the shore of Lake Union toward the base of Queen Anne Hill. Shortly after exiting, you meet a motorcade of three BMW sedans and a black Ferrari, traveling at great speed: the rich boys returning to affluent suburbs after a night of harassing the down and out. You flush with fury at the memory of their yanking your pants off—if, in fact, it was them. One more subject you must postpone thinking about until you are in clover.

Because Belford may have reported the Lincoln stolen—unlikely but you cannot risk it—you park his car at your building and transfer the monkey and your bag of supplies to the Porsche. "Remember this nice car, *mon ami?* You screwed it up royally with your stupid vitamins. But don't worry, Auntie Gwen forgives you. You don't have to ride in the nasty ol' trunk."

Immediately after starting the engine, you hear a shout and in the rearview mirror see a shadowy male figure dashing toward you. Without a second thought, you pop the clutch. For a second or two, he appears to be gaining on you, but once you are in the street, the Porsche makes a noise high in its throat, like an enraged Prussian baron about to run through his wife's lover with a saber; lays down twin streaks of that acrid testosterone jam that teenage boys love to spread on their asphalt, and leaves the pursuer behind. Probably it was poor Belford, but it just as easily could have been the Safe Sex Rapist. A girl can't be too careful. Making the Porsche bray and sway, you drive as fast as you think you can get away with without attracting undue attention, and, after stopping briefly at Thriftway for one final requisition of banana Popsicles, zoom off to Ballard and the Thunderbird Bowl.

FIVE TWENTY-FIVE A.M.

The stock market is scheduled to open in fifty-five minutes. You wonder if it will. Crossing the Ballard Bridge, you switch on radio news, but so annoying is the static that you switch it right back off. What do you care about the market, anyway? This day there is to be no "Sears, Philip Morris, Merck, General Electric." No "Westing-house, Walt Disney, Procter and Gamble." No "I . . . B . . . Mmmmm."

This day there is to be "Van Gooo-gh."

FIVE TWENTY-SEVEN A.M.

After circling the bowling alley once, you park in the rear (that being the west side of the building), adjacent to the long, narrow, ground-level window in Twister's "tipi."

"Get a grip on yourself, André. Be patient. You get to have some more fun, but it'll take a minute." The macaque is all aflutter, though whether in anticipation of another heist or because you are withholding his treats, you cannot know.

With an X-Acto knife, you trim a piece of heavy poster board until it forms a rectangle approximately fifteen inches by eleven. Then you go to work with a thick black crayon. You have had no formal art training, but your brother is a professional sculptor in San Francisco, and your mother had a talent for rendering in ink the mutilated unicorns and crumbling gravestones with which she often illustrated her poems, so your genes have provided you a facile touch with a sketch. Obviously, nothing is required here beyond the crudest approximation of the original, merely enough of a resemblance to inform the little thief what he is to snatch, yet you tax your memory—you have only seen the drawing once—to position the figures correctly; and once you have smeared the copy with fingertip and spit, you fancy that your cartoonish peasants possess some of the coarse dignity with which Van Gogh endowed his originals. Your appreciation may be enhanced by the light, or rather the lack of it: the sky is all huckleberry and nasturtium, the color of God's linoleum, but it is not yet bright enough to permit clear vision.

"Here we go, baby. Please hurry, okay?" You lead André to Twister's window, wag a Popsicle under his nose, and hand him the drawing. "This is what Auntie Gwen wants. It won't fit in your cheek pouch, but you can do it. And, hey, I'll pay extra for a rush job. Express, okay? Go! Now! Go!"

To be sure, Twister's window is shut and locked, but this monkey is supposed to be a master of the break-in, an animal criminal genius. You have every faith, yet it is strained when André, after fiddling with the window for a while, lies down beside it and begins to whimper. *Good grief!*

FIVE THIRTY-EIGHT A.M.

You *could* smash the window glass with a tire iron or something. Your desire, however, is to have this look like an inside job. When Twister returns from the airport to find his precious drawing gone, he and the investigators will have scant choice but to blame Larry Diamond. They'll straighten it out in a few days, so no harm will be done, and by then you should be well beyond easy reach.

That was the plan. Now, as desperation mounts, you look around for an object to heave through the pane. *Voilà!* What's this in the weeds? A bowling ball! My, my; some low-class oaf with a marginal existence must have logged such a pitiful score that he threw his ball away in a fit of proletarian pique. You pick it up. Ick! It's filthy. And heavier than you had supposed. It's the first time in your life that you have ever handled one of these "moons that orbit Milwaukee," and you suspect that merely lifting it has compromised your dignity and reduced your IQ. Straining to hold it away from your body, you walk toward the window.

Suddenly, however, as if he has been struck by an actual thought, the monkey springs to his feet and commences to shinny up a drainpipe. He is heading for the rooftop, perhaps in search of a ventilation shaft. Okay! Marvelous! This is more like it. You knew you could count on the simian scourge of the Côte d'Azur. You drop the bowling ball in disgust, massage your pained neck, and return to your car for the nerve-racking wait.

FIVE FORTY-FOUR A.M.

The time is five forty-four. Since you cannot conceive of there having been a prolonged farewell at Sea-Tac, it is reasonable to expect Twister within the next five or six minutes. To steady your emotional wobble and to prevent further gnashing of your bitten-down nails, you examine once more your packet of airline tickets—the fresh tickets that you acquired in the Sea-Tac exchange.

Seattle to New York. Good. The flight leaves in a couple of hours.

New York to Amsterdam. Excellent. If the Dutch industrialist was offering two million and change for the Van Gogh drawing, you certainly ought to be able to get half that from one of his fellow collectors. A little research. A little of your celebrated salesmanship. Bingo! You have allotted yourself a week. Then—

Amsterdam to Manila. Perfect. Grandma Mati will shelter you for as long as you might wish. Even if something has gone wrong and the authorities are after you, there is no extradition treaty between the United States and the Philippines. And once there, things could go very well, indeed. In her last letter, Grandma Mati wrote that there are a number of ambitious young politicians maneuvering to fill a power vacuum in the Filipino government. A young Filipina as well-educated, moneyed (your grandmother believes you are prosperous), sophisticated, and pretty as you (your unfortunate Anglo nose is a flaw they could persuade themselves to overlook) would be a catch, a definite boost to their political aspirations. You might very well, she wrote, become the new Imelda Marcos.

Personally, you would rather become the new Gwendolyn Mati, but, hey, "the new Imelda Marcos" has a prosperous ring.

FIVE-FIFTY A.M.

Jesus jumping Mary!

André is back. You neither heard him approach nor saw where he came from—Twister's window remains closed and intact—but here he is, perched on the bumper that wraps around the bulbous Porsche like a licorice whip curved around an ostrich egg. At first, you fear he must have failed to gain entry, but when he bounds backward off the bumper and launches into his spastic victory dance, your heart soars.

But wait a minute. That prize he is waving above his head, as if it were a championship trophy at Wimbledon or something—it's too small to be the Van Gogh drawing.

385

Too small. Too small. It is, in fact, not much larger than a tarot card.

André! You stupid beast!

You jump out of the car. He surrenders his loot and reaches for his sugary reward. You brush aside his paw. "What the . . ."

It *is* a tarot card. One of the oversized ones that tarotmancers usually reserve for special occasions.

You turn it over. At this point, what else *can* you do. Somehow, you are not surprised that it's the Fool.

What does surprise you is that something appears to be written on it, a message scrawled across the upper right corner, across the sovereign and paternalistic sun, across the innocent white rose, across the hermetic hobo bag in which are concealed, awaiting his recognition, all the things the Fool might require to facilitate his skip into the waters of the wild unknown.

In the weak dawn light, and with your weak vision, the message is difficult to read. Nevertheless, you squint and strain at it, for you can make out, to your supreme astonishment, that it is wrought in Q-Jo Huffington's wispy script and with Q-Jo Huffington's favorite silver ink.

When it comes into sharper focus, this is what it says:

See you in Timbuktu!

Author's Note

Readers desiring more detailed and scholarly information about the Bozo-Dogon-Sirius connection should consult *Le Renard Pâle* by Marcel Griaule and Germaine Dieterlen, *Ethnoastronomy: The Newest Oldest Science* by Verzig Dommer, *African Worlds* by Daryll Forde, and, especially, *The Sirius Mystery* by Robert K. G. Temple.

Exhaustive dental research has led me to conclude that George Washington's false teeth were actually carved from hippopotamus, elephant, and walrus tusks. The teeth were attached to plates made of gold (upper) and ivory (lower) by wooden pegs the diameter of toothpicks, and it is probably those pegs that gave rise to the notion that Washington had wooden choppers. I feel compelled to report the facts in this matter, although personally I much prefer the apocryphal.

—T.R.